Tomb for an Eagle

by

Lexie Conyngham

First published in 2018 by The Kellas Cat Press, Aberdeen.

Copyright Alexandra Conyngham, 2018

ISBN: 978-1-910926-44-4

Cover illustration by Helen Braid at www.ellieillustrates.co.uk

ACKNOWLEDGEMENTS

To my lovely readers, Kath, Nanisa, Jill, and Bryony, for all their input. To Fran and Raggie, for information supplied. To Peter Barton, old neighbour, who gave me the idea. And to M and E as always, for everything.

CAST OF PRINCIPAL CHARACTERS

Ketil Gunnarson, formerly of Heithabyr

At the Brough:
Thorfinn Sigurdarson, Earl of Orkney
Ingibjorg, his wife
Asgerdr, his daughter

At Buckquoy:
Einar Einarson, the chief
Rannveig, his wife
Hlifolf and Hrolf, his advisors
Helga, Hrolf's wife
Bjarni Hravn and his mother Ragna
Sigrid, a widow
Gnup, a farmhand
Tosti, a priest
Snorri, a skald

At Kirkuvagr:
Brodir, Thorfinn's man
Eirik

Lexie Conyngham

Scholars have speculated that the Brough of Birsay in Viking times was more firmly attached to the mainland than it is today. For the purposes of these books, that attachment has been reconstructed.

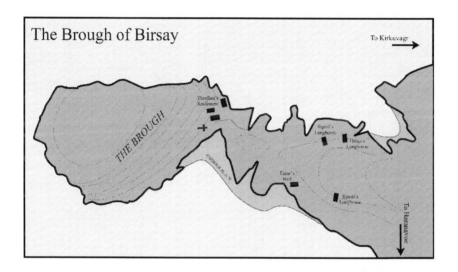

EIN

I

'Odin's bloody beard!'

Ketil tilted his head slightly. The soldier fell silent at once, but rubbed his stubbed toe vigorously. Ketil listened. In the crisp starlight, eye-wateringly cold, he could hear only the incessant wind, and the waves slapping on the shore. Threads of smoke still twisted through the air, and his clothes were thick with it. He glanced up the beach. He could just make out Thorfinn, stocky and dark, slipping forward, his own commander, the man to whom Ketil owed his fealty. Somewhere further inland Thorkell Fostri and Einar, two long ghosts of men, would be stalking their prey, moving in parallel, Thorkell Fostri sniffing the air like a hound. Kalf had taken his men ahead, the other prong of the pincer. After a moment, Ketil lifted a hand for his own few men to follow, keeping them down near the waterline. Somewhere ahead was their prey. Rognvald had to have seen them. He had to know they were coming, and why. He had run, after all.

Running away on these rocks would be a fool's game at night. Rognvald would be hiding somewhere, hoping that between them they would miss him. He would have covered his head, no doubt, to stop the starlight fingering his bright gold hair. Ketil scanned the lumpen darkness, his feet feeling each step, his fingers flexing and easing round his sword pommel, so that the cold did not numb them before he had to fight. Behind him a man slipped and gasped, but did not cry out: Ketil smiled to himself. They were learning.

Then, in the surge of wind and waves, one sharp sound cut through. A dog, barking.

They were there in seconds, surrounding the little hollow in the rocks, but standing back, letting the senior men do their work. Kalf had doubled back as expected, blocking the way, eyes glinting, darting from man to man. Thorfinn stood solidly in charge, sword at the ready, but it was Thorkell Fostri, pale and sharp, who leaned down and seized the crouching figure by the shoulder. The hood fell from Rognvald's golden head, and he made an effort to calm his breathing, Ketil could see, while the little lapdog who had betrayed him growled threats at his master's attacker. For a moment only the lapdog moved. Then, stiffly, Thorfinn nodded. Rognvald's eyes widened, bright blue in his white face. And Thorkell Fostri struck.

He made sure, running his sword right through with a crunching, scraping sound that everyone there knew too well. Blood bubbled dark through the robe Rognvald had grabbed to disguise himself in his escape, and the blue eyes dulled even as he sucked in a last, desperate breath and sagged, slicing unfeeling hands on the sword blade. After a moment, Thorkell Fostri bent again, took firm hold of the sword in his skeletal fingers and pulled it free with a nasty little liquid sound that the waves almost, but not quite, drowned. He wiped the sword with a rag, fitted it back in his sword belt, drew his knife, then snatched up the incredulous lapdog.

'No,' said Thorfinn, breaking the silence between them. 'Enough.'

He reached out his hand, and took the little dog from Thorkell Fostri's thin arm. Tucking it under his own, he gave Rognvald one last look before turning and slithering away over the rocks, back to dry land. He passed Ketil without seeming to notice – why would he? But Ketil saw his face, black and white in the starlight. It was empty.

Thorkell Fostri and Einar, insubstantial again, slipped silent in his wake. Their men had melted into the darkness of the machair. Kalf followed. He stopped fractionally, as though surprised to see Ketil. Their eyes met: Kalf's were still dancing, then his gaze slid away and he moved on, after the others. Ketil turned abruptly and stared for a moment at the waves: the tide was on the turn. Then he glanced back at the soldiers behind him, and jerked his head. There was a body to clear up.

Papa Stronsay, at Christmastide two years ago. Papa Westray for the burial. The names repeated in his head like a bad taste at the back of his throat. Things that should not have happened, deeds that should never have been done. That was the last time he had set foot on Orkney, mainland or island. But now he could see the islands growing through the fog – oh, he remembered the fog. If he had held to the old traditions he might have thought he was in Nifelheim. As it was, he peered distrustfully at the green grey shadows of land ahead. Islands were unchancy places, neither one thing nor the other, where evil could slip in unnoticed through the cracks in the world. Surreptitiously, he slipped one hand under the mist-damp folds of his cowl, and crossed himself.

The navigator of the small kvarr tasted water he had scooped from the sea in a cup on a string, and nodded even as he spat. Ketil was grateful for his certainty in the fog, and the steersman adjusted the course slightly. The broad-beamed cargo ship wallowed briefly and the sail rippled in wind strong enough, you would have said, to blow away that fog – strong enough anywhere but Orkney. His hood was pinned to his close-cut hair, blown from behind, but he stood easily in the steady kvarr, well used to wilder crossings in faster, narrower ships. It was more the anticipation of his arrival that made his blood run swiftly through his veins.

If he had not been studying the land so closely, he might have missed it: not that he thought it of any importance then. A fold of mist thinned and vanished, and he found himself peering through a window at a little scene towards the left of their path. Above the level of the waves, where a small stream had cut a cleft down the crumbling ginger cliff, a woman was working on the shore. What was she doing? It was heavy work, by the shape of her back as she bent and struggled. As he watched, fascinated by landwork after hours at sea, she let something solid drop to the ground, and straightened, stretching her back. Then her arms went up, bare and weathered, to adjust her headcloth – the knot must be slipping. He thought she glanced towards him for a moment, then looked away again, and as if a curtain dropped over the window the mist swept back, and she was gone.

By the time the mist really cleared, only minutes later, he had all but forgotten about her. They had rounded the broad headland, and tucked behind it was the harbour of Birsay, a sandy beach nestled under a broad scattering of buildings on the headland. Now the sun shone on it, the green sward that spread above the cliffs was remarkable, the detail suddenly clear: he could see longhouses scattered on the uplands to left and right, sheep grazing apparently at random, a few cattle enjoying their spring freedom, and people, people everywhere, around the longhouses, up on the headland, and most of all around the busy harbour. Three merchant kvarrs were already anchored nearby, and countless small vessels, fishing boats, tiny things that one man could use to skip from island to island, anything that went by water. Even, he was interested to see, a longship, though it had an unused air, pulled high up from the waterline. The raiding season was not yet upon Birsay.

The sand swooped and jerked beneath his leather boots as he steadied himself, finding his land-legs again. One of the crew nudged his shoulder and handed him out his second bag, eyebrows raised. He had almost forgotten it: he was not used to travelling with so much luggage. He nodded his thanks, handed over the agreed payment in a rattle of hacksilver, and turned to look around for some source of local information. One hand lingered on the wood of the kvarr's small boat's prow, saying farewell.

At a first, furtive glance he could see no one that he knew: he was not sure, yet, whether that was good or bad. It would have to be a stranger, then. There were plenty of possibilities. The little harbour area, tucked under the low, jagged cliff, was noisy with boat repairs and hauling of cargo, and with a persistent metallic tapping, somewhere up above them, that he only gradually noticed. It drew his attention properly at last to the headland, and he leaned back a little to look up, taking in the scuttling figures, the heaps of flat stones, the wooden hoists and the low, uneven walls. Someone had the builders in, it seemed.

An arm's length away from him, a stocky man with his back to the bay was repairing a barrel – urgently, apparently, as a slithering river of fish was sliding out of the finger-clutch of its remaining staves. Ketil approached, rounding the man to see his face.

'Good day to you.' He did his best to sound friendly. 'Who's in charge around here?'

The man glanced up at him, hands still busy with hammer and wood.

'In charge of what?'

'Well,' said Ketil, 'this.' He waved an arm awkwardly, still holding one bag over his shoulder and the other dangling against his leg. The man blew sharply upwards, as if trying to clear his fringe from his eyes. He did not appear to consider Ketil either useful or decorative.

'If you want the earl,' he said, 'that'd be Thorfinn. Thorfinn Sigurdarson, up on the Brough.' He jerked his head towards the headland above them.

'Thank you,' said Ketil, beginning to move away.

'He's not there, mind,' added the man, when Ketil had gone a few paces. Ketil stopped.

'What was that?'

'He's not there. Not up yonder.'

'I heard he was on pilgrimage. To Rome. If it's that Thorfinn,' he added quickly, not wanting to sound too familiar with him.

'Oh, he's long back from that,' said the man, unimpressed. 'He's away just now, though. Over on Stronsay, I hear tell.' He spat, though whether this was a reflection on Thorfinn's absence or the man's own feelings about Stronsay was not clear.

Ketil tried to remember. Stronsay, he thought, was about as far from here as you could get, to the east, and still be in the islands. He was on the western tip of the mainland here. He drew breath to ask if Thorfinn Sigurdarson was expected back soon, but the man looked up at him again from his barrel, kicked at the fish in irritation, and let go of a vital stave. The skeletal shape collapsed. The man swore. Ketil moved away fast.

The path up to the headland, the Brough, was obvious, from all the traffic: people and carts, and even a few horses, were wearing it deep into the earth. It was steep enough to be sheltered from the wind that skimmed across the long tongue of the headland, but once he had reached the top, rising between well-built stone walls that held back the earth on either side of the path, the breeze struck him again, snatching his hood from his head. He had to blink a few times before he could clearly see the settlement on the headland's rounded green cap.

Ahead of him and to right and left, stepping away at some distance, was a series of longhouses, comfortable and established, turf roofs shaggy with a few years' growth. Smoke, sweet peat smoke, rose from them, then slid away fast in the wind, leaving him with tantalising hints of hot midday meals cooking inside. Closer to hand and to his right, though, linked by newly cut drainage channels yet to be covered, old and new building mixed:

all sorts and shapes of structures rose angular with the local flat stones, tan and grey in variegated layers. He turned towards this area, following the bulk of the traffic. He noted that no one paid much attention to him: strangers must be common enough around here. Perhaps that meant that a meal would not be too difficult to find, even if he had to use more silver to pay for it. He was suddenly starving.

One completed building stood out, once he had sorted the shapes before him. Taller than most of the others, though not huge, it was clearly the local hall: even if Thorfinn really was away, someone there should know where he had gone and when he might be back. He began to make his way to it.

But by contrast with the buildings around it, busy with construction and cooking and general living, the hall stood quiet and empty. Ketil surveyed it from a few paces away: strong carved front doors, stone walls, wooden beams peeking out from under roof-turves. He tried the door, and it opened smoothly. Inside all was much as he would have expected, but unpeopled: a long table, a great chair, carved wooden pillars, and a number of barrels dotted around the walls. Curious, he stepped over to the nearest, and shifted the loose lid. Water. Of course: Thorfinn had had personal experience of how well halls could burn, when encouraged. Sensible Thorfinn.

'Who are you?'

The voice came from the other end of the hall, where a smaller doorway led out to one side. Beyond it, a safe distance away, were presumably the kitchens. He peered across the dusky room to the patch of sunlight there. A girl, it seemed, or a woman: hard to tell in this light.

'I'm a trader from Heithabyr. Ketil is my name. I'm looking for Thorfinn Sigurdarson.'

'He's away.'

'So I hear. When is he expected back?'

'When he comes.' She glanced over her shoulder, back through the little doorway. 'He says he's going to stay here, and then off he goes again. What's your business with him?'

'Oh ... trade, trade,' said Ketil airily. 'Buying and selling.'

'Buying and selling what?' She took a few paces in his direction. Girl, then, by her step. And her head was uncovered: her hair was thick and very fair, so he had half-taken it for a white headcloth.

'Whatever comes my way,' he said, but sensing that she was unimpressed, he added, 'Cups, mostly, that my brother makes.'

'Show me?' She came a few more paces forward, and he had to lay down his packs and pull open the end of the heavier one. He crouched and drew out a cloth, unfolding it to show her three carved ash cups, pale in the dim light. She touched the nearest, then took it up in her two hands, cradling it. The handle nestled between her thumbs. 'Not bad,' she said carelessly, knowing how to deal with a trader, though her eyes, now he could see them, were full of admiration.

'He loves his wood,' Ketil acknowledged, with a hint of admiration himself.

'What would you take for it?' she asked, eyes still on the cup.

'Just now,' he said, 'a hot meal and a bath.'

She looked up at him, assessing.

'And in the future?' she asked, cautious.

'A word with Thorfinn Sigurdarson,' he said innocently, 'when he returns.'

She nodded, considering.

'Well, then, Ketil from Heithabyr,' she said, 'I'll show you to the bath house, then you can join us to eat.'

The bath house was the public one, and busy enough though it was early even on a Saturday for the weekly wash. Ketil had seen much worse. Great fires of dried seaweed boiled water for generously sized tubs where men sat scrubbing and pondering in a row, chatting and staring out at the building work over the half-wall. The women's baths were presumably more enclosed, somewhere on the other side. Ketil wondered idly if the girl bathed there, or used a private bath house somewhere. She had spoken with some authority. Could she be Thorfinn's daughter? He had no idea.

'New here, are you?' The man in the tub next to him leaned over a little, friendly.

'Visiting, yes.'

'Trader?'

'From Heithabyr, that's right.'

'Heithabyr?' the man whistled softly. 'That's a way.'

'Not so far, really,' said Ketil. He had travelled much further, in his time.

'I've been to Dublin, myself,' said the man proudly.

'Raiding?'

'Oh, aye. There's nothing like getting away in the fine weather, and fetching home a few nice things for the winter. The wives like it too, eh? I'm sure your wife likes you out from under her feet, let her run things her own way a month or so, eh?'

'Sole purpose of trading,' Ketil agreed comfortably, though he had no wife. 'You'd be Thorfinn's man, then?'

'Oh, aye. I was Rognvald's once, too – they were kin, and then they had a falling out. I liked Rognvald fine, but I don't know. There were ill-done deeds, eh? And I ended up with Thorfinn. And now Rognvald's dead, not that that will mean anything to you, but, well, I'm Thorfinn's man. But now he's talking about not going raiding this summer, and where does that leave me?' He sounded dismayed, and Ketil turned to look more closely at his broad face. 'Or the wife, eh?' The man laughed, seeing him look, but there was still some undertone of dissatisfaction there. Ketil wondered, too. Thorfinn not raiding? Was he ill?

'I hear Thorfinn's away. Who's the man in charge while he's off?'

'That'd be Einar.'

'Einar Einarson?'

'Tall, thin fellow? That's the man. He must be better known than I'd thought to be heard of in Heithabyr?' The man gave him a dubious look, and Ketil quickly asked,

'Where's Thorfinn off to? Somewhere local?'

The man was easily enough distracted.

'Oh, aye, he's away over to Stronsay, they say, some case of sheep stealing they wanted him to decide on. He'll be back in a day or so, no doubt. He can't leave his building work for long at the moment.'

'Careless builders?' Ketil asked, warily. He had seen the calluses on the man's hands.

'No, the builders are fine,' said the man hurriedly. 'He just can't keep from supervising, eh?' He grinned again, sure of sympathy. Ketil smiled.

'What is it he's building?'

'Och, new everything. A new hall, a new longhouse for himself, a new enclosure wall, new bath house with hot steam, if you ever heard such a thing – and of course, a new church. A fancy big one with a roundy end – you never saw the like. Well, I haven't – you've travelled, of course.'

'Roundy ends are not the fashion in Heithabyr, I can tell you,' Ketil reassured him.

'Aye, well, of course Thorfinn's been all the way to Rome,' said the man, eyes wide. 'Who knows what he's seen?'

'Who indeed?' agreed Ketil.

Bathed and wearing a clean shirt, he folded his filthy travelling cope into his pack and pulled out his everyday blue cloak, pinning it over his right shoulder. He felt he had properly arrived. His damp hair bristling and his shorn jawline singing in the cold air, he returned to the buildings around the hall to follow the scent of food. The girl had previously shown him the doorway of the longhouse where dinner was being served to a random selection of household servants or slaves, in some cases difficult to distinguish. She herself had vanished. Ketil joined a queue with a bowl in his hands and received a dash of broth from a large central pot, and he retreated to a corner of the wooden bed platform to eat it with his own horn spoon. His packs he tucked safely behind him. The staff had little time for talk, and he had asked all the questions he needed to for now. His only real question was for himself: should he go and see Einar? Would Einar remember him?

On the other hand, he had failed to negotiate a bedspace for the night, too, in exchange for his brother's fine wooden cup. Not much of a trader, he told himself, with a wry smile. But Einar might put him up, whether or not he remembered him. Perhaps he'd be more likely to if he failed to recognise Ketil at all.

He nudged the man next to him, and asked him for directions to Einar's longhouse.

To his surprise, the directions took him along the wide tongue of land that linked the brough to the rest of the mainland. But Einar, it turned out, had lands and a hall of his own, at Buckquoy nearby, follower of Thorfinn though he was. His hall and longhouse both were nestled in the root of the tongue where it joined the slope of the mainland, with a view each side of the spit of land – not a bad defensive position, Ketil thought, as he approached. The north side of the spit was defended by long claws of rock, sharp edges upmost, as he had seen on the approach earlier. On the south, the Brough curled round to form a bay with the west coast of the mainland. Less crowded here than on the Brough itself, a scattering of longhouses showed where the farmers lived that tended to the sheep he could see on the bright green sward. These would be Einar's men, no doubt, farming in spring and autumn, and raiding with him in the summer months. He might have to tread carefully here.

A smaller version of Thorfinn's arrangement on the Brough, Einar too had his smithy, his brewery, his wellhouse here. Ketil picked his way through a wandering flock of hens, passed a stiff-legged dog resting in the sunlight, relished again the lingering fragrances of the midday meal. He wondered if he should enquire at the hall, tall beside the squat longhouse next to it, or at the longhouse itself, when he noticed a woman marching determinedly towards the same buildings. There was something about her that told him that whatever business he might have with Einar, she would have her turn first: on the other hand, she clearly knew where she was going, so he followed. He had the impression that she was the woman he had seen from the boat, though he had no idea why. Long-legged, he was only a few paces behind her when she decisively entered the hall, time enough to see her march up to where Einar, as thin as Ketil remembered, sat on his chair. Her head was high and though she was small she managed to make the room, with its dozen or so people, fall silent. Ketil slid round to one side, so that he could more clearly see her face, as Einar blinked slowly at this interruption to business – or perhaps to his midday meal.

'Sigrid? What is it?'

But Ketil hardly heard him. He was staring at Sigrid's face.

TVEIR

II

Standing to adjust her headcloth that morning, Sigrid had watched the merchants' kvarr approach the Brough without much interest. It was one of many.

She looked down critically at the flat stone she had been shifting. It abutted the previous stone quite well, she thought, though she gave it another little kick, and stepped firmly on to it to settle it lower into its bed. It seemed fairly steady. She brushed her hands together, examined a cut on the back of one knuckle, and picked up the cloak she had cast aside, warmed by her work. The mist was damp again on her face and she would chill quickly. She fastened the cloak on to her shoulder brooches, and began to climb back up by the tumbling stream to the top of the rough cliff. A clump of willow dug its stools into the damp earth here and she used the pliant branches to push herself up the slippery path: she had a sudden recollection of cutting last year's stems at the turn of winter, her fingers stiff with cold, her feet frozen in the soaking earth, tears icing on her cheeks. It had been only days since she had buried Thorstein and Saebjorn – her little Saebjorn. She swallowed now, and pushed on up the narrow cleft, toes gripping and hands reaching for the tough grass on the brow.

Once up, she turned and stood for a moment at the head of the cleft, feet planted firm in the springy turf, the wind a steady barrage that pressed her skirts and cloak against her. Her skin was cold, but inside she was warm, especially when she shut her eyes against the wind's draughty fingers. She stood, eyes closed, for a long time. She was so tired. Would it matter, she wondered, if she just let go, let the wind take her over the edge? Thorstein was gone, Saebjorn was gone. The croft and its sheep would be absorbed into Einar's lands or given out again to some deserving follower. She would be with Thorstein and Saebjorn, and for a moment she allowed herself to imagine again little Saebjorn safe in her arms, warm and soft.

But she had work to finish, before she could go. How could she meet Thorstein in the afterlife, and tell him she had let go before her work was done?

Reluctantly, she opened her eyes to the cold once more. The sea was bright and sharp. She squinted, turned, and headed home.

Almost at once she was aware of movement somewhere nearby that the wind had hidden from her ears before. She was glad she had not surrendered to any weeping, when she saw her neighbour Helga, bright and energetic, skipping up the path from the direction of the Brough, a basket of who knew what delights and novelties on her back. Helga liked the fine things in life. She would have every visiting merchant ship noted and listed within hours of its touching the land. Seeing Sigrid, she waved cheerfully.

'Good morning, friend!' she cried, and grinned. 'What have you been up to? You look as if you've been wading to Westray!'

Sigrid glanced down at her wet feet and skirt.

'It's cheaper than the boat-fare,' she conceded, straight-faced. 'Have you been down to the harbour already this morning?'

'Three boats in,' Helga confirmed, holding up a suitable number of fingers. 'One from Shetland – some lovely soapstone dishes, Sigrid, look!' She swung her basket down and pulled out a long, rectangular dish. 'Not the same quality as the Norwegian ones, of course, but I love the shape!'

Sigrid dutifully stroked a finger along the edge of the dish. To her certain knowledge, Helga had more dishes in her longhouse than she was ever likely to need: she could have hosted a feast for everyone in Birsay and given each their own plate.

'Very nice,' she said. Helga was undaunted by her tone.

'And look! This will interest you more, no doubt. Wool – very fine wool, don't you think?'

This time Sigrid's hand went out of its own accord. A hank of fine fibre, unspun but dyed a rich, bright reddish brown. Helga could keep her soapstone dishes.

'Where is this from?' Sigrid asked.

'Oh, there wasn't much of it, I'm afraid. I think it's from somewhere Frankish? Maybe? Or was it Saxon?'

Sigrid's mouth turned down at the corners, even as her fingers delighted in the wool. She could never afford something like that, but even so, she wanted to know more about it than that it was from somewhere vaguely south. Helga's sense of geography was not a keen one, but then Sigrid was fairly sure Helga had never left Orkney. She realised Helga was watching her.

'I wondered,' said Helga, a little smile in her eyes, 'if I spun it, would you work it into something? A little bag, perhaps?'

Sigrid considered, fingers still amongst the fibres.

'I could use it as the weft, and something stronger as the warp,' she suggested, already picturing it. 'That way it will wear better, and this little bit of wool will go further.'

'Perfect!' said Helga. She eased the wool out of Sigrid's fingers, and popped it back into her basket. 'I knew you'd like it.'

Sigrid nodded. Working it was all she wanted, really. And Helga could be relied upon to spin it well enough. She was grateful. They would discuss terms later.

Helga turned her gaze up the hill, and sighed.

'I'd better go and make the meal,' she said. 'They'll be hungry. Do you think this mist will lift soon?'

'You never know.' But even as they spoke, the wind shredded the fog around them, and they could see Helga's longhouse high on the smooth brow of land. Both women smiled. Helga nodded farewell, and turned to go. Sigrid, whose house was further inland and a little downhill, set off towards it, blinking in the sudden sunlight.

When she could focus properly, she glimpsed a movement at the corner of her own house. Gnup already? No: it was too big for Gnup. A figure, tall, she thought, in a blue cloak – but blue cloaks were common as gulls. She glanced back but Helga, head ploughing into the wind, was already out of earshot. She poked stray strands of her own hair back to her billowing headcloth and squinted, trying to identify the figure, but at that moment the man rounded the corner of the house, his cloak caught the wind and bucked like a turning sail, and he was hidden from view. Frowning, she brushed earth from her skirts, and set off briskly across the hill. She had no wish to lose a customer, whoever he was.

When she reached the house, though, there was no one in sight. She sighed. She must indeed have lost him. The sudden shelter of the building's lea deceived her into warmth and she paused, settling hair and headcloth and taking a moment to look about, unchallenged by the breeze. Already the pasture, under the spiky blonde strands of last year's grass, was astonishingly green in the morning's abrupt sunlight. She would never, she thought, quite grow used to this early spring. When Thorstein had first brought her here, when Einar Einarsson had granted him the land, she had been dazzled: the treeless swards, the plump sheep and cows, were like some dreamland from a poem. Not so much of a dream, it had turned out, for her. Or for Thorstein.

A chinking movement behind her made her jerk round.

'Sigrid? Oh, it is you!'

'Bjarni Hravn! Who did you expect in my house?'

The man laughed in the face of her irritation, and she had to smile back.

'I thought perhaps someone else was here to employ your talents before I could snatch you.'

Sigrid looked about her, ironically, at the empty pastures.

'I don't see a queue, today. You must have caught me at a quiet time.'

He grinned, pushing back the raven's wing of glinting black hair that had earned him his nickname.

'I know you keep busy enough, Sigrid,' he said, 'and I reminded my mother that she might have to be patient.'

Bjarni's mother was indeed a good customer. Sigrid relaxed a little, sure that payment in some form would follow.

'You'd better come in,' she said, giving the sunlight a regretful glance. 'But I have to set the stew over the fire for Gnup first.'

'I wondered what that wonderful smell was.' Bjarni stooped to follow her into the longhouse. 'Lucky Gnup.'

'He's a hungry boy by midday,' said Sigrid, rousing the central fire. The cooking pot was ready, the stew already cooked and only requiring warming through. She glanced up at Bjarni. He was outlined by the bright doorway, but the firelight showed his face and his keen interest in the appearance of vegetables and flakes of salt fish as she stirred through the thick gravy. 'But if you're lucky,' she said, relenting at last, 'he might leave you a bowlful.'

'That would be perfect!' Without further hesitation Bjarni

tucked up his cloak and settled himself on the edge of the wooden platform with her wools and loom, only glancing at them before focussing more intently on the pot on the fire. His broad feet established themselves on the stone-flagged floor, quite at ease.

For a few minutes, Sigrid also concentrated wordlessly on stirring the stew, making sure that nothing was sticking to the bottom of the pot to burn. She added a little more water, contemplated the fire, and sat back, wriggling the knot of her headcloth against her neck. Even after all this time, she was not comfortable talking business.

'Well,' she said, 'does Ragna want me to make something for her?'

Bjarni glanced up again from the pot, and back at the wools behind him.

'She's talking of a braid to weave from,' he said. Even when his face was bland, his light voice had a smile in it. 'She knows you don't often make them, but she wants a particular one, in black and white only.'

Sigrid pursed her lips.

'Could she not just stitch the braid on to the finished cloth? Weaving from a braid – it's not just me, it's really not often done these days.'

'She says she'll come and talk to you about it if you're not sure. She said something about a smoother finish?' He shrugged. No doubt he would be the recipient of whatever his mother Ragna was making, but the process did not concern him. 'Or you could go to her?'

That sounded more like Ragna. She preferred people to go to her.

'How long does she want it to be?' she asked. 'Only there's not much white wool around at the moment. There's a farmer in Rousay has a few white sheep, but he won't want to be shearing them yet.'

'She didn't say.' Bjarni put on a dismayed face, but Sigrid doubted its sincerity. Bjarni was all too good at setting off on some errand that took his fancy, without any of the necessary preparation. People were usually forgiving.

A scurry at the door interrupted her thoughts.

'Sigrid!'

Bjarni laughed, and Sigrid turned to see a small boy in the doorway, his breeches muddy and his cloak askew, dirty fair hair poked into a coxcomb not quite central on his head.

'Ah, good, Gnup, your meal is nearly ready. Let's see your hands?'

Automatically Gnup came forward to Sigrid with his hands out flat in front of him. Now he was no longer against the light, she could see that the mud on his breeches was the least of his problems. His face was smeared, and his hands were filthy, and that new hairstyle smelled distinctly of sheep.

'It's that old yow, Sigrid. She won't come up from that gully down by the cliff. You know what she's like.'

Sigrid gave a resigned laugh.

'I do indeed.' She sighed. 'What's she doing down there?'

Gnup twisted his mouth.

'I think maybe she's dropped her lamb down there. But if she has she's not looking after it. She's just standing there keeking at me down her long nose.'

'Oh, yes, that would be her.' Sigrid was already on her feet, flicking out her cape and pulling the pot of stew back off the fire. 'We'd better go and show her the error of her ways. Again.'

'The gully down by the cliff?' said Bjarni, as if he had only just worked out where they were talking about. 'That's rough enough to put any sensible sheep off. Surely if you just leave her she'll come home on her own.'

'Well, one, Bjarni,' said Sigrid, fetching a long stick from beside the door, 'if she's dropped her lamb and there's something wrong with it, she'll never shift from there till we've seen to the lamb. And I can't afford to lose both of them. And two, I've never seen any proof this ewe's remotely sensible. Sorry about the stew – maybe another time?'

At last Bjarni realised that he was not to have his free meal, and pushed himself up to his feet, broad hands on his knees. He seemed about to ruffle Gnup's hair, then reconsidered, thoughtfully wiping one hand down his cloak. He grinned at Sigrid, and waved them both farewell.

'Be careful down there, though, Sigrid. You may not want to lose the sheep, but we can't afford to lose you!'

It was lightly said, but it pleased her: she held the warmth of his words to her as she and Gnup turned and headed back across the hill to find the reluctant ewe.

The gully below the cliff was an awkward little place, and one she did not much like, though she could not have said why. It was certainly not particularly safe, as Bjarni had hinted: crooked into rocks at the north side of the Brough's tongue of land, part of it had fallen away in a storm five or six winters ago. One end of the sheltered scoop was broken, loose and fragmentary. Yet it was a pretty place, on a bright day: from the cliff above you would scarcely know it was there, but a gap in the rocks revealed a little grassy trail downwards. If you followed it, hardly a bootwidth across at first, stony corners catching your ankles, you came to a place where the savage rocks cradled the grass, broader now, in a hollow where the wind never seemed to venture, knotted with sweet pink arbies and other hardy flowers, on a spring day like this one. It caught the sun, too, and they often found a sheep dozing there, too near the brittle edge for comfort. Yet Sigrid found it a melancholy place, that drew from the salt-smarting air thoughts of sad times and losses and failures. Even thinking of going there cast a little gloom over her sunny day.

Going there was not to be easy, in any case. The narrow path was entirely blocked by a single ewe. A ewe, moreover, with both weight and determination on her side.

'I tried to shift her, Sigrid, but she wasn't for moving,' said Gnup anxiously. 'I don't think she's broken a leg or anything. She just doesn't want to move.'

'She hasn't trapped a foot, anyway,' said Sigrid, examining the ewe's legs. 'Did you try pushing from behind?'

'Um, yes,' said Gnup, and made a face. Sigrid looked back at him, taking in once again the layers of gutter and sheep muck. She nodded.

'I'm going to get past her, and see if I can find a lamb down there,' she decided.

The ewe might not have wanted to move, but she had no objection to Sigrid squeezing and scrambling half across her: she had a way of looking at humans that suggested she would not be surprised, whatever levels they stooped to. Sigrid, breathing faster, stood at last on the little path behind the animal and looked about. The rocks here were jumbled, but it was easy enough to see that no lamb had been born just here recently. She stepped carefully down the steep path towards the gully. She had not been down here, she thought, since last autumn at least. She could not help a shiver. The smooth grass of the hollow always seemed too perfect.

But today it was not perfect at all. In fact, a broad oval in the centre of the hollow had been cut away, the grass only beginning to grow back. Temporarily forgetting to hunt for lambs, she walked forward for a closer look. A few flat stones had been heaped on one particular spot, not large ones, just, it seemed, whatever had been to hand. Frowning, she squatted down, tucked her skirts out of the way, and lifted the nearest one. What she saw made her catch her breath, and for a moment she nearly lost her balance. Then she gently replaced the stone, and stood, thinking hard. Then with a nod that was not quite as firm as she might have liked, she turned and climbed the narrow path again, shoving past the ewe at the top.

'I can't see a lamb. Gnup, will you stay here with her? If anyone comes by, don't let them briz past her, all right? I'll be back as soon as I can.'

'Where are you going?'

'I'm going to see Einar.'

Einar had always shown respect to the wives of his followers, and she walked with confidence into his hall where he and some of his men were finishing their midday meal. Only vaguely aware of a tall figure following her, she had a fleeting guilty thought about Gnup's dinner, before she marched up the hall to seize Einar's attention.

'Sigrid!' said Einar, blinking at her. 'What can I do for you? Are you well?'

'Very well, thank you,' she said, 'but – you know the gully down below the cliff? Up to the north?'

Einar frowned, but two of his men nodded, nudging each other.

'That hollow that broke in the storm, yes?' asked one, plump and assured.

'That's the place.' She looked back at Einar, who also nodded, though she was not quite sure he yet knew where she meant.

'Is it damaged again?' he asked.

'Well, someone's been digging in it,' she said, her voice sharp at how everything seemed so slow. 'They've buried a man there.'

THRÍR

III

Ketil watched her face closely. Was it really her? It had been so long, and he had not thought of her for years, let alone expected to find her here. Her hair was covered, of course – she would be married now, no doubt – so he could not see if it was still the same untidy fair jumble. Her figure had filled out as it ought, and no more. Her voice was lower. How could he even begin to recognise her? But the face was the same, or an adult version of the same, serious and watching, jarring memories free in his mind. Her lips were still a little open, as if the words had spilled out before she could quite stop them. But the words were out. She could not put them back now.

'A man?' Einar queried. 'Who is it?'

'I don't know: I could only see the top of his head,' Sigrid admitted. 'In fact, it might, I suppose, be a woman, but the hair is short.' Her voice broke, just a little, and she shut her mouth abruptly. He could see her determination not to cry. That had not changed.

'Well,' said Einar, looking about him with wide eyes that still had not noticed Ketil there in the shadows. He raised a thin hand to gesture towards Sigrid. 'Does anyone know anything about this? Has anyone claimed manslaughter?' He waited, but no one spoke: there was an almost audible shrug. Einar pursed his lips a little, and went on. 'Is anyone missing?'

There was a pause. Ketil looked about the hall: it was possibly the smallest he had ever visited, but the high roof was still dark, and a few torches flickered to light the lower spaces. There was no central fire on this mild day, but the men had definitely been eating, the food probably brought in from Einar's longhouse. They sat about Einar's seat with various expressions of satisfaction on their faces, and dishes on their laps, more ready for sleep than for a puzzle.

The plump man, arranged to advantage at Einar's side, drew his lips together in thought, but his friend next to him shook his head.

'No one recently, I'm sure. Not around here.'

'What about the Brough?'

The plump man shrugged.

'There are so many strangers there at the moment, who could tell?' He smiled. Why would anyone care if a stranger found himself buried in a deserted gully?

His friend gave the matter more consideration, though.

'I have had no word of anyone missing,' he announced, stroking his thin, curling hair back from his forehead importantly. 'I'm sure I would have heard.'

'You didn't look at the face?' asked the plump man, staring at Sigrid as if a little disappointed with her. 'How long do you think he had been there?'

Sigrid's shoulders stiffened.

'I had no wish to look particularly closely, Hrolf. There's an arrangement of stones over the head, and I moved one and found what I found. Then I came here, so that Einar could see it as it was, not half dug up.' There was no threat of tears now in her voice, Ketil noticed. She clearly did not think highly of Hrolf, anyway.

'Ah, yes,' said Einar. He stretched his long legs out, leaning back perilously in his chair. 'I suppose I ought to take a look.'

'We'll go if you like,' Hrolf offered with easy generosity, speaking for himself and his thin-haired companion. Einar's gaze fell softly on him, and for a moment he seemed to consider the idea. Then he folded his legs back, and stood abruptly.

'We'll all go,' he announced.

Inevitably it took a few minutes for the men in the hall to gather themselves together. Sigrid vanished into a huddle of Einar, Hrolf and Hrolf's friend. Ketil recognised Einar's wife, though he could not remember her name, clearing dishes out of the way and making sure Einar had his cloak on properly: she had always, he recalled, been an organiser. He found himself on the outskirts of the busyness, wondering whether he should follow everyone to see Sigrid's discovery or not. He certainly wanted to talk to her, and this might be his only chance.

'Hello, I don't think we've met before?' came a voice from

behind him. He turned to find a broad, well-made man, almost his own height, with a slick of dark hair over his handsome brow. Ketil nodded his head.

'Ketil. I'm a trader from Heithabyr, looking for Thorfinn Sigurdarson, but I hear he's away. Someone directed me here.'

'Sounds as if you didn't arrive at a good moment for talking trade. I'm Bjarni, by the way: I live up the hill.' He gestured, his arm clinking with bangles. Some of them, Ketil thought, were gold.

'Good to meet you, Bjarni. No, my timing is unlucky.'

The crowd began to move towards the door. He and Bjarni were in the way, and it was natural for them to shift through the doorway to clear the path. Once outside, it made sense to keep walking with the others: Bjarni seemed to belong, anyway.

'What do you trade?' asked Bjarni, happy enough to carry on their conversation.

'Whatever is available in one place, and wanted in another,' said Ketil frankly. 'But my brother makes wooden cups, and I help him sell them.' He had left his packs tucked to the side of the hall: he hoped they would be safe, or at least unnoticed. No doubt Einar's wife would have them tidied away even as he was leaving the hall. 'I can show you one later,' he added, remembering to fish for custom. 'He's a good carver, one of the best in Heithabyr.'

'I'll take a look,' said Bjarni easily, not committing himself to anything. 'My mother likes a fine cup, if the design pleases her.'

'Oh, he'll carve to a customer's request, too,' said Ketil, 'though of course that could take a while to fetch for you.'

'From Heithabyr? Yes, I should think so!' Bjarni laughed.

They were at the back of the little crowd, and following the leaders up and across the hill at the neck of the land bridge. The brightness of the day seemed to have passed now and cloud crept high over the hill, ready to drop about them at any moment like cobwebs from a turf roof. Ketil looked around him while he still could, mist-free. Ahead, over the brow of the low hill, was the sea he had crossed earlier, the horizon less sharp now as grey blended into grey. The lack of trees, not what he was used to, made the land look barren, but the grass was much brighter than he was used to further north. Only when he glanced around to take in the whole hillside did he realise that they were not quite the very last of

Einar's court crossing the hill.

He stopped, taken aback. Bjarni paused, but walked on slowly, smiling.

A man was following them, a man whose shaggy white head reached only the middle of Ketil's chest. Ketil's first impression was triangular: the man's broad shoulders looked strong enough to uproot substantial trees, but below them his body tapered sharply down to a pair of withered legs that could do little more than help him to balance. His weight was pressed into two thick crutches, on which he swung himself competently over the rough turf.

'That's Snorri,' Bjarni called back with a grin. 'Snorri, keep your hand on your silver – this man's a Heithabyr trader, out for custom.'

'Good day to you,' said Ketil, wondering at the man on crutches. 'You're one of Einar's men?'

'Ha!' Snorri let out a snort of laughter. 'Aye, well, I am, but you'll not expect me to head off on a raid, will you?'

'Well, no.' Ketil turned to walk alongside Snorri, slowly. Snorri's beard bristled, as if it had gone untrimmed all its life. Tucked between it and a pair of eyebrows almost as bushy, a hooked red nose and a pair of glinting blue eyes invited conspiracy. Despite his rough appearance, his voice was deep and mellifluous.

'I'm his skald,' said Snorri at last, clearly disappointed at Ketil's patient silence.

'Of course.'

He could feel Snorri assessing him from the depths of the forest of hair.

'It's fine, lad, you can relax. No one would expect a trader to be any good at verse.'

Ketil smiled.

'Thanks, that's a relief.' He thought for a moment. 'How long have you been Einar's skald?'

'Oh, I think this is nearly three years, now. Since he settled down a bit.'

'Settled down?'

'Oh, yes,' said Snorri, with a whistle for emphasis. 'Used to be some warrior, our Einar, or so I'm told. Fought all round the place with Thorfinn, over to Ireland, the Western Isles, down as far as …

er, Gippesvig, is it called? Foreign parts, anyway. Maybe further. Then Thorfinn – well, Thorfinn headed off to Rome – by land, if you please! - and left Einar in charge here. You'd have thought Einar would just keep raiding, but he seemed to lose the taste for it. He doesn't go for as long as he used to now. Makes it easier for me, though, staying put: at least that's one of us happy – though there aren't so many heroics to make verse about.' He gave Ketil a sideways glance, as if expecting him to draw his own conclusions. 'And he's learning to read.'

'To read? You mean runes?'

'Latin.'

Ketil was shocked. In Snorri's fine voice, the word fell like a stone. Ketil almost wanted to laugh. He told himself to remember he was not supposed to know much about Einar's past.

'Well,' he said, 'I've never met a warrior who could read Latin. He must be an interesting man.'

Snorri nodded, slowly.

'You might want to catch up, if you don't want to miss anything,' he said, one shoulder gesturing to where the others had drawn ahead of them. 'Don't worry about me: I'm making verses in my head.'

He felt dismissed, and did as he was bid, hurrying on to catch up with the others. Bjarni had already joined Hrolf and his friend, leading the way. Einar and Sigrid were walking together, and Ketil edged up behind them, hoping for the chance of a word with one or the other.

'Bjarni, perhaps, or Hlifolf,' Einar was saying. Ketil wondered who Hlifolf was.

'I don't think so. Not yet,' said Sigrid, her voice calm. It seemed unlikely that this conversation had anything to do with the body they were going to see: Bjarni, after all, was still alive, if it was the man he had just been talking with. He was wondering if he could interrupt, when it became apparent that they were near their goal. Hrolf slowed, and turned to wave helpfully to Einar.

There were rocks ahead, and from here you would say there was nothing beyond them but the cliff edge. But now that he was near the front of the crowd, Ketil could see a small boy emerge from amongst them. He seemed to have been bathing in tan-coloured mud, and one skinny arm was around the neck of a large ewe with a dismissive eye. The boy looked with surprise at the crowd approaching.

'Och, surely it'll not take all that lot to shift her, Sigrid?' the boy called, though by the looks of the ewe it might. The ewe, however, swiftly assessed the situation, and strolled off to one side as though she had quite intended to leave just then. The boy gave a yelp, and followed her.

'Just keep an eye on her, Gnup, would you?' Sigrid called. 'And try not to let her go down towards the gully again.' But the ewe had no further interest in the gully, and was clearly heading home. Sigrid watched her thoughtfully. 'I'm not even sure she's dropped her lamb,' she added, half to herself.

'The gully, Sigrid?' Hrolf called. Sigrid favoured him with a stony look, and led the way along a little path through the tilting rocks. Einar followed.

'Hrolf, Hlifolf,' he called back, 'you two next.'

So the friend with the thin curly hair was Hlifolf, then, Ketil thought. It suited him, a scrawny breath of a name, more usually a woman's. Following him, Ketil could see his scalp greyish through the curls, which lay lank over his shoulders as if he thought they could make up in length what they lacked in bulk.

The little crowd was filtered to a single file, slithering as the grass grew muddier with their steps. As they descended below the level of the hillside they had left, rocks to waist height on their right, Ketil felt himself tensing: it was the perfect place for an ambush. But why would anyone want to ambush them?

The gully at the foot of the path was lush and grassy, balmy almost in the lee of the cliff. Everyone gathered just where the path ended, crowding to see but not quite wanting to move forward. In the centre of the grass was a patch which might have been bare all winter, but now, as if they sensed a sympathetic spring, green threads of grass were beginning to litter the dark earth. A tumble of flat stones, none bigger than a man could lift easily enough with one hand, lay heaped at the far end. Ketil found himself with a clear view as Einar and Sigrid, followed importantly by Hrolf and his friend Hlifolf, moved carefully forward. Sigrid slipped between the two followers and the stones, and with Einar on the other side of them Hrolf and his friend were forced to wait while she squatted down, skirts tucked back, and gently lifted away the first stone.

Einar had his back half-turned to Ketil, and Sigrid's head was bent: he could see Hrolf's face, though, saw the look of revulsion surge across it, saw him jerk back almost knocking Hlifolf sideways. Hlifolf grabbed his arms from behind, steadying himself, his long fingers surprisingly strong. Neither took their eyes from whatever was revealed beneath the heap of stones.

Sigrid, with a swift glance up at Einar, continued to move the stones until they were all set aside. There was a little shift forward in the crowd, and Ketil felt himself pushed a pace or two nearer the burial. Einar was crouching now, beginning the slow sweep of earth from the rest of the body. With every pass of his hands, a little more became clear.

The man lay on his side, curled up, wrapped in a blue cloak, facing towards Sigrid and with his head towards the sea and the Brough. His hair was short, but not cropped too close, and darkish fair, though it may have been lighter when he was alive and not covered in earth. Ketil edged to his left, discreetly. A shivery, prickly feeling had begun to creep up the back of his neck. He craned forward, caught sight of the profile of a grubby, sunken face, and felt himself freeze.

He took a step backwards, flicking a look to left and right. No one was taking any notice of him except as a potential obstruction to their own view. He made himself focus once again on the grave before them. Blue cloak, hunched shoulders folded forward, the cuff of a shirt in brown linen that must once have been white, a knee, breeches ripped across, bent and peering from under the cloak's edge. It was scarred by some predator, tempted even by that bony flesh. He pursed his lips, and made himself look at the face once more. The eyes and lips were gone, he saw now: he had imagined his impression of them at his first glimpse. And now the smell of decay, released by the earth's disruption, oozed about them, caught in the gully's airless trap. What he could not see, his mind began to fill in for him: the blackened stomach, the gaunt nails, the falling flesh: he knew all too well what would be under that blue cloak.

'How long do you think he has been here?' Einar asked. Hlifolf regarded the corpse thoughtfully.

'It's been cold, up to recently. He could have been here since the end of the autumn, beginning of the winter. The earth has settled, and you see that grass growing.'

'When were you last down here, Sigrid?' Einar asked.

'The autumn,' she replied quickly enough. 'I've had no cause to be here since. But it's been mild weather this past month or more. I think he might not have been here so long as that. He could have been killed in the early spring.'

Hrolf and Hlifolf, behind her, exchanged a look that Ketil could not understand. Einar caught it too, and frowned.

'Well, between late autumn and early spring. It's a good cloak: this is not just someone's slave disposed of here, and anyway he's been buried. Does anyone recognise him, from here or elsewhere? Could he have been a visitor over on the Brough?' He steadied himself with long fingers on the earth as he looked up at his followers. Ketil held his breath. 'No one?'

'I don't know,' said Hlifolf at last, his head on one side. 'There's something slightly familiar about him. Could he have been a visitor over on the Brough?' It was an odd little echo of Einar's question, and Ketil wondered if Hlifolf were hard of hearing.

'Well, you would know if he had been, wouldn't you?' said Hrolf. Hlifolf nodded solemnly. Einar waited for any further response, then carried on dusting damp earth away from the body. His hands were surprisingly gentle.

'What shall we do with him, then?' he asked, lifting loose soil from a pair of stained leather boots, long laces treble-wrapped over the stiff ankles.

'Couldn't we just leave him here?'

Sigrid's suggestion seemed to surprise everyone. Einar blinked at her.

'Wouldn't you mind? He's on land you graze.'

'It's not going to be pleasant to move him. He might as well lie here as anywhere.'

'What if he was a Christian?' asked Einar mildly. 'We could take him to the new churchyard.'

'He's not lying like a Christian,' Hlifolf remarked.

'Has he a cross?' asked Einar, then, as no one else moved he leaned over the corpse, lips firmly closed against the smell, and delicately touched the man's chin and neck. His fingers flew back suddenly, stained black.

'Of course,' he said, almost to himself. 'Of course.' He looked up at them all, stuck there in the gully's neck like dunters in a rockpool. 'His throat is cut.'

Well, obviously, Ketil thought. The man had not buried himself up here, far from public view. What had they all thought? What had Einar thought?

'Then he was murdered?' Hlifolf was the first to put it into words. 'But who would have done that?'

'Maybe someone killed him in a boat, and hid him here?' suggested Bjarni. It was the first time any of the crowd had spoken since they had arrived, and everyone jumped.

'He's not a small man,' Sigrid objected. 'It's a hard climb even without carrying something. I know, I tried to rescue a sheep that way once.'

There was general agreement, as if Bjarni's interjection had given them all permission to have opinions. Bjarni, too, had gained confidence.

'Can we turn him on to his back, so we can all see his face? And his right arm, too. Is he holding a weapon? Is there anything else that might tell us who he is?'

Thank heavens for someone with a bit of wit, Ketil thought, watching as Sigrid and Einar between them eased the man's shoulders back, turning his head. The gash in his neck was black and filthy, and there was some damage to the cheek that had lain on the earth: whatever had eaten his eyes and lips, no doubt, a softer meal than that knee. His right hand was lying in a mound of some kind, tucked partly under the tail of his cloak. Sigrid disentangled the fabric carefully. She pulled it clear, laying the border of the cloak over the man's legs. A length of stained braid edged it, the colours only a little faded in the dirt. Left bare, the odd mound seemed to shiver in the air. She gave a little cry.

'What's that?' gasped Einar, with a start. Hlifolf peered over Sigrid's shoulder, as the crowd, breathing heavily, leaned forward. Ketil could see feathers, gaunt but strong, yellow bone, and the edge of a fierce beak.

'It appears to be an eagle,' Hlifolf said.

'An eagle? What's it doing there?' snapped Einar. But that, for once, seemed to be a question that not even Hlifolf could answer.

FJÓRIR

IV

Sigrid swallowed: the smell from the body had been ripe enough, but the eagle, oddly, uncovered, had released a curious aroma all its own. She straightened and stood, staring down at the ruptured grave. In her mind were other bodies, other deaths, fresh in her memory. She turned away, edging out from between the grave and Hrolf's assured stomach, and went to lean on the rocky hillside that formed the back wall of the gully, cushioning her neck on her headcloth. The sea beyond the gully's sill was ashen, the sky a grey glare.

Einar was organising a couple of the men to fetch a hurdle to carry the corpse back to the hall – along with the eagle, she assumed. She would have happily left man and eagle here together, in this gully, and blocked the path off with rocks, and never come here again, let them rest peacefully – until the sea took them, anyway.

'I'll see what I can find out,' Hrolf was saying to Einar. 'It should be easy enough to work out who he is, where he's come from. Don't worry about it.'

It should, she thought – it would be even easier if he knew what she knew. But she was not even sure she could find the words to say it. Any possible connexion with her ... she shivered at the thought.

'And I'll make enquiries on the Brough,' said Hlifolf. Any excuse, thought Sigrid, and Hlifolf's off to Thorfinn's court, rubbing shoulders with his important friends. But the thought only danced across the habitual surface of her mind: underneath it, she was still trying to reason, to work out who this man in the grave could possibly be. If she could work it out before Hrolf could, even with Hlifolf's connexions to help him, then she would know what to do. Or at least, she would be better placed to make a decision. She shivered again. The sky was growing darker.

Einar noticed it too, and began to herd his little court back out of the gully. As they were trying to climb the path, the two men he had sent for a hurdle reappeared, and for a moment there was confusion as they simultaneously tried to slither back down to the corpse. Sigrid watched, half-amused, half-irritated. The rain began, subtly at first as if sneaking in from the sea like a night raid. It damped down the sickly smell, but made the ground muddier for the last of the disinterment. The men with the hurdle swore, unplugging their feet from the soft earth with nasty sucking sounds.

Then she noticed the tall man at the neck of the gully – a stranger. Who was he? She vaguely remembered him in the hall when she had arrived to tell Einar her news. If he had been interested enough to follow them here, was he connected with the court in some way? Might he have some idea who the dead man was? He stood there, a little hunched, hands folded lightly in front of him, taking in all the details of the corpse and its attendants as if he were trying to memorise the scene. He was quite still, though she had the impression of action waiting to happen. His close-cropped hair was almost white-fair, the shape of his skull obvious: he did not even have a beard. She wondered if he was a priest or a monk, yet he wore a blue cloak like an ordinary man.

As if at last acknowledging her scrutiny, he lifted his head and met her eye, with the slightest of smiles. And suddenly she knew him.

Or had known him. Old memories surfaced as she felt herself smile and frown at once.

'Ketil?'

'Sigrid.'

'It is you!'

No one else paid any attention: apart from the two men fastidiously rearranging the corpse on their hurdle, cloths over their muttering mouths, everyone else was now at least at the top of the gully path, out of earshot. With a last glance at the corpse, Ketil gestured her to go up ahead of him, and followed. Once on the headland, the wind nipped at them again, flinging rain, but she turned to stare at him.

'Ketil Gunnarson! What are you doing here?'

'Trading. I've just arrived,' he said, nodding his head in the vague direction of the harbour.

'Oh, you must have been on one of Helga's ships,' she realised, then explained. 'My neighbour never lets a trading ship go without a thorough inspection of its cargo. You'll have met her - though you may have mistaken her for a tax officer.'

'I don't think I saw her. I was travelling alone – well, I had a passage on a kvarr, of course. She may have appeared after I left.'

'What are you selling?'

'Wooden cups, mostly.'

'Oh, yes: Gunnar was a woodworker, wasn't he?' Images of the Heithabyr of her childhood blinked through her mind, tight-packed with people and animals, with a noise and smell to match. Breathing the sea air, she turned to face the green pasture that lay between them, Einar's hall and her own longhouse. She assumed Ketil was going back to the former. He walked beside her, though she thought he would find her short strides a little restricting. 'I mean,' she said, catching up with her own thoughts, 'perhaps he still is?'

He shook his head briefly.

'My father died a few years ago. My brother has the business now. But what are you doing here?' he asked her. 'You clearly live here, you aren't just visiting. I thought you went to Norway.'

'I did,' she said. 'I went to my aunt when my parents died. I lived not far from the old Kaupang place until I married.'

'A trader?'

'A soldier.' She gave a shrug. 'The glamorous life! He was one of Einar's men, and so we settled here.'

She thought he was about to say something, but he must have changed his mind.

'It seems a fine place to settle,' he said instead.

'It's not bad, I suppose,' she agreed easily, heedless of the fine rain that was now misting her face. 'The farming is good. Crops grow tall, and sheep grow fat. Plenty of land without having to clear it. Not too many trees.'

'None at all, that I've seen,' Ketil said. 'I'm not sure how my brother would fare here. So your husband is Einar's man?'

'He was. He died last winter.'

'I'm sorry.'

'Mm.'

They walked in silence for a moment. They could see the others up ahead, Hlifolf and Hrolf clustered around Einar, like a pair of sheep sharing a lamb, Snorri swooping behind on his crutches, talking with Bjarni. She had not realised that Snorri had followed them, too. He was not a stupid man, she reflected. She remembered Ketil beside her, and cleared her throat.

'Is this your first time in the islands, then?' she asked.

'Ah, yes,' he said after a moment. 'We mostly go to the Norwegian coast, and to Sweden. This is a new venture, a bit further than before.'

'I'm glad it brought you here, then,' she said. 'We can tell each other tales of the old days. I must have been … nine? When I left for Norway?'

'I think so: I was ten, I remember.'

'Then there are some years to fill in! Are you staying at Einar's hall?'

'I don't know yet: I had only just arrived when you appeared. I've only spoken to the skald – Snorri, is it? – and that tall man who's talking with him.'

'Bjarni,' she said at once, her eyes turning to the man in question. 'Well, I'll introduce you to Einar now if you like, but I can't stay at the hall for long. I have work to do, and I want to go and tell my neighbour about the body.' She at once felt unfriendly. She should have been prepared to make more time for him straightaway. But Ketil solved the problem.

'Well,' he said, 'if you'll come and square things with Einar for me, maybe I could walk with you to your neighbour?' He gave a little cough. 'I'm always on the lookout for a new customer, and she sounds ideal.'

She glanced at him. There was the least smile on his lips.

'Yes,' she said. 'Why don't we do that?'

The others had disappeared into the hall, presumably to discuss the corpse in the gully. She gave a little sigh: some of them were all too ready to sit around the hall these days, and Einar wasn't helping. The ones who looked forward to the summer's raiding were growing impatient: they should have been busy already, training, making preparations, but instead they sat at Einar's fire, eating Einar's food (which, to be fair, mostly came from their own farms) and drinking Einar's beer, and growing fat and lazy and cross. It would not surprise her if one of them had in a fit of restless temper slashed some stranger's throat. In fact, she told herself firmly, that was probably what had happened.

She led Ketil into the hall, and up to face Einar's seat. Einar was already sprawled there, his old fighting fingers now delicate on the leather cover of some book he kept by his chair. He did her the courtesy of looking up as she approached.

'Einar, may I present a man of my acquaintance from Heithabyr? He is here to trade and seeks somewhere to stay.' She turned to wave Ketil forward, and was surprised to see him hang his head and come only reluctantly into the light of the lamps around Einar's seat. He had, she remembered, been a confident boy, proud in his bearing. Of course, that had been years ago.

'Your name?' asked Einar.

'Ketil Gunnarson, sir,' said Ketil in a low voice, hardly looking at Einar.

'What do you trade in?'

'My brother makes fine wooden cups,' said Ketil. 'I can show you one, if my packs have not been moved.' He glanced over into the shadows of the hall.

'Later, perhaps,' said Einar carelessly, though his wife, Rannveig, filling Einar's horn cup with fresh beer, gave Ketil an assessing look, as if she could tell the quality of his brother's cups from the cut of Ketil's shirt. And perhaps, thought Sigrid, knowing Rannveig, she could. At a nod from Einar, Rannveig fetched another cup of beer and handed it to Ketil, and he was allowed to sit. Rannveig waited in the shadows behind the chair, though Sigrid knew well that her servile position was the best one from which to hear exactly what was going on, for the purposes of discussing it with her husband afterwards. She liked Rannveig: spiky, sharp, clever, and moreover with the taste to buy and wear that short dress over her gown, the one that Sigrid had woven from purple Dublin wool. Rannveig was careful with her purchases. If she bought one of Ketil's cups, every other woman on the island would, too.

'You can sleep here, of course,' Einar was saying to Ketil, with casual hospitality. It would be draughty, thought Sigrid: hardly anyone else was sleeping in the hall at the moment, and though it was small it was not warm in the spring winds.

'Are you sure that's wise, Einar?' Hlifolf was not happy. 'Remember we have a dead body being brought here. A stranger …'

'That's true,' said Hrolf. He cast a glance at Ketil which was notable for its lack of enthusiasm. 'We already have a dead body. Should we be welcoming a stranger into our midst?'

'I think Hlifolf meant that it would not be congenial for Ketil to share the hall with a rotting corpse,' said Einar mildly. 'And Ketil has only just arrived: it seems unlikely that he killed our stranger, who has been dead for some time.' He sighed, regarding his two counsellors with what looked like mild amusement. 'Hlifolf is right,' he said at last. 'You should come into our longhouse, Ketil.'

'You are more than kind,' said Ketil.

'Not at all, not at all.' Einar waved a long hand. 'It's our Christian duty, of course.'

'Of course.' Ketil blinked. 'I am honoured to be its beneficiary.' He kept his head low. Sigrid frowned.

'Ketil, if you want to take that walk with me we'd best make a start,' she said. 'Do you need to fetch your pack?'

Ketil nodded, and was on his feet in an instant. He slipped around the back of Einar to return the cup to Rannveig with a small bow.

'Are my packs …?'

'Just there,' said Rannveig, clearly pleased with his manners. Ketil vanished into the dark corner of the hall for a moment, and reappeared with a neat bundle on his shoulder.

'Hey, Ketil!' Bjarni waved a friendly beer cup in his direction. 'We'll be doing some training soon, warming up for the summer raiding. Want to join us?'

Ketil paused.

'I'm only a trader,' he said, sounding unsure of himself. 'And I'm not sure how long I'll be here.'

There was the least movement amongst the men in the hall, and Sigrid tensed. Lazy they might be, but they enjoyed finding someone weaker than themselves.

'I'm sure you'll be far too busy trading, anyway, won't you?' she asked briskly. She glared at Bjarni, who grinned back, and led Ketil back to the door, letting him go out before her. She felt an arm on her elbow, and turned to find Hlifolf's face in her own.

'Take care, Sigrid!' His eyebrows high, he blinked his pale eyes hard at her, as if trying to give her some kind of signal. His breath was fragranced with rosemary and beer. 'Strangers, yes?'

'Yes, Hlifolf,' she said quickly, hoping he would let her go. But he clung on, eyes still on hers, until she dutifully nodded back. 'Yes, I'll be careful.'

Ketil had walked on a few paces, and turned while she caught up, shaking the feel of Hlifolf's fingers from her arm.

'Something wrong?' he asked.

'Just Hlifolf being nervous.'

'I meant generally.' She did not reply, and he went on, as if she needed more explanation. 'I'd heard that Einar was a mighty warrior, one of Thorfinn Sigurdarson's closest allies, but this place feels – well, lifeless. Unless you're so used to finding dead men around the place that today was nothing out of the ordinary.'

She sighed.

'I know. Well, he used to be. Thorstein – my husband – admired Einar above all men, I think. That's why we're here.'

'Then what happened?'

'I suppose … I suppose it was Rognvald.' She looked sideways at him, but his face was blank. 'Rognvald Brusason, Thorfinn's nephew. Orkney's golden boy. I won't tell you the whole story – it's fit for one of the longer sagas – but Rognvald ruled half of Orkney and Thorfinn the other half. Thorfinn, as I'm sure you know, has lands in Scotland too which keep him busy, so for the most part Rognvald and his father before him had full control here, and they raided together in the summer. Thorfinn loved Rognvald like his own son, and the rest of Orkney practically worshipped him. I saw him once,' she said, 'and he looked like Baldur and the Archangel Gabriel rolled into one, but the man could fight, too! Never to be forgotten.'

He looked round at her, eyebrows raised, and she frowned.

'He was just like that: he had that effect on anyone who saw him. But then they fell out.'

'What about?'

'What about is not really important. Well, I don't think so, but I think I know who was to blame, even if not what the bone of contention was.'

'Oh, yes?'

She paused to negotiate a boggy patch of ground, chewed rough with sheep's hoofprints.

'Thorfinn has a wife, Ingibjorg. She's ...' She stopped. Her opinions of Ingibjorg were not strictly relevant at the moment. 'Well, anyway. She has an uncle, Kalf, who fell out with the King of Norway and came here because – well, I suppose because she was here. He offered his help to Thorfinn and Rognvald. He has ships and men, of course.'

'Of course.'

She glanced at him, but he seemed to be listening attentively.

'All this must be tedious history for you,' she said, apologetically.

'If it affects what's happening now, it affects trade,' he said, slightly sententiously. She had the impression he'd been practising the phrase. Was he really a trader? The thought caught her unawares. She considered, abandoning her narrative for a moment. He certainly walked easily with his pack, striding across the hill as if he had walked miles with it, the soft jingle of his armrings under his sleeves telling of financial comfort, and caution. He had been a gangly ten-year-old, but now he was muscular, confident – except when she had presented him to Einar. She shook her head, not willing to pursue such thoughts at the moment. Her head was busy enough.

'Helga's longhouse is up beyond mine – that's mine, there,' she nodded across to a largish, well-kept roll of a building, snug under a turf roof.

'Have you family, then?' he asked.

'No.' She heard herself say it easily, while her other self, her inside self, froze.

'But that boy with the sheep – Gnup, was it? I thought he was with you.'

'Oh, Gnup! No, he's Bjarni's cousin, or nephew, or something. He helps me with the farm.'

'And it's your farm?'

Heavens, would the man's questions never end? She dug her fingernails into her palms, telling herself that he was just interested, just polite, just finding out the lie of the land for his trade. She didn't remember him like this, constantly poking and prodding.

'It's my farm,' she said, her voice tight. 'Our son died, shortly after his father.'

'Oh, of course. I'm sorry,' he said, and sounded as if he meant it.

She drew a deep breath, and tried to remember where she had left her story of Rognvald and Thorfinn. That at least she could tell without racking her heart.

'Anyway,' she said. 'Kalf was working with Thorfinn and Rognvald, and then Thorfinn and Rognvald fell out. And Kalf turned from one to the other, fighting for Thorfinn, then fighting for Rognvald, then back again, or holding off entirely and just watching them beat each other senseless.'

'Because he felt loyalty to both of them?' Ketil suggested reasonably. 'If he had fought with both – sometimes when friends fall out it's hard for a mutual friend to take sides.'

'You don't know Kalf,' she said. 'Kalf is friends with no one but himself. And I'm quite sure he not only took advantage of their quarrel, he started it – spreading rumours about Rognvald and Ingibjorg.'

'He spread rumours about his own niece?'

'That's what made them more convincing, of course! Oh, poor Ingibjorg, the injured party, seduced by the golden boy Rognvald! Anyone who didn't know them would believe it, if they looked at Thorfinn and at Rognvald. They wouldn't see Rognvald's sparkling glamour, how unreliable it was. They wouldn't see that Thorfinn was the safe and steady one, the strong one. And anyway, of course there was no proof the rumours started with Kalf. It just seems to me the most reasonable source.'

'You always were interested in how people fitted together, weren't you, Sigrid?' Ketil smiled. 'I remember you used to watch our neighbours …'

'Never mind that,' said Sigrid sharply. 'I was a child then: I've seen more now of how people work. And Kalf works for Kalf, and no one else. If he sometimes sat back and helped neither side, it was because he was saving his energies for some point where they would serve him better – and no doubt amusing himself at the spectacle.'

'So what happened to Rognvald, then?' asked Ketil, nodding acknowledgement of this.

'The quarrel escalated: Rognvald and Thorfinn were both good men, at heart, but when rumour and devious men nibble away at their hearts and minds, like mice at a barrel, they get through eventually. Rognvald tried to kill Thorfinn, and nearly succeeded – burned down his hall during a feast. Thorfinn and Ingibjorg only just escaped. So Thorfinn took his revenge, followed Rognvald when he went to Papa Stronsay – that's a tiny island off Stronsay, which isn't that big itself – where he had gone for Christmas supplies. And Thorfinn killed Rognvald.'

'So that was that?'

'For Rognvald, perhaps.' She stopped to catch her breath: the last rise up to Helga's longhouse was rough and muddy. She turned, surveying Einar's settlement and the path they had taken. Ketil waited beside her, seemingly unaffected. She should get out more, she thought. Too much time spent over her loom and her tablets. 'Thorfinn hasn't been the same since. Nor has Einar. Einar, perhaps, received too many blows to the head over the years: he's learned to read, and talks with priests, and takes his ease, and shows no inclination to go raiding, which makes half his men restless and impatient – and poorer. But Einar will head off in the summer, eventually, reluctantly. Thorfinn's raiding days are over. He has never recovered from Rognvald's death. He went on a pilgrimage to Rome!'

'To Rome? Well, some do. And, well, there are lots of Christians about, these days.'

'Well, yes, of course. Most of us here are Christian. But he has become … it's as if no other belief can allow him to be guilty,' she said, feeling her way around the words for something she had been considering for a while. 'He's devout. Einar is scholarly, but Thorfinn is on his knees every day – and I think he's still asking forgiveness for Rognvald's death. He's building a huge new church on the Brough, there.' She pointed to the distant building works, mistily visible on the broad green tongue of land. 'He has monks coming to live there, and a priest, and he's settled there. I mean really settled: he's not taking his court around the islands any more, he's established an agent in the Western Isles to look after them for him and when he finds someone he can trust he'll probably do the same for his Scottish lands. It's not popular here.'

'No? Won't it bring a bit of prosperity to the area?'

'It'll bleed us dry,' she said frankly. 'There isn't enough here to feed a court all year round. He'll need to sort something out, some supply routes from his other lands, or we'll all starve.'

Ketil blinked, evidently considering the problem.

'Who is Thorfinn's agent in the Western Isles?' he asked at last.

'Well,' said Sigrid, 'you know how when you're sick of the sight of someone and all trust has broken down between you? You send them as far away as you can, don't you?'

'Yes,' said Ketil warily.

She smiled.

'Well, Thorfinn sent Kalf.'

FIMM

V

A wave of smoke swept down the turf roof of the longhouse before them from some cooking fire inside, flowing through a smoke hole near the ridge. Ketil's stomach felt strongly that it had been a long time since his midday meal. The wooden door stood open but a leather curtain covered half the aperture, probably blocking out a good deal of the available light. But through the gap he could see that lamps had already been lit: it looked warm and welcoming. To complete the image, he was sure he could hear singing from within, a woman's voice, high and sweet.

'Is that Helga, then?' he murmured to Sigrid.

'It is. Not sure why,' she added. 'I wouldn't sing if I were married to Hrolf, but there we are.'

Hrolf – the plump one with the cap of fair hair and the little beard.

'Maybe it's a lullaby?' he suggested. He was still trying to digest all she had told him of Thorfinn and Einar and Kalf – all the new information, anyway. 'Sending the children to sleep?'

Sigrid grinned suddenly, taking him by surprise.

'Not with that song! But maybe, knowing Helga …'

With the slightest of chuckles, she led the way up the path to the door, and slapped her hand against it. The singing broke off.

'Helga? It's Sigrid.'

'Come in!' It was the same sweet voice, certainly. Ketil stooped to enter the longhouse behind Sigrid, feeling at once the promised warmth on his chilled face and hands. The cooking smell was wonderful. Perfectly placed to appreciate it, perched on the wooden ledge near the fire, were three smallish children, two boys and a girl, each clutching a dish in anticipation and staring up at the new arrivals. Sigrid they clearly knew, so it was Ketil who came in for their attention. The little girl in particular, the smallest of the three, inserted her thumb between her lips and sucked hard as she contemplated him, eyebrows twisted curiously, in a manner Ketil began to find a little intimidating. Sigrid and Helga seemed to have fallen swiftly into a discussion of wool, and he took a moment to look about him – anywhere but at the children.

Lamps scooped from soft soapstone hung from the wooden roof posts, and more dishes were stacked on a rack against the wall where he would have expected to see the household loom. As far as he could see, this was an extraordinary thing – a loomless household. There was cloth aplenty, though: curtains, pushed back for now, would divide the room into separate sleeping quarters at night; rolls of wool and linen fabrics, with furs and skins, banked the walls, pushing the beds out towards the central walkway. The beds themselves were heaped with blankets that oozed comfort and warmth. Other goods hung from the roof posts under the lamps: wooden cups and bowls, toy boats and animals (all well carved, to his expert eye), soapstone weights and shapes, odd metalwork he thought was from the East. He had never seen a longhouse so cluttered, though everything his gaze fell on was of fine quality. Sigrid was right: Helga must buy something from every ship that landed.

'This is Ketil, a friend from Heithabyr,' Sigrid was saying. 'We knew each other as children. He sells wooden cups.'

'Does he?' was Helga's instant response. Sigrid met Ketil's eye with a wink, but he was already turning towards the purchaser of this vast collection of goods.

Helga had removed her headcloth to reveal long, curling red hair that caught the lamplight and almost twinkled. Her eyes certainly did. She barely looked old enough to have the three children that sat by the fire, but Ketil could see the shape of her eyes repeated in each of them – luckier, he thought, than taking after their father, plump Hrolf. He bowed his head to her.

'Well, Ketil, come and sit by the fire,' said Helga. 'Children, move up! Let the man sit down. Will you take some food? It's only fish stew, and some bread.'

'It smells very good,' said Ketil, finding his dish already in his hands. Helga moved close to him, beads swooping low, to spoon stew on to it, then added a round of flatbread. The bread was warm and soft and fragrant. He pulled his spoon out and started when the children did: none of the plates stayed full for long.

'Oh, Sigrid – some stew?' Helga was asking, as Ketil wiped the last of the stew with the bread. Ketil had almost forgotten she was there, and cast her an apologetic look. She made a face at him that suddenly took him back twenty years. Sigrid accepted the dish from Helga, and settled herself beside Ketil on the wooden ledge.

'No Hrolf yet, then?' she asked, though they had left him behind them at Einar's hall.

'No, he'll be ages yet. My husband's an adviser to Einar Einarsson, you know,' she explained to Ketil, who raised his eyebrows and nodded as if impressed.

'I think he will indeed be ages, particularly tonight,' agreed Sigrid. 'You won't have heard the news, then?'

'News? Since I saw you earlier?'

'Oh, yes.' Sigrid paused. 'I found a dead body, Helga.'

Helga was pouring another helping into Ketil's dish. She raised her eyes to meet his with a smile, unexpectedly dark lashes lush around pools of blue, then glanced to Sigrid.

'A dead body? What do you mean?' She straightened gracefully, checking to see if the children needed more bread.

'There was a dead man, in a shallow grave in the gully.'

Helga sat back sharply, and Ketil watched her with care. Something about that had shocked her more than the initial idea of a dead body. Or was it only that Sigrid's words had taken a moment to sink in?

'In the gully below the cliff? But who would –' He was right, he thought. It was something about the gully. Too close to home? 'But there's no one gone missing, is there? Not in years. Had it been there a long time? Has the sea taken more of the gully away, was that it?' Her eyes were wide, speculating, seeing, Ketil thought, not them but the gully. 'Sigrid, who was it?'

'No one seems to know.' Sigrid's reply was calm, but he saw how watchful she was. Ketil sat motionless: there was more to this conversation than he was hearing, and he very much wanted to hear it. Sigrid took a spoonful of stew, and chewed it thoughtfully before going on. 'It was a man, as I say. But he wasn't there in the autumn. It looks as if he was killed since the winter.'

Or in the late autumn, thought Ketil, but he did not feel he could interrupt. He saw again that white, soapy flesh, gashed black. He knew corpses. It could easily have been older.

'My!' Helga, looking back at Sigrid as though she had just remembered she was there, crouched to stir the stew. It was almost as if she had shaken herself. 'Sigrid, another spoonful?'

Sigrid held out her dish. Helga slipped another flatbread beside the stew, absently arranging it at the perfect angle.

'You don't remember anyone visiting the area around that time, do you? I mean, any time since the winter? Between your visits to the harbour and Hrolf's position with Einar, I know you hear most of the happenings around here.'

Helga frowned.

'Who visits us here?' she said. 'Unless it was someone who knew one of us – like you, Ketil,' she added with another smile. The tension that had bound the conversation was gently released, as she let her light voice hurry on. 'Visiting Sigrid, I mean. Everyone else goes up to the Brough, don't they? That's where things happen, up around Thorfinn and Ingibjorg. Has Sigrid shown you all the new buildings yet, Ketil? Everything rebuilt and improved, even the smithy and the bath house! And a huge hall! It will be magnificent! Ingibjorg's talking about the hangings she wants for it – no expense spared, I can tell you!'

Sigrid gave Helga a peculiar look, which Ketil could not quite interpret.

'Well, whether it was on the Brough or here –'

Helga interrupted.

'If you want to find out about strangers on the Brough, you'd better ask Hlifolf. He's the one who knows everyone over there. He's always going on about his cousin or whoever it is, sending him word of every little thing that happens.'

'I might just do that, if you can't help,' said Sigrid with a sigh. 'I'd hoped you might know and save me going to see him.'

'Oh!' said Helga with a giggle, 'Hlifolf would love you to go and see him!'

'Hlifolf might, yes,' said Sigrid, with a twist of her eyebrows. 'Anyway, someone must have met this man, for he didn't bury himself.'

'Are you sure?' asked Helga, serious again. 'Perhaps there was a rock fall or something. You know part of that gully was washed away already.'

'Yes, but he was buried, deliberately, in the earth.' Sigrid's voice was heavy with conscious patience. 'And his throat was cut.'

A movement amongst the children drew their attention. The older boy's eyes were wide, but the other two were more intent on their dinner. Helga skipped around the fire to hug the child.

'Hush, Sigrid! You'll upset them!'

Ketil thought the children looked far from upset. Indeed, there was a suppressed chortle between the two younger ones, and a nudge flickered between all three.

'It's the ghost!' squawked the younger boy, and the girl gave him a mock scowl.

'Shut up, Eini!' she hissed. The older boy drew some dignity from his seniority, and hushed them both, but Ketil was already paying close attention.

'What ghost is that, then?' he asked, aiming for a light tone.

'The ghost! Everyone's talking about the ghost,' said the younger boy.

'That's rubbish,' the older one dismissed him.

'You mean there is no ghost?' asked Ketil, casually wiping up the last of his stew with his bread.

'I mean … well, I don't know about the ghost, but it's a secret. Not everyone knows.'

'So who does know, then?'

'Only me and those two,' said the boy, 'over here. We met a boy from Kirkuvag whose father had been to Lervig and he said there was a ghost but he told us not to tell. And we haven't, not till now.'

'Why not?' asked Ketil. In his experience, the more you told people not to tell, the faster a secret spread.

'Well,' said the boy, 'he was a lot bigger than us.' Ketil nodded, appreciating the potential problem. 'And anyway, we came straight back here. There's not been anyone to tell,' he added frankly. The little girl in particular seemed to feel this as a loss, nodding sadly. Ketil looked at them sideways. If he had been on his own with them, he might have asked them if they had heard whose ghost it was. Perhaps he would catch one of them later. For now, it seemed best to leave it.

'Well anyway,' said Sigrid, after a weighty pause, 'Hrolf is helping Einar try to work out who the man was, and who might have killed him. So no doubt he'll be late home.'

'I'm sure he will,' said Helga, neither resigned nor disappointed. 'Now, I should pop these three off to bed while they're warm.' It was an abrupt dismissal, though she softened it with another smile for Ketil, at least. 'You'll have to show me your cups another time, Ketil!'

'Of course,' he said. He was already on his feet, and turned to help Sigrid off the low platform. When they reached the doorway, they pushed aside the leather curtain and left, with a wave to Helga. She hurried to them at the last moment, holding out a discreet cloth bundle for Sigrid, who thanked her quietly. Behind them they heard the door shut and latch, and the curtain swish back to cover it. Their shadows on the path in front vanished into dusk as they walked away.

'Well,' said Sigrid, 'that came to a sharp end.'

'Hm. She seemed pleasant enough to me,' said Ketil, remembering that flash of blue eyes. He could still smell the soft flatbread. 'What's in the parcel?'

'Bread,' said Sigrid. 'She makes the best bread here. We have an arrangement: she bakes for me, and I weave for her.'

It seemed a sensible idea, but even in the dusk Ketil could see that Sigrid was frowning.

'What's wrong?' he asked.

'Oh … she has some new wool, but not very much of it. I was just thinking what could be done with it that she would find useful.'

'Do you make tablet braids still?' Ketil asked, a sudden memory of bright bands darting back from his childhood.

'Yes, yes I do,' said Sigrid. 'Quite a number, actually.' She seemed on the point of saying something else, but fell silent. He let the silence lie, hoping she might go on, but she did not.

Sigrid left him where the path led to her own longhouse, and he walked on down the hill to Einar's collection of buildings. The little hall was almost in darkness: when he stepped inside to fetch his second pack, he knew at once that the body had been brought in to lie here. The choked decay was heavily overlaid with smouldering herbs, but the four lamps about the corpse showed him, at a sensible distance, a kneeling figure with a tonsured head and eyes blearing with smoke. The priest seemed dazed by the smell, or half-asleep. Ketil took a deep breath and approached the body. The man had been laid out on a table, like the first course of some dreadful feast. The impression was not helped by the ungainly body of the eagle with which he had been buried, which was now lying on a long soapstone dish at his feet. It must have seemed appropriate to arrange him in the middle, though the table was a long one so that the pools of lamplight arranged at the head and the foot barely reached him. They showed, in sharp-cut shadows, how his cloak had been drawn respectably round him, his pin on his right shoulder glinting dully, his legs straightened as much as possible, his arms in the awful staining of his shirt laid by his sides. A sword and scabbard and a knife, set aside at the end of the table as if forgotten for now, also showed the signs of having been buried for months. Ketil peered at the knife, which had a curling leaf pattern on the handle, and shook his head slightly. Returning to the body, he leaned forward to examine the pin and the rings and bangles on his right arm – the left was hidden by the cloak. There was nothing unusual in the patterns of the silver, nothing to pinpoint the man's name or his origins. Ketil breathed out and in again steadily, and looked at the man's face.

'Is it someone you know?'

The soft voice from the shadows made him jump, and he turned thankfully from his examination. The priest, a younger man than he had first thought, had risen silently to his feet and stood opposite him, hands clasped easily. His eyes, sideways to the lamps, were in shadow.

'I wondered,' said Ketil. 'It might have been someone I had met on my travels. But I don't think so.'

'He made someone his enemy, anyway,' said the priest, without judgement. 'For that reason, if for none other, I should like to know his name.' He caught Ketil's questioning look, and smiled. 'Even if this man is not one of those I think of as my family here, it seems to me likely that his murderer is.'

Ketil bowed his head for a moment, thinking. At last, someone here seemed to be asking the logical questions about this murder. His eyes were drawn irresistibly back to the face of the corpse, disfigured and foul, and the great black gaping gash, edges lapsed with decay, that hauled the throat open. He swallowed, trying to find the right words.

'Do you think, whoever did this, do you think they were following the old beliefs?'

The priest smiled.

'You mean the eagle?' He nodded towards the undignified heap in the soapstone dish. 'I'm afraid it may have been dead even longer than our brother here. Bits ... fell off, when it was moved. And of course there was a sword and scabbard. But I wonder if it was all just a bit coincidental? A rushed job, perhaps?' He turned a quizzical look on Ketil, genuinely interested in sharing thoughts. When Ketil did not respond, he gave a tiny sigh. 'We'll bury him as a Christian, anyway, just in case.'

'Have there been other ... happenings like this in the area?'

'Others?' The priest seemed puzzled.

'Yes, other murders, maybe?' He shrugged. 'I just wondered: Einar and his men seemed very calm when they found the body.'

The priest was silent. Ketil became aware of the wind outside, the little draughts that tickled the candle flames into life, the small sounds of creatures in the turf roof.

'There has been nothing like this here in my time,' the priest said at last. 'Not at all.'

'Oh.' There seemed nothing more to be said just now. 'Thank you. I'll leave you to your vigil, father.'

Ketil bowed his head again over the corpse, adding his own prayer for the lost, then nodded to the priest and heaved his pack out into the fresh air. He hoped he was imagining that the smell of decay had already soaked into it.

It was only as he stumbled towards the shadow of Einar's longhouse in the dark that he considered. He should really have asked the priest who, amongst those he thought of as his family here, he felt might be a murderer.

The longhouse was cosy and well lit, a much pleasanter place for a social gathering than the draughty hall and, as Sigrid had rightly pointed out, infinitely more comfortable to sleep in. The space for the animals, to the left of the door as he entered, was almost empty, with only one young cow weightily in calf shifting from hoof to hoof, and hens murmuring in the straw. He was impressed by the airiness of the room: the bedspaces were divided not by wooden slats, as at home, but by curtains, most of which were drawn back. To the right the furthest bed curtains were closed, probably concealing sleeping children or the frail, but Einar's wife was already on her feet, drawing him towards the central fire with a firm smile. The women around here, he thought, were very welcoming. Were they as kindly to all strangers? Had they welcomed the man with the eagle?

'Ah, here's our visiting trader!' Bjarni, with the raven-black lick of hair, grinned a greeting. 'Sigrid been showing you around?' he added, as Ketil sat down beside him.

'A little,' Ketil agreed.

'How is it you know her? From Heithabyr, did she say?'

He wondered if he was imagining more than an edge of interest in Bjarni's voice.

'We were neighbours as children. Two of the Norwegian families in Heithabyr, but she left to go back to Norway years ago.'

'And you haven't seen her since?'

'Not till today.'

Bjarni considered.

'Been to Orkney before?'

Ketil shook his head, sipping the ale that Einar's wife had given him. He had hardly noticed it earlier, but now he realised how good it was. Bjarni noted his appreciation and nodded.

'Rannveig's brewing is excellent, isn't it?'

That was her name: he remembered it now. She had the reputation of a skilled supporter of her husband, in hospitality and also, it was said, in the planning of raids. He did not expect that she would remember him.

'Very fine,' he said. Bjarni patted him on the shoulder, and turned to some word from the man on his other side. Ketil, under cover of his horn cup, took the opportunity to look about him.

Einar sat on the other side of the fire, at his ease, a book on his lap. To Ketil's eyes it still did not look right: it should have been a sword, the long hands polishing off the glour of the day's work, not toying with the metal clasps on the leather binding. In one respect he had not much changed, anyway: he took little part in the conversation, allowing it to flow around him. His gaze moved almost lazily from man to man and once or twice caught his wife's eye with a little smile or a nod. He had always been more of a watcher than a speaker, not needing to tell everyone his opinion.

The same could not be said, it seemed, of Hrolf and Hlifolf to Einar's left. Hlifolf was listing aloud, from memory, every visitor to the Brough and to Birsay for the last year, to judge by the look of boredom on some of the faces. At least, Ketil thought, they were making some effort to identify the stranger, unless they had simply become distracted by this feat of recollection.

'Well, Kalf Arnason was there more than once, that I can tell you,' said Hlifolf, as if someone had been unwise enough to argue. 'After all, he is Ingibjorg's uncle. I'm not likely to forget him!' He simpered, delighted by the opportunity to express such acquaintance with Thorfinn's wife.

'Kalf Arnason was there more times than Thorfinn wanted him, anyway!' laughed a man Ketil could not see.

'Nonsense,' said Hlifolf at once. 'I can tell you on good authority that Thorfinn trusts Kalf as his right hand man. Why else would he send him to the Western Isles to steward his lands there?'

Ketil remembered what Sigrid had said, and privately thought she might be right: trusting Kalf to steward distant lands and wanting him on his doorstep were not necessarily the same thing for Thorfinn. He jumped, as he felt a nudge in his ribs. He turned to find a boy of ten or twelve kneeling on the bed shelf behind him.

'Will you play a game with me?' asked the boy.

'What do you play?' asked Ketil, wary.

'King's Table?' The boy proffered a tray full of brown and yellow pieces, and a board that had had the markings carved into it, then been smeared with soot to show them up clearly. The pieces were of good quality, but the boy had a melancholy look.

'Yes, of course,' said Ketil. 'Can you set it down here, and sit on the ledge? What's your name?'

'Asgrimr,' said the boy, as if he had been cursed with it.

'I'm Ketil.'

'I know.'

The boy sat down at once, and busied himself arranging the pieces on the board. Ketil had to turn his back on the others, but listened still to the conversation. He hoped that it might make his listening less obvious.

'Do you want to play the king, or the attackers?' asked the boy. Behind Ketil, a couple of men whose voices he did not recognise were putting the case that the body had been there in the gully for several years. Bjarni, he noted, jumped to Sigrid's defence, and that of her late husband.

'You don't seriously think they wouldn't have noticed that before now?' he was demanding. 'And surely you don't think that either of them killed him?'

'Why don't we decide by lot?' asked Ketil into the short silence, taking a brown piece and a yellow piece, one in each hand, and hiding them behind his back. 'Left or right?'

The boy won the king's side, and waited, fingers drumming, for Ketil to make the first move. He did so, starting conventionally enough. The boy considered briefly, allowing Ketil time to note the slick blue eyes and the cap of yellow hair. This must be one of Hrolf and Helga's children, one old enough to stay with the men along with his father. The boy made a sensible move, and looked up at him expectantly. Ketil shifted again, protecting his men in a cautious attack. The boy examined the board.

'You don't have to be kind, you know. I'm a very good player.'

'Perhaps I'm a very bad one,' said Ketil mildly. 'You might easily beat me whether I'm kind or not.'

'Bound to be someone straying from the Brough,' Hrolf was saying. 'No one ever visits us here unless they're related to someone else.'

'Someone on their way to Kirkuvagr?'

'By land? It would be as easy to go by sea.' Hrolf spoke with careless authority. The boy, probably his son, struck out with equal assurance across the board, taking one of Ketil's pieces wordlessly. Ketil made a defensive move, and the boy gave a little snort.

'You are quite a bad player,' he agreed. 'So far.'

'I did warn you,' said Ketil. Behind him he heard a discussion of Eynhallow Sound, and whether or not it might deter someone sailing to Kirkuvagr.

'And what about the eagle?' asked one of the unknown voices. 'Who buries a man with an eagle these days?'

'Well, it wasn't a Christian burial at all, was it?' Hlifolf agreed, as if he had already made that point. 'All curled over like that. Father Tosti would never have allowed it.'

'Yes, but when people were buried with eagles,' went on the unknown voice, 'it meant something, didn't it? What was it?'

There was uncertain murmuring, but inevitably Hlifolf had the answer.

'It was a particular family sign, that's what it was. They had an eagle on their shield or their scabbard point, and they were buried with eagles. That's all.'

'So it should tell us who he was, then, shouldn't it?' asked Bjarni.

'It would,' said Hlifolf, with a voice like bottled vinegar, 'if anyone knew which family it was.'

Ketil had been paying too much attention to the conversation. The boy won his game comfortably, and was wise enough not to crow, shaking hands solemnly with Ketil across the board.

'Did he win?' Bjarni's voice came over Ketil's shoulder.

'Yes, he did.'

'He's a good one, that! You play, then?'

'Only a little, as he'll tell you,' said Ketil with a nod at the boy. Bjarni frowned, regarding Ketil thoughtfully.

'We're going to start some competitions tomorrow, training for the summer – I think I mentioned it earlier,' he said. 'If you want to join in you'd be very welcome.'

'Ah, I'm only a trader,' said Ketil. 'I'd hardly be worth your while.'

'Oh, come on!' said Bjarni, his boyish face enthusiastic. 'We're always looking for new men to make up the numbers! You'll enjoy it.'

'Well …'

'That's the man! It's great fun. And what's the worst that can happen?'

SEX

VI

The fire she had so hastily left earlier to go and deal with the old ewe was almost past reviving. Sigrid crouched, patiently sliding embers here and there, rousing their red glow, and added dried moss and twigs as delicately as if she were feeding a sickly infant. The cat, a plump mouser, watched with interest, and Sigrid spared the occasional finger to scratch her on the head. Sigrid was chilled, and a little of the stew she had made for Gnup earlier would warm her. As the flames curled up around the cooking pot, teasing out the details of her home around her from the darkness, the cat settled against her skirts to wash, and she held out her hands to warm them, staring into the thick stew as if willing the bubbles to start rising in the rich broth. In her mind, though, was the man's body in that ill-luckid gully.

If he had been killed since the winter, then everything would be all right.

Well, not for him, she reminded herself. And not, in the end, for whoever had killed him. But for her, it mattered.

A rustle at the animal end of the longhouse did not disturb her at first, for like Einar she had, amongst the roosting hens, a cow there ready to calf. This cow was an old lady, mother of many, her ribs splayed permanently to accommodate generous pregnancies, and it was only from affection that she was allowed to stay in when she was quite capable of giving birth on the hillside unimpeded by human interference. That light breath was not hers, though, and Sigrid turned abruptly to find Gnup, straw in his desperate hair, emerging blinking from behind the calm mother.

'Gnup! You should have been at home long since!'

'I was tuim – I had no dinner,' said Gnup, without reproach. 'And I was barkit with dirt. Ragna would have given me a hod if I'd gone home. I washed my hair in the barrel, and my head was cold, so I came in. Then I fell asleep. I tethered that old yow behind the house: she would never come in with the cow here.'

'I hope you tethered her well,' said Sigrid, giving the stew a stir. Was that the start of a bubble? Her stomach rumbled.

'All four feet,' said Gnup with a sigh, 'and a rope around her horns, too.'

They exchanged a look, one that spoke of long experience with the old beast. She might be there in the morning, and she might not.

'If you'd gone home at dusk, you'd have been fed by now,' Sigrid pointed out. 'Ragna will be wondering where you are.'

'Grandma won't care,' said the boy, without much emotion. 'She might not even notice. And Uncle Bjarni won't be home yet.'

'That's probably true.' Gnup was Bjarni's nephew, one of Ragna's many grandchildren. Gnup's parents were dead, and to judge from the way he was treated they had not been amongst Ragna's rare favourites, anyway. That he could make himself useful helping Sigrid with her croft was, in Ragna's eyes, his only virtue. But Sigrid, who even to herself admitted she was not good at tolerating company, liked the boy. 'Do you know what they found in the gully?'

The boy's eyes were bright.

'Nobody told me,' he said carefully.

'They found the body of a man, buried, but not far down.'

'A man buried in the gully?' Gnup considered, and Sigrid was impressed at the role he played of hearing this for the first time. He would have been hanging around, as much as the ewe would let him, to hear what the men were saying. 'Do they know who he was? He can't have been there for long.'

'No one seems to know. When were you last in the gully?'

'Ages ago,' said the boy. 'I never fancied that place much, even when I was peedie.'

Sigrid nodded.

'Since the winter?'

'No, I don't think so. Why would I? End of last summer, maybe? But I can't think what I would have been down there for, even then.'

'Can you bring those bowls here?' Sigrid spooned stew into the bowls she had set out at midday, and handed the larger one to Gnup. It was not so long since she had eaten Helga's fine fish stew, and the boy must indeed be starving. 'Do you remember seeing any strangers around in the last year? Or can you think of anyone who has disappeared, that you might have expected to see?'

Gnup was spooning stew into his mouth with remarkable speed and precision, but his eyes filled with thought.

'If it's a year you're talking about,' he said, pausing for breath, 'there would have been a few. Visitors to the Brough going to Kirkuvagr, or the other way around. Priests, I remember, or monks, maybe?'

'He wasn't a priest,' said Sigrid quickly. 'Or a monk. He might have been a merchant?'

'Or a soldier?' asked Gnup. 'Maybe he got into a hassfang with someone and they were stronger than he thought and they fought back and he died?' For a moment his eyes glowed with excitement, then he considered. 'But if he lit on them first, then they had only to say, to Einar or to Thorfinn. It would be manslaughter. There would be no need for them to bury him and hide.'

'No, no need. And in an awkward place, too,' she added, her thoughts marching on. This was going to have to be dealt with, before rumours began to spread and fingers began to point. Her very life might depend upon it.

Gnup stayed the night, curled in the warm straw by the cow. Sigrid made him wash again in the water barrel by the door, paying particular attention to his wilful hair and his filthy hands, before marching him off with her, shivering, to the hall by Einar's longhouse. It was the Sabbath, and the priest, Tosti, who had been watching over the stranger's body, was to officiate there before returning to the Brough for the rest of the day. In view of the smell in the hall, Einar suggested they hold the service outside, and Tosti readily agreed, blinking in the daylight. A table was brought out, and a white linen cloth, and the comforting rituals began, Einar and his men standing protectively at the front, and the women herding the children at the back. Ragna, Bjarni's stately mother, nodded to Sigrid and raised her black eyebrows at the freshly scrubbed Gnup by her side. Father Tosti, small and bright-eyed, offered up prayers for the souls of the dead man and of his murderer, an addition that caused a little stir amongst his flock. Hlifolf in particular tutted loudly, causing the priest to hesitate. All the conversation after the final blessing was of dead bodies, and wandering strangers, and reasons to kill.

She told herself she should stay and talk, and listen, to see where people's thoughts were going and to direct them, if she could. But where should she begin? She nodded to Helga, to Einar's wife Rannveig, to Bjarni's confident grin, and tried her best to avoid Hlifolf and Hrolf, settled like conjoined twins by Einar's side and issuing facts to enquirers with all the authority of the Pope in Rome. There was no sense in trying anything in their vicinity. Turning, with a jolt, she recognised Ketil watching them, too. She had forgotten all about him. Catching her eye, he slid over through the crowd, his height hidden in a slight, self-deprecating hunch.

'Good day,' he said. 'I hope you slept well after yesterday's events.'

'Yes, thank you, and you?'

Ketil's lips twisted.

'Eventually, yes, thank you. And Rannveig's ale is very good.' He rubbed his forehead with his fingertips, as if easing tension away. Sigrid noticed that the skin of his fingers was toughened, as if he did some kind of manual work. It must be all that carrying of packs, she thought, remembering with slight resentment his ease in carrying his pack up to Helga's longhouse yesterday.

'She has a reputation for good ale,' she said. 'I've been lucky enough to receive a small barrel now and again, when I've done some weaving for her.'

'That's your business now, then, is it?' he asked. 'Weaving? And tablet-braids?'

'And nalbinding.' She edged away from the thought of tablet-braids. 'It helps. The croft is not large, and I am not by nature a baker nor a brewer.'

'Oh, I'm sure you are,' came a new voice. They had not noticed Hlifolf, his thin hair brushed back to its Sunday best knot at the back of his head, his face drawn up in something like a smile. Somehow he had become detached from Hrolf, though Sigrid was sure there must be a connecting strand of wool somewhere binding them together. 'I have had fine meals by your fire, Sigrid. In fact, I was about to ask you if I might join you for your midday meal today.'

Sigrid felt her eyes widen in surprise. Random thoughts tumbled through her suddenly gaping mind: was there enough stew left from yesterday? Where had she put the flatbreads Helga had given her? Why did Hlifolf want to eat with her? And why could she not think quickly enough of an excuse to get rid of him?

'I hope you won't be bored,' Ketil was saying politely. 'Sigrid and I have old family and friends to discuss over the midday meal.'

Hlifolf had a thicker skin than that, though, Sigrid knew, even as she applauded Ketil's effort.

'That will be fascinating!' Hlifolf was saying. 'It's always a delight to learn more about old friends. It helps us all draw closer, doesn't it?' He bestowed a kindly look on Sigrid, sending a shiver creeping up her spine. Then he turned to proffer her his arm. 'Shall we go now?'

Helpless to resist without actually hitting him – which was sorely tempting - Sigrid walked alongside him, in a slipstream of rosemary oil. To her relief, Ketil, so recently forgotten, attended closely on the other side. She would have liked him better if there had not been the slightest look of amusement on his face. Two men coming to eat – she really hoped there was enough stew left. Gnup, she noticed with relief, had been snatched into the regiment of grandchildren surrounding Ragna, and would at least be fed in his own home. How many flatbreads were there in Helga's parcel? She had not even looked.

Hlifolf released her arm as they approached her longhouse, and hurried ahead to hold the door open for her, and for Ketil, as if he owned the place. She bit her lip, more worried about the fire and the meal. A glance at last night's cooking pot told her that rations would be thin. No food for her, then – unless … Yes, Gnup had collected the eggs before they had set out for church. There were eight. She pushed six into the hot ash at the edge of the fire to bake, and shifted the stew pot back over the centre of the fire. The parcel of flatbreads, still fragrant, was on a shelf hanging overhead. She fetched it down and unwrapped it: there were four, and again she reserved one for later, arranging the other three on plates. What a mercy that Helga was such a good baker.

And that Rannveig was such a good brewer. She poured out a

cup of ale from her small barrel for each of her guests, indicating to them where they should sit opposite her at the fire. Hlifolf took a long swallow of the ale, and sighed with satisfaction, wriggling himself into a more comfortable position. He waved a hospitable hand about the longhouse.

'You see here fine examples of Sigrid's work, Ketil. No doubt she has developed her skills since you saw her last.'

Sigrid watched Ketil's interested scrutiny from the corner of her eye as she stirred the stew, trying to hide the darker lumps she was scraping from the pot's base. She would much rather be braiding, weaving or binding just now, she thought fervently, Sabbath or no Sabbath. In solitude, for preference.

'She was always very skilful,' Ketil remarked. Hlifolf nodded proudly.

'I myself have two cloaks woven by her, with very fine braiding in several colours.' He smiled at Sigrid. Yes, she thought, looking away, but I didn't do them as favours for you, despite your hints. You paid me well in the end – in hens, as I recall. She resisted a glance at the hens in question, but poked one of the eggs in its ash bed.

'But then, I have to have a certain distinction of appearance in my position as Einar's counsellor,' said Hlifolf.

'It must be a difficult job,' said Ketil, sympathetically. 'I saw how seriously you were discussing matters last night, while some of us were able to relax and enjoy our evening.'

Sigrid cast Ketil a look. Was he teasing Hlifolf? For a moment she wondered.

'Well, exactly,' said Hlifolf earnestly. 'As if our lives were not busy enough, arranging all that has to be organised! Then we come upon this mysterious body!'

'And all the responsibility of investigating who he was and how he died falls upon you. And Hrolf, I suppose,' Ketil added.

'Oh, yes, Hrolf has his uses,' Hlifolf agreed. 'Of course his mind is not as strong as – as some. He lacks the discipline of thought.'

'His son plays a fine game of King's Table,' said Ketil.

'Because I taught him!' exclaimed Hlifolf, with a triumphant grin. 'An accomplished teacher makes all the difference!'

'Of course,' said Ketil humbly. 'I hope he realises how lucky he is.'

'But we must not allow such pleasures to distract us from the matter at hand,' Hlifolf went on. 'This man we found – on land that is grazed mostly by your animals, Sigrid – have you any idea who he might be?'

Sigrid sighed.

'My animals graze that gully as little as possible, Hlifolf,' she said. 'I've never liked it down there, and we try to keep the sheep away from the cliff edge. I haven't been down there since last summer, as far as I can remember, and there was nothing out of the ordinary there then.'

'But did you recognise the man?'

'The man? Well, it would be difficult, with his face all ...' She swallowed, remembering that face all too clearly. 'I have no idea who he was. And I can't think of any strangers who passed this way that looked anything like that. Sometimes people walk along the cliffs on their way between the Brough and Kirkuvagr, I know, but we often don't pay them much attention. They don't usually pass this close by, unless they come to ask us directions or stop to exchange news.'

'You sit outside in the summer, don't you? And warm days, braiding?'

'Of course, to get the light.'

'So you can watch people passing.'

'I can see them,' she corrected, 'if I look, if I'm not too wrapped up in what I'm doing.' What did he think she was, the local watchman? Or worse? The stew gave a rumble, and began to simmer. She tried to be patient, and allow it to cook properly, rather than serve it lukewarm in a hurry to be rid of Hlifolf. Then again, she thought, it might put him off if the food was bad. It wouldn't be very fair on Ketil, though.

Then struck by a sudden idea, she said,

'Surely you are well aware of anybody who comes here, in the normal way of things, Hlifolf? There's no one whose passage through Einar's lands, however brief, you don't know about.'

Hlifolf was quick to take this seriously.

'That's quite right, you know.'

'So all I can imagine is that whoever he was, he didn't come here in the normal way of things. He may even have been brought here already dead.' She managed to meet his eye, trying to impress the idea on him. It worked.

'Not the normal way ... perhaps at night, or could he have reached the gully by boat?' He was not expecting an answer from either of them, but working through the idea himself. 'He may have been dead when he was brought here!' he exclaimed at last. Sigrid bit her lip.

'Yes, I think you could be right, Hlifolf! What a clever idea!' she managed to say. She could not look anywhere near Ketil.

'So therefore ...' Hlifolf was really thinking hard now. Sigrid thought she could nearly hear the beat of oars in his head. 'Therefore we should be looking for someone who perhaps came here at night ... with a boat? Or with a cart, even?' His eyes wide at his own genius, he looked to each of them for approbation. Sigrid took his bowl from him, plopped a ladleful of stew into it, and helped him to a flatbread.

The remarkable advances in Hlifolf's thinking on the murder kept him relatively quiet for the rest of the meal, allowing them to eat in peace. As soon as he was finished, he scurried off, after enveloping Sigrid in a limp embrace, to share his new conclusions with Hrolf and apply them to their investigation. Sigrid sighed with relief, and quickly brushed the crumbs of Hlifolf's bread off the place where he had sat, as if to deny he had ever been under her roof. Returning to the fire, she was irritated by the look of amusement on Ketil's face.

'You have an admirer there, then?' he asked.

'Ugh,' was her comment. 'He's harmless enough, he's just a bit of a pest. And he needs someone to sit around tending to his needs and agreeing with his every utterance.'

'You'll not be weaving him a shirt any time soon, then?'

'I'll weave him all the cloaks he wants if he pays for them,' she said, 'but never a shirt. There are some round here,' she added, trying not to sound entirely peevish, 'who think a woman's husband needn't be in the ground more than a day and a night before they have to marry her off.'

Ketil did not comment, but looked about the longhouse.

'You look as if you keep yourself busy enough.'

Sigrid too looked at the looms, the yarns, the dyepots that she kept aside in a corner where the smell was least likely to offend. If she did marry again, where would she fit a husband? She smiled a little.

'I enjoy it,' she said, slightly to her own surprise. 'Between this and the croft – and I have Gnup to help there – I'm occupied enough.'

'It sounds as if your work is appreciated, anyway.'

'I've been very lucky. Ingibjorg and Rannveig like it, and if Thorfinn's household and Einar's household want my work, then everyone will. Including Helga, and that's a very good arrangement.' She waved the last piece of her flatbread, and smiled again. 'Now, then, what about your work? You've left your packs down at Einar's, I know, but a good tradesman always has a sample to hand.'

Ketil made a face, but reached into a small bag concealed under his cloak, bringing out a neat wooden cup. He set it on the flat of his hand, and held it out to her.

Sigrid took the cup, and examined it closely. She weighed the pale wood in her hands, ran a thumb over the carving and around the lip, then upended it and rubbed the base with her fingertips.

'It's good,' she said at last. 'Your brother – Njal? Njal always had a way with wood, didn't he? I remember now.' She studied the carving more closely. 'An elk, eh? Very nice. You, however,' she set the cup down delicately beside her and viewed it again, as if getting to know a new acquaintance. 'You had no great skills in that direction, did you?'

'That's why Njal is in the workshop back in Heithabyr, and I'm here,' said Ketil.

'Married?' It was a natural question for an old friend.

'He is. I haven't, as yet. He has three boys, already slicing open their fingers on the chisels. His wife despairs.'

'Weren't there three of you, though?' she said suddenly. 'Njal the eldest, then Ketil, and then a little one – what was his name? He could only have been five or six when I left. What became of him?'

'He's gone. I mean,' he added quickly at her look of dismay, 'I mean I don't know where he is. He's a man now, or he was two years since.'

'A soldier?' Sigrid asked sympathetically.

'No,' said Ketil. He swallowed, as if he were about to confess something awkward. Sigrid was surprised when he only added, 'He's a priest.'

'A Christian priest?'

'Of course.'

'Well, you never know. There's all sorts in Heithabyr. But a Christian priest, now, that's good. So where did he go?'

'To Rome, we think – or he set out that way. For the first couple of months we had messages back, and then nothing. You know how it is. People go, and either they come back, or they don't. There's not much you can do, except to go on praying for them.' He made the words light, but he took a sudden gulp of ale, as though his mouth were dry.

'He always looked up to you, I remember. Followed you around.' She smiled again – three times in a few minutes! Her lips felt stiff with disuse, but a small answering smile touched his own mouth.

'He did. But he's gone his own way now.'

'So,' said Sigrid, feeling it was time to leave the subject. She wanted to know more, though: something did not quite fit all she remembered of the boy that had been Ketil. 'A priest and a cupmaker. And – you. What are you, Ketil?'

'I told you, I'm a trader.' His eyes were very blue in his pale face, but something told her he was not quite at his ease.

'A trader who came from Heithabyr through Norway and Shetland to here – did you look at the soapstone work in Shetland?'

'I did.'

'Buy any? Good quality stuff it is, and they make such perfect circles: it would sell well in Heithabyr, I'd have thought.'

'Yes, bought some, and sent them back. No sense in carrying heavy soapstone all around the place,' he said smoothly. She nodded, as if agreeing, though she added the evidence to her list. Shetland soapstone was not as good as Norwegian, and they made rectangular dishes, not round ones. Why was he lying? She persisted.

'So, travelling all that way, and selling your brother's excellent cups as you went, and you still have, if I'm any judge of your pack last night, thirty or forty? If nothing else, I'd have thought you'd be giving them away, tired of carrying them. If you're a trader, you're not much of one, my friend.'

'And you haven't changed much, Sigrid,' he retorted. 'If I'm your friend, how cruel are you to your enemies?'

This time she truly grinned, deciding to leave it for now.

'You always said that to me! It really is you.' She sighed. 'It seems such a long time since Heithabyr. So much has happened.'

'Not too many dead bodies like this one, though, I hope,' said Ketil, and she blinked at his eagerness to return to the topic. But his next words shook her even more. 'Do you know something about him, Sigrid? About the dead man? You praised Hlifolf's knowledge of all that goes on, but I remember you: you were always the clever one. I can't believe someone was killed or buried or both so near your home, and you knew nothing of it.'

Sigrid met his eye. He would be the easiest person to tell: he had no connexions here. But the habit of secret keeping was a hard one to break. She shook her head, and he looked away.

SJAU

VII

'Anyway,' said Ketil, unfolding his long legs from beneath him, 'Thank you for the food – I'm sorry I forced my way in.'

'No, it was very kind of you not to leave me with Hlifolf, as I think you know!'

He nodded, but gestured to the door.

'I have to be heading back to Einar's place.'

'Another engagement?' She seemed reluctant to move from the fire.

He shrugged.

'I've been asked to take part in a ball game this afternoon. Part of the training for the summer raids, apparently.'

'If they go,' said Sigrid, making a face. 'I haven't seen any enthusiasm on the part of Einar, and now Thorfinn's filling his time with local matters and building schemes, he seems less inclined, too.'

'Well, Bjarni seemed keen. And the others were all going to play today, anyway.'

She gave him a quizzical look.

'Some of them are quite good, you know.'

'Are you suggesting I might not be?'

'Well ...'

He waited, interested to see what she would say. Did she think that a trader would not be able to compete with Einar's followers? If so, he must be acting his part better than he thought.

'Well,' she said at last, 'enjoy yourself. Try not to let them do you any damage!'

'That would certainly be one of my priorities,' he acknowledged, and left her longhouse, smiling to himself.

He arrived at the open space in front of Einar's hall just in time: the men of Einar's little court were emerging into the pale sunshine in a fizz of excitement. Some wore shirts with shorter sleeves than usual: others had bound their sleeves with leg bindings, and they had discarded cloaks and kirtles. Only Hlifolf was wearing a woolly hat, and he seemed to be in charge.

'Ah, Ketil, I was hoping you hadn't forgotten! You can join this team, here.' He gestured to his left where a group of half a dozen men had gathered, wiping their noses and adjusting their shoes. It included Hrolf's son, the King's Table player, who standing came up to just past Ketil's waist; a couple of thin-faced lads who shivered in the breeze; and a hunched man with an undernourished grey beard. The group to Hlifolf's right, by contrast, included Bjarni, Hrolf, and several other promising individuals that Ketil would have been pleased to have behind him in a battle: they looked as if they would row to Ireland in a day and then wrestle an army to the ground without pausing for breath. Ketil could not see men like these resting easy all summer if Einar did not take them raiding.

Hlifolf was giving directions, his light voice snatched back and forth by the breeze, and two of the large men were bringing a ball, and a couple of half-barrels. They set one at one end of the open space, by Einar's longhouse, and the other, slightly uphill, at the other end. Ketil watched with interest. The ball was about a handspan across, leather-clad, and apparently weighty. He noted automatically which parts of the playing area would be affected by cross winds, and where the sun might blare in the eyes of an unsuspecting player. A few men, even older than the greybeard in his own team, found themselves sheltered perches where they could see the play, and a handful of small children had gathered themselves on the other side of a paddock wall, ignoring the charms of a pony in favour of watching what was going on.

Hlifolf gathered the men to him with an imperious hand.

'Listen!' he said. 'The goal for each team is to get the ball into the barrel defended by the other team. The ball should not go outside these lines – along the front of the hall and on to the longhouse, along the longhouse to the paddock, along the paddock to the path, and back from the path to the hall.'

Some of them followed his waving gestures, while others just nodded, impatient to be playing.

'When the ball goes into the barrel, we change sides and start again.' His voice was growing squeaky with effort. Ketil looked about at his team mates, memorising their faces. They were an uninspiring lot, but perhaps they kept their skills hidden. 'Right, is everyone ready? Hrolf, your team's playing that way to begin with. Ulf, the other way.'

Greybeard – Ulf - glanced at his team's barrel, and nodded. He jerked his head at his men and led them out on to the playing area. Hrolf did the same, and both teams arranged themselves generally in a defensive block. Ketil cast off his own cloak, pushed back his sleeves and joined his side. There was a brief, breathless pause, everyone on their toes. Then Hlifolf hurled the ball across the yard.

Play burst out like seaspray off a rock. At once there was running and yelling, kicking and diving, all the pent-up energy of winter, it seemed, flooding out in a few mad seconds. Even the weakest boys on Ulf's team hurled themselves into the action, scowling and grinning as the play moved back and forth – mostly back, for them, as Hrolf and Bjarni's powerful team forced everyone away from the longhouse end, towards Ulf's barrel. Finding the ball unexpectedly just in front of him, Ketil tried to step forward but found a foot in front of his ankle and a fist in his ribs and the ball flew from him as he landed face first on the ground, rolling up fast so as not to be trodden on. In a moment there was a flash and a thud, and Bjarni cheered as the ball landed hard in the barrel. He reached in a long arm and tossed the leather lump back to Hlifolf, who caught it clumsily.

'Change ends!' called Hlifolf. 'One point to Hrolf's team!'

Bjarni, Hrolf and their friends slapped one another's shoulders and assembled again. Ulf's team, more surprised than anything at the speed of the point, shuffled to the other end of the yard. Ulf looked stiff, as if this were his first exercise since Christmas, but there was a determined glint in his eye. Ketil brushed himself down and gave the lads an encouraging smile, but it was not returned.

The ball was thrown back in, and play began again. This time Ketil was slammed over the wall of the paddock, elbows smacking into stone. One lad crawled off into the shelter of the hall doorway, bleeding. Two of the heavies ran for the ball at the same moment, and bounced off each other, sitting down hard. In a few minutes, Hrolf's team had scored once more, and they changed ends in resignation.

'Not much use bringing you in, new man,' said one of Hrolf's friends as they passed. 'Don't think you've even touched the ball yet.'

Ketil grinned, trying not to rise to the taunt. It was all part of the game, no doubt.

This time, old Ulf seemed to have warmed up. The minute the ball hit the court, he was after it, short legs flying. Bjarni tackled him, trying to grab his arms from behind, but the old man shook him off, blundered into one of the big men, shook his head to clear it and powered towards the barrel. From three paces away he slammed the ball hard down, with an echoing thud, and turned with his arms triumphantly high.

The yard fell silent. It was his own barrel.

Laughter shot up, and Ulf, realising his mistake, slapped his face with both hands. He staggered away from the barrel, lurching as the other team slapped his back appreciatively, and made faces at his own team mates to show his regret. Bjarni rescued the ball again and threw it back to Hlifolf, who was bent double, cackling helplessly. A distinct distance to one side of Hlifolf, Snorri the bard was sagging on his crutches, watching with interest. Hlifolf, recovering, staggered over to the bard and slapped him on the shoulders.

'Come on, cripple, laugh! Just because you can't play!'

'I'm that sorry, lad,' Ulf said to Ketil. 'I'm strong enough still when I get going. But all this changing back and forth – man! I cannot keep track of that at all!'

Ketil nodded sympathetically, and took his place again to play the next round.

The other team won two more points. Ketil, trying to balance polite enthusiasm with a desire not to draw too much attention to himself, ran about the yard encouraging his team mates, sighing as the unevenly matched teams edged further and further apart. Then the ball pretty much fell into his hands, followed, thunderously, by two of the large players from the other team, and Bjarni.

Instinctively, Ketil spun to protect the ball, and ran. He felt, rather than heard, the beat of three great pairs of feet pounding after him, and spared a second to wonder where the last vast warrior was. Then he saw him, moving fast from his left to intercept his rush with the ball.

The man's shoulder, mountainous with muscle, lowered like some siege machine and rammed into Ketil's ribs. He swerved at the last moment, just too late to avoid any damage at all, but felt only a scrape along his chest, heard the ripping of linen. A wild arm grabbed, slowed him for a moment to let the others catch up. He could feel breath on his neck, and with a great spin of his shoulder he sent the ball in a sweet arc, hard and true, towards the opposing team's barrel. It shot straight in, and the sturdy barrel shook with the shock.

Stunned, his own team stood about in silence for an age, almost as if they expected the point to be disallowed. But Hlifolf, readjusting his own jaw, held up one hand, and Ulf gave a roar of delight. He scooped out the ball and punched Ketil hard on the elbow, grinning like a troll.

'That's the way to do it!' he cried. 'See that, lads? We have a good one here!'

'A moment of good luck,' said Ketil hurriedly. He had not intended to score so spectacularly. 'Was it all right?'

'All right, lad? It was the best point of the game so far! Right, come on, lads, you've seen how to do it now! Hi, Hlifolf, we're ready now!'

Hlifolf gave Ulf a look that should have crossed his eyes, and waited pointedly until the other team was also in place. The ball was once again tossed in, and play resumed, with Ulf's team now in rather better spirits and consequently more confident. Ketil held back, but the youngsters, more through unpredictable play than anything, scored three more points in between the usual skilled points from Hrolf's team.

Nevertheless, Hrolf's team won comfortably enough, and Bjarni gave Ketil a sympathetic slap between the shoulder blades as they went to recover their cloaks and kirtles.

'Enjoy that, then?' he asked with a grin.

'Very entertaining,' said Ketil.

'You showed some skill – or was it beginner's luck?' Bjarni gave Ketil a sudden, sharp look.

'Definitely the latter,' said Ketil. He felt his shoulder carefully, as if it might have pulled out with the effort. 'I don't think I'll be trying that again.'

Bjarni laughed, apparently relieved.

'Another epic battle?' Snorri asked as they approached the hall doorway.

'Fit for a saga,' Bjarni agreed, and they both laughed.

'We're not going into the hall, are we?' Ketil asked, surprised. 'Has the man's body been buried?'

'Oh, no,' said Bjarni, and Hlifolf, catching the question, spun busily to explain.

'We heard that Thorfinn's soon to be back on the Brough,' he said, 'so Einar thought it best to let him and some of his men see the corpse, just in case they recognised it.'

'When is he expected?' Ketil had barely uttered the words, when a lad he recognised as one of Hrolf's younger children came hurtling across the yard.

'Thorfinn's ship is just landed! Thorfinn's back!'

Given the state of the body in the hall, it was wise to act quickly. Einar, emerging from his longhouse to receive the news of his earl's return, fastened his own cloak about his shoulders and nodded to Hrolf and Hlifolf, inevitably. Then as an afterthought, he sent the same boy running again to fetch Sigrid from her home. Perhaps she had expected the summons: she appeared in no time, her Sunday overdress still smart and neat, her back cloak swinging briskly.

'Since you found the body,' Einar explained as she approached.

'If it won't be too distressing for you,' Hlifolf added solicitously. Sigrid cast him a sardonic look.

'Telling Thorfinn Sigurdarson about it is probably going to be less distressing than coming upon it in the first place, don't you think?'

Hlifolf smiled greasily, as if she had thanked him for his concern. Ketil attached himself undemonstratively to the end of the small group, behind Sigrid, and ambled up on to the tongue of the headland in their wake. Sigrid glanced round at him.

'You survived your game, then?' she asked.

'It was very entertaining,' he replied. He could feel his ribs begin to ache as expected. 'And relatively few injuries.'

'Well, there's a blessing. Let me guess: Hrolf's team won?'

'Mm, yes.'

She nodded.

'I would have been surprised if it had been otherwise. Ah, well, one of these days some stranger may come along and beat them hollow.'

'Or the younger lads will grow up and learn from experience.'

He caught her glancing sideways at him, but said nothing. She had not queried his adding himself to the little procession, but perhaps she was wondering.

There was a path down to sea level at Einar's end of the tongue of land, but Einar ignored it, and Ketil assumed that though it was less sheltered, the path was easier across the top. Einar strode out, the wind seeming to slip by his thin form without noticing. Hrolf stamped along behind, and Hlifolf took advantage of any shelter they gave him. Sigrid and Ketil, too far in the rear, did not benefit.

Almost at the Brough itself they stopped, and Einar stared down at the harbour to see Thorfinn's boat. Ketil could see the little boat for the kvarr on which he himself had arrived, pulled high and safe on the shore, and beside it a small longship, so finely made for slicing waves he could almost imagine it itching to be back in the water. Nearby was a small assortment of people, mostly men, clustered about a solid, dark figure that even from this height Ketil recognised at once.

'Thorfinn's still down by his ship,' Einar declared. 'Let's intercept him there. If we're lucky, he'll be interested enough to come straight back with us.' He started down the path to the harbour, and now that they were dropping below the worst of the wind Ketil could hear that Einar walked as silently as he ever had, as if his feet never landed on the stones at all. He shivered. He had always found Einar unsettling.

Thorfinn's broad shoulders marked him out even when they were on level ground with him: Ketil remembered that wide-legged, solid stance, feet planted steady in the sand, knees a little flexed as if he were about to spring, or were back on his ship taking the swell in his stride. His elbows were bent, too, hands ready to wield sword or axe or knife – but to Ketil's surprise, tucked under one of them, taking him back abruptly to that dark beach on Papa Stronsay, was a small dog – Rognvald's dog. As he watched, the dog stretched up to lick Thorfinn's clipped beard, and Thorfinn glanced down with an absent, fond look. Ketil shook his head hard, sure he was in some dream land. Einar reading, and Thorfinn with a lapdog? Was this some kind of upside down Ragnarok, where the world ends in cosy furs, and warm fires, and sweet love stories? Or maybe he had hit his head in the ball game this afternoon, and had still not come round. It seemed more than likely.

To add to his confusion, the person he saw Thorfinn greet first was the little priest who had taken the service this morning at Einar's, and had spent last night praying over the murdered man.

'Tosti!' Thorfinn slapped the priest's shoulder with his free hand, and Father Tosti staggered. He managed to keep smiling, though, clearly well used to Thorfinn's strength. 'Listen, Father, I've been thinking – if the building work was done, could we be into the church, and it blessed and all, for Holy Week? It seemed to me that if we could begin in it then, it would be a good devout way to go on. An example, if you like, for how it should be.'

'That's an excellent idea, my lord,' said Tosti at once, 'but you'll have to square it with the builders, of course. They might not see it the same way.'

'I'll have a word with them,' Thorfinn agreed. Ketil was almost relieved to see a ghost of the old ferocity in Thorfinn's face, though he felt sorry for any builder who delayed. Tosti cleared his throat.

'Another slight problem – though it needn't delay things, it just means it might not be as perfect as you would like, my lord …'

'Out with it!'

'Yes … The relics and other ornaments you arranged to have brought from Rome: they haven't arrived yet.'

'Still not?' Thorfinn scowled. 'And no word?'

'None, my lord.'

Thorfinn extended his lower lip and blew resignedly upwards. Ketil recognised the movement, and knew that Thorfinn was reminding himself to be patient: he was not, by nature, a patient man.

'I hope they are travelling safely with it, and just delayed somewhere. But I should have thought, by now … They were to come through England to some monastery and collect a contribution from there, too, I remember. Oh, well.' He blew again, for longer this time. 'If it is God's will that they arrive in time, then they will. And if it isn't, well ... then it isn't, is it?'

He looked around at his followers, as if suddenly surprised to see so many of them come to meet him. He blinked at Einar.

'Einar! Good of you to come down to the shore, sir. Or were you sailing, yourself?'

'No, my lord,' said Einar, floating forward reluctantly. The light breeze in the harbour toyed with strands of his long white hair, giving him the look of a giant seedhead. 'I wished to be the first to advise you of something a little out of the ordinary – something Sigrid found.'

He turned and tugged Sigrid forward by her sleeve: Ketil could see by the twist of her eyebrows that she was less than impressed by this treatment. She tugged her arm away and stood facing Thorfinn.

'Sigrid?' Thorfinn narrowed his eyes. 'I hope you're going to tell me that what you've found is a new husband. Is it Hlifolf here?'

Sigrid managed to keep a straight face.

'I've found a murdered man, my lord. Buried on land my sheep graze.'

Thorfinn's gaze sharpened and he looked to Einar.

'No claim for manslaughter?'

'None, my lord.'

'And who's the man?'

'We don't know.' Sigrid answered, more ready to explain than Einar and closer to Thorfinn than Hrolf and Hlifolf, though Ketil saw their mouths opening and shutting like fish. She was not going to allow them to tell her story, clearly. 'But the body is in Einar's hall, and awaiting reburial – urgently – and I hope you will think it wise to come back with us and see if it is anyone you know, my lord.'

Thorfinn considered.

'Urgently, you say?'

'Unless winter returns tonight, yes.'

He wrinkled his nose, and sighed.

'Very well. Ingibjorg will be busy with her plans for

decoration anyway: she won't have time for me till the evening meal. I'll come now.'

Decisive still, anyway, he turned to follow the path they had come by, setting the little dog down to follow, and gesturing Sigrid to walk with him. Einar and his men followed, and Ketil joined the little procession thoughtfully.

'Still not sure about the victim, then?'

He glanced round to find the little priest, Tosti, walking alongside him.

'I knew Sigrid as a girl: I'm coming because she's going,' he explained.

'From Heithabyr, then? I hear it's a Godless place.'

Ketil gave a small smile.

'Not godless as such, no: there are plenty of gods represented there. Perhaps too many.'

'But you came to the service this morning.'

'I'm a Christian.'

Tosti nodded, not surprised.

'Not an easy choice in Heithabyr, I'd have thought.'

'Not easy, no.'

They reached the gateway to the Brough, and turned from it to walk back inland towards Einar's hall.

'I'll leave you here,' said Tosti. 'If Thorfinn says the church is to be finished, it might be best if I have a word with the builders first.' He gave Ketil a wry smile, his eyes innocent. 'I'll be over tomorrow, no doubt, for the funeral.'

'I'll see you then, I hope,' said Ketil, and nodded goodbye.

The party spread out on the wide land-tongue, the wind catching them sideways. Ketil walked alone, half-listening to words blown past him from the others.

'She spoken to you about weavings yet?' Thorfinn was asking Sigrid.

'Dined with Sigrid today,' Hlifolf was telling Einar. 'A well-kept house, but needs a man about it.'

'Makes sense,' Hrolf added. 'A nice bit of land like that, and a competent woman to manage it for him while he's away in the summer.'

'If she really wants gold thread, it'll be expensive,' said Sigrid. 'And I don't much like working with it, either.'

The little dog trotted at Thorfinn's heel, only occasionally distracted by a tempting scent. Ketil watched it, wondering how it felt about its life, wondering why Thorfinn had rescued it from the hand that had killed its master. On the outside, you would say that Thorfinn had not changed at all, but to hear him talk ... What had happened to him, that night on Papa Stronsay? Ketil had thought they had gone there to kill Rognvald, maybe a few of his followers. And they had succeeded: there had been a score or more bodies to bury afterwards. But the Thorfinn he had known had not returned, either, it seemed: he too was buried somewhere in the islands, far away.

Almost without his noticing they had reached Einar's buildings, and now they followed Thorfinn's assured step into Einar's hall. Ketil took a last breath of the fresh breeze. Inside the air was heavy with burning herbs and eye-stinging smoke. The body, attended now by Rannveig and a couple of other women, lay as Ketil had seen it last, though someone had evidently been poking about at the eagle. Decaying feathers patterned the table. Ketil suspected the little priest, Tosti, had been trying to tidy it up.

Thorfinn paused, lowering his head, as the others followed him in and spread about him. Ketil realised with a start that he was praying, and it reminded him to follow suit. The others did, too, an impromptu funeral congregation. Then Thorfinn strode forward to the man's head, propped his hands on the edge of the table, and subjected the body to a keen scrutiny.

After a moment, Hlifolf teetered obsequiously forward.

'We have his sword too, my lord,' he said, offering up the blade. 'And a plain scabbard.'

Ketil looked on with interest. It looked as if Hlifolf had cleaned them well for the occasion: you would hardly know they had been in the ground. Thorfinn cast a glance over them, but dismissed them.

'There are a hundred such,' he said. 'They can tell us little, I think. But the man himself ... someone must know who he is.'

'No one has come forward,' said Einar, his voice hollow behind Thorfinn. Thorfinn rubbed his nose on his sleeve.

'You'd better bury him. Have someone note all there is to be noted about him, though: height, colouring, clothing, in case someone does claim him. How long would you say he's been dead?'

'Since the winter,' said Hlifolf confidently. 'Probably the beginning.'

'Or maybe the end,' added Sigrid. 'It's been cold.'

'True, true,' said Thorfinn thoughtfully. Hlifolf frowned, and Hrolf scowled at Sigrid. 'Late autumn to early spring, then. I'll see if anyone on the Brough knows about it – maybe one of the builders? Though he does not quite look like a builder.' His eyes had not left the body, taking in every detail. Ketil took a deep breath.

'I believe I know who he is, my lord,' he said.

It took a moment before the words sank in. Then everyone turned to look at him. He straightened, facing his captain.

'Ketil? Ketil Gunnarson?' Thorfinn's face was a mask of surprise – and, Ketil hoped, pleasure.

'My lord.'

'You know?' Hlifolf's voice was thinly dismissive. 'What do you know? You're just a trader.'

'Well, who is he?' Thorfinn ignored Hlifolf.

'His name is Herleif. He's one of my men.' He was keenly aware of Sigrid's gaze on him like a binding nail. He would have some explaining to do. 'He was sent here with a message for you. And now he is dead.'

ÁTTA

VIII

Sigrid, out of the corner of her eye, had the great satisfaction of seeing Hrolf's and Hlifolf's jaws drop in unison. Not that she had entirely guessed what Ketil was up to herself, but she had at least spotted a few moth-holes in his trader story – and, she told herself, if she had not had all the distractions since his arrival, obstinate sheep and Hlifolf and dead bodies in gullies, no doubt she would have worked the whole thing out much faster. As Hrolf and Hlifolf clearly had not.

She reassessed her old friend now, watching him stand before Thorfinn's silent surprise. That strongly muscled body, the wear on his hands, the discreetly hidden wealth in his sleeves – those were not the results of pack-bearing and unsuccessful bartering, were they? And his eyes, much too assessing for the kind of trader he had claimed to be. The only wonder was that he was not more scarred. Heavens, Thorstein had had his share of gashes and breaks in his time, and he had not been badly off, till that last wound. Ketil was not only a warrior: he must be a skilled one. Or very lucky.

'He had a message for me?' Thorfinn said at last, his wary gaze back on the poor corpse, as if it could tell him now. Yet he was calm enough: there was no reason why a message from Norway should cause him anything other than curiosity, surely.

'He did. As there was no response, and he did not return, I came to find out if something had gone amiss. As it happened, I arrived just as his body was found. I take it, since you did not recognise him, my lord, that the message did not reach you?'

'I've never seen him before in my life,' said Thorfinn flatly. 'Nor received any message. The message was from you? Or from the Norwegian court?'

Ketil shifted.

'A little of both.' He stopped, and although he did not look at Einar and his men, it was clear that he was not quite comfortable speaking in front of them.

'You want to speak to me alone?' asked Thorfinn, more blunt than Ketil.

'If I may, my lord.'

'Come on, then.' Thorfinn jerked his head, and Ketil followed him into the darkness at the far end of the hall, behind Einar's chair. Einar looked after them and then away, sighing, clearly eager to be back with his books. Hrolf and Hlifolf, furious to have been so deceived by their erstwhile trader, or perhaps even more at being excluded from his secret conversation, whispered angrily together.

'I'm just off to have a word with Rannveig,' Sigrid announced to no one in particular. The men paid her no attention whatsoever, and she slipped out through the main door, scuttling at once around the side of the building. At the back was the door through which Rannveig and her women brought food and drink into the hall: Thorfinn was probably unaware of it and Ketil may not even have thought of it. She clutched her cloak close around her to stop it or her pleated Sunday skirts billowing, and edged up to the doorway, pleased to find it open, ready to greet Rannveig heartily should she happen to appear from the longhouse – not that Rannveig would disapprove of a little tactically accidental overhearing. But no one appeared: they would likely be starting to make the evening meal. She could smell seaweed burning, and the beginnings of meat cooking. She held her breath, and offered up a prayer that the wind would stay easy. Then she wondered, with a twinge of conscience, if God would be likely to be merciful to an eavesdropper. It was not as if she had even made an excuse, even to herself. Because her old friend owed her information, after his deceit?

'Herleif Erikson,' Ketil was saying steadily. 'He'd been here before, said he was happy to come back and be messenger. He'd stayed on in the islands for a time after … after Papa Stronsay.'

'He'd been with you a while, hadn't he? I know the name, though I wouldn't have known his face. Not like that.' Thorfinn's voice was sombre, sympathetic. To lose a good comrade was a great sorrow.

'Six years we'd fought together.' There was a little silence.

'The message he was to bring you, my lord, was of a rumour that was rife in Norway even until I left there myself, and I find there is some trace of it here, too, or so it seems.'

'Herleif was killed for a rumour?'

'That's how it seems.'

'How could a rumour be so important?' Thorfinn's tone was light, puzzled.

Sigrid could almost hear Ketil draw breath, and she held hers, not wanting to miss a word.

'The rumour, my lord,' said Ketil, 'is that Rognvald is back.'

Thorfinn's next words echoed Sigrid's own incredulous thoughts.

'Rognvald Brusason?'

'My lord.'

'Back? *But he's dead!*'

Sigrid shivered violently. Thorfinn's words were uttered with such agony, such despair, such hope, that she felt tears spring in her eyes.

There were sounds of blundering movement, and Ketil, pitching his voice to be heard by Thorfinn but not by Einar and his men, went on quickly.

'I know, my lord. I saw to his burial. My men took his body from Papa Stronsay that night and laid it in a ship, and the next day we bore it through the Fall of Warness and the Westray Firth and into the North Sound to Papa Westray.' He recited the names as if they had been burned into his mind, as if the details themselves would prove it was true. 'And the priest there said his prayers over Rognvald, and we stayed until he was buried. I know what we did. I cannot think that at any point the body could have been exchanged, or was anything other than dead. He was dead, my lord.'

It must be Thorfinn breathing so heavily, with that great bull chest of his. She prayed his heart would not burst. It seemed to take an age until he was able to speak again.

'You're sure?' He was whispering, but she caught it.

'I'm sure, my lord.'

'Then what is this? His ghost?'

'Some of the rumours say so.'

'Some of them?'

'Some say that he was a saint, and has been brought from the dead.'

Thorfinn gave a brief, breathy laugh.

'A saint! Well, he wasn't that, anyway.' There was a thump, and Sigrid imagined he had kicked the back of Einar's chair. Then a heavy sigh. 'But they loved him. They loved him enough to think him a saint. Even I loved him, you know, before – before everything that happened.' He drew a shuddering breath. 'And then I killed him.'

'Had him killed, my lord.'

'It's the same bloody thing!'

Ketil was silent.

'Where has he been seen? Surely not in Norway? That would make no sense.'

'No, my lord. The rumours came from here, from these islands. And a little in Shetland, I found, as I passed through.'

There was a long pause again, and the faint sound of boots on stone. Thorfinn must be pacing as he thought.

'Right,' said Thorfinn at last. 'If these are just rumours intended to alarm me, then there would be no point in killing your man Herleif. So it looks as if someone, somewhere is up to something – raising Rognvald's followers again, to oppose me. That would be my guess. And they would rise, if he came back to lead them.' He cleared his throat sharply. 'So we need to find out who killed Herleif, and what they're trying to hide.'

'Yes, my lord.'

'Can you do that?'

'I have very little local knowledge, my lord. And surely it's the responsibility of the people here, under Einar?'

'True, but I trust you. You were never Rognvald's man. Anyone here might have fallen under his spell.'

I didn't, thought Sigrid sharply. Golden-haired charmers were never my choice. Whatever his faults, and there were many, she had always preferred Thorfinn's blunt solidity. She felt more inclined to trust him – on the whole. And to have Rognvald back as the earl of most of Orkney, that would not be good. Rognvald meant glittering instability, luxury and poverty, wild dreams and cold morning light. No, no: they needed Thorfinn.

'I had already portrayed myself to Einar's court as a trader.

They will be even less inclined to trust me with their confidences now,' Ketil was making his case, echoing her thoughts. Sigrid agreed with him. Why would anyone trust him – a lying outsider? She was not that pleased with him herself.

'Einar and his two men won't talk – if they know what's good for them,' said Thorfinn brusquely. 'Tell them that. No – I will. Einar barely speaks, anyway.'

'There's the woman, as well,' said Ketil tentatively, and Sigrid felt an unexpected shiver up her spine. 'Sigrid. She's from Heithabyr, but she was married to one of Einar's men. She's been here for years.'

'Heithabyr? I know Sigrid: I didn't remember that. Isn't that where you're from?'

'Yes, my lord. By chance, we knew each other as children.'

'She doesn't look Danish. Well, then, tell her to keep her mouth shut, too. If she's a widow she won't have a husband to go telling, and she's not the gossiping kind. I think. So Ingibjorg says, anyway.'

Sigrid bristled at the thought of Thorfinn's self-satisfied wife Ingibjorg discussing her behind her back. And 'tell her to keep her mouth shut'! What did they think she was? Someone's leftover slave?

'In fact, if she's an old friend,' Thorfinn was going on, 'no doubt she'll help you with that local knowledge you need. Orkney was Rognvald's base: his followers, what's left of them, will be here. You say this is where the rumours started, where the rumours say he's been seen. Get to the bottom of it. Find out who's making use of this, and who killed your man, and bring them to me. Right?'

'My lord.'

'Let's go and have a word with Einar and his men, then.'

Sigrid's legs wobbled under her as she relaxed, hearing their footsteps retreat down the hall. There was a lot to take in. Ketil was a soldier – well, that fitted better with her recollection of him than his being a trader. Presumably he had pretended to be one in order to find out discreetly what had happened to his man, and thereby avoid anything similar happening to him before he delivered the message to Thorfinn. Nevertheless, he could have told her! How long had he known her? All their lives.

She shivered, and turned to look at the sea to the south. Dusk was coming, and the water was shining silver from the land to sharpen dark grey on the horizon, and Einar's duck pond was stone white, reflecting the sky. The sloping pastures had faded to lichen green. What should she do now? Go home without saying anything to anyone? She had only come out to tell Thorfinn what she had found, and that was done. He had not seemed to want to ask her any further questions, for which she was thankful, and just at present she had no particular wish to talk to any of them. She should go home and have her own evening meal, whatever food might be left in the house. It was not as if there was not plenty she had to do at home, both for her own survival and for Thorstein's eternal life. And plenty to think about, too: did Ketil's news mean she no longer had to worry? No – that, unfortunately, made no sense.

Determined not to be caught at the hall's front door, she slipped around the back of the building, between it and fresh peat stacks and a few shadowy outhouses. Dotted around were a small longhouse where an old, childless couple lived who had done some service with Einar's father and merited his charity, Rannveig's famous brewery, sweet-smelling and warm, a feedstore stale by comparison, almost empty now in the spring, with animals in the fields and the hay scraped nearly clean. Skeldro, sharp black and white with their bright bills, posed on the roof ridges, their insistent cries quiet at last as the sun went down. The wind caught her now out of the lea of the hall, and whipped her cloak out behind her, but the evening was still mild and she enjoyed the feel of the breeze on her face. She slipped away as softly as she could towards the worn path to her longhouse.

She was halfway there, in the middle of the pastures, when she heard her name called. She did not break stride, but in a moment the call came again, and reluctantly, deliberately reluctantly, she stopped and turned.

It was Ketil, of course. His long strides meant that he caught up with her easily: he could probably have sprinted the distance, with a sword in one hand and a wooden shield weighty in the other. And a pack of cups on his back. She made a face, then tried to straighten it, but it was too late.

'You're angry,' he said, reaching her.

'I knew there was something not quite right about you. Shetland soapstone doesn't make good round dishes, you know.'

He blinked, then gave a wry smile, turning his head away.

'I should have been better prepared, I know,' he said. 'I'm sorry I lied to you.'

'I remember now you were never to be trusted,' she said carelessly, though it was intended to bite. It was not quite accurate, either. 'Was anything you said true?'

'My brother has taken over the business, and he's married, with children, and my parents are dead, and my younger brother is a priest if he's still living. But I left Heithabyr too, when I was about fourteen, and went back to Norway, like you. Then I met Thorfinn, and joined his followers.'

'Why have we never seen you in Orkney before, then?'

'I have been here. But only that time when Rognvald was killed. I usually – work in Norway. For Thorfinn, that is.'

She would not give him the satisfaction, she thought, of asking him any more questions. She found she was surprisingly annoyed at him. There seemed to be nothing to say.

'You'll be off to the Brough, then, with your Thorfinn.' It came out more petulantly than she had intended, and she hoped he had not noticed. 'I'm away home. Good night.'

She turned, and walked off, listening intently for footsteps behind her. For a moment there was nothing, then she caught the slightest scrape of boot on stone. It was already closer than she had expected. He was quiet.

'I said I was sorry.'

'I daresay.' She paced on, not looking at him, but not hurrying, either. He said nothing. She sighed. 'What was your friend's name again? Her something?'

'Herleif. He was one of my band.'

'Large band?'

'Eight of us. Seven, now.'

'What was he like?'

'Popular. He liked a laugh and a joke, and a drink and a woman. He fought well, but if he could find some way of taking the hard work out of it, he would.'

'Married?'

'No,' said Ketil. 'He used to say he liked women too much to marry one.'

'Nothing out of the ordinary, then,' said Sigrid, and two paces later regretted it.

'Perhaps not,' said Ketil. 'But we shall miss him.'

She bit her lip. She wanted him to go away: her head felt tired. She might not bother with a meal tonight: bed was calling her, and she was at her very door. She should just go inside, and close it behind her. The rudeness would be satisfying. But he stood there, very still, not quite looking at her.

'Listen,' he said eventually. 'I've delivered my message to Thorfinn, but I'm not going straight back. Thorfinn has asked me to see if I can find out what happened to Herleif. So it would be useful ...'

'If no one mentioned you were Thorfinn's man, and not just an unsuccessful tradesman from Heithabyr?'

His lips pressed tight together for an instant.

'Pretty much that, yes.'

'You should have thought, before making a grand announcement in front of Hlifolf and Hrolf.'

'Yes,' he said slowly. 'I realise that. I wasn't sure at the time what else to do. I knew Thorfinn would recognise me.'

'Why didn't Einar?'

Ketil shrugged.

'I have no idea. I don't suppose he ever took much notice of minor officers, unless he needed to.'

'And with you slouching there with your head in your chest when I presented you – you certainly didn't look very warrior-like.'

A smile tweaked the corner of his mouth. She sighed. Her hand was already on the door latch, but she could not seem to make either of them move.

'Look, I won't tell anyone, all right?'

He bowed his head, but just as she thought she had dismissed him, he added,

'And would you be able to introduce me to some more of your friends? As you did with Helga – a travelling merchant, selling cups, someone you know from your youth.'

She poked at the knot of her headcloth, then folded her arms, considering.

'There's Ragna, I suppose, Bjarni's mother. Or is there someone in particular you want to meet?'

'I don't know. I want to pick up some local knowledge, generally.'

'Anyone could give you that. You don't need to go bothering me.'

'No,' he said, straight-faced, 'but I do need someone I trust.'

She frowned at him.

'I'll see. In the morning, though. I've had enough today.' She turned firmly to her door this time, and pushed it open. There was still a glow at the bottom of the fire. 'Go away, Ketil. And remember in the future, that if you want to trust someone, it's a good idea not to lie to them in the first place.'

She closed the door, without waiting to see whether or not he was indeed going away. The cat brushed about her legs, purring, and not bothering to light a lamp she reached down a scrap from a hanging shelf to feed it before going to check on the cow at the end of the room. She had not yet given birth, but stood there, solid, as if she had not moved since this morning. Sigrid made sure she had water and hay, trying not to disturb the sleeping hens. She also made sure Gnup was not tucked into some cosy corner. She wanted to be on her own.

He had clearly been, and done his evening tasks, but he was nowhere to be found. She relaxed at last, pulled off her head cloth to free her hair, and sat down beside the fire, attending to both it and the cat. Should she bother to eat? There were still a couple of eggs, and one piece of Helga's flatbread, and salted fish, but it all seemed too much effort. From the busyness of the day and her anger at Ketil, she found herself sinking into a melancholy, unable even to shift herself to go to bed, staring into the crimson embers of the fire. The longhouse was almost silent, with only the fire, the cow, and the soft sighing of the wind brushing about it, as if the house itself were breathing. It had been built for a family, and now it was just her. And if she lived here on her own much longer, she would not be fit to share it with anybody else. She valued her solitary life too much. And who would want to live with her, anyway? Apart from Gnup, and he was only escaping neglect at home.

Torn between self-pity at her lonely state and her desire to stay that way, she was too miserable even to laugh at her own lack of logic. In the end, only the thought that sleeping in her Sunday overdress would not be good for it roused her enough to prepare the fire for the morning, and undress for bed.

She slept better than she would have expected, and at first light had the fire lively and fresh eggs boiling, and the stew started for Gnup's midday meal. She might be able to go on with her work by the stream later, if she was lucky. By the time Gnup arrived, prompt and cheery as ever, she was sitting at the front door working, bare-toed, on a half-finished tablet weaving. It was a complex one, and she paused to greet the boy.

'All well at home?' she asked.

'Aye, well enough,' he replied. 'Ragna says can you talk to her about that braid that Bjarni told you about?'

'Oh! Yes, that was two days ago. It had gone right out of my head.'

'Oh,' said Gnup, 'I thought Bjarni was the one who had forgotten! It's usually him.'

'Hey, show some respect to your uncle!' Sigrid told him off, but they exchanged a grin. Bjarni was not known for his reliability. 'Oh, the yow's escaped, by the way: you might go and see if you can find her, when you've done your usual jobs.'

'Aye, well, the old skon's never happy unless she's causing someone misery,' Gnup remarked in resignation. 'She's probably away to that gully again.'

'I hope not!' said Sigrid. 'If she is, don't go down there on your own. I'd rather lose her than you.'

'Thank you!' said Gnup with a bow, and laughed. He squeezed past her to go into the longhouse and see to the cow, and she heard him singing under his breath as he worked. Ragna's braid: black and white, she seemed to remember. She wondered if that farmer she knew had any white wool put by from last year. Trust Ragna to want something awkward, but at least her payment would be a good one, and possibly in silver. She might go down to Einar's hall and see if Ketil wanted to come with her to visit Ragna. It would be convenient: she had no particular wish to go twice if she could avoid it.

She laid her shuttle down beside her and looked at her pattern, stretching the broad band between her two hands and squinting to judge the effect. It was a pattern she had made up herself, complex and lively, using twenty bone tablets in a row twisted in sequence. Admiring it, she thought of all the braid she had made over the years, even since coming to Birsay. Miles of it, she thought, more than likely. Braid for Helga and Ragna and Ingibjorg, for their menfolk and for her own, for Rannveig and her women, for Thorfinn's court. If she were asked to account for it all, it would be impossible, wouldn't it? Yet a day might come, she thought to herself. That day might come – and soon.

NÍU

IX

Ketil stirred and woke next morning, listening to the room before opening his eyes. It had become a habit lately, a quick assessment of his situation before letting anyone else see he was awake. All he could hear was Hlifolf's emaciated snoring from the other side of the thick wool curtain that divided their bed places. He grimaced. Wooden slats would be better, after all. Hlifolf and Hrolf had spoken to him as little as possible the previous night, and he had spent an hour or so playing King's Table with Bjarni – fairly evenly – before turning in.

Then he heard movement about the centre of the longhouse, and made himself decent before pulling back his portion of the curtains. Rannveig was squatting at the fire, settling a pot of water over it to boil.

'Good morning, Ketil!' she said at once, her smile friendly. 'Sleep well?'

'Thanks, yes.' He stretched, and went to the doorway where the wooden door was already ajar, grey light spilling across the stone floor. Outside was a water barrel, and he used the icy water to sluice down his head, face and hands. When he blinked his wet eyes open, he found Rannveig beside him, holding out a cloth to dry himself with.

'Einar told me last night,' she said, keeping her voice low. 'You're one of Thorfinn's men?'

'That's right.' Einar was not supposed to have told anyone.

'I thought I'd seen you before. Don't worry,' she added, 'I'll not spread your secret. But if you need any help, let me know. Einar's – well, he doesn't do as much now as he used to. But if you need information, or a word in someone's ear, don't think that it's not women's work, eh?'

Her dark eyes caught him firmly, making sure he took her seriously. He nodded.

'Thank you.' Was there something he should ask now, while he had the chance? 'I know the men say they never saw Herleif, but did you? Or did anyone mention to you that they had seen a stranger of his appearance?'

'Herleif, was that his name?' She considered, tapping her front teeth with a fingernail. 'I've been thinking, of course, and I cannot remember anything of the kind. When would you have expected him to arrive here? He left you in Norway, did he?'

'Yes. Late autumn, that was when he went. He expected to arrive before the weather worsened, and I thought he might stay the winter if things were bad. When he did not reappear in the spring, I wondered.'

'So he could have been hiding all winter, or he was killed in the autumn, when he first arrived.'

'The second seems more likely,' he agreed.

She nodded, frowning.

'I'll go on thinking,' she said. 'If anything comes to mind, I'll tell you. And be careful! This would normally be work for Einar and his men. I don't want – well, I don't want Einar looking bad in front of Thorfinn.'

She gave him another sharp look, then vanished back into the house with an energetic twist of her skirts. Ketil rubbed his face again with the cloth, staring out to the west and the Brough on its green spit. Was he in danger? Now he had told Thorfinn what Herleif had come to say, he thought the immediate danger had been removed. No one could kill him now to prevent word reaching Thorfinn. But there was more to it than that, of course. Where and what was Rognvald's ghost? Because whoever had raised it had not just done it for fun.

The hall was to his right as he looked out to the Brough, and in a moment Einar himself slipped round the corner, heading back to the longhouse. When he saw Ketil, he gestured him to meet him halfway.

'The funeral of Herleif will take place today,' he murmured, tilting his curtain of hair back at the hall. 'He has been prepared, and the priest Tosti arrived late last night to watch with him.'

'Of course, sir.' It had to be soon, certainly, but he wished someone had told him last night. He would have watched, too – but of course, others might have wondered why he should wake a stranger. 'May I go in now to pay my respects?'

'Hm?' Einar's mind was spinning off on to other things. 'Oh, yes, of course. Carry on.'

Ketil found the dim hall much as before, except that now Herleif's body was lying on a bier, and wrapped tightly in a stitched shroud. The women had been busy: he had been straightened, it seemed, and tidied. Tosti rose from his knees when Ketil entered.

'It's a good job,' he remarked, nodding at the body. 'Nobody wants him to fall apart as we lay him in the grave!' He glanced sideways at Ketil. 'Einar says you were the one who gave him a name? So it was somebody you had met?'

'Yes, in the end,' said Ketil. Einar's discretion so far was not impressive.

'So you'll be coming to the funeral? That's good, that's good. We'll bury him at the Brough church.'

'I thought it wasn't finished yet?'

Tosti grinned.

'No, the old one. We had a church already, you know! Oh, there have been people living on the Brough long before Thorfinn took a fancy to it.'

'Probably not Christians, though,' Ketil said.

'Ah, well, no, probably not, for the most part.'

'Have you eaten this morning?' Ketil asked, used to making sure others were fed. 'I'll stay here if you want to go.'

'Would you?' Tosti's eyes lit up. 'I'll not be long!'

He trotted out, and Ketil knelt by the bier to take his place. His mind was not entirely on his prayers, though, and he found it difficult to keep his eyes closed. Herleif's cloak had now been laid to one side with his sword – there was no longer any sign of the rapidly decaying eagle – and he wondered if there was any information that might be found in them.

'Herleif,' he thought, almost aloud, 'I wish you could tell me what happened, man. Did everything become too complicated? You were always one for a straight fight, and home in time for a feast. Other people's trickery was never something you appreciated, was it?'

Of course the shrouded figure did not respond. His gaze wandered again to the cloak, neatly folded, the braid bright on one side and dulled on the other by its time in the earth. The sword was as clean as Hlifolf had made it, and laid separately from its wooden scabbard. Was there anything else? He could not see in the dim candlelight without going over to examine it. He listened for footsteps outside the hall, heard nothing, and sprang up irresistibly to take a closer look.

Sword, scabbard and cloak – this must have been all that was worth retaining. Everything else, even his boots, had probably been burned, and Herleif would go to his maker cleaner than the day he died.

A sound at the door attracted his attention, and in a second he was back on his knees by the bier. Tosti entered, wiping his lips with his fingers.

'That was good of you, thank you!' he said. 'You want to go and have something, too?'

'No rush,' said Ketil, though he sat back on to his heels. Tosti came to kneel beside him.

'So whereabouts did you say you were from in Denmark?'

'Heithabyr, a long time ago.'

'Me too! Well, not Heithabyr, but Denmark. And a long time ago, too.'

'Where have you been in between?' Ketil asked.

'Oh, nearly everywhere! Rome, Frankland, Ireland, all about England, even Spain, once. I'm hoping to stop here for a bit, though. If God will let me!' He gave a cheery laugh, then looked apologetically at the bier.

'I don't think Herleif would have minded a bit of laughter,' said Ketil. 'I remember him as a happy man.' He rose to his feet, bowed a final prayer in Herleif's direction, and went to break his fast.

The men of Einar's household gathered themselves together slowly that morning, drifting in under grey skies from their various farms. Some had dressed for the occasion: Bjarni wore a cloak of very dark blue, and a sealskin kirtle dyed sombre red. Hlifolf and Hrolf had bright clean shirts and breeches, and Hlifolf's boots were laced an extravagant number of times about his calves. Ketil wondered if he had lost weight recently: his shirt bagged out at the sleeves in a way that did not quite accord with his otherwise smart appearance. They assembled outside the door of the hall, where they had played the ball game, and when Einar seemed to feel that everyone had arrived four men were selected, Ketil among them, to enter the hall and, following Tosti, bring out the bier. Tosti had his cheerful face under control and paced solemnly, leading the short procession over the spit of land to the Brough.

The bier was an old one, but well-maintained, the wood a precious commodity. The handle sat smoothly on his shoulder. Despite the women's efforts and the wind, the thick smell of decaying flesh was strong around them: the bearer behind him choked, hawked and spat more than once, and Ketil tried hard to breathe through his mouth, not his nose.

Their cloaks and Tosti's robes whipped about them as the wind flung handfuls of rain against their bare heads: to their right, Ketil was distracted by the constant white frothing of the dark sea, relentless lines of foam making for the shore. Would Herleif be happy, buried here? He was a soldier: he would never have had expectations of a quiet death and a burial near home. But there was a difference between death in battle, fairly come by, and a knife across the throat in a secluded gully. Had one of the men here today done that? He could not look round at them, not while he was carrying the bier, but he thought of Bjarni, and Hlifolf, and Hrolf, and Einar – and Tosti? A priest? He was a small man. Snorri the bard? His arms were powerful enough to kill anyone, as long as he did not have to pursue them. One of the hefty warriors from the ball game? Or someone he had not yet met? Or – and his mind danced over Helga and Sigrid and Rannveig, capable women who would run their farms and manhandle livestock while their husbands raided – could a woman have killed Herleif? He almost smiled: he thought that Herleif might almost have liked that idea.

A few people joined the procession when they reached the Brough, more from curiosity than anything else, he thought. It was not far to the churchyard, where the grave was already dug in the ginger soil. The building work beyond the low walls stopped, the builders standing on a heap of loose earth to bow their heads in respect. One man pulled himself up out of the grave of some foundation pit to rest his hands on his spade. Tosti said his prayers, his Latin sounding clipped and precise, as Ketil and the others lowered Herleif into the ground, and men he did not know came forward to tip the earth back in over him. Hlifolf, explaining to

Tosti some mistake he had made during the service, handed round a flask of sharp spirit, and they broke some bannocks between them, before setting off, empty-handed, back to Einar's hall.

As always, the crowd returning were less solemn than the procession going. There was some laughter and gossip, but Ketil was only half-listening, his mind on Herleif. He jumped when a hand touched his arm, and he turned to find Hlifolf and Hrolf walking beside him.

'We're sorry for your loss,' Hrolf muttered, as if the words were hard to say.

'We are,' added Hlifolf. 'We were shocked when you told us who –' he swept a dramatic look behind him, checking to see they were not overheard, 'who you really were. Thorfinn told me you were going to be looking into your friend's death. If I can be of any help, of course, you have only to ask.'

'Thank you. That is very kind,' said Ketil, not at all sure that it was. 'Of course I don't have your local knowledge, and I was not here at the time, so I'm sure I'll find your help very valuable.'

'Good work, Ketil!' came a voice from his other side. Bjarni had caught up with them. 'Good of you to do the service for a stranger, too.'

'I'm sure he was happy to,' said Hlifolf.

'I was wondering, though,' Bjarni went on, 'if we were right to bury him in the churchyard. I mean, there he was, on his side with his sword and an eagle – maybe he had stayed with the old beliefs?'

There was silence for a moment, or as much silence as the wind and the kitticks would allow.

'I'm sure Father Tosti preferred to be safe than sorry,' said Ketil, wondering at Hlifolf not finding something to say.

'But anyway,' Bjarni said, 'the other thing that made me wonder was, if he was a follower of the old beliefs, why whoever killed him didn't just burn the body? I mean, they did that quite a lot, didn't they? So I've heard. And then we'd never have found it and no one would have been any the wiser.'

'I suppose,' said Hlifolf, 'people might have noticed the smoke.' He gave Bjarni the kind of look reserved for unpromising children.

'Well,' said Hrolf, 'it's done now. We can get back into the hall tonight, if the women have cleaned it up. And back to a bit of preparation for the summer, eh, Bjarni?'

'Oh, yes! Ketil, will you join us again? We're going to have some sword practice this afternoon. I can lend you a spare one, don't worry!'

'I'm not sure swordplay is really –'

'Oh, yes!' Hrolf was suddenly enthusiastic. 'Bjarni will teach you a few tricks, won't you, Bjarni? He's one of our best swordsmen – and you never know when something like that will come in handy, even for a trader.'

'Well …'

'That's my man! I knew you weren't in a rush to travel onwards just yet. Plenty of customers here, eh? And not far to Kirkuvagr and Hamnavoe for markets, too.' Bjarni seemed keen enough to keep him.

'Then you'll be wanting to move on, come the summer,' Hrolf added, a little too quickly. 'When we go raiding, there'll only be the women and the old men left. That would be very dull for a trader.'

Ketil looked at him, wondering if Hrolf wanted him to move on for a specific reason – was there something he might more easily discover when Hrolf had gone? But they had arrived back at the hall, where the doors were flung open as they had left them, and the women had indeed been cleaning away all traces of long-dead strangers from their meeting place. Rannveig ushered them inside where a fire burned in the central hearth, and they put their damp cloaks aside and were welcomed with warm ale and broth.

The women stayed in the hall with them: Ketil saw Helga, bright and busy with a cheerful wave for him, and Sigrid, who would not meet his eye. To judge by the way people circulated and spoke to each other, at least one of the warriors from the ball game had a wife here, and old Ulf had a daughter, but the society was still strange to him though the faces were becoming familiar. He must learn faster, he thought, and not waste any more time: the sooner he did the work Thorfinn wanted, the sooner he could return to Norway and his men. Yet even as he thought that, the notion flickered through his mind that he would never see Norway again - that he would never leave Orkney. He shook himself, cross, but the thought persisted – islands were unchancy places.

Near to Einar's chair, Hlifolf was making a great show of examining the dead man's sword.

'Often,' he declared, his thin voice penetrating the rest of the conversation, 'a sword can give clues to the identity of a person.'

Well, yes, thought Ketil. That was fairly obvious.

'And here we have the scabbard, too. The metal tip here, that protects the scabbard from damage – the chape, it's called.'

As probably every man in the room knows, Ketil thought, and most of the women, too.

'Often it will have some kind of insignia on it. This one, though, does not. Could that be significant in itself?'

Or could it be that Herleif brought his second best sword and scabbard, having left his best one for mending with the smith in Trondheim. He had been annoyed, Ketil remembered, but Ketil had told him to pull himself together and board the ship. They were probably the last words he had exchanged with the man. He felt a hand touch his arm, and half-turned. It was Sigrid.

'Here,' she said, refilling his cup from a large jug. 'The man with the scarred face there is Afi,' she went on quietly, pointing with a tilt of the shoulder to the ball-playing warrior who had carried the bier behind Ketil. 'Over there, green overdress, that's his wife, Gullaug.' Gullaug was spinning wool and chatting with her neighbour, paying no attention to her husband or anyone else. Plump woman, wind-beaten face, Ketil noted, though he was sure he would forget again. 'Woman beside her,' also spinning, Ketil saw, 'that's Geirny, Ulf's wife.' She had probably spun enough wool in her years to wind a thread right about the islands: her face was wizened, her pale eyes tired. Next to her was a younger woman with the same squat nose, broadly pregnant. 'Aud's their daughter. She might buy cups, she's not long married. That man, only three fingers on each hand – careless – is Ingvar. Wife dead. Two of the young lads are his. Probably not interested in cups, though.'

Ketil gave a little smile.

'I said I wanted useful local information, not an arrow-storm of facts.' He would be glad, though, to see the back of the cups – but he owed it to his brother to dispose of them usefully. Sigrid was right: he was a rotten trader.

'And there,' she nodded slightly, ignoring his complaint, 'is

Ragna. Bjarni's mother, and queen of all she surveys.'

Ketil had already noticed the woman – he remembered seeing her at the service the previous day. Ragna's headcloth was double-layered, white below and a rich blue above, and it flowed past her shoulders and down her back, unknotted and improbably perfect. She did indeed hold herself like a queen, her narrow shoulders straight and sharp, her hands at peace on her lap, not occupied nor resting but simply at ease as if she never lowered herself to the kind of work that kept all the other women constantly active. Her brows were jet black, her eyes dark.

'Danish?' he asked, wondering at her colouring.

'Orcadian,' said Sigrid, still keeping her voice low. 'They say her family was here before the Norse came, long ago.'

'Is that a badge of honour?' asked Ketil, curious at the woman's clear self-assurance. She certainly had a presence.

'I've never quite worked that out,' Sigrid admitted. 'But she's related to Ingibjorg, Thorfinn's wife, too, so that helps.'

'It explains Bjarni's ease, too, I suppose,' Ketil murmured.

'Oh, in Bjarni's case it's three parts natural charm, and five parts laziness,' said Sigrid with a smile. Ketil gave her a quick look: her expression was almost indulgent. So that was Hlifolf's rival, was it? Well, Bjarni was a handsome man.

'He has no wife, then?' he asked, as casually as he could.

'No.' She did not look at him, keeping her gaze moving about the room, watching her neighbours. 'His wife died in childbirth, years ago. He never remarried – couldn't be bothered, I think.'

'Mother looks after the house?'

'Well, she oversees it. Bjarni's two sisters, who are both widows, do most of the work. And there's plenty, with their children around the house. But they have slaves, too. It's a large household.' She gave a sly smile. 'Plenty of people to use cups.'

'I'd forgotten how annoying you were as a child,' Ketil told her. 'I suppose I need to see all of them.'

'But here's one you've seen before,' Sigrid nodded, her voice louder again. Ketil looked up as Helga, skirts swinging easily, passed through the crowd to reach them.

'Are you staying to eat, Sigrid?' she asked.

'No, I think Ketil wants to see if Ragna will buy any of his cups,' said Sigrid quickly. A meal here would take an age, and she wanted to get on. But Helga's eyes had brightened.

'Hello, Ketil! Weren't you at the funeral? Hrolf said they were going to ask you to help with the bier, being used to carrying packs and so on.'

'I did help, yes,' said Ketil, a little surprised.

'You must be very strong!' she said, but before he could respond, Hrolf himself was beside them.

'Oh, yes: Ketil's going to join us in our training later!' he announced. 'We thought we would give him some beginner's lessons in swordplay. He was on the losing side in the ball game, but maybe we'll find something he's better at!'

No doubt, thought Ketil, smiling politely, Hrolf was trying to reinforce Ketil's impression of a humble trader. He was being a little heavy-handed.

'Oh, look,' said Sigrid, nudging Ketil. 'Ragna and Bjarni are leaving.'

'Ragna never stays,' Helga sighed. 'I think she's very lonely, you know.'

'If she is, it's her own fault,' said Sigrid. 'She doesn't think any of us are good enough to be her friends.'

'I suppose so,' said Helga, her pretty eyes sorrowful as she watched Bjarni escort his mother from the hall, a stately progress. Ragna walked as if men were bowing to the floor as she passed.

'Should we follow?' Ketil asked quietly. Hrolf's eyebrows were questioning. 'Sigrid is kindly going to introduce me, in case Ragna might want to buy some of my cups.'

'Of course. Helga, have you seen Ketil's cups? Are they something you think you might like one or two of?' Hrolf asked his wife. His tone was still rather superior.

'I haven't seen them yet, my dear,' said Helga. 'I'd be very happy to inspect Ketil's merchandise, any time that is convenient for him.'

He met her eyes quickly – was he imagining that tone in her voice? He looked away, and away from Hrolf, too. How had a man like Hrolf managed to marry a woman as pretty as Helga? And keep her?

TÍU

X

'Hey, Hrolf!'

Sigrid, who had been watching Helga with interest, jumped as Afi slapped Hrolf on the shoulder. Hrolf himself staggered forward against Ketil, shoving him backwards, but it looked exaggerated. Sigrid frowned. Afi, a great giant who barely knew his own strength, snatched Hrolf back and propped him upright, patting him a little too hard on the back. Hrolf coughed, and Afi's great scarred face looked dismayed.

'Here, are you all right?'

'Yes, yes,' said Hrolf, eventually, catching his breath. 'See if our poor trader is harmed, though: he's not used to brawls.'

Afi gave Ketil an anxious look, but he seemed uninjured, putting up a hand to ward off Afi's gentle ministrations. Afi grinned, and turned back to Hrolf.

'He's tougher than he looks. I hit him the other day in the ball game and he never complained. And I hear he's no a trader, either!' He winked laboriously, the heavy scar tissue making a struggle of it. 'Look, Hrolf, we were just talking over there. Remember back in the autumn we found the wreckage of a boat, just north of the cliffs? Not far from the gully, anyway.'

'Did we?' Hrolf looked puzzled. Sigrid's heart was busy: back to the autumn again! Why could the man not have died in the spring? Surely it was more than likely.

'Aye, we did. Remember, the people who salvaged it divvied up the wood between us? There wasn't much, it must have been a small boat. And we never found a body, either. We thought the fellow must have drowned. But maybe it was this man we've buried today. What do you think?'

'You used all the wood between you?' Ketil's voice was interested, innocent. 'That's very economical.'

'Aye, well, when you've near no trees at all, or not the kind for building, you have to take what the sea gives you, eh?' Afi laughed, propping his hands on his hips.

'For firewood?'

'Never! Not unless it's no good for anything else. We'll use it for doors or frames or – well, whatever needs it. That bier we were carrying earlier – that came from driftwood. I mind my father cutting the wood for that when I was only peedie, and though we've replaced the bindings since it's still good and strong. Comfy enough on the shoulders, too, did you not think?'

'Oh,' said Ketil, 'yes. Very.'

Sigrid decided to rescue him.

'If we want to talk to Ragna about your cups,' she said, still amused at the thought of Afi ever having been peedie, 'this would be a good time to go. She'll be home before we get there, but not settled to anything.' Ketil looked at her blankly for a second, then nodded. She let him go ahead of her out of the hall, aware of Helga and Hrolf still watching them. And someone else, too: she could feel a sharp observation, so keen it almost made her stumble as she walked, but when she looked to see who it was she saw only Rannveig, gathering cups from the tables, giving her a bright farewell.

'Are you being organised?' she asked, when they had gone a few paces from Einar's buildings. She was guiding Ketil back towards the mainland, towards a distant longhouse in the lea of the same slope that protected Einar's place. The path was worn a darker green in the sandy close-cropped grass.

'I'm being organised by you,' he replied, fairly mildly.

'That's not what I mean,' she said, tutting. 'I mean, do you know what it is you are trying to find out, and where you might need to go to find it? What are you hoping to find out from Ragna, or Bjarni?'

He stopped. She had thought as much – he had no idea what he was doing. And she must not allow him to be distracted with talk of the autumn. If she could not be at home working on her braid (and how cross she had been when Helga and Hrolf came along to tell her it was the funeral that morning!) then at least she could try to guide Ketil's inept investigation. He was no better at this than he had been as a trader: she had always had to help him when they were children. It was a wonder he had found his way out of Heithabyr on his own.

A sheep fank by the path provided a flat piece of wall, golden with lichen, and she hopped up to sit on it, arranging her cloak beneath her. There was no one in sight in any direction, no one to question what they might be talking about.

'Herleif was killed by someone who cut his throat, but didn't steal his cloak.'

'Or his sword,' Ketil added. 'It was a good sword, too, before it was buried.'

'Not a thief, then.'

'No. He still had his cloak-brooch and rings on his arms. I don't think he could have been robbed.'

'What's the business with the eagle?'

Ketil shrugged.

'I have no idea. Herleif always liked birds, though. It was a strange thing with him, but it came in useful once or twice, knowing their habits and spotting them acting out of their usual way.'

Sigrid frowned. The eagle had been very dead: it would not have told Herleif much.

'Well, anyway, it's a puzzle.' She dismissed the eagle, and moved on. 'And it wasn't manslaughter, or his killer would have told someone.'

'Yes, within three houses.' Ketil glanced back the way they had come. 'So most likely they would have gone to Einar's hall.'

'It would have made most sense. But nothing here fits with manslaughter, so it's murder.' She eyed him, but he did not seem particularly upset. He was a soldier, and used enough to sudden death. 'Now, why was he here?'

He looked at her, not speaking.

'Did Thorfinn tell you not to tell me?' she asked.

'Not exactly ...'

'Not at all, in fact! But you think I might be a Rognvald supporter, and betray you!'

His jaw dropped.

'You were listening!'

'I was.' She folded her arms, quite defiant – or at least, she hoped that was how she looked. She did feel a little guilty.

'You … You can't be trusted, can you?'

'Says the man who told us all he was a trader!'

'That was a necessary deception, for my own safety.'

'Well, maybe I thought it was necessary to hear what you and Thorfinn were saying, for my own safety!'

'How could what we were saying possibly affect you?'

'I didn't know whether it did or not. That's why I listened! And the body was found nearest to my house, on ground my sheep graze, and I found it! So there was a good chance it would affect me, wasn't there? And now you're using your old acquaintance with me to inveigle yourself into this place, so it definitely does affect me! So there!'

Oh, that wasn't good, she thought, stopping abruptly as her words hovered in the air. That was her nine-year-old self quarrelling with the neighbour's boy. The question was, was the neighbour's boy grown up enough to ignore that little slip into the past, and not mock her for it? He was very still, even when he was angry: she could suddenly picture him on a battlefield, cold and controlled.

There was a long pause. She could see a tiny twitch of Ketil's eyebrows, but whether he was trying not to laugh or beginning to frown she could not say. At last, he drew a deep breath.

'Are you a supporter of Rognvald? Or were you?'

She shook her head emphatically.

'No, I never was. Nor was my husband, though he wasn't there when Rognvald died – he had taken a bad injury to his leg by then, and Einar had given him the farm. But we were always Thorfinn's supporters, through and through. He's not perfect, but I never trusted Rognvald. Too good to be true.'

'And what about Einar?'

'Einar?' She was taken aback. 'We supported him, too.'

'No, I mean Einar, or his household. What did they think of Rognvald?'

'Surely you would know that better than I. You were there when Rognvald was killed, weren't you? And me telling you the whole story the other day – you must have been laughing! But wasn't Einar there, too? With Thorfinn?

'He was, and Kalf, and Thorkell Fostri. Thorkell did the actual killing. The rest of us – well, there was a hall to be burned, followers to pursue. We killed about ten of the others. Rognvald nearly escaped, in disguise, but we found him, and closed in, and Thorkell killed him, on Thorfinn's nod.'

'Einar?'

'Stood by, watched, did nothing. We were all Thorfinn's men, that day. But some had changed sides a few times before that. Do you know if Einar ever did?'

She screwed up her face, concentrating.

'I don't know,' she said at last. 'Einar was always the older man. I think if I thought anything of his sympathies, it was that he thought the fight between Thorfinn and Rognvald was childish.'

'I see.' He considered. 'And what about others in the place? Hrolf? Hlifolf? Bjarni?'

'Those three in particular?'

'Those three to start with. Then the others. But let's start with Bjarni, since we're on our way to his house. Where did his sympathies lie?'

'With Bjarni,' she said, with a smile.

'Apart from that.'

'Bjarni and Ragna ... well, Ragna resents Einar, because she thinks her household should be the central one around here, not his. I suppose Bjarni agrees with her, to an extent, but it would all be too much effort for Bjarni to lead. He would rather follow, as long as it didn't go against what he wanted. Whether Ragna would have supported Rognvald just to oppose Einar, that I don't know. I suspect she might.'

'All right, then, that's a start.' He was standing straighter again, looking more soldierly, though he always had the slight hunch of a man over-conscious of his height. 'Now, you said she had two widowed daughters living with her. What of them? What were their husbands?'

'One drowned, the other fell from the cliffs fetching birds' eggs. Local gossip sometimes suggests they weren't up to Ragna's exacting standards, and she somehow cursed them. But there was nothing odd about their deaths, really.'

'Rognvald's men? Thorfinn's men?'

'Thorfinn's, I should have said.' She thought back, fiddling with a strand of tungrass that wriggled out of the wall, lying low out of the wind. One of the men she had scarcely known, the other had lived down south, she remembered.

'The drowned man was a Scot. He must have been Thorfinn's,' she said. 'The daughter went away south with him, over the water, but came back when he died, with two of her children. The other man was not a local, either, he was from Hoy, but he came here to live till the cliff accident. I didn't see much of him. They had a few children, too. There always seem to be children at Ragna's, though she finds them more irritating than anything.'

'And this is where your boy Gnup lives?'

'Yes!' she said, surprised that he remembered. 'And some slaves – I'm not sure how many. Bjarni's always buying new ones.'

'Would the children at Bjarni's speak much with the children at Hrolf's?'

'I've no idea. Probably, at the hall, sometimes. Maybe after church. Why?'

'Because Helga's children had heard a story about a ghost, and I want to know if it's Rognvald's ghost. I need to try to trace that story to its source, and work out who is spreading it, and why. Because no ghost of Rognvald's is likely to be a friend to Thorfinn.'

'And probably killed your man Herleif,' Sigrid added. It did not need saying, but the look on Ketil's face had sent a shiver down her spine, and she had to say something to dispel it. Then she could not resist going on as she slipped down off the wall. 'You'll want to go back to Helga's, then, anyway, to talk to the children again.'

'Back to Helga's,' he repeated, looking past her. 'Yes, I should probably go back to Helga's. Soon.'

She gave a wry smile, mostly to herself, and set off again along the path to Bjarni's longhouse.

Bjarni's longhouse was substantial and busy, with its own bath house and a complex of walled enclosures for various animals, including a pair of fine horses. Slaves in the usual rough clothing were sowing bygg in a ploughed field, the youngest of them dancing barefoot behind to keep the birds off. The family did not seem to be outside, though, and when Sigrid chapped at the door,

Bjarni's voice called her in.

The slaves and children must already have finished their midday meal but the family adults were still seated at the fire, the widowed daughters nearest it to tend to the pots, Bjarni long-legged at the far end, and above him, stately in a chair little different from Einar's, sat Ragna, as if attended by her court. Sigrid gave Ketil a sharp nudge and nodded towards it, hoping it only looked as if she were directing his attention to Ragna. He kept his face blank, but in a moment she knew he had seen what she had seen – the back of the chair was carved from the prow of a small boat, and Sigrid was fairly sure it was part of the wreckage found last autumn. It was new, anyway: Bjarni had no doubt been amongst the salvage men. That kind of brief, profitable excitement would suit him well.

'Sigrid!' Bjarni rose elegantly to his feet, arms wide. 'And Ketil! If we had known you were coming after us we would have invited you to join us!' He beamed the easy smile of one who does not have to do the extra cooking. One of the dark-haired daughters – Sigrid always had trouble remembering which was which – rose to bring the guests forward towards Ragna. Bjarni might have greeted them, but it was more than clear who was in charge in this household.

Sigrid presented Ketil, her trading friend from the cup markets of Heithabyr. Now that she knew for a fact this was a lie, she found a surge of giggles in her throat, but she managed to contain it. Lying and eavesdropping in one week! Her husband would have been shocked.

'Ah,' said Ragna, inclining her head. Her robes and headcloth sat perfectly, as if she were carved out of wood like the chair. 'Ketil from Heithabyr. Yes, I have heard of you. You may show a cup or two to her.' She pointed to a daughter, who rose obediently, face blank. That was why she could never tell them apart, Sigrid thought. She barely heard them speak, and Ragna appeared to allow them no character of their own. Ketil retreated with the selected daughter to the doorway where the light was better, and Sigrid heard the clunking of cups in Ketil's bag. She hoped he would manage at least one sale, if only for appearance's sake. 'You, though, Sigrid – have you come to find out about the braid I desire? I sent Bjarni to speak with you last week.'

Sigrid ignored the hint of reproach in her voice. If you apologised every time Ragna expressed her dissatisfaction, the conversation would be very dull indeed.

'Yes, Ragna, I've come just to make sure I have the details all correct.'

'Well, first it must be black and white. As white a white as you can find.'

'I'll make enquiries, but that might mean a delay. The farmer on Rousay ...'

'And I want you to weave it so that the cloth is integral to the braid.' The limitations of the farmer on Rousay and his sheep were of no interest to Ragna.

'Ah. Well, as I tried to explain to Bjarni ...'

She hesitated. Ragna was scowling terribly, so terribly that Sigrid feared Ragna was about to scream at her. The woman looked furious. Then Sigrid saw her eyes, and there was fear in them – fear, and something else.

'You must – you must –' Ragna struggled, swallowing hard, teeth clenched. Then she suddenly rose from her seat, staring at nothing, and vomited violently all over what remained of their meal.

In the stinking confusion, Sigrid was the first to reach the woman, catching her about her narrow waist and lowering her back on to her seat. Ragna was ash white, eyelids sagging, but Sigrid, still supporting her, could feel that her stomach was heaving. The shudders shook them. Sigrid, trying to breathe through her mouth, held Ragna's clammy forehead as Ragna leaned forward, braced on the chair, and was sick again, just missing her black fur cloak tails. Ragna gasped for breath, but the breaths eased now and slowly, reluctantly, she pulled herself back into her chair, sagging down as if she would almost slide off it. She looked twenty years older than she had when they came in, reeking sweet and sour at once.

'Have you a cup of ale?' Sigrid turned to the nearer daughter. The daughter scurried off and fetched one that was far from the scene of destruction. Sigrid held it to Ragna's lips. Ragna took a mouthful, swilled it about her teeth, and spat it out into the filthy mess before her. The last trail of it dribbled down her chin, but she ignored it, proof more than anything to Sigrid that Ragna was really ill.

'You should probably lie down, Ragna,' Sigrid suggested, ready to be rejected at once. But Ragna nodded slowly.

'I should.' She stopped, and cleared her throat, a noisy business, and probably painful. She swallowed again, and swiped at her chin at last. 'We must talk of braid another time. You and your friend should go now.'

Sigrid bowed her head, as she often found herself doing with Ragna, and went to the door where she and Ketil left quietly. The family, shocked, were clustering round Ragna as Sigrid looked back, but Ragna's hand was raised in instruction and Sigrid was fairly sure she was already recovering. She and Ketil walked slowly down the path, back the way they had come.

When they were clear of the infields, Sigrid remarked,

'Well, that was interesting.'

Ketil looked sideways at her.

'What?'

'Didn't you smell it? You were too near the door, perhaps. That thick scent of meadowsweet, and I think – I think – tungrass.' Ketil was still staring at her, puzzled. 'It's too early in the year to need meadowsweet for the midges. It's a herb to bring on the flux, though, and tungrass empties the stomach.'

'You mean someone made her ill?'

'Yes,' said Sigrid thoughtfully. 'I think someone did.'

They walked on, still at a gentle pace.

'To kill her?'

'They're not deadly poisons. Well, if someone has too much, no doubt, and the vomiting and flux can't be stopped, then they might well die. But Ragna was already getting better when we left, I think.'

'Then to stop her talking to us?'

'We're assuming it had anything to do with us,' Sigrid pointed out. 'Maybe one of her daughters just wanted to see her suffer a bit.' She considered. 'If I were one of her daughters, I'd be sorely tempted.'

'They didn't look very happy,' Ketil agreed.

'Well-dressed slaves,' said Sigrid. 'Did you sell a cup?'

'With the woman in charge spewing over the midday meal? The circumstances were not conducive to good trade.'

'Maybe she was poisoned by the gods of good traders!' said Sigrid, and earned herself a painful dig from Ketil's elbow. It was like being nine again. 'Anyway,' she went on, 'if someone wanted her not to speak to us, they would have needed to plan this in advance, made sure the stuff was ready, put it in something she was going to eat, in time to take effect when we were there. It acts quite quickly, particularly if it's a large dose, but they would have wanted it to happen with us as witnesses, to say yes, she is sick, we shouldn't disturb her. How would they know when we were coming and what we might be asking about? Bjarni wasn't in the hall when you confessed all in front of Einar and Hlifolf and Hrolf.'

'No, but I don't think Einar's followers are very good at keeping secrets, do you?' Ketil asked mildly. 'That ogre Afi hinted that he knew I was not a trader.'

'Oh, that's true. So you think word is out?'

'It wouldn't surprise me,' he said.

'Does that mean,' Sigrid frowned, 'that your life is in danger? I mean, if they killed your friend Herleif ...'

Ketil grinned, but she could not see his eyes.

'Herleif died to prevent him giving his message to Thorfinn. Thorfinn now knows what Herleif knew. The only way I could be in danger of death would be if I were close to finding his killer. At present, I'm so far from that, I might live forever.'

Sigrid laughed, but then a thought struck her.

'You said that Thorfinn knows all Herleif knew. Well, Thorfinn knows what you know, but who's to say that Herleif, in the time he was here, didn't find out more? You said the rumours came from Orkney. What if he couldn't speak to Thorfinn straightaway – maybe Thorfinn was away – so he decided to do some investigation on his own account? He maybe even worked on it all winter, knowing it was easier to wait for a passage back to Norway in the spring, and if he spent all that time on it, who's to say what he found out?'

Ketil said nothing for a moment. Then, keeping his eye on the path, he uttered the words she had hoped he would never think to utter.

'You're very determined, Sigrid, that Herleif died in the spring. Why might that be, then? What do you have against him dying in the autumn?'

Despite herself, she felt her face redden. The strain of the last few days bubbled to the surface, and hot tears spilled down her cheeks.

'What is it, Sigrid?' His voice was almost gentle.

'My husband died in the late winter. If Herleif died in the spring, then my husband could not have been to blame. But if Herleif died in the autumn ... then I honestly don't know.'

ELLIFU

XI

He stared at her, at first not sure what she meant. Hadn't she told him that her husband was loyal to Thorfinn? Why would he have killed Herleif? In his confusion, he said nothing, which seemed to be all that was needed to encourage Sigrid to speak.

'Look, Thorstein was – well, he wasn't too bad when I first met him. I mean, I loved him, and he loved me, and he fought with Thorfinn and Einar and I stayed with the women, mostly in Caithness, sometimes here. It was a good life for him, and I suppose I enjoyed joining in with the weaving and braiding and so on. He came home now and again, and carried on drinking and fighting with his friends, and I didn't really see that much of him, truth be told. It was only when he was wounded that we ended up spending time together.' She made a face.

'He took a sword wound in his right thigh, a kind of downward slash that took the flesh from the bone as if it was a filleted fish. Someone bound it up on the battlefield, and it began to heal, but it could never be right: he had lost too much flesh. Then he had an infection in it that weakened the bone. But the rest of him was fine, and he came back here, for Thorfinn was moving his court to Orkney, and Einar gave him the croft, and he retired and we began to live here – there,' she said, pointing towards her longhouse.

'Not good at retirement?' Ketil suggested softly, when the silence went on too long.

'Not at all good at retirement. It seems Thorstein needed violence, the way other men need ale or the sea. He tried it on me, but I told him what to do with that idea.'

Not easily, Ketil thought, seeing the way her gaze turned inwards, back on bad memories.

'I thought that it would be enough to train with the other men, but friendly violence seemingly was not the right kind. He killed a man in a fight.'

'Manslaughter?'

'He claimed self-defence, and paid compensation to the family. But it was expensive: I had to work hard that year to make actual silver from braiding and weaving, to pay the fee. He was full of apologies, contrite, and I believed it would not happen again. But it did.'

'He killed again?'

'He injured someone, badly. It was a fellow at the harbour, just landed from Shetland, and Thorstein took offence at half a look. I don't know. The man lost an eye and an arm. More compensation, and a stern talk from Einar. Thorstein was under threat of banishment.'

'Exile ...' It would be hard, away from friends, away from support and land. 'And then?'

'Then not long after last Christmas he began coughing, and in January he – died.'

'Along with your boy?' He made his voice as gentle as he could, slipping the words in.

'Along with my Saebjorn. As if their chests were full of water – green water, that never ended. They couldn't breathe. And Saebjorn was only small ...'

She was small, too, standing there so forlorn. He suddenly wanted to take her in his arms and hug her, but he felt she might not take it well. And he needed the rest of the story.

'But you fear he might have killed again, and not declared it?'

She shrugged, pulling herself together.

'He would have known we couldn't afford to pay more compensation. And it was on our grazing land – Herleif was. No one was likely to see it happen down there, as long as no one was passing in a boat. And it wasn't –' she broke off and frowned hard. 'It wasn't an obvious place, that's all, for anyone to look for anyone.' She mumbled the last words, and he was sure she had intended to say something quite different.

But was this the answer? Had Sigrid's Thorstein killed Herleif, just because he was there? It sounded more than likely. That would be the murder solved, and he could go back to Norway.

Except that he still needed to find out about the rumours of Rognvald's resurrection.

'I'm hungry,' he said at last. 'I wonder if there's anything left over in the hall?'

'I'd made a stew,' said Sigrid, hesitantly. 'Gnup will have heated it up, or eaten it cold, if he's desperate. And Helga brought me flatbread earlier.'

He wanted to get away from her just now, to give himself time to think about what she had said. But perhaps if he went to her house she might give him more information. Could Herleif have been killed in a random act of uncontrolled violence? The idea clearly frightened Sigrid, so that she had had to brace herself to tell him. She must think it was a strong possibility, or she would never have said it. And she had been trying to direct his thoughts to a spring death from the start, he remembered.

She was waiting to see if he was going to eat with her. Her expression was unreadable: perhaps she had invited him against her better judgement, too.

'That would be good,' he said at last. 'Thank you.'

'Well, the bread will be good,' she conceded with a half-smile.

They cut across the pasture towards her longhouse. When they arrived at the door, the fire was already bright, and Gnup was stirring at the pot with some vigour.

'Hallo!' he said, looking up brightly. 'You're Ketil, aren't you? Everyone's talking about you!'

Ketil was not filled with joy at the thought. He nodded, however. This was the boy from Bjarni's house, and Ketil was interested to see what he was like. The first answer to that question appeared to be that Gnup was mostly damp.

'What have you been doing, Gnup?' Sigrid asked, presumably noticing the steam rising from Gnup's clothes. 'It's not raining.'

'Ah, well, I needed a bit of a wash,' said Gnup, looking pleased with himself. 'But it all came out right in the end. Except the water barrel's not quite as full as it was.'

'Go on, Gnup,' said Sigrid, her tone resigned.

'Kari's had her calf!'

Sigrid whipped round to look at the dark end of the longhouse. Ketil squinted in the same direction. A large beast chewed solemnly, ankle-deep in straw, watching them as if she could not think of anything more interesting to do. In a moment, a wet nose and two dark eyes emerged around her chest, and Sigrid darted off to look more closely.

'A heifer! Wonderful!' she said. 'And all looking well, too. She's suckling all right?'

'She is now,' said Gnup with satisfaction. 'She came out in a bit of a rush, though.'

'Was she hurt?'

'No, no,' said Gnup. 'I broke her fall.'

'With straw?'

'No, with me.' He looked up from the cooking pot. 'Hence the bath.'

'Well done,' said Sigrid, and Gnup gave a secret grin back to the pot.

Sigrid spent a few minutes assuring herself that the calf was all right, while Gnup found bowls and served the stew. Sigrid went to wash her hands, and Gnup took down flatbreads from a hanging shelf and offered one to Ketil.

'So is it true that you're Thorfinn's right hand man?' he asked, settling back with his stew bowl in a manner that implied that he was far too old to be excited by such things, but it would be useful to know, nevertheless.

'I work for Thorfinn, yes,' said Ketil. Presumably the whole island knew by now.

'And the man who was killed was your friend?'

'Yes, he was.'

'So is the man that killed him going to kill you too?'

'Gnup!' exclaimed Sigrid, sitting to take her bowl on to her lap.

'Well ...'

'I'd like to think not,' said Ketil lightly. 'What about you? You work on the land around here – did you see the man when he was alive? Or anyone acting in some way that made you suspicious of them?'

'I don't think so,' said Gnup. 'Sigrid asked me the same question. What was the man's name, anyway?'

'Herleif.'

'I don't think I've even met anyone called Herleif.'

'Gnup, do you talk to the children in Helga's – in Hrolf's household?'

Gnup considered.

'Well, if I have to.'

'Why would you not?'

'They're very young.'

'Oh, of course.' What age was Gnup? Eight? Nine? 'Have you heard this ghost story that seems to be going around?'

'A new one? There was one in the winter. Though maybe Hrolf's bairns have only heard it now.' He turned his mouth down, pitying his juniors for being so far behind the fashion.

'What was the one you heard in the winter, then?'

'Well, it wasn't a proper ghost story. It was only a story about a ghost, if you see what I mean.' He paused to wipe his dish clean with the last of his bread, stuff the bread into his mouth and lick his fingers thoroughly. It took a little while.

'I mean that it wasn't someone sitting at the fire telling a whole yarn, it was just a rumour that some people had seen a particular ghost in Kirkuvagr.'

'What ghost was that, then?'

Gnup looked at him, waiting to be mocked. He was older than he looked, Ketil decided.

'Rognvald Brusason – you know, the man Thorfinn killed a couple of years back. His nephew.'

Ketil did not smile.

'Did you believe the story?'

'I'd say if Thorfinn kills someone, they stay killed,' said Gnup seriously.

'When did you last hear the story?'

'Oh, sometime in the winter,' said Gnup. 'I'm not sure when. No, I tell a lie: I heard it again last week. There, see? It seemed such a silly story I'd forgotten!'

'Where did you hear it this time?'

'Oh, someone on the Brough, I think, or going to the Brough. I think. I can't really remember. Though it might have been at home.'

Gnup was careless now, and Ketil wondered if he was lying. There was little he could do about it just now, if so. He did not imagine that Sigrid would appreciate him threatening her farmhand. But he had to ask at least one question.

'At home? You live in Bjarni's longhouse, don't you?'

Gnup made a face.

'Yes, I live there. I don't spend much time there, though. Not if I can help it.'

'But long enough to have heard traces of a rumour?'

'I think that's where it was. In fact, I'm almost sure.' Gnup was more definite this time, yet there was something still not quite right about the candid way he met Ketil's eye.

'I should go,' said Ketil. 'I promised Hrolf and Hlifolf I'd do swordplay with them this afternoon, before the light goes.'

'You've plenty of light left yet,' said Gnup, but Sigrid was on her feet.

'Well, if you have to go you have to go,' she said, nodding. Ketil, taken by surprise at her abrupt move, scrambled up too.

'Thank you for the meal. Thank you, too, Gnup, for your work on it. I hope the calf does well.'

'Thank you.' Sigrid cast a pleased glance in the calf's direction, and Ketil left.

Back at Einar's hall, the space outside where the ball game had been played was now the arena for swordsmanship. Not that it had been roped off: a few stones marked the lines the swordmen were not supposed to cross, running in front of the longhouse and opposite it with the hall's door in the centre. At the door Einar sat, reading his book just in the door's shelter, with Hlifolf inevitably beside him. Along with Hlifolf stood Hrolf, Afi, Ulf and others, familiar from the ball game, and surprisingly Bjarni was with them.

'I hope Ragna is much improved,' Ketil said to Bjarni as soon as he was near enough.

'Has Ragna been injured?' asked Hlifolf at once. 'She can't be sick: she was fine this morning.'

'She took ill later,' said Bjarni smoothly. 'I'm afraid she's still very weak, as you can imagine, Ketil. She was grateful for Sigrid's help, though.' He smiled full into Ketil's face. 'Sigrid is always very much welcome in our household.'

And I'm not? Ketil wondered. Or does his welcome to Sigrid include, perhaps, marriage?

'Sigrid is welcome anywhere,' said Hlifolf, warm in his response. 'Now, Bjarni, since you're here from your mother's sickbed, perhaps you'd like to play your match and return to her? I have you down to fight Ketil first.'

'Oh!' said Bjarni. 'But that was when I thought he was only a trader! He's far too good for me now, you know.' He smiled again, self-deprecating, unwilling to put himself forward. Hlifolf snorted.

'Then Afi can fight Ketil,' he said waspishly, and ignored Bjarni's blink of disappointment. 'Bjarni, you can fight with Hrolf.'

'Ah, a worthy opponent!' said Hrolf warmly. He drew his sword with a smart clatter, and swished it back and forth, examining the play of the blade with care. It seemed to meet with his approval. 'Perhaps later, Ketil, you and I might exchange one or two blows. As soon as you're ready, Bjarni!'

'I'll need to fetch my sword,' said Ketil. There was no point in trying to pretend any more that he was a humble trader: he might as well be armed.

'Oh, do you have one?' asked Hlifolf. 'I was going to give you your man Herleif's belongings – that's that bundle there, by the door – and there's a sword in that.'

'I have my own,' Ketil assured him. What warrior would not rather have his own sword than one that had been buried in the earth for months? He was not sure yet that Hlifolf really believed that he was not just a trader – either that, or standards had really slipped at Einar's court. He hurried to the longhouse where his bundles lay in the place he had slept last night. He snatched out bindings, and bound his sleeves, then it was a matter of a few seconds to retrieve his sword, scabbard and belt. He slung them on, and at once felt real again.

When he edged past Einar into the daylight again, Bjarni and Hrolf were already sizing each other up a little to the right of the doorway. Ketil rested his left hand on his hilt and prepared to wait, but Hlifolf looked round and saw him.

'Afi's ready, too, or he will be in a moment,' he said. 'You two can fight over there.' He pointed towards the left of the doorway. Afi, his sword lying carelessly on the ground beside him, was dunking his great head into the water barrel by the door. Hlifolf watched him, then turned back to Ketil. 'A little too much ale today,' he explained.

Afi's head surged out of the barrel grinning. He shook it like a dog, spraying water droplets the length of the yard, and bent to grab his sword. Ketil blinked. The weapon seemed nearly twice the length of his own, yet it fitted sweetly into Afi's hand. This was definitely a warrior you wanted on your own side.

'Come on, then!' said Afi, nudging him hard. Ketil struggled not to stagger, and followed Afi to their side of the arena. Afi stopped and turned, not far from the wall of the pasture, and Ketil waited as close as he dared. Hlifolf called over,

'We try not to injure each other too much – remember that, Afi! He doesn't know his own strength! – but the aim is to disarm the other man or bring him to the ground.'

'Right,' said Ketil, not taking his eyes off Afi. The big man looked happy.

'Will we start, then?' he asked, and immediately began to circle.

Ketil moved too, thinking fast. There was a scurry of swords clashing behind him – Bjarni and Hrolf making contact – but he put it out of his mind. If he was to get past the reach of that great sword of Afi's and do anything to him at all, he had to be clever.

His main advantage here was that he was an unknown quantity. A warrior, yes, but they had no idea if he was good or bad, or left or right handed, or straightforward or tricky. But then, apart from the sheer careless size of the man, he knew little about Afi, too.

Afi flicked his sword up and tapped Ketil's blade, testing him. Well, there: Afi was impatient. Ketil would have waited longer. He edged his blade out of the way, not quickly, but easily enough. He kept his eyes on Afi's eyes, and let whatever sixth sense it was he possessed watch the blades between them. The eyes would tell you before the blades moved. Afi tapped again, and again Ketil shifted his blade so that Afi's ran harmlessly along it. The attack would come soon: Ketil could almost see the spring wound tight in Afi's cheerful face.

He was right. Still grinning, Afi's eyes suddenly took on a bright glare and he plunged forward, sword sweeping at Ketil's chest height. Without a thought, Ketil brought his own blade up to block, deflecting the blow so that his hand and arm were not jarred. But the sheer length of Afi's sword made it harder to judge where he should apply any leverage, and all he achieved was survival, no damage to Afi. Afi nodded, acknowledging Ketil's reaction, and backed to start circling again.

Now Bjarni and Hrolf came into Ketil's range of vision, hacking away at each other with apparent satisfaction. He took a moment to note that Hrolf was doing most of the work, and whatever his abilities at swinging and assessing his weapon, he was not particularly good at wielding it. Bjarni seemed to be allowing him to tire himself out as he himself struck manly attitudes in front of him. Those not fighting at the moment shouted advice, usually best ignored. Ketil focussed again on Afi.

Afi's patience really was not his strong point. He struck again, with one of his great sweeping blows, a repeat of his last attempt. Ketil's deflection was quicker and cleverer this time, twisting the hilt in Afi's hand but not quite releasing it. Afi frowned, considering. Ketil wondered if that was Afi's main stroke, one that would slice an unsuspecting opponent in half in battle. If so, he was trying to come up with a different one now: Ketil could see him thinking hard as he paced sideways again. Hrolf and Bjarni vanished from Ketil's sight, though he could still hear their swordplay, quick and busy. He put it out of his mind.

Afi had reached a decision. The great sword blade heaved up in both his huge hands, sweeping up above his left shoulder. Then, relentless as a falling tree, down it came.

How was that supposed to disarm without injury?

Ketil watched, as if the world had slowed down just for them. The blade caught the light, dancing grey-white, well kept. Afi's face broke once more into a grin, eyes burning on Ketil. His feet danced upwards as the sword came down. Ketil waited.

At the last possible second, Ketil thrust his own blade up and out, elbow pressed into his ribs. The great sword seemed to buckle and spring, flicking from Afi's shocked hands and flying into the pasture over the wall. Afi bellowed, and Ketil fell to the ground.

'Did you see that?' Afi was yelling, delighted as he scrambled after his sword. 'Did you see what he did?'

There were people around him, he knew, but the world looked suddenly blazing. Pain shot through his calf, and he clutched it.

'Oh, man, did I get you?' Hrolf was standing over him, sword dangling bloody in one hand. Bjarni laughed, then broke off. Ketil felt blood oozing around his hand.

'Did you see what he did?' Afi came bounding back with his

sword in his hand, waving it dangerously. 'Oh! What happened? It wasn't me!'

'No, it was Hrolf,' said Bjarni, serious now. 'I think he was distracted by your play, and he tripped and fell. His sword went into Ketil's leg. How are you doing, Ketil? Let's get you some bandages, shall we?' He helped Ketil to rise to his feet, and supported him off the field. Rannveig, ready for anything, was at the door of the longhouse waiting almost as if she knew something was going to happen.

'Thanks for the fight!' called Afi, dismayed, tapping his sword on his hand. 'Did you see what he did?' he asked again, in the hope that someone might hear, but Bjarni, Hlifolf and Hrolf were already discussing the next pair of fights.

Ketil said nothing as Rannveig cleaned and bound his wound as best she could. He knew he was going to have to rest it if he wanted it to heal properly – and he needed it to heal properly. But he also needed to get on, to find out about Herleif and Rognvald's ghost – what could he do, if he were confined to Einar's longhouse?

And besides, he had seen Hrolf's face, bending over him as he squatted clutching his leg. Accident or not, Hrolf had no regrets, that much was clear. Had he intended more than just a leg wound?

TÓLF

XII

Ketil had barely left the house earlier when Sigrid had grabbed her weaving tablets and made for the doorway. Untangling the work as she settled down, she kicked off one boot and looped the knotted end of wool over her big toe, wriggling it in the cool air. The braid that was already completed she slipped through a belt round her waist and secured, then paused to see just where she had left the pattern that morning. Then she set to work, flicking tablets around, sliding the shuttle through the shed between the taut yarn and beating down the weft as she went. Gnup, wiping his mouth with his fingers, stopped for a moment to watch the pattern emerge, then went about his work with a sack of bygg seed under his arm. He knew better than to stand over her for too long: she had blamed him for several mistakes in the past.

Gnup vanished to the field they had ploughed last week, and she sighed, happy to be alone. The damp wind was gentle as it crossed from sea to sea in front of her, tickling her toes, and she leaned back, making herself comfortable against the longhouse's stone wall. It was not warm, but it was light, and she needed to make the most of it. Thorstein had not left her well off.

As her fingers flew, her thoughts took her back to her conversation with Ketil. What had he thought about her theories? He had hardly seemed to react at all, even when she had brought herself to suggest that her own late husband might have murdered Ketil's friend. And she still had not told him the other thing, the thing which would link her and her household even more firmly with the dead man. Maybe it was just a detail, but it loomed large in her mind.

Yet she knew that the mystery of Herleif's killer was not all Ketil had to sort out here. Even if Thorstein had killed Herleif last autumn, that did not solve the matter of Rognvald's reported ghost. Was it just mischief-making, or a silly winter story that had accidentally grown out of its original fireside purpose? Or was someone definitely spreading the rumours with malevolent intent? If so, what was that intent? When even Thorfinn had not recovered from ordering Rognvald's death, it was more than likely that plenty of sympathy for the golden-haired boy still existed in the islands, but who was going to benefit from that?

Her thoughts were busy and her eyes were only on her work when a movement distracted her, and she realised suddenly that someone was approaching from the direction of Einar's house. She squinted, trying to refocus – was it Ketil? No, nowhere near as tall. It was Hrolf's eldest son, Asgrimr, the clever one, but his expression was urgent.

She laid down her shuttle before he had the chance to greet her.

'Has something happened?'

'I was told to tell you it was nothing fatal. It's just your friend, the trader man from Heithabyr.'

'What about him?' She wanted to spring to her feet, but tablet-weaving was unforgiving of disruption. She began to disengage herself from the work, telling herself she was cross to be interrupted yet again, as the boy caught his breath. He was not used to moving fast.

'Wounded in the leg,' he said. 'Father said you'd want to know.'

'Thank you. Wounded how?'

'Sword fight.' Asgrimr shrugged. 'Rannveig's bandaged him up. You don't need to come down or anything,' he added, just as Sigrid slipped her boot back on. 'It was just in case you were expecting him, or anything. He'd be best off his feet for a day or two, at least.'

That was not good news, not for Ketil. She considered, even as she wound up the wool. He would be well looked after down at Einar's, no doubt, but if he wanted to make any progress in his investigation … He might not want her to visit him, but she thought she should. And anyway, even if Thorstein had killed again, working out the puzzle of Rognvald's ghost would distract everyone from Thorstein, and perhaps, if she were very lucky, from the possibility that she might be responsible for compensation to Herleif's family on her late husband's behalf. She could not possibly afford another payment, not if she wove braid from dawn to dusk without these constant interruptions.

'Oh, I'd better go down and see him,' she said aloud, making herself sound resigned, 'in case he needs something. You're heading home?'

'That's right. Father's staying at the hall for the evening.'

'Of course.'

The boy carried on up the path towards Helga's longhouse. Sigrid pulled off her shawl and reached a hand inside the house for her cloak. She hooked it into her shoulder brooches. Then she picked up a basket with a bundle of nalbinding in it. If she were going to sit with Ketil, she might as well not waste her time.

'What have you done now?' she asked when Rannveig showed her to Ketil's sleeping place in Einar's longhouse. Ketil, sitting in comfort on his bedding with one bandaged leg on a pad of blankets, raised his eyebrows at her. A leg of his linen breeches was sliced off at the knee.

'It's only a flesh wound,' he said.

'But a deep one,' added Rannveig. 'I've told him he's not to think of getting up for at least two days. It will just open up again.'

'Did you have to stitch it?' Sigrid asked.

'Yes, but there, he was a big brave boy!' She grinned at Ketil, who gave a rather forced smile. 'Milk?' she asked Sigrid.

'Yes, please. I'll keep him company for a bit. That will teach him.' Sigrid settled herself at Ketil's bedside, and waited until Rannveig had brought milk for both of them and hurried away about her business. The longhouse was quiet: no animals left in this one.

'What happened?' she asked. She took out her nalbinding and began twisting wool around her thumb.

'An accident, I think,' said Ketil. She was not sure whether to be relieved or not: he was still injured. Ketil described, as best he understood it, how the fight had ended.

'So you didn't notice how close they were?' Sigrid asked.

'They were close all the way through the fight. At the last, they moved very quickly, I think,' Ketil said. Sigrid was doubtful. Hrolf never moved very fast. 'And then Bjarni seems to have tripped Hrolf, so that he fell forwards with his sword.'

'That seems more than likely. Bjarni's better than Hrolf, by quite a way. You were lucky to beat Afi, though: he's skilful, too, never mind being enormous. Is the cut really bad?'

'She's probably right. I should probably let it heal a little before walking much.'

Sigrid sniffed. She had suspected he would take the chance to rest for a couple of days.

'I suppose you want me to go round asking questions for you, then?' she said.

'I'm sure that won't be necessary.'

'Nonsense. You need to make progress on this. You know what Thorfinn is like when he starts on something. He'll be asking for new information twice a day, and three times on Sundays. Poor Father Tosti is running round in circles trying to make sure the new church is ready for Easter, with Thorfinn after him all the time.'

'I'm sure Thorfinn can be patient, when it's something like this. And anyway, there hasn't been a new mention of ghosts for a week or so now, as far as I can judge.' His words were light, but something in the way he was sitting, still and watchful, made her wonder. Was he trying to cut her out now? Was it because of what she had said about Thorstein?

'Thorfinn and patience have never been easy bedfellows,' she said, trying to sound as light as he did, but the words were hardly out of her mouth when a voice came from the open doorway.

'Rannveig?'

'She's out somewhere. Who's that?' Sigrid leaned back, trying to see past the curtain and against the light.

'I'm just over from the Brough,' said the man, hovering doubtfully in the doorway. Sigrid knew his face, at least. 'Thorfinn sent me. He's says you've all to come tonight to his hall.'

'A feast?' Sigrid was surprised. 'But it's Lent.'

'Thorfinn said it wasn't really a feast. It'll be fish, and eggs, and cheese.' The man's voice had turned thin: it clearly was not his idea of a good night out.

'Well, you can't go, anyway,' Sigrid turned to Ketil. But the man had ventured further into the longhouse, treading warily on the clean, brushed floor, and overheard.

'Are you the fellow from Heithabyr? Karl? Ketil?'

'Ketil, yes.'

'Thorfinn said you had to come particularly. He said you'd know why.' The man leaned perilously forward to wink in Ketil's face. To judge from Ketil's expression, the man's breath was not as fragrant as it might be. Sigrid gave Ketil an I-told-you-so look.

'He's not going anywhere,' she told the man. 'Can't you see he's injured?'

'But Thorfinn said ...'

'I don't care what Thorfinn said,' she announced. 'Ketil is not going to any feast. Or excuse for a feast.'

The cart that Thorfinn had sent over rumbled along the path that linked Einar's place to the Brough. Ketil's expression spoke of gritted teeth, and Sigrid marched alongside, cross but curious. Thorfinn clearly expected Ketil to learn something from the people Thorfinn was gathering that evening, and Sigrid wondered what it might be.

True to instruction, nearly all Einar's followers accompanied the cart across to the Brough. Feast or not, they wore their best clothes, and the fine pleating in Sigrid's skirt had to be gathered in both hands to keep the wind from billowing it against the cartwheel. Einar, Hrolf, Hlifolf and Bjarni led the way as always, the women and the less important men following at various paces behind, excited or resigned at the break in routine. The elderly couple that lived behind Einar's hall shared the cart, along with the smallest children. Snorri swung himself along on his crutches, ignoring the benefits of cart travel. Even the dogs followed, excited at the outing. It crossed Sigrid's mind that if anyone wanted to attack Einar's place, this evening would be a good time.

At Thorfinn's hall, Afi lifted Ketil down from the cart and carried him into the building. Sigrid tried not to grin: she was quite sure that Ketil had not asked for his help, but Bjarni's face was also unnaturally straight, and Sigrid was sure he had instigated the move. The men of Einar's court were so competitive - anyone new had to be put in their place.

The hall itself was already hot and crowded, most people still standing and chatting rather than finding themselves seats. The arrival of Einar's party, shedding their cloaks by the door, seemed to shake everyone into settling down. Sigrid went to join the women who were not serving the meal, clustering around where

Ingibjorg sat next to her husband at the head of the hall. If she was lucky, Ingibjorg would not trouble to speak to her. From a distance she watched Ketil being deposited, not too gently, about halfway down the men's table, where he seemed to be struggling to make his leg comfortable. He really did seem to be in pain, she thought. Had the wound been deliberate?

'Is Ketil badly hurt, then?' Helga's eyes were wide.

'That's why he was on the cart,' said Sigrid.

'Hrolf said he'd injured him. He feels really badly about it,' Helga said. 'He said he was just a better swordsman than Ketil and couldn't help it.'

Sigrid bit her lip and said nothing. She had no idea if Ketil was any good, but Hrolf certainly was not. She wondered which man was lying, but if Hrolf were really better than Ketil, Ketil must be dire. Thorfinn, seeing Ketil stuck in his seat, had left his chair to speak to him. They were too far away in the noisy hall for Sigrid to hear them this time, but it could not, in the circumstances, have been a private conversation. Bjarni and Afi were nearby. Hrolf was attending Einar closely, basking in reflected status. Sigrid looked around for Hlifolf and found he was in the midst of Thorfinn's men, no doubt gathering the latest gossip.

Gradually people found their places, Thorfinn returned to his high seat, and Ingibjorg nodded her long head to her women. They distributed platters of bread and cheese around the tables, then paused, watching her. Ingibjorg nudged Thorfinn, who in turn waved to Tosti. Tosti stood, looking a little self-conscious, and said grace. Sigrid admired the way Thorfinn had finally trained his men not only to wait for grace, but also not to dive straight into the food the moment Amen had been said, like starving ravens on a dying sheep. The women served bowls of fish soup, and the meal began.

'Sigrid!'

She heard the voice through the chatter, and turned reluctantly.

'Yes, Ingibjorg?'

'I need to talk to you about hangings for the new hall. Tomorrow, yes? Come early: I'm busy.'

So am I, Ingibjorg, thought Sigrid as she inclined her head to the old sheep. Ingibjorg always had what Ingibjorg wanted – and she thought that people obeyed her because the women admired her and the men adored her. In that, thought Sigrid, she was definitely mistaken.

She let the gossip and laughter swell and ebb around her, half-listening to Helga's commentary on a good-looking young man she had spotted in Thorfinn's following, half-watching Bjarni chatting with Rannveig where the men's tables and the women's tables met. Einar had a vacant expression on his face: no wonder Rannveig sought conversation elsewhere. Later, certainly, Rannveig would comb the Brough women for the latest news, more subtle in her approach than Hlifolf with his self-importance, and use it to her husband's advantage. She was a clever woman, no doubt about it. Sigrid was fleetingly envious, then considered how bored she might be if she were as clever as Rannveig, without a husband to organise and promote.

Ketil, she noticed, was listening to conversations, too. He was good at listening, she thought. Like Einar, he seemed to feel no great need to have his own voice heard, which always helped. At present, as he spooned up his soup, he seemed to have one ear on his neighbour, a sturdy dark-haired man with large, muscular hands, and the other on two of Ingibjorg's women behind him, who had paused for a word. Every now and again he nodded to the dark-haired man, which was all that was required to keep the man talking.

There were no honey cakes after the meal, as there might have been outside Lent. Instead there were last autumn's apples, wizened but still sweet, and more bread and cheese to go with them. It was a plain feast, but satisfying for men who were already working in the fields as well as preparing for the summer's raids. The dishes were abandoned on the tables as the rate of eating eased. People polished off their spoons and knives, tucked them into their belts, took up their ale cups thoughtfully, and prepared to digest food and conversation, elbows on the boards. Thorfinn surveyed his hall, exchanging low words first with Ingibjorg, then with Snorri, Einar's bard, who often worked in Thorfinn's hall, too. Seeing the bard rise from his seat, the guests allowed their conversation to lull a little, as they waited to see if the entertainment was starting.

'We're to have no dancing, as it's Lent,' Snorri announced, and if he grimaced at the idea, he had his back to Thorfinn. Some of the drinkers were relaxed enough to groan out loud, and were nudged by their more sober neighbours. 'But if anyone wants to give us some verse, my lord Thorfinn will be pleased to hear it.'

Thorfinn nodded as if his mind were on some other subject. Rognvald's little dog jumped up on to his broad lap from his place under the table, and Thorfinn fed him scraps of cheese and, as far as Sigrid could see, some unLenten meat. The dog licked his fingers with enthusiasm, then curled up abruptly to sleep. The hall had begun to smell more of ale than of food as the torches and the fire flickered hot. Some of the women rose to join their particular men, while the others chattered around Sigrid, a few excited, a few dozing already. Helga was still bright and interested, eyes on the men across the hall. Sigrid glanced at her. Helga's gaze did not seem to be on Hrolf.

One of Thorfinn's Brough men stood up, only a little unsteady, and announced that he had a verse. Snorri beckoned him forward, and the man scrambled out from his place on the long bench to take Snorri's place before Thorfinn's seat. He raised a hand to still the friendly jeers, and recited some skaldic verse so quickly that only its familiarity let Sigrid know what he had said.

'Heard it before!' cried a couple of voices from the sides of the hall.

'But it's a good one!' acknowledged a lone voice.

'Aye, if you can make out the words!' came the response. The man made an elaborate bow, wobbled a little at the base of it, and returned carefully to his seat.

'I have one, if anyone would care to hear it.' Hlifolf had taken advantage of a little ebb in the noise to allow his thin voice to be heard. There was a polite silence, as he bowed his head modestly, waiting to be called forward. Snorri grunted.

'Hlifolf, then, up you come.' He retreated from his spot, muttering. Hlifolf stepped forward, arranging himself and his cloak to best advantage. Sigrid sighed. Hlifolf did enjoy his skaldic verse.

He drew breath to begin, and at that exact moment someone on the men's benches emitted an enormous belch. The hall dissolved in laughter, and Hlifolf forced his furious glare into something more like amusement. He patted the crowd quiet again, and began properly.

Lithest linen-oak, lissom leaf-lake,
Marvel-mother, matchless, match-made,
Hard-helmed hero heart-held, handfast,
Storm-strong shield-shaker, sure as stone.
Close-coupled, conquerors in conquest,
Sword and sheath in shakeless standing,
Thorfinn, thick-thighed, thewed in thunder
With winsome woman wedded – wonder!

There was polite applause at the end, and a considerable wave of coughing. When Hlifolf turned to bow to Thorfinn, the earl, red-faced, gave him a look that was some kind of acknowledgement of the compliment, then covered his mouth, turning away from the table to clear his throat at length. Hlifolf seemed satisfied, and with a smug smile he returned to his seat. Tosti turned a little towards Ketil.

'I'm not sure,' he said, smothering laughter in his turn, 'that I should be seen to approve of some of those images.'

Ketil, whose skin was crawling at the very thought of the verse, nodded fervently.

'Right,' called Snorri, grimly. 'Anyone want to top that?'

'What about our new man?' came a voice from the bottom of the hall. Squinting down into the darkness, Sigrid was not sure who had spoken – Bjarni had been sitting in that direction, but then Hrolf was moving about, too. What was clearer, though, was that they meant Ketil. Even the Brough men seemed to know enough of what had been happening to turn immediately to where Ketil sat, his face stony.

'Will you favour us, Ketil Gunnarson?' Snorri asked, with the best bow his crutches could afford.

Sigrid expected him to refuse. What would Ketil know of verse? It seemed that everyone wanted to find out: the hall fell silent. Then Ketil, delicately moving his injured leg, rose to his feet.

'Of course, if you wish.'

Walking with care, he stepped out into the centre of the room, and Sigrid noticed Snorri pat Ketil's shoulder and murmur something, as if offering him support. Ketil nodded, and stood for a moment hunched over, as if calling something to mind. Then he cleared his throat and looked up.

From pine pitch paint to prow point
I watch the wild and wander wave-wood
Mist-marked maiden, or metal molten
I've trod and tilled the turbid tear-turf
Sky spray sombre, sky seared umber
Stormlight shadow, seal field sallow
Ardent for all airs and aspects
I steer my sea-sword surfborne sunward.

His voice, raised to fill the room, was clear and pleasant, and when he fell silent there was a moment's appreciative silence before the applause began. Helga punched Sigrid in the arm, and hugged her suddenly: her eyes were very bright. Sigrid found she had been holding her breath, and let it go. He had not disgraced himself.

'Well,' said Snorri, 'that's all very touching, but what about a laugh now?'

There was a general surge of approval: no one wanted to be touched for too long.

'Go on, then, Snorri, what have you got for us?' someone called out.

'Well,' said the bard, adjusting his crutches thoughtfully, 'I thought I might give you a new mansongvar.'

'Ooh!' An appreciative murmur swelled and sank.

'Whose slave have you been eyeing up?' called a wit, and a few names were shouted. Laughter broke out here and there, and a man choked on his ale and had to be thumped on the back. Snorri maintained an expression of superiority, though his eyes were glinting.

'A poet can observe another man's behaviour, you know,' he said, 'and if I have observed, well, a fondness in a man towards a lovely young slavegirl, then I might well assume his character, for the sake of the verse. Here we are.' He took a stance, turned his gaze innocently up towards the invisible roof, and raised his voice a little as the hall fell silent once more.

Lint-lapped lady, silk-slipped
The edge-storm urges, blood-warm
Heedless of helm-height, home-heart
To elk-float no eel-field need yield
To lip my love-lake linen-oak
Though seldom sword-breeze sapped ease
Red cave, rune-carved I'll run
To weave wave-hair with cup-capped care.

Snorri gave a bow, a smile twitching at his hairy mouth as the audience began to discuss the kennings, trying to work out which man he was speaking for, and which low-born woman he might mean. Sigrid looked about the room. Ketil's keen eyes were watching, too, skipping from conversation to conversation: if there had been gossip before, now everyone had a theory. Ketil met her gaze, eyebrows raised, and tilted his head very slightly. She looked where he was indicating, towards the back of the hall. At the same moment, someone else solved the puzzle with a tremendous shout.

'It's not a woman at all!' he cried. 'It's Hrolf and Hlifolf!'

Snorri nodded in satisfaction, and the hall erupted.

THRETTÁN

XIII

There was a kind of squawk above the laughter. Ketil looked about in alarm, then found the source. Hlifolf was laughing, and loudly making some comment about wide-sleeved shirts and the fashions in Trondheim.

Beside Ketil, Tosti visibly relaxed.

'Praise Heaven,' he murmured. 'That could have gone badly!'

'Is Hlifolf not known for taking a joke?'

'He'd sooner take pigswill in his ale,' said Tosti, then caught Ketil's eye and gave a boyish grin. 'If you'll excuse the phrase.'

Ketil grunted.

'Was Snorri just trying to provoke him, then? As a joke?'

Tosti took a sip of ale.

'I wouldn't like to say. But look at Hlifolf's shirt sleeves – if he wears them loose like that, he's bound to cause talk.'

Ketil glanced quickly at Hlifolf's baggy sleeves, allowing his gaze to travel on past him at once. It was true, Hlifolf's clothes tended towards the effeminate.

'And Hrolf?'

'Hrolf is happily married.'

'To the lovely Helga, indeed.' This time Ketil did allow his gaze to linger. Helga's headcloth had slipped a little, showing a glint of that curling red hair. The dark lashes were wide, as she tilted her head, throat pale and perfect, back to listen to something Bjarni was saying.

'Still married, yes,' Tosti's reproach was mild. Ketil grinned. Bjarni's hand, Ketil noticed, was on Sigrid's shoulder, easy and possessive. Sigrid sat almost directly beneath one of the torches, her face half in shadow, light catching on her fine cheekbones. He had to admit she was as pretty as Helga, really, though his mind flickered between Sigrid as he saw her now, and Sigrid as he had said goodbye to her as a child, still rounded with puppy fat, bossy and cross. Bjarni bent to say something to her, his dark hair sweeping forward, and the angle of a smile creased her cheek. They made a handsome couple. Ketil gave a slight snort. Hlifolf really did not seem to stand a chance – assuming he wanted one. But then Sigrid offered advantages other than being a comely wife: there was the farm, and all that weaving.

'It's a small community,' Tosti said, unemphatic. 'And whether or not you add in all those who travel through, there'll be courtships and jealousies, loves and hates. People are people.'

Ketil eased his injured leg, expressionless, still watching the exchange across the room.

'Tell me about Sigrid's late husband,' he said. 'Did you know him?'

'Thorstein? Oh, yes, I knew Thorstein. And little Saebjorn, of course. I christened him. And buried him.'

'What killed them?'

'An illness of the chest. Thorstein had it first, then Saebjorn caught it, too. The child was far too young to survive. Thorstein was tougher. It took him longer to die, though he went first.' He sighed, and sipped his ale.

'What kind of man was he?'

Tosti seemed to take a little while to consider. Around them Thorfinn's guests were moving from place to place, calling across to each other, accepting generous refills of the strong ale. Ketil toyed with his cup, eyes busy, aware of who was behind and beside him at any given moment.

'He was – not a man at peace with himself,' Tosti said eventually.

'A violent man?'

'Most men are violent, at the right time.'

'And did Thorstein keep to the right time?'

Tosti made a face.

'No, he didn't. I think you've heard a few stories, have you?'

'You mentioned that this is a small community. How did Thorstein fit in, if he – let's say if he was unable to keep his violence under control?'

'It was beginning to be a problem,' Tosti admitted.

'Courtships and jealousies? Loves and hates?' Ketil tossed Tosti's words back to him. Tosti gave a quarter-smile.

'Jealousies and hates, yes. As far as I could ever tell, he was faithful to Sigrid and he never went dabbling in another man's domestic concerns.'

'So what made him angry? I know he had a crippled leg. But I mean what kind of thing would set him off?'

Tosti shrugged.

'Jealousies and hates.'

'But not jealousy of another man's wife?'

'No, more of another man's wealth, or good fortune. Thorstein resented the fact that he could no longer go raiding. He liked what he could bring back. He'd travelled a long way in his time, you know: the Baltic, down round Spain, over to Ireland and the Western Isles. He brought things back, too, wealth for him and for Sigrid. Staying at home watching his wife doing the work was not Thorstein's dream.'

'So then he killed a man.'

'Someone's been telling you all the stories!'

'He did, though, didn't he?'

'Yes, and injured another. It was when Sigrid was expecting their child, though I don't know if that has anything to do with it. Of course, he had to tell Einar. I'm not telling secrets out of the confessional here, though I saw him there, too.'

'Do you believe that that was all he did?'

Tosti blinked at him. He was not stupid, for all his look of innocence.

'Do I believe he killed again? Yes. Yes, I do: he swore he would not, to me, to Sigrid, to Einar, even to his God. But I don't think he could have helped it. I'm sure he killed again, or if he didn't, it was pure good luck that no one put themselves in his way. It would never have lasted, if he had lived.'

'And do you think,' said Ketil carefully, 'that he might have killed my friend Herleif?'

'Oh!' Tosti flung a look across at Sigrid. 'You aren't looking for compensation, are you? Because ...'

'She can't afford it, I know. No, I'm not looking for compensation. Herleif had no family, anyway. But I need to know who killed him. Would Thorstein have killed him, and hidden the body? To avoid owning up to breaking his oath not to kill again?'

Tosti considered.

'He might have,' he said. 'He was ashamed when they had to pay before – when Sigrid had to pay. And then …'

Ketil let the pause lie. To call it a silence would not have been accurate: the noise in the hall was now considerable. Tosti drummed his fingers on his cup, his lips twisted, then made his decision.

'Sigrid's building a bridge.'

'What?'

'Sigrid.' Tosti nodded across at her. 'She's building a bridge. And you know what that means.'

Ketil sat back and looked at Tosti.

'You mean,' he said, 'a bridge for Thorstein?' Tosti nodded. 'To atone for his sins? Help him through Purgatory?'

'That's what she told me, anyway. And she's saving up to have a stone carved to mark it.'

'Did she say what sins?' But he knew the answer even before Tosti shook his head.

'She wasn't specific. We both knew he was far from perfect, and I didn't feel I could discuss it further.'

Ketil looked away, back at Sigrid across the hall. This time she caught him looking, and frowned, gesturing to his leg with a question on her face. He shrugged, and she turned away.

'Where is this bridge, do you know?'

'Somewhere down by the sea, I think. I don't know exactly.'

Ketil remembered seeing the figure, struggling with a flat stone as his kvarr approached the Brough the day he had arrived.

'I think I know where it is,' he said.

They both jumped as two great muscular elbows landed hard on the table in front of them.

'That verse of yours was no bad,' announced Snorri, the bard. 'Where'd you hear that one?'

'Oh,' said Ketil, 'somewhere in Heithabyr, I think. It's a while ago.'

'You're a lying bastard, if a modest one,' said Snorri. 'You made that up yourself. I can tell. Though I thought "aspects" was weak. You need to work on it.'

Ketil avoided that.

'That was a clever one about Hrolf and Hlifolf,' he said. 'You were lucky they took it well.'

Snorri spat on the floor with volume and emphasis.

'Luck doesna come into it. There's as much courage in the pair of them put together that might make an ordinary sort of a man. And Einar likes me,' he said, standing straight again, pride in his eyes despite his dismissive tone. 'They'll never touch me while I have his favour.' He snatched up a reasonably clean cup, and stopped the nearest serving woman to have it filled with fresh ale. Balancing against one crutch and the table, he knocked the drink back in one go, shaking his head to clear drips from his beard. 'Anyway, you'd ken all about that. I could see you were no just a trader the minute you scored that point in the ball game. Now that was poetry.' Hairy eyebrows expressively mobile, he slammed the cup down on the table, and clutched at his other crutch.

'Ketil was asking about Thorstein,' said Tosti.

'Sigrid's Thorstein? Well, he's dead,' said Snorri. 'He'll no get in your way if you want to make a bid for her.'

'Nothing further from my mind,' said Ketil. 'No, I wondered if there was a chance he could have killed Herleif. My friend, the one they found in the gully.'

Snorri directed a bright, sharp look at Ketil, then at Tosti.

'Someone been telling you stories?' he asked.

'They will, if they haven't already,' said Ketil. Snorri nodded.

'Aye, I'd say there was a good chance Thorstein killed him. He'd killed before. The only wonder would be that he didn't rob him, too, unless he couldna think of a story to tell Sigrid about the plunder. Aye, a good chance. So who's been telling you stories, then?'

'Ah, well, that would be telling, too,' said Ketil, easily. 'But you like stories. Have you heard the one recently about the ghost?'

'The ghost?' Snorri's gaze became even sharper. 'What ghost might that be, then?'

'I think you know,' said Ketil. From the corner of his eye, he could see Tosti watching them both, puzzled.

'Do you maybe mean a ghost Kirkuvagr direction? One,' said Snorri, lowering his immense voice, 'with golden hair to his bonny head?'

'That might be the one I mean, yes.' Ketil met his gaze. Snorri seemed almost to be about to speak, then he shook his head.

'I canna hear my own ears in this place. Listen, I'll talk to you later. What are you doing in the morning?'

'Nothing I can't change,' said Ketil. 'As long as I don't have to walk too far.'

'Oh, that would be me, too,' said Snorri with a grin. 'I'll see you then. Let me think ... I'll see you round the back of Einar's hall. It's sheltered there, and we can see anyone coming from most directions. Just in case, ken?' The grin broadened, a great slice through his beard, and the eyes glinted wickedly. Ketil half-thought he was being lured into a trap. Snorri might be a cripple, but Ketil had no doubts about his intelligence, and the strength of his arms. If he wanted to dispose of Ketil, he would find a way. Would Tosti bear witness that they had arranged this meeting?

'Tomorrow, after breakfast,' Snorri nodded, and swung away on his crutches. Tosti turned to Ketil.

'Did you really make up that verse yourself?' he asked.

'Everyone has to have a feast piece, at Thorfinn's court, don't they?' Ketil said. 'Or are priests exempt?'

'They're not usually expected to make verse, certainly.'

'Tell me,' said Ketil, 'what do you make of that eagle in the grave?'

Tosti's eyes widened in surprise at the turn of the conversation.

'It looked a bit like the old religion, to me,' he said.

'Are there many around here who still adhere to it?'

Tosti paused, then looked casually around him.

'Some,' he said. 'Not very openly. Not since Thorfinn came home from Rome, anyway.'

'You mean it's not a good move to advance your career?'

Tosti gave a little smile, though he was not looking at Ketil.

'Something like that, yes.'

'Were there eagles in graves round here? Is it a local practice?'

Tosti shrugged.

'They've found old graves with animals in them, of course, but not always eagles. But that's very old graves, from the people here before us.'

'Of course.' Ketil let the words lie for a moment, then asked, 'Would it be something you would expect Thorstein to do, if he were burying a stranger?'

'I wouldn't expect Thorstein to bury a stranger!' The priest considered. 'No, I don't think it is. I wouldn't have expected him to go to much effort at all. Kill the man, panic, bury him. Why add unnecessary details?' Tosti pushed himself away from the table, swinging his legs over the bench. 'I'd better go and have a few words with people before they're too drunk to remember I spoke to them. Some of them,' he added thoughtfully, 'I'll leave till later, when they *will* be too drunk to remember I spoke to them. I'll see you some time.'

Ketil nodded, propping his chin on his hands and surveying the room. He knew, slightly, about half a dozen people here, though plenty of them seemed to know who he was. How on earth was he going to be able to work out what had happened last autumn – or in the spring – and what was happening now? Thorfinn should really ask someone local, Hlifolf or Bjarni, or someone from the Brough. Who remembered who had been where sometime last year? If it really had been Sigrid's husband – though why would he go to the trouble of arranging a burial according to the old religion, when Herleif was if anything Christian? – if it really had been Thorstein, he was dead anyway. Ketil had no wish to pursue it. And if it had been someone else, someone connected with the rumours of Rognvald's return, how could he ever know? It would take him years to find out anything, by which time, if they were really unlucky, it would be too late.

Tosti moved about the hall, quiet, innocent, and Ketil idly watched his progress. He spoke to Hlifolf and Einar: Einar looked tired and bored, but he perked up a little as he chatted with the priest. Ketil's gaze slid on, as he toyed with his ale cup. He had not drunk much. The ale was not as good as Rannveig's. Ingibjorg had grand ideas, but he remembered that her best talent was delegation. His eyes wandered on around the hall and settled for a moment on Ingibjorg. She caught his eye, nudged Thorfinn, and together (sword and sheath, he involuntarily thought, and tried not to laugh) they beckoned him over. He went to the back of their table, where he would not have to shout across it. Ingibjorg laid a hand on his arm, widening her unremarkable blue eyes at him.

'Ketil! Thorfinn said you were here. It's good to see you!'

'My lady,' said Ketil.

'Well, Ketil, who have you spoken to?' Thorfinn demanded.

One hand rested on the lapdog on his knees, but he waved the other. 'I've given you a room full of suspects!'

'I've been watching,' said Ketil, 'seeing who is friends with whom, and which people don't seem to get on. And I've had a long word with Father Tosti, and the beginnings of a conversation with Snorri. I'm meeting him tomorrow.'

'Tomorrow?' Thorfinn was puzzled. 'I thought he was off to Kirkuvagr tomorrow. But then, that's skalds for you. They have minds of their own.' He gave a bark of laughter at this, and Ketil smiled dutifully.

'But I hear you've hurt your leg?' said Ingibjorg.

'A small cut.'

'Who dressed it? I hope you didn't dress it yourself!'

'Rannveig did it,' said Ketil, firmly, hoping that would be the end of it. But Ingibjorg, to his horror, rose from her chair.

'Let me see,' she commanded. She knelt down beside him, and he felt her fingers on his calf. They did not limit their exploration to his injury, and he tried very hard not to pull away, keeping his gaze somewhere past Thorfinn's left ear. Possibly disappointed by his lack of reaction, she stood, rather too close, gazing up at his face.

'Rannveig's salves are no good,' she said, with a sly smile. 'Let me give you one of mine.'

'I have – ah, thank you, my lady,' said Ketil. He had Sigrid's salve, but he suddenly did not want to put Sigrid up against Ingibjorg. It might be bad for his old friend's business. Ingibjorg waited until he offered her his arm to settle back into her chair, then nodded to a girl beside her.

'The salve, dear.'

The girl – the one he had met when he arrived, he realised, and indeed one of Thorfinn's daughters – raised her eyebrows at him cheekily and glided off into the darkness at the back of the hall. Her thick fair hair was shadowy. Ketil hoped she liked the cup.

She was back in a moment, beckoning him further away from her father's seat. In her hand was a small bundle.

'I'd better put it on. It does no good in the jar, you know.'

'I suppose not.'

She drew him to a bench at the very back of the hall, pushed him gently down on to it, and crouched beside his leg, fingers already undoing the bandages.

'So, Ketil of Heithabyr, I hear you're no trader at all?'

'No.' He sighed, and leaned back against the wall. At least this one was not already married.

'One of my father's warriors, I hear?'

'Yes.'

'How dull. Nearly every man I meet is one of my father's warriors. To meet a trader was pleasantly refreshing. Really quite … tantalising.'

He met her eyes, unreadable in the dim light.

'I am sorry to be a source of disappointment for you,' he said lightly.

'You have not even asked my name!' she said, taking a scoop of salve and touching it to his wound, not as gently as she might have.

'I daresay I could find it out from anyone here.'

'Now you make me sound common property!' The wound suffered another jab.

'That was never my intention,' he assured her. 'Perhaps you had better tell me, then, if so few know you.'

'My name is Asgerdr.' Her neck straightened as she said it, proud.

'I feel privileged to hear it.'

'You should. There, that's bandaged again, properly this time. Your breeches are very fine.'

'Thank you, though I'm not sure it's appropriate for you to be commenting on them.'

'Well, they're very close to me, down here.'

'Then allow me to help you up.'

He stood and handed her to her feet with a bow. She was dangerous, married or not – Thorfinn's daughter was Thorfinn's gift, not her own property nor his to take. And he had his own reasons for keeping clear. He made a little distance between them.

'Take care of that wound,' she said. 'My father no doubt finds you more useful with two legs.'

'I'll do my best. Thank you for your attention.'

'One does one's duty.' She had dismissed him, vanishing back into the darkness, but he thought he had caught the twitch of a smile on her face.

153

He turned back to see if Thorfinn wanted any more conversation with him, but as he did so he became slowly aware of a tension in the hall behind him. He was just feeling for his knife when there was a terrific shout and a clatter. He spun.

Snorri the bard was leaning over a table, readjusting his hold on his crutches. His hairy face was thunderous. Near him, breathless, excited, was Hrolf, his cap of hair pushed back from his shiny brow. Snorri straightened, but before he could sort out his balance, Hrolf thundered against his chest, throwing punches as random as leaves on the breeze. But Snorri was strong. All he had to do was push himself forward hard on his crutches, and Hrolf staggered backwards. But now Snorri was away from the table, and he needed the crutches to stand. Hrolf knew it, and tried to break his grip. He grabbed dishes from the table and slammed them against Snorri's knuckles, moving faster than Ketil would have thought he could. The crowd shouted, some for Hrolf, more for Snorri. Snorri let out a roar as the edge of a soapstone dish caught his thumb, and lurched back towards the safety of the table. Propped against it, he lifted one powerful arm, blood dripping, and swept his crutch around. The first time it caught on the ear of someone seated behind him, and there was a groan of shared pain. Blood spurted on to the table, but Snorri paid no heed. He swung the crutch again, spilling cups from the table, and smashed the crutch into Hrolf. Hrolf's hands rose to protect himself, but too slowly: the crutch slipped beneath his elbow and into his ribs. Hrolf reeled. Bjarni, confident in the pause, stepped forward and caught Hrolf neatly, pulling him back from the range of that crutch. Hrolf screamed, half-pain, half-frustration. Bjarni looked around for help. Helga sat, her hand slapped over her mouth, and beside her, Sigrid scowled. Snorri, gasping for breath, shoved himself away from the table, swayed for a perilous moment, then swung himself to the door of the hall and out into the night.

Hlifolf's snoring, rough and catching like a boatbuilder with wet wood and a saw, woke Ketil the next morning. Einar's hall smelled of old ale and cold smoke and unwashed men, and since there was only himself and Hlifolf there, Ketil quickly hauled himself on his good leg outside to wash. To his delight, the bath house was hot, and though he could not submerge his wounded leg yet he was able to sluice himself all over with steaming water, shave, and change his clothes.

When he emerged, feeling red and fresh, he met Rannveig carrying a couple of dishes.

'Since there were only two of you,' she said, 'it seemed easier just to bring it over like this. Is Hlifolf awake?'

'Not this side of Ragnarok, I think,' said Ketil. 'Though if you wave that food under his nose, he might rise. But I'll take mine outside, if that's all right.'

'Of course,' said Rannveig, tipping her head towards the hall door. 'Like that, is it? Maybe I'll leave Hlifolf's outside, too.' But she was better than her word, though she certainly did not spend long in the hall. In a moment she was out in the fresh air again, and disappeared back to the longhouse with a wave of her hand.

Ketil ate his breakfast in a leisurely fashion, relishing a few moments of peace. The air was light and fresh, the sea blue-grey and seemingly calm, and several of the sheep he could see on the sloping pastures had long-legged lambs about them. He was not much of a country man himself, but he could appreciate the idea of it, when the weather was fine. He grinned to himself, cleared his dish, and took it back to the longhouse.

'Have you seen Snorri this morning?' he asked, as Rannveig thanked him for the dish.

'Snorri? No, I haven't. After that fight last night I wondered if he had stayed on the Brough for a bit of quiet.'

'Licking his wounds. Maybe you're right.'

He turned away. It might be best to check behind the hall anyway, and if he had to go back to the Brough later to find him, then so be it. He would have to find a cart, though, he thought, still walking carefully. He could feel his leg was healing, but it was not the kind of injury to be careless with.

He rounded the corner of the hall. The path, which would be a much-used one, was paved with those flat local stones, pale grey while they were dry, easy to limp on. To his right were various outbuildings and a small longhouse, almost more of a cottage. A pig snuffled in a small enclosure. Against the wall of the hall were a few low bushes of some kind – Sigrid would know what they were, he thought. There was no sign of Snorri.

He walked on a few paces, just to make sure that the bard was not snoozing on the ground behind the bushes. He was not, but something else caught Ketil's eye, from this new angle. One of Snorri's heavy crutches was propped against the wall of the pig's enclosure.

Ketil glanced around. No one else seemed to be in sight. He crossed the path to the wall, and examined the crutch. It was undamaged, left there as if the owner expected to come back for it shortly.

Could Snorri manage on only one crutch? Ketil did not think so. He took a deep breath, pulled out his knife, and leaned over the wall.

The other crutch lay on the mud, where the pig's excited trotters had churned up the earth. Snorri lay face down, mercifully. The pig had not left much of his hands or the back of his neck. Ketil would not have liked to have seen his face.

FJÓRTÁN

XIV

'That's very strange.'

Sigrid had provided Ketil with a cup of fresh milk, and quickly returned to her tablet weaving, feeling her usual urgency. She eyed Ketil's injured leg dubiously as he used his arms to swing himself down to a spot on the other side of the doorway, but he seemed not to need help. Propped there at his ease, he leaned his forearms across his knees and relaxed.

'I'm not sure you should even have walked up this far, though I'm grateful you brought me the news. If that wound opens and goes nasty, you won't be walking at all.'

'Oh, don't worry,' he said. 'I have one of Ingibjorg's salves.'

'Ingibjorg's?' She managed not to snort, but suspected her face gave away her feelings on that matter. 'Oh, that's right, don't waste time waiting for something foul to get into your wound – stick it straight in yourself. Throw that salve in the midden.'

Ketil smiled slightly, and she stopped herself. Maybe he liked Ingibjorg – she had forgotten that he probably knew her before coming here. She should really be more discreet. Then she reflected that if he did like Ingibjorg there was no hope for him, and he deserved all he got. Certainly Ingibjorg had been flirting shamelessly with him last night.

She realised that her mind had wandered away completely from his awful news. Snorri could not really be dead, could he? The skald was always larger than life.

'You're sure it was Snorri?' she could not help asking.

'The pig hadn't touched his legs. Only his hands and the back of his neck.'

She made a face.

'No pork down at Einar's for a while, then. Good thing it's Lent.' She laid down her shuttle. 'Oh, poor Snorri! Do you think he was more badly hurt than everyone thought? His hands were a terrible mess. Could he have passed out and fallen into the sty?'

'I don't remember seeing Hrolf hit Snorri's head, and he couldn't have lost so much blood that he was dizzy.'

'No … and I've never seen Snorri so drunk he couldn't stand up. Yet how else could he have toppled into the sty?'

Ketil cleared his throat. Sigrid half-knew what he was going to say, but she did not want to hear it.

'I think he had help,' he said, and met her eye. 'Pigs don't tend to leave a furrow of broken bone straight across the back of the skull, and anyway, that pig doesn't seem to fancy eating hair. The wound was pretty much undisturbed.'

'Couldn't he have hit his head when he fell?'

'There's no mark on the wall. And anyway, how could he have fallen? If he had really tipped accidentally, surely both his crutches would have been left outside the sty. He wouldn't have pulled one in with him.'

'He might. You saw how hard he held on to them in the fight.'

'You're being obstinate,' he said with a sigh. 'You know what I'm saying. Snorri was murdered.'

'But who would have killed Snorri?'

'Well, Hrolf seems to be the obvious suspect, wouldn't you say?'

Sigrid laughed.

'Snorri broke three of Hrolf's ribs. Even if he hadn't, I couldn't see him lifting Snorri over a wall, could you?'

'Oh. Fair point.' He thought about it for a moment, watching her hands flick the bone tablets back and forth through the wool strands, a small, controlled wave on a well-ordered river. 'Are those dragons?' he asked.

'Deer!' she snapped. 'Look.' She turned part of the finished braid so that Ketil could see it the right way up. 'See? Antlers.'

'It's very good,' said Ketil, but now she thought he was just being polite. 'I've seen people wearing braids like that, but I've never seen them being made, not such complex ones.' She nodded. He had redeemed himself.

'I've had a lot of practice,' she said, allowing herself a little pride. 'Most people round here buy my braid for special garments.'

'And the braid on Herleif's cloak in the grave – you made that, didn't you?'

His voice echoed around her head, making the wall sway behind her. She closed her eyes, but all she could see was that stained braid along the cloak's edge, the pattern one she had invented herself, the very wool familiar to her fingers.

'Yes,' she heard herself say, as if she were very far away. 'Yes, I wove that braid.'

'Sigrid! Sigrid.' He had leaned closer, and he seemed to need some kind of response, but in her mind's eye she was weaving that braid once again. The green was a colour she had been particularly proud of, bright and true, but the other colours were strong enough to balance it, blue and red, black and a touch of white. The pattern was geometric, but complex. She had found it particularly challenging: she was fairly sure she had never done one like it again. But who had bought it? Who? She frowned so hard it almost hurt, as if she could squeeze the information out of her memory. Who had taken it? What had they said they would use it for? People usually did. But had they said this time? Had they said they would stitch it on to the cloak of a man destined to have his throat cut and die in a gully, so that she would find it again?

'I have no idea who bought it, though,' she said at last, opening her eyes. He was indeed close, staring at her face.

'Are you sure?'

'I've been wracking my memory. It could have been anybody. I remember the braid, but not the customer.'

'Was it a commission?'

'I don't think so. I think I wove it to see if I could, then sold it later.'

'But not to Herleif?'

'I usually sell to women. I think I would have remembered selling it to a strange man.'

Ketil sat back. The braid on his own cloak, she noted, was quite narrow and unassuming, and the silver brooch holding it to his shoulder was really very plain. If she focussed on it she felt less sick.

'Before or after your husband died?' he began again.

'Before. I made it last autumn, I think.'

'Could your husband have taken it, for whatever reason, and given it to Herleif?'

'No! Why on earth would he do that?'

'Compensation for injury? Payment of a debt?'

'He left that kind of thing to me.'

'If he didn't want you to know about it?'

'I don't know!' She swallowed hard. 'I don't remember noticing it was missing. I'd never known him do such a thing. I don't remember who I sold it to, if I sold it. I don't remember! I make more lengths of braid than you've killed men in battle. If I manage to recognise my own work, it's the most I can do. I don't keep every transaction in my head – as long as I'm paid I can forget about it. I have no idea how braid that I made ended up on your dead friend!'

After a moment he breathed out, and turned away. She blinked back tears from her eyes. He was dead a season, and still Thorstein's violence haunted her. No doubt it would go on. Ketil would never understand.

'I'm bothered,' he said at last, his voice deliberately lighter, 'about that eagle.'

Sigrid sniffed, and wiped the back of her hand over her eyes while his gaze was still elsewhere. Like her, he seemed to find the view from her longhouse door appealing, the broad sweep of land to the Brough with the sea blue on either side.

'What about the eagle?'

'Why would someone in this day and age give Herleif a burial that was not Christian? That harks back to the old beliefs? I wouldn't have said that Herleif was a particularly devout attender at church, but nor was he interested in Thor.'

'Perhaps the person who killed him was?'

'That's what I was wondering. Is there much of that around here? Lingering old beliefs?'

'I suppose there must be some,' said Sigrid cautiously. 'It's not against the laws, is it? But it might be soon. Thorfinn's favour would not come easily now to someone who was not openly a Christian.'

'No, indeed. Nor, more locally, Einar's.'

'True enough. So whatever there is it's not much talked about.'

'Was – I'm sorry to keep coming back to your husband – was he a Christian?'

'He was, yes.' She was determined to keep her voice from

cracking again. 'I never saw him wear a hammer pendant, or buy a charm, or anything that might have made me wonder. His parents were Christian, and he'd never worshipped in any other way.'

Ketil sighed, and eased out his leg.

'I don't know what to do, Sigrid,' he said, and she looked across at him, surprised. He caught her eye. 'How can I resolve this? How can I say who killed Herleif, when it was on some unknown day from last autumn to this spring, and I don't even know the people here, let alone who among them might have been here on that unknown day? And no one has mentioned a ghost, apart from the children remembering something from months ago, since I arrived. Has it faded away? If so, is there any point in trying to find out where it came from in the first place?'

'I thought Gnup said he'd heard the rumour of the ghost again last week.'

'Hm,' said Ketil. 'I'm not sure Gnup was being entirely accurate.'

'Gnup's a good boy!'

'Even good boys sometimes find it convenient to – reorganise the truth.'

She could not disagree. She concentrated on her weaving, and hoped that Gnup was not within hearing.

'I wonder why he would have found that reorganisation convenient, though?' she asked.

'I have no idea. But he was hiding something.' He sighed. 'And then there's Snorri. He asked me to meet him this morning, so did someone kill him to frighten me off? To try to have me accused of his death? To stop him telling me something? Or even to stop him going to Kirkuvagr, because Thorfinn thought he was going there today? Or was it just something that happened, a fight he had with someone, that has nothing to do with me or anything I want to find out?'

'I think you ask too many questions,' said Sigrid, her head beginning to spin with all the possibilities. 'You're only going to confuse yourself. Let's think what questions you really need to answer, for Thorfinn's satisfaction or for your own.'

'I need to know where the rumours of Rognvald's return came from. That's the main thing.'

'And in Norway it was thought they came from Orkney?'

'And from Shetland. But I stopped there on my way here, and any rumours there came from here, too. There's always an Orcadian link.'

'From the Brough specifically, though?'

Ketil shrugged.

'It was somewhere to start. And I had to see Thorfinn, anyway. But no, I don't know more specifically. The man died on Papa Stronsay, and we buried him on Papa Westray. I could start in those places. But how do I look for a ghost?'

'You're not looking for a ghost,' said Sigrid firmly. 'You're looking for a rumour. All you need to do is to find someone who heard it, and ask them where they heard it from. Then go to that person, and ask them. And so on, backwards, like a line of descent in the sagas, or in the Bible. You know, so-and-so the son of so-and-so the son of so-and-so?'

'You make it sound very simple,' Ketil conceded. 'But what if someone can't remember? Or lies?'

'Deal with that when it happens,' she said. 'You can always go back and find a second cousin, and track it back instead.'

He smiled a little.

'I wish I could be as sure as you are. Anyway, Gnup didn't seem inclined to tell me where he had heard it.'

'Maybe I could get him to tell me,' Sigrid suggested. 'Is that him coming now?'

She had heard light footsteps approaching the longhouse and looked past Ketil to the corner. But it was not Gnup that appeared, but Helga. She was wearing her second best dress and overdress, and carried a neat little basket on her back. Sigrid glanced quickly at Ketil, but his face was bland. Helga was undeniably very attractive, but she was not going to leave Hrolf for some wandering warrior: she would hate to see her old friend hurt.

'Good day!' Helga called cheerily, and perched herself uninvited on a low stack of flat stones. 'Good day, Ketil! How is your poor leg?' She waved a hand very close to it, without actually touching: Sigrid saw Ketil brace himself against the contact. 'Is that my braid you're working on, Sigrid?' She darted a look at the wool, then bestowed a shining smile on Ketil.

'No, it's the one before yours. People will keep interrupting me ...' said Sigrid, but Helga may not have heard. 'Where are you off to?'

'Oh! Well, I thought I'd better go and see how poor Ragna is, since she was too ill to go to the feast last night. Have you heard anything of her today?'

'No, nothing,' said Sigrid. 'Have you, Ketil?'

'Nothing,' he agreed.

'That's good of you, Helga,' said Sigrid. 'But I'm sure she's fine, with two daughters bowing to her every command.' She gave Helga a searching look, then returned to her tablets.

'Well,' said Helga, trying to look innocent, 'I hear there's a trader coming north up the coast from Hamnavoe, with some pretty silverware. I thought if I caught him before he made it to the Brough I might have a better choice, and maybe even a better price.'

'Ah! Of course - clever you,' said Sigrid, grinning to herself. That sounded much more like Helga: she was not much for visiting the sick.

'Will you come with me to Ragna's, though, Sigrid? It would look much better if you were there, too.'

'How better?'

'Well, Ragna always tells me I'm useless at medicines and things. If you come along she'll be much more welcoming. And anyway – you and Bjarni …'

Bjarni and I … Sigrid's mind, half on the yarn before her, skipped a little sideways. Bjarni and I. It seemed that suddenly everyone thought they were close to betrothed. And Bjarni himself – she could still feel his large hand on her shoulder last night, casually possessive. Did he think they were close, too? Yet he had never said anything. If he did, what would she say? He was handsome, yes, and wealthy, and easy going – maybe a little too easy going – but was he worth giving up her independence for? It was not a wealthy independence, but it was, she thought, a good one. If she had to live in the same longhouse as Ragna, one of them would be dead in a week.

Dead, like poor Snorri. The thought brought her abruptly back to the present. She did not think she had been missed: Helga was chattering to Ketil about the silverware trader, and Ketil was listening, content, it appeared, to watch her as she talked. He did seem to be smitten. Silly man, she thought. Even were she free, surely he could do a lot better than Helga. She really would need to have a word with him, before he made a complete fool of himself.

'Well, then, are you coming to Ragna's?' Helga demanded. 'I don't want to miss the trader!'

Sigrid looked down at the braid. It had been interrupted so many times already, and in spite of herself her curiosity was tugging at her. She had thought, the other day, that Ragna's vomiting had been brought on deliberately – but why was she still sick? Maybe she herself was not the only one who was appalled at the thought of living with Ragna. Maybe one of her silent daughters was at last making her presence felt. It would be interesting to find out.

'Oh, all right,' she said at last, bending to unloop the yarn from her toe. She bundled the work carefully so it would not tangle, and set it into its basket.

'Shall I come too?' asked Ketil. Sigrid glanced from him to Helga.

'You'll go back to Einar's hall and rest your leg,' she informed him. 'Or you can stay here as long as you like. You aren't marching off around the countryside any more than you have to until that has healed a bit more.'

To her surprise, he took that quite well. Ketil sat back against the doorpost, and raised a hand in farewell as they set off towards Ragna's longhouse. His leg must hurt more than he was allowing his face to show.

From outside, Ragna's house looked as busy as usual. In the farthest outfield they could see Bjarni supervising the mending of a broken wall – Helga nudged Sigrid hard in the ribs as Bjarni lifted a flag into place, as if they were girls eyeing up the local lads. There was no doubt he was a good-looking man, and more than competent with a sword or in a fist fight. When she had occasion to watch any of the competitions the men had, she had noted his effortless strength and accuracy. He was quite the dream of any romantically-inclined young lass. She said nothing, as they approached the longhouse door.

One of the interchangeable daughters met them at the door, and hurried them backwards at once.

'My mother is resting!' she said, with more force than Sigrid ever remembered seeing in any of the family apart from Ragna herself. 'You mustn't disturb her!'

'Oh, well, then,' said Helga at once, happy to turn from the door, but Sigrid caught her arm.

'We only came to ask how she was,' she explained. 'We were worried when she didn't come with the rest of us last night.'

'She's not at all well,' said the daughter sternly, but she was interrupted by a weak word from indoors.

'Is that Sigrid?'

'Yes, mother, and Helga.'

There was a rustling, as if Ragna were rearranging herself in her blankets.

'Tell them to come in, then.'

In an instant the daughter bowed her head and allowed them to pass. Sigrid wondered if any warrior leaders had thought of taking lessons from Ragna, as they, too, did as they were told and stepped into the house.

It was dim inside, with fewer lamps lit than usual. Ragna beckoned them forward from her bed, then set her long pale hands back amongst the thick bear fur of her blanket. Her face was thin and grey, a decade older than she had looked only a few days ago. Sigrid was shocked, though, sniffing discreetly, she could smell nothing other than the usual herbs that freshened a winter longhouse. Had she imagined that Ragna's illness was not natural?

She felt Helga's surprise, too, but neither of them dashed to sit by the bed and comfort the invalid. Even ill, Ragna was not that kind of patient. Standing awkwardly in the central aisle of the house, Helga handed fresh bread from her basket to the nearer attendant daughter, and Sigrid dug out a pot of fragrant dried herbs that were supposed to deter nausea, that she had made last year for her son and never used. The daughter turned away with them, as Ragna said waspishly,

'There, Olvor, the neighbours know how terrible your bread is, that they need to bring me their own.'

'That's not what I -!' Helga began to exclaim, but Ragna cut across with a change of subject.

'Who was at the feast last night?'

'We were sorry you missed it,' said Sigrid, seeing that Helga was watching agonised as the daughter arranged her bread on a dish. 'I think everyone else was there. Bjarni will have told you, no doubt.'

'I have scarcely seen Bjarni today. He was doubtless too drunk to walk further, and stayed at Einar's hall last night.'

Sigrid did not remember Bjarni being particularly drunk even in Thorfinn's hall, but not wanting to provoke Ragna she kept her face expressionless.

'I think everyone else was there. Your absence was keenly felt,' she added, knowing the words sounded stiff. 'But it wasn't really a feast, not with it being Lent. Thorfinn just wanted to see us all, I think, since he's been away.'

Ragna gave a faint snort.

'How was Ingibjorg?'

'She seemed well. She only spoke with me briefly.'

'Of course.'

Sigrid kicked herself. Ragna would not expect Ingibjorg, her kinswoman, to speak much to the lowly Sigrid. The two women were alike only in their superiority: if Ingibjorg looked like a sheep, Ragna was a hawk. Just now, though, she was a hawk in moult.

She half-emerged from her thoughts on hawks to realise that no one was speaking. Had Ragna asked her a question? To judge from the expressions on Helga's and Ragna's faces, they had simply run out of something to say. Sigrid rushed to fill the silence.

'Does anyone know of anyone around here who is still sympathetic to the old beliefs?' The moment she opened her mouth, she knew it was a stupid question, and quite possibly rude. Ragna looked at her as if she had proved how unworthy she was to talk with Ingibjorg. The daughter-attendants, mute over the fire, glanced up in surprise, and Sigrid felt herself redden like the young girl she had imagined being earlier. Helga alone seemed unbothered, and came quickly to her rescue.

'I don't know of anyone ordinary who still holds to those beliefs – not completely, anyway. I mean, you hear of men going for a charm before they go raiding, don't you? That kind of thing happens all the time, I think.'

'Do you?' asked Ragna, her voice sharp as an axehead. Helga seemed gripped by the same panic that had hit Sigrid.

'Yes, of course you do, all the time! The men go to that old woman that lives at the old house by the Loons. You know, down

TOMB FOR AN EAGLE

at Skorn. By the marshes.' She was beginning to gabble, and Sigrid, a little recovered, laid a hand on her forearm. Helga took a deep breath. 'Well, so I've heard,' she added, and swallowed hard.

'Well, it's very good to see you looking so much better, Ragna,' Sigrid said. 'But I'm sure you need your rest. We'll let you be, now. Thank you for your hospitality.'

They stumbled out of the longhouse, with Ragna's granite-hard gaze on their backs and a daughter at each side, blank-eyed as they waved them goodbye. Sigrid and Helga scuttled down the path through the infields, not even looking around for Bjarni.

'Why do we bother?' Helga snapped at last. 'She's just an old tarf corbie. There's never a word of thanks, or a smile of welcome.'

'It's the daughters I feel sorry for,' said Sigrid in agreement.

'Will you come with me to see the silver man?' Helga asked, clearly trying to cheer herself up.

'No ...' Sigrid looked about her, choosing a path as they reached a crossroads. Helga's was the path to the left. 'Was it near Skorn you meant? Where the old woman lives?'

'That's right. If you're looking for a curse for Ragna, I'll give you silver towards it.'

Sigrid tried a laugh.

'No, it was something else I was thinking about.'

'Love potions?' Helga was coming back to life, a twinkle in her eye.

'Maybe the opposite!' Sigrid said, with a significant look intended to amuse, rather than inform. 'I'm off to Einar's place. Good luck with the silver man. I hope you find a bargain!'

'Thanks – I usually do!'

FIMTÁN

XV

Ketil sat in the sun, his leg stretched out. It was well bound up, and he could feel that it was healing, whatever Sigrid's concerns. But it had only happened yesterday: she was probably right that he should not have walked to Ragna's house just now – and anyway, he had other plans.

He thought again of Snorri's corpse, lying there filthy and blooded in the sty. He had not asked about any family Snorri might have had, but skalds were wanderers, staying for a while at any court that paid them, moving on when the inspiration ran dry. Trouble-makers, many of them, sweet as honey to the lord they flattered, but insinuating themselves into court politics like a lever between rocks, ready to break allies apart. Had Snorri done that? He had certainly caused trouble with Hlifolf and Hrolf, and no one had seemed much surprised. But Snorri was also by necessity a watcher, an outsider, particularly when it came to the ball games and mock fights. What might he have seen amongst Einar's or Thorfinn's men that he had planned to tell Ketil? Or had he planned it at all? But then, Ketil thought, Snorri had at least been in the place they had arranged to meet. It looked as if he really had intended to tell Ketil something. But was that why he had died?

Ketil was no further in his thoughts when he heard footsteps, and a cheerful whistle. Gnup had appeared at last. The boy rounded the corner of the longhouse, and started when he saw Ketil propped comfortably at the doorway.

'Hallo!' he said, though there was a wary look in his face which assured Ketil. The boy had indeed been hiding something. He jerked his head. 'Sigrid inside?'

'Sigrid's away,' said Ketil, expressionless. 'Sit down a moment, will you, Gnup? I want a word.'

He was right: the boy was nervous, much more nervous than when they had first met. Gnup hesitated, his gaze anywhere but

169

Ketil's face. Ketil waited, silent and still, and Gnup sat, almost as if his legs gave up.

'I don't know anything!' he said, his voice trembling.

'Then this won't take long,' said Ketil. 'We spoke yesterday about that rumour you had heard. About Rognvald's ghost?'

Gnup, confident young man, had shrunk back to boyhood. He clutched his knees against his chest and nodded, though it was hard to see it.

'I'd like to be quite clear where you heard that rumour.' He waited. Gnup said nothing. 'Was it at your home? At Bjarni's house?' Again he waited, this time allowing time to pace past one slow step at a time. Gnup's eyes flickered to Ketil's hands, loose on his lap, and he mumbled something.

'What was that?'

'I don't want Sigrid to marry Bjarni,' Gnup said. He glanced up quickly at Ketil's face, to see if he understood. 'If Sigrid marries Bjarni, I'll have to go home. I hate home. I want to work here. With Sigrid.'

'Right …' Ketil tried not to show his puzzlement. At the same time, he thought here was another person who thought Sigrid was going to marry Bjarni! He would be a guest at the wedding before he left Orkney, if things were moving this quickly. Assuming he and Sigrid were still on speaking terms. 'So you told me you had heard the rumour at home, to try to bring blame on Bjarni, is that right?'

Gnup nodded frantically.

'It doesn't sound like a good rumour to me,' he said. 'What would Thorfinn do if Rognvald came back? What would Thorfinn do if people even thought Rognvald was coming back? See? It's trouble, start to finish. And if you went poking around at Bjarni's, well, it might be enough to drive Sigrid and Bjarni apart.'

'You really think they're going to marry?'

'Well … everyone says so.' Gnup swallowed. Ketil imagined being the lowest and least loved child in the house where Ragna was in charge, and felt a wave of sympathy.

'I understand. But if you didn't hear the rumour at Bjarni's house, where did you hear it?'

'From a fisherman from Tingwall,' Gnup said quickly enough, but not so quickly that it sounded like a lie. 'He came into the harbour here one day when the wind was wrong to go home, and I was down fetching some special wool for Sigrid.'

'How long ago was that?'

'A month or so. No, longer: before Lent began, because he gave me some dried beef he had with him while we talked. I was hungry,' he added, and Ketil remembered keenly the perpetual hunger of being nine or ten.

'Did you know the fisherman? Was it someone you had met before?'

'I'd seen him in the harbour before, but we hadn't spoken.'

'Do you know his name?'

Gnup thought.

'It might be something like Olaf, but I'm not sure. But he lives in Tingwall.'

'That's along the coast?'

'Yes: there's an old house there – no, two, I think, and it's past Eynhallow.'

'Did he say where he had heard the rumour?' Ketil had not moved, keeping Gnup pinned with his gaze.

'I'm not sure. I think he mentioned Kirkuvagr, but we were talking about different things and I might be wrong.' Gnup must be feeling safer now: he seemed to be growing up before Ketil's eyes, after shrinking so far down. Ketil sighed, and pulled his legs up, easing his knees. Gnup relaxed. 'Is that all you need to know?'

'For now.'

Gnup grinned, and ran a hand up through his haystack hair.

'You know you're really scary? How do you do that? You didn't even move, and I thought you were going to stick a knife in me!'

'That was the general intention.' But he was very glad he had not had to. He liked Gnup, and it would have been hard to explain to Sigrid. And anyway, he was never sure he could rely on information obtained at knifepoint. A blade behind the ear always made people unnaturally happy to oblige with whatever they thought you wanted to hear. He was sure Gnup had been telling the truth.

He had rested long enough. He pushed himself to his feet, dusting out his cloak and adjusting the angle of his sword.

'I'll leave you to your work,' he said. 'I'd better get back to

Einar's place.'

'No doubt you'll be back soon,' said Gnup. 'If I remember the name of that fisherman, I'll tell you. Olaf it was, or something like it …' He wrinkled his brow.

'Thanks.' Still wary over his leg, Ketil glanced down to Einar's hall to get his bearings, and set off in the sunshine. It was far too fine a day to be considering death and conspiracy, but it had to be done. He found himself thinking about Bjarni, and his shiny black hair. Was Sigrid's first husband that dark-haired, Danish type too? He tried to picture his old friend in Ragna's household, obedient to that imperious woman, and for the first time in days he laughed out loud.

At Einar's place, he found that Snorri's distorted body had been cleaned and laid in the hall, and that he and Hlifolf had once more been removed to the longhouse. Hlifolf, who still had the look of a man who had drunk too much ale the night before, was sorting through his own belongings on his bed.

'What a thing to wake up to,' he said when he saw Ketil. 'Terrible news. You found him, didn't you?'

'I did,' said Ketil.

'You didn't see anyone about?'

'Not a soul, just then.' But he had not been there very long, Ketil knew: he remembered the dull warmth that was fading from Snorri's shoulder as Ketil turned him over. It had been unsettling, somehow, and made him search his memory for any sight of Snorri that morning, or sound of a struggle at the back of the hall. But there was nothing.

'He was a skilful skald,' Hlifolf was saying. 'He'll be much missed.'

'You weren't so impressed with him last night, if I remember,' said Ketil.

Hlifolf looked round at him.

'Ha! No, I wasn't. But we all took our turns to be the butt of his humour: it was just our night! I'm sorry, though, that it should happen to be the night before he died.'

'Were you surprised at his death?'

'What an odd question!' Hlifolf sat back, considering. 'He was always a heavy drinker, but he could usually hold it. I didn't have the impression at the time that Hrolf had done him much harm in that fight, but maybe there was a blow to the head that I didn't see. He just toppled over the wall, I suppose, and maybe hit his head again. Accidents happen.'

'They do, but this was not an accident,' said Ketil. 'There was indeed a blow to the back of his head, but it did not happen in the fight, and I'm convinced someone pushed him over that wall. It was too high for him to topple over on his own.'

'What if he was sitting on the wall head?'

'It would have been a struggle for him to get up there, and worse to get down later,' said Ketil, unable to picture it. 'And why would he? He could easily have sat on the ground by the wall instead.'

'If he was drunk, though ...'

'He had had plenty of time to sober up. He died this morning.'

Hlifolf jerked back, staring.

'This morning?'

'Yes, didn't I say? He was still warm when I found him.'

'Oh. Oh, my ...'

Hlifolf had gone very pale. Ketil waited with interest to see what he would say, but whatever had shocked him Hlifolf drew a deep breath, and said,

'I hadn't realised. I assumed it was last night. Dear me.'

His colour, such as it was, returned, and Ketil looked away, disappointed. Hlifolf turned back to sorting his belongings.

'Look,' he said, after a moment, 'we were supposed to give you these. It's your friend Herleif's cloak and sword, and what's left of his scabbard. Now everyone seems to know you knew him, you'd better take them. There's nothing useful to be learned from them, anyway.'

'Thank you.' Ketil accepted the bundle of stained cloth and the second best sword, setting them down with his own pack. He would decide what to do with them later. 'Wasn't there a knife, too?'

'A knife?' Hlifolf looked about him, as if it might have fallen. 'Do you know, I think there was? Now, where could it have gone?'

'It'll turn up, no doubt, or someone is making use of it anyway,' said Ketil, a little more easily than he felt. He remembered the knife, with its leaf pattern, but he would have liked a longer look at it. He decided to change the subject. 'By the way,' he said, casually, 'do you know if there is much following of the old beliefs around here?'

Hlifolf looked back over his shoulder, but carried on with what he was doing. He seemed to have abandoned any search for the knife.

'The old beliefs? I suppose there might be something still, though it's not a matter I concern myself with, not unless Einar asks me to do something about it.'

'Is that something he has done in the past?'

'I don't think so. Einar's very devout, and I think he probably believes that all his hird are, too. He's probably right. Everyone comes to church on a Sunday and feast days. I don't think we cause Father Tosti too many sleepless nights around here! And of course, Thorfinn keeps us all on the right track: all his court follow the true faith.'

As it is in their interests to do, thought Ketil, touching the cross at his own throat. Political faith was not quite the same thing as personal faith, though it was often expedient.

Rannveig stuck her head around the longhouse door.

'Are you both decent? You have a visitor!' she called, and vanished again.

'Not that she would care one way or the other,' Hlifolf grumbled, but he smiled when he looked round. 'Sigrid! What a pleasure to see you this fine morning!'

'Oh, hello, Hlifolf,' said Sigrid, blinking in the dim light of the longhouse after the bright sunshine. 'Ketil, can I have a word? What on earth are the pair of you doing squatting in here on such a sunny day?'

Ketil took that as an instruction to follow her back outside, away from Hlifolf's eager attention, and obeyed. Sigrid led the way briskly across to the paddock wall opposite the door of Einar's hall, where no one else could hear their conversation.

'I think I've found someone to talk to about the old beliefs,' she said quickly. 'There's an old woman over at the Loons, and I hear people visit her for charms and such. It's only two or three miles away. We should go and see her. Except I don't think you should.'

'Well, that's clear enough,' said Ketil. 'I should but I

174

shouldn't.'

'What have they done with poor Snorri?' she asked, ignoring him.

'He's lying in the hall, like Herleif. He's been cleaned.'

'Poor Rannveig is not having a pleasant time at the moment,' she murmured. 'Do you think anyone would mind if I paid my respects?'

'I'm sure no one would. Would you mind if I came too?'

'Of course not. Come on.' She stepped briskly across the yard and he followed again. It struck him that his most familiar view of her was the back of her head.

The hall was dim after the sunlight, except for the lamps lit once again as they had been for Herleif. A couple of Rannveig's women waited in the shadows, kneeling close together in a way that suggested communal prayer but had probably been the result of a low-voiced gossip together. They nodded at Sigrid, and blinked at Ketil. Snorri's body, massive from head to waist then dwindling away, lay with a sheet over all but his face on the long table. His crutches were propped beside him, as if he might swing up and seize them again.

'Poor Snorri,' murmured Sigrid, crossing herself and touching him lightly on the forehead. Ketil did the same. The women had worked hard on Snorri's hair and beard, and they flowed peacefully at last, not so wiry and aggressive as they had been in life. Snorri looked older, but calm. 'He could be very insulting,' Sigrid went on, 'but you knew you just had to take it on the chin. There was nothing personal in it.'

Ketil wondered. He had seen the devious look on Snorri's face when he began that verse last night. It had undoubtedly been malicious, and deliberate. His gaze wandered, playing over the crutches by Snorri's side. He wondered if they would be buried with him, or was such valuable wood more likely to be repurposed. He ran his eye down the wood, judging its strength, and noticed a dark stain on one of the poles. He crouched on his good leg.

'What is it?' asked Sigrid.

'Not sure,' he said. He straightened, lifted the crutch and took it to the hall door. Sigrid followed. 'Look.'

The stain was, as he had suspected, dark red, and in one place still a little tacky. He touched it, and showed Sigrid his finger.

'Blood,' she said, confirming his thoughts. 'A murder weapon?'

'We'll need to lift him.'

She looked at him in mild disbelief.

'He'll be heavy. And stiff, by now.'

He shrugged, and carried the crutch back into the hall.

'Bring that lamp over,' he told her. 'And take the crutch. You'll need to look while I lift. Don't mind us,' he added to the two women at the side of the hall. He stood by Snorri, turned the sheet back a little, and braced himself. Then he leaned over, and pulled the heavy shoulder towards him, showing Sigrid the back of Snorri's weighty head. She peered closely, looking intensely from crutch to wound, and at last nodded. Ketil laid Snorri back as respectfully as he could.

'It's the weapon,' she said bleakly. 'He was killed with his own crutch.'

'The killer was very strong, or took him by surprise.' Ketil tried to picture the scene. 'Perhaps Snorri had fallen asleep out there.'

'He was growing a little deaf,' Sigrid said. 'He might have missed someone creeping up on him. Oh, poor Snorri.' She sighed, gently rearranging the dead man's hair where their investigations had disturbed it. 'We need to find out who did this, Ketil. This was not –' she turned quickly to glance at the women, still watching them in wonder, 'this was not Thorstein's doing this time.'

'Of course not. There is much more to this, whether he planned to speak to me or not.' He watched her as she adjusted the sheet again, fingers nimble, forehead creased. There must have been relief at this proof that her husband was not wholly responsible for the violence here, but it did not show: there was only sorrow, and determination. Suddenly he was glad she was here, and ready to help him.

'We need to work out how to get you to the Loons,' she said, giving Snorri's hair a final tweak. 'Do you think you could ride?'

He had been considering the matter.

'Perhaps, if the horse was easy going. I'm not sure I could grip hard with both knees.'

'What if you ride, and I lead it? There's no real path for a cart to go safely, but I'm sure Einar would lend us his old mare. She's very gentle, even if you're not used to horses.'

'I'm quite used to horses, thank you,' he said, a little more smartly than he had intended.

But it was Einar's old mare that they took, as gentle as Sigrid had said but slower than a snail and stopping to admire every other animal along the way. Sigrid tugged the reins to distract her each time, and led them along the path with him lopsided in the saddle like an old man. He was glad none of his men could see him now.

'It's the road to Hamnavoe,' Sigrid threw back over her shoulder. 'Good thing that it's a fine day.'

To their right, the sea glittered dark blue below them, and Ketil could see more of the jagged claws of rock stretching out into it. They headed south from Einar's place, closer to the coast as they rounded the bay where Thorfinn's harbour was tucked. Ahead the land rose again, a broken headland high to the right, and hills more rounded to their left. Sandy grass, dry from last summer, flickered in the wind over brighter green fresh growth, and walls built of the grey and ginger flags surrounded sheepfanks and infields by the scattered longhouses in their shallow valley.

The road was almost straight, directly to the south.

'I hope we've missed Helga,' Sigrid said. 'She was coming out this way to meet a silver trader walking up from Hamnavoe. She probably found him in one of the farms along here. No one would trade silver in the middle of the road, I suppose.'

'I suppose not.' He glanced around pointlessly, just in case of a sight of Helga with her basket. Silver today – there must come a point when Helga's longhouse could take no more, surely. She would be an expensive wife to keep, however pretty she might be.

The sun was high, and almost hot, the wind a soothing chill on warm skin. The mare, settled into her work, paced quietly along the path. Sigrid was silent, presumably wrapped in her own thoughts, and Ketil's mind wandered. When would he be able to go home to Norway? He would have to break the news of Herleif's death to his other men. Had Thorstein killed him? It seemed more than likely, but why would Thorstein have buried him, and why would he have buried him curled up, with that eagle? How, though, had he come to be wearing a braid made by Sigrid? Did she really not remember who had bought it from her?

'Do you need a rest?'

The words roused him from his dwam.

'Where are we? How far is it from here?'

'We're – well, that's Skorn down there.'

He looked about, absently noticing that his leg had begun to ache again. He had had worse, more than once. The hill they had been banking, to their left, had descended to a saddle before the road continued between two more hills ahead, moving away from the coast. Sigrid was pointing down to the east of the saddle, where Ketil could see the sunlight glinting on a small loch. Between it and them, the low ground was wet, pools of water lying flat between tufts of muddy green land. Even as they watched, the sun slid furtively behind a cloud. Sigrid shivered, as a frantic wave of marsh birds rose suddenly, crying to the sky. Redshanks tumbled upwards, and down where Sigrid had indicated he could see duck on the water. He thought about Herleif and his odd love of birds – had he come this far? He would have enjoyed it.

'That's the place she's supposed to live.'

'Supposed to?'

'Well,' Sigrid's shoulders had an uncomfortable hunch. 'I've never been here. It's not something I know much about. It was Helga that told me, as if she thought everyone must know. I don't even know the woman's name.'

Ketil looked about. The sky was darker, and the place had a wary air. He shook himself. On a road like the one they had just travelled, he would usually have been on the alert, watching for anything hostile. Yet he had half-slept for the last mile and a half, at least. Now, though, all his senses were alert, prickling. Was it a real threat, or was it something to do with the light changing? His instinct was only clear on one thing: he should not take chances here.

SEXTÁN

XVI

Sigrid sensed Ketil wincing, his hands tight on the saddle bow, as the horse's uncertain descent jarred his leg. She tried to guide the mare a little sideways, so the path was not so steep, but the mare had her own ideas and clearly just wanted to get the whole thing over with, stiff-legged on the tufted hillside. But when they reached the wet ground at the foot of the hill, the mare refused to go any further at all.

Ketil swung his good leg over, and slid off the horse's back without apparent resentment. They stood for a moment, level now with their goal, and surveyed the wetlands before them.

The Loons, they called it, as though there were no other marshland in the islands. And it was not just marsh here: there were pools and islands, reedbeds and even a little useful pasture, though she had always wondered if the cattle had webbed feet instead of hooves. Those who lived near knew the ways to work the land, sometimes on foot, sometimes in little boats, but she preferred her hillside and her sheep, and dry feet of an evening.

Those who lived near had their limits, though. Those who lived near did not come to this end of the marsh, not to where the old house was.

Though the hills around were low, this end of the marsh felt enclosed, almost stuffy, overlooked. She noticed that Ketil's quick blue eyes were darting about, checking all angles, as if he thought there might be an attack threatening from some higher ground. She knew how he felt.

'"Wolves in the bog", eh?' he said sideways to her. It was an old saying, but it was certainly creepy here.

The old house, once you saw what it was, was stonebuilt, of course, but it looked as if it had grown out of the wetland around it. Shaggy turf roofed it, and banked against the flag walls. The doorway was low, a rathole in the side facing them, a dark socket in a skull. Around the house, swirled pools of water lay like blind eyes, grey under the stony sky. A small apple tree, many of its branches broken or cut off, stood forlorn – she remembered that apple twigs had been used for telling fortunes once. Still, by the look of this. Sharp bird cries echoed all around, as if the air itself could not relax, and the agitated sawing of sedge warblers added to Sigrid's nervous pulse.

'Do you think she does human sacrifice?' she found herself whispering to Ketil, half-hoping he would not hear her. He gave a little snort. 'Well, you know, they did, in the old beliefs. Look at Uppsala – that's what they say.'

'It happened in some places, yes.' He was whispering, too. It did not reassure her. 'Wouldn't you have noticed if people had been sacrificed around here? At least noticed they were missing?'

'I don't know. I'm beginning to wonder.' She made herself busy for a moment, knotting the horse's reins into a low bush. Her fingers fumbled. Then she straightened, trying to look ready for whatever was about to happen. Her breath caught. 'What is that smell, though?'

'Just wet earth, I think.'

'It's not the kind you'd want to plant something in. That smells rotten.' It was sickly sweet, tendrils winding into their faces, around their hands, soaking into bare skin and cloth. She shuddered.

'Come on, then,' said Ketil, touching her arm. 'We're here now.'

Sigrid thought it would be easy, even at this stage, to be somewhere else quite quickly, but she could not allow him to go in on his own. It was not the kind of thing she thought he would be any good at. Swords, maybe, she thought, as she followed his shallow footsteps across the marsh, though she hadn't seen any evidence yet. And as it turned out his verse had not been too embarrassing - quite nice, really – but he wasn't much of a talker. There he had been the night before at Thorfinn's, everything set up for him to question all kinds of people, and she had watched him spending nearly the whole evening chatting with Tosti, then a quick word with Snorri and off to make sheep's eyes with ewe-mouthed Ingibjorg (more fool him). He would be better with Helga, if it had to be one or the other. At least Helga could cook.

She had just managed to distract herself nicely when he stopped abruptly in front of her. Her nose brushed his cloak, and she stepped back hurriedly, peering round his arm, clutching at her shoulder brooch to dull the jingle of knife and keys. She could tell that his left hand was already at his sword.

A flock of loopwinged teeicks shot out from behind the old house, angry and letting everyone know it. From here the building looked like an ancient grey egg, overgrown, the smoke from some invisible fire lying low over the turf roof like a mist. She knew now it was not strictly one of the old houses, but one of the tombs that people sometimes found, and usually left alone, their bones white and abandoned, witness to beliefs even older than the old beliefs they were seeking. She swallowed hard, and jumped at a movement beside the house that was definitely not made by a bird.

The figure moved slowly, so hunched it almost seemed to be rolling along. Claw-hands clutched a stick, straight in front as it walked, and long white hair streeled down from a filthy leather cap with things tied to its peak, things that Sigrid did not want to examine too closely. The figure took its tiny, shuffling steps all the way to the hole that served as a door, then stopped, and turned to face them. Sigrid held her breath.

'Well? What do you want?'

The voice was harsh but surprisingly strong.

'We want information,' Ketil called back. Sigrid wanted to poke him in the ribs, tell him to keep quiet and come away now, but he stood his ground and she could not move.

The figure raised its head as far as it could, tilted to one side, examining them. The white hair trailed over its wizened face, but it made no effort to push it away. Then abruptly, it turned.

'Come on, then. No point in shouting over a bog.'

Ketil stepped forward. It was as much as Sigrid could do not to grab the back of his cloak in handfuls and pull him back. Instead, she found herself, feet numb, following him.

She missed seeing how the creature scrambled into what was really little more than a cave. Ketil had to fold himself right over, pulling his injured leg in last, and then she had to crawl in herself. If the smell outside was bad, inside it was much worse.

She found she had already pressed the back of her hand against her mouth, fighting the rising nausea. The figure – surely female? The bones were fine, under everything, she thought – turned and let out an ungenerous cackle. Sigrid snatched her hand away and clutched it behind her back. Ketil was looking around the dwelling, coolly examining the contents though he was bent double.

They were in a central chamber with two smaller ones, one to each side, hardly large enough for a child to stand in. One was full of peat for the fire that burned brightly at the back of the main chamber, overheating the still air and emitting some strange aroma that gummed up at the back of the throat. The other chamber held a jumble of rubbish, though Sigrid caught her breath when she saw it included several white bones and a clearly human skull.

The woman squatted down on a heap of rags, a rock beside her for a table. She waved her filthy hand at them.

'Sit, sit! You are too tall!'

Two other rocks, flat-topped, served as seats on either side of the door. Sigrid took one quickly, and Ketil angled himself down on to the other. Perhaps it was that the roof was too low, but he seemed to be leaning into the doorway, his head almost in the fresh air, relaxed Sigrid found herself resenting how comfortable he looked.

'What do you want?' the woman asked again.

'Information,' said Ketil again. 'We have some questions.'

The woman laughed her cackling laugh again.

'I'm sure you do! What is it, then: love potion?' Her eyes, darkly obscured by the dangling hair, flicked between them. 'A poison for your husband?' she asked Sigrid. 'Or for your wife?' she added to Ketil. 'But no: you have no wife, and her husband is already dead. How convenient for you both! How did you dispose of him, my dear?'

Sigrid scowled.

'This has nothing to do with my husband,' she snapped.

'No ... well, I have a hand in plenty of things around here,' said the woman. 'Sick men, sick cattle ... There are plenty here who still respect the old ways. A man I know,' her voice became odd, singsong, 'a man I know has a bonny wife: he tries the love potion on her, but little does he know she's a customer too: she hides his potion, and uses it on her own interests. And he struts around all bigsie-prinky, no cockerel but a cuckold!'

A local man? Sigrid blinked, but she would not ask, not while the old woman had that beady eye on her for her reaction. She looked up and away from her. The room seemed to be darker than it had been when they came in. Odd things were suspended from the roof, dead birds littering feathers on the stone floor, a Thor hammer pendant one could find in any market in Heithabyr or a thousand other places, something that caught the light – a crystal? It moved suddenly, caught perhaps in a draught, and brightness darted about the room before the crystal stilled again. And were those dried frogs? The eyes, still round and staring, seemed to grow larger as she looked. She swallowed hard.

'We're not talking about potions,' Ketil was saying, his voice very far away. 'We want to know who round here still follows the old ways. Odin, Thor, Frygg maybe.'

'Not here,' said the woman, and she looked away from them now, toying with something on the stone beside her, as if her mind was wandering elsewhere. 'Not them here.'

'Who, then?' Sigrid asked, curious at last. Her head felt thick.

'Ullinn, sister of Ullr.' The names rolled out, soft in the warm air. 'Lover of animals, skilled huntress, far-sighted, cunning sailor, protector of sweet pastures, bringer of peace and order. That is who we worship here, though her home is across the sea.'

Ullinn ... The name seeped into Sigrid's mind. A good goddess to have on your side, loving animals and pasture, bringing peace and order to the land. It was peaceful here, too, warm by the fire, the stone comfortable against her back. Her eyelids felt heavy and her head had begun to ache: after that long, sunny walk she deserved a little rest.

'And who still worships her around here? I'm sure,' Ketil's voice was challenging, 'I'm sure there aren't many any more. Not with Thorfinn and his Christian church.'

'Ha!' The woman shrieked, and Sigrid gave a groan. Why couldn't they keep quiet? 'Thorfinn knows nothing. Clinging to his Christ! He's weak.' She spat, but the spittle caught on her hair and dripped unheeded on to her lap. 'And Einar's worse,' she added as an afterthought. 'There are plenty left, plenty left. A charm for love, a charm for death, a charm for good fortune in battle!' She chuckled hoarsely, swaying a little backwards and forwards on her rag pile.

'Who, then?' Ketil raised his eyebrows at her. 'Go on, you must know some good names!'

A sly look passed out from among the locks of dirty hair. Yet, thought Sigrid distantly, it was not as dirty as all that. It looked more as if dirt had been smeared on it. And when she thought about it, though there were several unpleasant smells in the little hut, rancid human was not among them. Maybe the old witch had just been bathing in the marsh. But she was dry ... oh, it was all too complicated.

'There's one that's close to Einar, and one who has no love for Thorfinn's peelie-wallie Christ, whatever that one says on a Sunday. And one who kens that Ragnarok is coming, aye, and no the Kingdom of Heaven. Do you feel it too, there, dearie?'

To Sigrid's alarm, the old woman was suddenly standing over her, leaning forward against her stick, her foul hair dangling in Sigrid's face. 'Do you see it? Do you see Ragnarok?' She bent closer still, and Sigrid gagged. 'Do you hear the wolves?'

Sigrid could hear no wolves, but outside the sniping and scraping cries of the waterfowl seemed to intensify, as if they were whirling about the old house, spinning up a storm, weaving a violent magic.

'That's enough.' Ketil's sharp voice broke across the room. The old woman was snatched away, spinning back to her rag pile. Ketil seized Sigrid's arm, half-shaking her. 'Come on.'

'You're a Christian!' spat the woman. 'I can smell it off you! What do you want with us? You'll never win!'

'Thank you for your information.' Sigrid gaped as Ketil turned to the woman with a polite nod. 'I'm sure we'll find it very useful.'

He pushed Sigrid before him through the rat-hole doorway, then slid himself out with rather more dignity. Sigrid's legs buckled under her in the fresh air. Ketil caught her elbow, and marched her back across the bog to where the mare waited patiently, blinking at them, a creature from the real world.

'Breathe deeply,' he told her. 'Rub your face.' He propped her against the mare's steady flank, and stopped her following his instruction by rubbing her hands himself. When she looked up at him he was watching her face carefully, but then he looked away, a quick check behind them and across the marsh. 'It was the fire, I think, something she sprinkled on it. I've come across something similar before.'

'I could smell herbs at first, but then I was just confused.' Sigrid's mind was clearing, and she shook her head, annoyed at herself for succumbing when Ketil had not. She remembered how he had leaned back into the doorway, where the air was no doubt clearer. b'Do you think she told us anything useful?'

'Let's get moving, shall we?' Ketil took the mare's reins and disentangled them from the bush. Sigrid pulled herself upright and walked slowly beside him, sideways up the hill to the saddle where they had first seen the Loons. He was limping, and she wondered what it had cost his leg to march so smartly away from the old house.

On the hillside, he paused by a rock, and used it to swing himself back on to the mare while Sigrid held her steady. The air was much clearer here, and she was grateful for the breeze blowing off the sea. She pulled off her headcloth and shook it out, smelling the last of the woman's reeks whipping away. The wind in her hair was a sudden delight, and she took her time refolding the cloth before tying it back on her head, heedless of Ketil waiting.

'She was not quite what I was expecting,' Ketil said at last, as she was ready to set off.

'There were plenty like her around Heithabyr, weren't there? I always thought they were creepy, but when I grew older I realised they did it on purpose.' Sigrid shivered. 'But I didn't like her at all.'

'I'm not sure I remember much about Ullinn. Or even Ullr,' said Ketil, using one knee to urge the mare into motion.

'No. I expected Thor or Odin, but different places had different allegiances, I suppose. Or perhaps they still have. Perhaps there's much more of it about than I ever suspected.' The thought made her deeply uncomfortable. She had thought she was happy worshipping with Father Tosti in Einar's hall or Thorfinn's church, but when she reflected on how she had felt down there, in the old house, with images of Ullinn smiling in her mind … She shook her head abruptly again, and though she was sure he was watching her, she kept her shoulders stiff and did not look back at Ketil. 'Well, she mentioned someone close to Einar, didn't she?'

'She did. And a proud man with a pretty wife, too.'

'I wasn't clear – well, I wasn't clear at all, in there – but I wasn't sure that that was the same man. Someone close to Einar would probably be Hlifolf, or Hrolf, or even Bjarni.'

'Or Snorri, perhaps?'

'She probably wouldn't know that he was dead,' Sigrid agreed. 'It could be Snorri, if a skald is ever thought to be close to anyone.'

'Which of the others seems most likely?'

Sigrid considered.

'I don't know. It could be any of them. Well, if she did mean the same man, then obviously it could only be Hrolf: Helga is certainly pretty, and he is certainly proud.' This time she did glance round at Ketil, but his face was expressionless. 'But I'm still not sure she did. And anyway, do you trust her? Do you think she was telling the truth at all?'

Ketil was silent for a moment.

'I think she was, yes. Maybe the man she meant is not as devoted a believer in the old ways as she says: there are plenty who worship Christ along with Thor, and maybe he's someone like that. But I believe her when she says that one close to Einar still follows the old beliefs.'

'One ...' said Sigrid, suddenly.

'Well, or more than one,' Ketil conceded.

'That's not what I meant. I mean she said "one". She didn't say "a man". Obviously, if it's the proud man with the wife then it's a man, but she didn't say "a man" when she talked of the one close to Einar. She didn't even say "he", I'm sure of it.'

She turned to look up at Ketil. The mare stopped, and for a long moment there was silence.

'Rannveig?' Ketil whispered at last.

'I like Rannveig: she's strong and she's clever,' said Sigrid hurriedly. 'And she's a good customer.'

'Yes, but if she followed the old beliefs ...'

'She could certainly be discreet about it. I doubt even Einar would know, if she didn't want him to.'

'I always liked Rannveig,' he murmured.

'Me too.'

'But you're right, she's clever.' Ketil nodded. 'Just maybe ... but why would she want to kill Herleif? Or resurrect Rognvald? I agree she's a possibility, but I can't see why, yet. We need to find out more.'

He nudged the mare on again, and Sigrid walked on. Her mind, after its involuntary rest, was busy.

'Of course, just because she follows the old ways – with or without Einar's knowledge – doesn't necessarily mean she's involved in any of this. There could be more than one person.'

'It needs to be someone with good connexions,' Ketil said. 'If you were a serf and fancied going back to having Rognvald as your lord, you wouldn't be able to do much about it, even if you conjured up a real ghost. It has to be someone who has enough influence already to make use of the rumours when they arise. Does that make sense?' he asked suddenly, and she was taken aback. She thought it through.

'Yes, I think so. Which means that someone at Einar's or Thorfinn's court is most likely. Assuming that the death of your friend Herleif and the source of the rumours are linked – and the death of Snorri, too, now.'

'If the rumours are still alive,' added Ketil. 'Whatever Snorri was going to tell me, there have been no rumours for a month. Maybe the person who invented them has just given up.'

They talked on as they made their slow progress along the shadowed side of the hill. Gulls rose from the cliffs to the east, catching the evening light as the sea seeped from blue to grey. Away from the marshes, the sun seemed to shine again. It was an easy conversation, she realised: there was no chance of anyone overhearing them, and ideas criss-crossed between them – not to any great advancement of their quest, but somehow satisfying: theories considered, ideas aired, Ketil's questions about local matters answered. It was often the case, Sigrid thought: talk was better on a walk than around a fire, or across a table, where you were watching the other person's face. She almost found she was enjoying herself: she had not thought about her tablet weaving since they left Einar's place. Then she thought of poor Snorri, food for Einar's pig. It was important for everyone that she and Ketil, if no one else, worked out what was happening. She had no desire to see anyone else, not even Hlifolf, end up in the pig sty too.

They had lapsed into a comfortable silence as they descended into the little settlement by the beach. The tongue of the Brough lay green ahead of them, the harbour curled into its armpit. Four or five longhouses had been built down here at the sheltered bay, clustered close like their boats drawn up below on the beach. It was usually a quiet place, the people keeping themselves to themselves, but today there was some disturbance, men and women milling about on the path that led through the settlement, talking together in worryingly low voices. Sigrid hesitated, feeling the tension in the air. What was going on? Had someone died?

'I'll ask,' said Ketil, slipping carefully off the horse to land on his good leg. He left her with the mare, but only took a couple of steps to approach a tall man with a net of grey hair spreading over his shoulders. 'Good day, sir – what's the news? Has something happened?'

The man turned to examine him, a frown on his face before he even spoke. Then he cast a glance over at Sigrid, and nodded recognition.

'You're with her?'

'She's a friend, yes,' said Ketil.

The man fingered his neat beard.

'You're not from around here, but she can explain to you. That fellow there,' he pointed to a small, anxious-looking man pressed against a cart by the crowd about him, 'he's just back from Kirkuvagr. And guess what he's seen? Or guess, maybe, who he's seen?'

Ketil shrugged. Sigrid found she was holding her breath.

'He saw Rognvald. Rognvald Brusason.' The tall man had a wild, confused look in his eyes. 'He says that Rognvald's back!'

SJAUTÁN

XVII

'Bjarni says I can get to Kirkuvagr before dark, and that the way is perfectly obvious.' He was not going to say it again.

'Bjarni doesn't have a daft mare and a gash in his leg you could put a hand into.' Sigrid was being unreasonable. The mare was perfectly all right, mostly, and she had not even seen the gash in his leg. 'You can't possibly go off to Kirkuvagr on your own.'

'Well, you're not coming with me, that's certain!'

'I certainly was not intending to! If you insist on this stupid expedition, it's on your own head!'

Elbows on hips, Sigrid stood in the middle of Rannveig's longhouse. He had only intended to pack a few things into a sack in case he had to stay longer than a day or two, but with the distraction of Sigrid's objections it seemed to be taking him all afternoon. And he did want to get to Kirkuvagr before dark.

'I'll show you the way, Ketil, if you like,' Helga put in. 'I'd like to see what's new in Kirkuvagr. The last time I was there it was almost a little village!' What she was doing in Rannveig's longhouse was anyone's guess, particularly as she was telling everyone she met how badly injured Hrolf was in last night's fight, but she was making herself useful toasting flatbreads on the fire. The firelight caught the sweet curves of her face, but her suggestion was ridiculous.

'I can find my own way, thank you both very much,' he said firmly, tying the neck of his pack. 'And if Einar's mare is rested, I'll be on my way.' He stepped past Sigrid and out of the doorway, then waited a moment for her to follow. He drew her to one side. 'You know this is what I was waiting for. If I don't chase this news straightaway, it will turn into ghosts and rumours like all the other stories.'

'I know,' said Sigrid. Her akimboed arms folded across in front of her, and for a moment she seemed more worried than annoyed. 'I just don't think you're fit to go, or fit to look after yourself when you get there. At least take Bjarni with you. Or Afi, though he's more brawn than brain. Either of them can wield a sword.'

'Are you saying I can't?' he asked, finding himself smiling. He had sharpened his sword that morning as usual.

She shrugged.

'Well, I've never seen you fighting. And I have seen them.'

'I'll manage,' he said. He had no intention of taking Bjarni, Afi or anyone. Not until he could work out whose side they were on.

Sigrid had given up on him and gone home by the time he left, but Helga waved him off. His grip on the horse was still uncertain, he knew, but it was improving all the time and the mare was indeed fairly biddable. They struck out from Einar's place for the second time that day, this time to the east. He turned to look back as the horse plodded up the hill, veering from sheep to sheep. Hrolf had joined Helga, who had stopped waving. Ketil smiled to himself. Hrolf, who was indeed walking painfully, really did not like him, but it was not Ketil's fault that Hrolf had a pretty and flirtatious wife.

The day was still fine, the sun warm on his back now. His leg ached, but bearably. As long as nothing forced him into setting a faster pace, he should be fine: he was only going to ask a few questions, discreetly, and finally make some progress in this matter. A small part of him was actually quite excited.

Keep the coast in sight, Bjarni had said: it would be a little longer, but an easier route to follow and not to stray. Redirected from sheep, the horse plodded in apparent content, leaving Ketil free to look about him. The hills were brown with last year's heather, and distantly to the north he could see other islands, looming and indistinct. He rounded the head of a loch to his right and the coast turned a little too, taking his road slightly to the south, just as Bjarni had described. The road was busy enough, and he was rarely out of sight of a longhouse or two: across the water now and closer than the previous islands he could see the small lump Bjarni had called Eynhallow, and the larger hill of Rousay behind it. He remembered the names from before, echoes from a time he would rather forget, but on a sunny day like this one the memories had less power to darken his mind. Ahead to the south east he could already see the pretend mountain called Hammars Hill, and he knew he had to turn south past it to find the path across the boggy land beyond. He was making fair time: the hill stood black against the westering sun, but the light was still good.

At Tingwall, where Gnup's fisherman had hailed from, he paused. He might have tried to look for maybe-Olaf, but Gnup's story was old compared with the news he now had. At the toun o' Firth, he forded a river. Bjarni had told him to look out for another hill here, the tallest on the mainland. He could stick to the coast leaving the hill to his south, or go round the hill in the other direction, a shorter but harder route over a saddle. The harder route, Bjarni had told him, was also the more populated. He considered, watching the mare as she took her chance to graze, and eating dried fish and cheese that Rannveig had given him. He would go inland, and when he reached the point where he could see water on both sides, he would cut down to the natural harbour to the north, where there would be plenty of boats hauled up to mark Kirkuvagr.

He arrived at dusk, leading the mare and only limping a little, inhaling the scent of low tide and cooking fires as he made his way to the hall near the harbour. Einar had given him the name of Thorfinn's local chief, Brodir - a safe pair of hands, Einar claimed, after Rognvald's death - and instructions to send his greetings. Ketil was pleased to see the hall already lit and warm for the evening, and when a lad came and took the mare from him he made his way inside, confident of the same welcome himself.

The moment he walked through the door, a thin man leapt from his seat at the head of the hall, and ran straight for him. Every eye in the place turned to watch. Ketil's hands went to his sword and at the last second the man, seeing this, backed off, fingers waving.

'No, no! I'm not attacking you!' He laughed, but it was a nervous, breathy laugh. 'Come in, come in! Have you come from the Brough? Have you a message from Thorfinn?'

'Ah, no,' said Ketil, moving up the hall, though his hands were still tensed. 'I left before I could speak to him. But Einar sends his greetings.'

'Oh, Einar! Excellent, excellent. Here, have some wine. It's quite good, really, though I'm sure you'll have better at Thorfinn's hall. Here, have a seat. Someone seeing to your horse? Or did you come by boat? Did you?'

'Horse. Yes, a lad took the mare away.'

'Good, good. Sit down, sit down.'

Ketil sat on a bench, where another man had moved up to give him room. It was hardly necessary: there were only about half a dozen men in the hall. All watched him like hawks about to stoop.

'We're just about to eat. You'll join us, of course? Oh, you'll want a wash after your journey – just there, there's water, see! And the towel, yes! Thank you, Margaret, thank you. More wine? No, not yet, of course. And how is Thorfinn? Of course, he came here last week – was it only last week? – on his way back from Stronsay to the Brough. But he's well, is he? He was looking well. He's such a good leader, we're lucky to have him, aren't we?'

'Ah, yes,' said Ketil, taken aback at the sudden stop in Brodir's flow of words. 'Yes, he's an excellent leader. In fact, although I didn't see him before I left, I'm here on his business.'

'Oh, aye,' said the man beside him in a low, rumbling voice. 'That's grand, then.'

Ketil looked at him, but the man did not look back. He had massive rounded shoulders and a bristling gingerish beard, which had been oiled for the evening. For all Ketil knew, he could have been talking to the table in front of him.

'Thorfinn's business? Oh, can we help? We're all Thorfinn's men here, you know. All Thorfinn's men.' Brodir glanced round nervously, his long hair slithering over his shoulders as if it wanted to hide in the folds of his cloak. But the other men in the room certainly nodded at Brodir's words. The man beside Ketil turned at last, and fixed him with a beady glare, but said nothing. 'What can we do to help?'

Ketil paused, considering his words, and in that pause the woman Margaret and her helpers brought in the food, hot fish, cheese and broth and bread that looked as if it had previously been ballast in a kvarr. He waited until the women had once again retreated, and no one else spoke. The room was as tense as a bowstring.

'We hear, on the Brough, that Rognvald has returned to Kirkuvagr.'

If he had hoped for any kind of shock or denial at these blunt words, he would have been disappointed. The half dozen men sighed, nodded, grunted agreement.

'There are folk who say they've seen him,' Brodir said sadly.

'But Rognvald is dead.'

'Yes, yes, I know: Thorfinn killed him. And it was the right thing to do, of course. But ... Well, they always see him at night, when the light's not good.'

'Or at dusk,' put in one man. 'My neighbour saw him in the harbour at dusk.'

'It's no just dusk,' said another. 'My own brother – he's away just now,' he added in explanation to Ketil, 'he saw him up on the headland in broad daylight. But no close up, you ken, just from the back. But that hair! He said it had to be him, couldn't be anyone else.'

Ketil took a spoonful of broth, and swallowed it. The room was very still.

'Has anyone here seen him?'

They looked about at each other, shaking their heads. Rumours again, Ketil thought crossly. The man was dead. He knew he was dead.

'Are there many of his supporters left around here?'

'Oh yes!' Brodir answered at once. 'There are plenty: this was his main hall – not this one, Thorfinn burned the old one – and there are lots of folk around here who favoured Rognvald. That's why we're here, really: Thorfinn's relying on us to hold Kirkuvagr for him! Particularly the harbour, of course,' he added, importantly.

'I'm sure you're doing a splendid job,' said Ketil. It explained the tension in the hall. These were soldiers manning an insecure border post: he had seen it before.

'So anything we can do to help, anything at all,' Brodir was still eager.

'I need to find some of these supporters of Rognvald,' said Ketil. 'Can you give me names? Places I might find them?'

'Oh, that's easy!' Brodir laughed, looking about at his men. 'They meet at the longhouse at the end of the harbour. It's Eirik's place and he's been bringing them there every evening, just as if it was a hall,' he ended a little sadly. 'There'll be a score or more of them there tonight, no doubt.' You could see him not quite glancing round at his mere half dozen.

Ketil sat back, examining Brodir's thin face.

'They're that open?'

'Just recently, yes. They're growing in confidence.'

'And you think that's because of these rumours that Rognvald is back?'

'What else could it be?'

'But Rognvald is dead. He can't be back.'

Brodir shrugged.

'Then someone is pretending to be Rognvald. You've no idea how popular he was around here. The people loved him. The day he and Thorfinn fell out was a bad day for Thorfinn, because he'll never get Kirkuvagr on his side while there's any hope of Rognvald coming back.'

Ketil was grateful for his meal – perhaps not for the bread – but he did not linger long after it. Indeed, they did not seem to expect him to, encouraging him with directions and advice and assuring him that the mare would be safe till his return. Brodir handed him a torch to find his way safely around the harbour edge, and sent him off with an enthusiastic pat on his shoulder. The hall door closed behind him, and he stepped into the darkness.

He had only reached the corner of the hall when he was spun about and pinned against the hall's stone wall. His head bumped painfully, and the torch was snatched from his hand. He was already gripping his knife when he realised that his attacker had not thrown the torch away preparatory to a fight, but was holding it high so they could both see. It was his neighbour with the oily hair.

'You didna think much of us, did you?' His voice was deep, and not friendly.

'I think you don't have enough men in the circumstances,' said Ketil frankly.

'And you were checking that, were you?' The hairy hand pressed hard into Ketil's chest twitched just a little, and the man fixed his hard eyes on Ketil's own. 'Listen son, I dinna ken who you are with your bare chin and your fancy ways, but if I find later you're supporting Rognvald, I'll have you minced on a flatbread for my breakfast, ken?'

'I understand.' Ketil tried not to struggle for breath. The man glared at him for a count of ten, then dropped him and handed back the torch.

'You're on your own, lad,' he said, and stamped off back to the hall door. There was a brief waft of broth, then darkness again. Ketil rubbed the back of his head, straightened his kirtle, and set off once again for the longhouse of the man called Eirik.

The settlement was quiet: he could hear the harbour waves lapping on the shore, but little else. It was a moment or two before something told him there was another person there in the dark with him. He tensed, but did not pause or shift the torch: his left hand was already on his scabbard. The oily-haired thug had definitely gone back into Brodir's hall, and he knew no one else in Kirkuvagr, so who was this? Someone out to attack an unwary traveller, or someone about their own business? The trouble was, they could see him and he could not see them. He stopped, set the torch against a low wall, and moved away from it, knife out, eyes flicking across the darkness for any sign of movement. All was still.

A tongue of movement in the air threw him the smell of unwashed clothing. He wrinkled his nose, and caught something else: smoke? But not ordinary smoke.

There was a scuff of footsteps behind him. The stone paths here were not as treacherous as the wooden walkways of the towns he had known in Norway: they gave little away, but now he knew the person was somewhere behind him. He backed at an angle, his senses on stalks. Reaching a wary hand, he brushed something hairy, something leathery, and grabbed. The person lost their balance, lurched back against him, and he had his knife to their throat.

'Well,' he snapped, 'what are you doing here, so far from your filthy bog?'

The stink of poisonous smoke was unmistakable now, but he held tight to her hair, his fist wound in its streels.

'They toast the old gods everywhere, fool!' she hissed. Her claws were scratching at his hands, but almost half-heartedly. He wondered if she had been seeking the chance to talk to him.

'Rognvald and his followers – are they your believers?'

'What if they are? Your Christ-belief only managed to bring

one man back from the dead. That is nothing to us. Odin died on a tree, too, and rose again. And we have ways of making sure he is not the only one.'

There was something so certain in her voice that Ketil's heart swayed. Had they brought Rognvald back from the dead? That was impossible. Wasn't it?

'Is that who you came here to see? Rognvald?'

'Rognvald is here,' she conceded, with a wriggle of her thin shoulders. 'But then, Rognvald is everywhere! The golden boy has returned! And Thorfinn and his Christ will fall again – for good, this time!'

And she let out a cackle of metallic laughter so loud, so sudden, that he jerked the knife away. She twisted from his grasp like an eel, and vanished into the darkness. He darted back to save the torch, and glanced down at his knife before sheathing it. There was a bright smear along the blade: he was right, he had caught her, just a little. That was going to sting, he thought, with grim satisfaction.

He raised the torch and looked about him. Was anyone else going to interrupt his short walk to the longhouse belonging to the mysterious Eirik? No one seemed to be about, but he elected not to sheath his knife after all. It was easier to manage with the torch than his sword.

The longhouse, one of unremarkable size, lay where he had been directed, the doorway facing the harbour. Dumping the torch at last in a hissing puddle, he simply followed the sound of voices as he slid up to the opening. The door was open, and despite the leather curtain he could feel the heat from the fire inside. The voices were not, he thought, those of abandoned feasting: instead there seemed to be intense conversation around the fire. For a moment he contemplated the old trick of setting fire to the place and standing by the door with his sword for elimination purposes, but he reminded himself that he was here to gather information – at this stage, anyway.

They were confident enough not to have posted a guard outside, but he sensed someone close to the doorway inside. He kept himself still, and focussed on the voices.

He could not make out the words at all. Instead, he tried to determine how many people were in there. One by the door, yes, and one authoritative voice by the fire, or thereabouts. Two more speaking with him. Murmurs of agreement – another three or four? But the room did not sound altogether crowded. Maybe ten men, all told? Too many for him to take on alone, but there must be something else he could do. If he could at least get inside – and preferably out again – he might be able to identify some of the faces later. He slipped his knife into his belt, and slapped the open door.

'Hallo! Are there any still awake within?' he called. There was a sudden silence, then a quick scuffle. He waited.

'Aye, who's there?' came a voice.

'A late traveller seeking shelter,' Ketil called. A hand shifted the leather curtain, a curious face peeped out.

'Come in, then!'

Ketil smiled his thanks, and followed the sentry into the longhouse.

Four men sat around the fire – considerably fewer than he had thought. On the other hand, two of the bed recesses were already curtained off.

'Welcome!' A fair-haired man stood and ushered him towards the fire. 'The women have retired for the night, I'm afraid, but there's ale and bread. Take a seat!'

'You're very kind,' said Ketil, perching on the stone edge of the bed platform. He made sure the curtained recesses were in front of him, and not behind. 'I've just walked from Hamnavoe, and mistook the way.'

'Easily done after dark,' the man said lightly. 'Here, take a cup. There's the bread, too. You're a stranger here?'

'Not long arrived from Norway,' Ketil nodded. 'I'm a trader – wooden cups. But I left my bundle under a dyke, thinking I was more likely to reach somewhere safely unburdened.'

The men nodded sagely. Ketil watched them over the top of the ale cup: all four looked handy men in a fight, young and strong, though the doorkeeper was only a lad. He tore off a piece of bread, and waved it.

'How's trade in Kirkuvagr, then?'

'Oh, fair enough,' said the fair-haired man. His hair, Ketil noted, was almost as short as his own, though his beard was long. It was an unusual combination. 'The safe harbour helps, of course.

We're always busy around here.'

'I'm glad to hear it –' Ketil's words were lost. The bed curtains whipped back, and three men sprang out, swords wild.

Ketil was on his feet, but the man beside him grabbed his cloak and tugged. Ketil seized his knife and slashed downwards, freeing himself as the man screamed. But the knife sprang from his hand at the impact. He drew his sword.

It was a damned stupid place for a sword fight. Hanging shelves impeded swordswing. Curtains caught and snagged. Though it was three against one – and the three had the help of their friends by the fire – Ketil knew he had a chance. And all he had to do was escape into the night. He pushed one man backwards into the fire, and slashed at another, using the back stroke to elbow someone behind him. The fair-haired man dashed ale into his eyes and Ketil spluttered, lashing out blind and catching someone by pure chance. He shook his head to see the man crashing back into the bed recess, foot caught on the edge of the stone platform. The third man grabbed a soapstone dish from the hanging shelf above him and spun it towards Ketil's head. Ketil ducked, but the dish glanced off his brow even as he swung and stabbed at his attacker. The man fell awkwardly with a loud grunt. Ketil skipped over him and ran to the door. The lad who had let him in had got hold of a sword, and stood breathless across the doorway. He was too young to injure.

'Let me through.'

'I won't!' said the boy, but there was a hint of anxiety there.

'You will,' said Ketil, reasonably. 'It's just a question of how much damage I cause on the way.'

The boy yelped, and Ketil flicked his sword out of the way. Then he sprinted into the darkness.

He was only a dozen paces back along the harbour, his bruises just beginning to tingle, his calf aching, when he felt rather than heard a movement behind him. Damning the loss of his knife, he swung his sword again. The impact was smothered in a cloak, and suddenly he was fighting once more, parrying invisible blows and trying to cause some harm himself. It was bewildering.

A low strike caught him across the calf, just beside the old stab wound, and he gasped, but thrust back and was rewarded with a cry, quickly stifled. There was a clatter as his opponent's sword hit the ground. Then something heavy hit him, and he fell, twisting, as his assailant lost his balance and landed on him. Something hit his right arm before Ketil scrambled out from underneath, still holding his sword. He reached the blade forward to feel for the other man, but even as he did so, the man must have staggered to his feet. Uncertain footsteps stumbled, then ran.

The first spits of rain tipped at Ketil's face as he stood, sword in hand, catching his breath as the pain gathered its forces in his arm. He sank to his knees, and knew no more.

ÁTJÁN

XVIII

Sigrid woke reluctantly the next morning, stretched, and hit her ankle on a lump of the stone wall.

Cursing and rubbing it, she opened her eyes and considered the day. It looked as if the weather was dull after yesterday's bright promise, and the air felt damp. The water in the barrel almost had an edge of ice to it, though she washed anyway. Her clothes felt stiff, and she jabbed her finger on the pins holding her dress. The cat sulked when she tried to stroke it, turning away from her extended fingers. The fire, when she poked the embers, was equally reluctant and smoky. By the time Gnup arrived, friendly and happy as usual, she was in a thoroughly bad mood.

'How's Ragna?' she asked, grudgingly trying to find something to say to him. At least he should know it was not his fault – or not yet, anyway. There was plenty of time for him to annoy her, too.

Gnup made a face, and the cat at once made for him, rubbing against his hands for attention. Sigrid glowered.

'Well, she hasn't been spewing, anyway. We all had a quiet night for once. As far as I know, she never shifted from her bed.'

'All right for some,' she muttered.

'You didn't sleep so well?' he asked, his smile kind.

'It's not funny. I've three braids on order, and every time I try to work on them something new happens.' It was not quite why she had not slept, but Gnup was not entirely in her confidence.

'You worked late? By lamplight?'

'A bit. But you know it's never as easy.'

'It's bad for your eyes.'

'Aye, Gnup, but I've managed without a mother now for twenty years. If I want a replacement, I'll let you know.'

He grinned anyway, irrepressible. She scowled back, not ready to be cheered up yet.

'Go on,' she said. 'Go and see to the hens. I shouldn't have to tell you what to do by now.'

He nipped off, leaving the cat purring treacherously, and Sigrid sat back, chewing on a piece of Helga's stale bread. Then she found her comb, and began the morning hair combing, scraping hard through the night's tats to her scalp.

Ketil would not be back yet, anyway. He would have arrived late. If he had any sense – which was in debate – he would have stayed overnight in Kirkuvagr, assuming he found Thorfinn's chief there, or someone else to stay with. But what if he had picked the wrong person? Found himself at the mercy of Rognvald's followers, or whoever was doing whatever with the rumours of Rognvald's ghost? She should not have let him go on his own. She felt responsible, as if he were her little brother. But he would not be back yet, anyway. He was not late. There was no need to worry yet.

So when, she thought, sorting out her braidwork, when would she allow herself to start worrying? Say he arrived in Kirkuvagr at dusk last night, and went straight to – what was his name? Brodir? It would have been too late to try to find out anything last night. He would have to stay today as well, at least. He had talked of staying longer. And the mare could do with the rest – she was not used to all this trailing about with full-grown – really overgrown, with the height of Ketil – men on her back. She should not start worrying until … this was Thursday, wasn't it? There was no point in growing anxious until Saturday at the earliest. In fact, if he was still there on Saturday he would probably stay until Monday, to avoid travelling on a Sunday. Days yet. She should just get on with her weaving, and be glad of the chance of a bit of peace and quiet. She had barely had a moment to herself since that man had arrived in Orkney.

She began twisting and turning the tablets. It was cold to sit outside today, but Gnup was quite right about the light. Should she fetch a shawl? No, no, concentrate on the work.

What if someone else was killed while Ketil was away? Whoever killed Snorri was no doubt still here: they wouldn't have gone trailing off to Kirkuvagr just because Ketil had gone there. It might be just as dangerous here as it would be asking questions about Rognvald's ghost in Kirkuvagr. Had Snorri really been killed

202

because he was going to tell Ketil something?

Well: it could not have been Hrolf, not with three broken ribs. It could have been Bjarni, or Afi, or several other large men well able to haul Snorri over the wall into the pig sty. It was unlikely to have been Einar, but he could have ordered someone to do it. Was it someone who knew more about Rognvald's ghost, or someone who knew more about Herleif's death?

She was trying to make the questions sound brisk and efficient even in her head, but she knew she was going nowhere. And Ketil would never be able to work it out on his own. He would be depending on her. Or would he turn to Helga for help? Surely not: Helga might have an eye for a bargain, and was indeed probably her closest friend, but she was at heart a silly woman. Rannveig, now, she was clever. If she involved herself in the business, no doubt it would be helpful. Rannveig probably already had her ideas about who had killed Herleif, and who was involved in Rognvald's reappearance. If it was in Einar's interest, she would have it sorted out. Now, she remembered, Rannveig had been talking with Bjarni at Thorfinn's feast that wasn't a feast, and Sigrid did not remember her singling Bjarni out for conversation before. Did Rannveig suspect Bjarni? If so, why? She should probably go and ask her, take a walk down to Einar's place once she had finished this particular sequence of weaving. And then she could see if Ketil was back, too.

Oh, she was going round in circles. She had told herself not to worry about Ketil until at least Saturday, hadn't she?

But talking the business over with Rannveig was, she thought, a good idea. Rannveig would know about things in Einar's hall of which Sigrid knew nothing. And they seemed to be making very little progress. Even the old woman at the Loons yesterday had told them hardly anything: vague hints at old beliefs among Einar's followers or Thorfinn's men, but nothing definite. And all that helped them towards was the person who had buried Herleif on his side with an eagle in his arms.

The old woman had not been what Sigrid was expecting, and yet she could not quite put her finger on what was odd about her. Charms for love, charms for death, charms to protect in battle, wasn't that what she had said? Maybe they had asked her the wrong questions.

For a little while, she let that thought play in her mind, while her nimble fingers slipped the yarn and turned the tablets on their own. She had absolutely no wish to go back to the Loons, and certainly not on her own. Who knew what might have happened to her yesterday, if Ketil had not pulled her out of that miserable hut? Even the thought of that fire and its insidious smell made her retch.

But the question lingered in her mind. She set her shuttle down and stared down the hill, considering. If she left now, she could be there and back by early afternoon – well, thereabouts.

And she would not linger at Einar's place on the way. She had told herself that she would not worry about Ketil until at least Friday. After all, the poor man would never achieve anything useful in only a day and a night. No doubt he was making himself comfortable at Brodir's hall and wouldn't be back for a week. And it would never occur to him to send any kind of message back, would it? No. Or not to her, anyway. Maybe to Helga.

She was not, she thought, as she disentangled the yarn from her toe, she was not going to ask Helga for news.

That turned out to be an easy vow to keep, as she did not meet Helga. Cloaked and booted, she strode firmly down to Einar's place and, with considerable resolution, walked straight past it and on to the Hamnavoe road without speaking to a soul. If she felt that dark cloud of foreboding, which had hovered over her since she woke, close down about her as she left Einar's place behind, she managed somehow not to let it break her stride. She drew her cloak close, and kept walking.

The walk seemed miles longer than it had in yesterday's sunshine. Each longhouse she passed seemed further from the road, and more lonely. The sea beyond the headland was obscure, mist threatening, toying with the coastline with long white fingers. By the time she reached the dip between the hills where she was to turn down to the Loons, she could barely see the next hill. She was shivering, despite her cloak. But she knew that if she paused she would never go down to the marsh again. She poked at her damp headcloth, straightened her dress, and let the slope take her down to the wetland below.

In the hollows of the marsh, the mist hung low, watching. She tried to focus on the dim shape of the little stone house ahead, but it was hard to keep her eyes from flicking anxiously from side to side, watching for any movement. The broken apple tree was motionless. Even the marsh birds seemed to be quiet today, their cries only distant pangs. Yet she knew that her progress was under scrutiny, and she walked more confidently than she felt, head high, praying she would not trip and fall flat on her face on the soaking ground.

This had been a stupid thing to do, she thought, as the walk across the marsh stretched endlessly, the stone house never seeming closer. She would be found drugged or dead, or never found at all, sinking slowly into the marsh to become one with the stinking decay.

But all at once, the hut was before her, its one rough doorway gaping.

'Hallo?' she called. Her voice did not sound as strong as she had hoped it would. There was no response. 'Is there anyone there?'

Still nothing. Yet she still felt eyes on her. Despite herself, she glanced nervously over her shoulder. The mist was growing thicker.

Right, well, she knew what was inside the hut, and she was increasingly unsure about what was behind her, so surely it would be best to go forward?

The idea sounded good in her head, but she was having trouble convincing her legs. She clenched her fists, shook herself, and moved determinedly forward.

The hut was empty.

Well, all the assorted things still dangled from the roof, and the stones that served as tables seemed undisturbed. But the dangerous scented fire was out, she saw at once, and when she crept over the rocky sill and examined the two side alcoves, there was no one there.

Half disappointed, half relieved, she crawled back outside and surveyed the marsh. The mist could be concealing a hunched figure easily enough, she thought, but where would she start looking? She knew the marshes could be treacherous to those who did not know them, and she certainly had no claim to that knowledge herself. She frowned. Almost against her better judgement, she decided at least to check the outside of the hut. After all, that was where the woman had emerged from yesterday, somewhere around the back.

The banked turf that bordered the stone walls meant that she had to move away from the hut itself to circle it. The ground was littered with bruck of all kinds, odd pieces of salvaged wood, useful stones, bits of wet leather. She picked her way through it, and reached the back of the hut. There was nothing there – a few blackish branches in a bundle of old cloth. And some kind of greyish grass, dead-looking. And – oh, and a hand.

Sigrid swallowed a yelp, and pressed the back of her own hand to her mouth.

The body was a woman's, wizened, tiny, old – but fresh enough. Sigrid braced herself to touch the filthy forehead, but it was stone cold. Nevertheless the smell of decay was sharp, now that she was close to the woman. She must have died not long after they had left yesterday. Could the death be anything to do with them? Surely not: unless they had somehow upset her, made her collapse in some way. But no: the matted hair just there, at the back, was black with clotted blood. She had somehow hit her head.

Sigrid crouched, considering. This was probably still Einar's land out here, but it might belong to another chief. She would have to go to the nearest longhouse and report what she had found. The woman looked so much smaller now than she had done, hunched as she had been, in life – really tiny. Sigrid frowned, and extended another reluctant finger to lift a lock of the grey hair away from the woman's face.

Grey hair, not white. And the woman's face was distinctly different from yesterday, sagging, not fine-boned.

Were there two old women living here? No one had mentioned it – and where was the one they had seen yesterday? She had been round the back of the hut where Sigrid was now. Sigrid's stomach contracted. Had it been a human sacrifice after all?

But she noticed that the woman's hair was matted and sticking to the top of her head, as if she habitually wore a cap – and there was no cap here. The other woman had been wearing a cap. Could she have killed her for her cap? She almost giggled at the thought.

The mist seeped around her as she stood. It would conceal anyone watching her, she thought. She shivered violently.

Oh, now she was turning daft. That was enough, she thought.

She would go and tell the people at the first longhouse she came to, and if they said it was still Einar's land, she would go on to his place and tell him. Then she would go home.

Einar's place was quiet. She slapped at the longhouse door, sure she was going to find Ketil inside, and discovered only a couple of Rannveig's women spinning and gossiping.

'They've all gone up to the Brough,' said one with a sigh. 'And left us here. Something about the new church?'

'No sign of Ketil coming back?' She could not help asking. The woman shook her head.

'Wasn't expecting him back yet, were you?' She nudged her friend.

'No, not today. He's away in Kirkuvagr, you know.'

Sigrid sighed, and thanked them. Her feet were tired, and it was tempting just to sit with them and spin, but she knew she had to take her news to Einar, whether or not he wanted to hear it.

At the Brough, she passed through the walled gateway and up amongst the buildings. There was a sweet smell of freshly cut timber, unusual around here. Thorfinn must have brought in supplies for his new works. The usual bustle surrounded her, but she could see no sign of anyone from Einar's place until she walked on up to the new church building. It had grown even since the last time she had been here. She had to walk round to the other end of the building to find a small crowd at the doorway, and obvious amongst them were Einar, tall and thin, and Thorfinn, twice his width and the dark centre for the crowd. The women at the near edge were looking about them, and it was only a moment before Helga and Rannveig spotted her.

'Sigrid, you're here! We didn't want to disturb you,' said Helga brightly, 'but the church is finished!'

'In time for Holy Week, just as Thorfinn said,' said Rannveig, a flick of her eyebrows mocking the efficacy of Thorfinn's decrees.

'There's just a bit inside to do.' Tosti was looking tired but relieved as he turned to them. 'But we have till Sunday.'

'Is Ketil back yet?' Helga asked. Sigrid shook her head.

'It's a bit early yet,' she said. 'I wouldn't expect him before Sunday. What's left to be done inside, Father Tosti?'

'Cleaning, mostly,' said Tosti with a grin. 'Some lamps need to be put up, and there's a man in there now painting a picture behind the altar.'

'Is there? Can I see?' Helga was happily distracted, as Tosti showed her into the church. Rannveig was looking at Sigrid.

'You're tired. Everything all right?'

'Hm.' She might as well report to Rannveig as to Einar. It was almost the same thing. 'I went down to the Loons to see that old woman – you know the one?'

'I do!' Rannveig looked surprised. 'I didn't know you did, though.'

'I only heard about her recently. Ketil wanted to see her to try to find out why Herleif had been buried with an eagle.' She paused. 'How do you know about her?'

'Oh, Einar's had problems with her for a couple of years. She's encouraging people to follow the old beliefs, you know?'

'Yes ... Well, she's dead now.'

'What?' Rannveig had turned sallow in a second.

'I found her lying behind her hut. She'd been dead maybe for a day?'

'I'll tell Einar.' Rannveig slipped away through the crowd to her husband. Sigrid stood for a moment, then went to sit on the low stone wall around the graveyard.

The people at the first longhouse had said they were Einar's people. They had given the impression of saying whatever would cause them the least trouble, and when she had told them what she had found, they had nearly pushed her out of the house in their hurry not to be involved. Well, she had tried. She had trudged homewards, hardly seeing what was around her, trying to rid her nostrils of the smell of decay once again. Two bodies in a week? What had she done to deserve it? But that was something on which she had no wish to reflect.

She tried not to close her eyes, sure that if she did she would fall asleep on the spot. She looked about her. There was still work going on: the church was not the last of the new buildings. Beyond it men were digging trenches and collecting flags, busy while the good weather would allow – some kind of monastery, they were saying. She wondered if Thorfinn would eventually cover the whole Brough with his town, and it would grow dense and stinking like Heithabyr. She prayed not.

The crowd, excitement over, was beginning to disperse. Helga and Tosti emerged from the church smiling, and Hrolf followed after, walking stiffly with his broken ribs. Sigrid looked about for Hlifolf, but it seemed that Hrolf was on his own for once. In fact, the crowd from Einar's place was rather smaller than usual – Bjarni and of course Ragna were also missing. Sigrid wondered if Ragna had taken a turn for the worse.

She spent the walk back to Einar's place in a weary three-way conversation with Rannveig and Einar. Both had questions about the body she had found – this week's body, as Einar rather unkindly put it. He must not have been counting Snorri in Sigrid's collection of corpses. Rannveig was inclined to think that the old woman had died accidentally, in a fall, perhaps – she was ancient, apparently – but Einar was not so sure. He wanted to send Hlifolf down to the Loons to see, but Hlifolf had gone out earlier, before the summons to the Brough.

But as they neared Einar's hall, Hlifolf was the first person they saw. A hooded hawk on his gloved right hand, he came to meet them as they approached.

'Ah, you'll have been up at the Brough!' he said, nodding. Sigrid grinned to herself. Hlifolf would be kicking himself that he had missed something, but nothing would make him admit his ignorance by asking what it was. 'I was too busy with this little beauty.'

'She's lovely,' agreed Rannveig, admiring the hawk. 'Where did you get her?'

'A man over at Dounby knew I was looking for a new bird. He usually gives Thorfinn first choice, but this time it was me. I've been out starting her training.'

The hawk sat alert, blind in its hood but catching every sound. She was beautiful, from her sharp beak to her savage claws. Hlifolf was good with birds, even Sigrid had to admit.

The bird suddenly started, wings jerking, and turned her head back towards the hall. Something about her movement caused everyone to look in the same direction. A lone horse with a bundle of some kind on its back walked, sure of its welcome, round by the longhouse, and only paused when it saw the people gathered by the paddock. The bundle, dislodged by the change in movement, slid off and fell to the earth.

Sigrid's blood stopped in her veins.

It was Ketil.

NÍTJÁN

XIX

He had been unconscious, he thought, only for a few minutes. When he woke there was still darkness all about him, the settlement was silent, and the rain fell cold on his face. It took him longer than he would have liked to remember where he was. The next thing he remembered was pushing his way past the lad in Brodir's stables, clumsily saddling the mare, then setting off in some direction he hoped was towards Birsay. He knew he had been muttering to himself: 'Keep the sea to the right. Keep the sea to the right.' But in the dark he had no idea where the sea was, though as the rain grew heavier he occasionally had the impression he had wandered into it.

'How did I get here?' he mumbled to the women around him. Surely someone would have seen him and stopped him on the way.

'Einar's mare likes her home stable,' said one voice – Rannveig?

'She probably followed a sheep.' Sigrid.

He tried to open his eyes, but the room was dim and full of skirts and sleeves. He smiled a little. That brought back a few good memories. His eyes sank closed again.

'He must have fallen off a few times on his way back,' came another voice. 'Look at the grass stains! And the mud! And it's been a lovely shirt, too.'

Helga, pretty Helga. So she was there, too.

'We should have given him new clothes when he arrived, as our guest,' came Rannveig's voice again. 'But to be honest, I had nothing that – tall and long – in the stores. I can give it to him now, though, when he needs it.'

'He needs another blanket more urgently,' came Sigrid's voice. 'He was soaked through.'

Had he fallen into that lochan, or was that a dream? It had woken him a little. He half thought the mare had tipped him in there deliberately to rouse him. His head pounded at the memory of the ice cold water hitting him.

'So, head injuries, front and back,' said Rannveig efficiently. 'Something – part of a sword blade? - stuck in his arm, and the stitches have burst on his calf again.' She sighed, but managed even to do that briskly. 'Astrid, bring me more hot water.'

Who was Astrid? One of Rannveig's team of women, no doubt, stitchers and spinners and servers and stridders. Stridders. Like Astrid. Was that where the name came from? Wait – was stridder even a word? What did it mean? He thought he knew, then the notion faded again. The room seemed very warm: his thoughts were melting. A hand on his forehead, dry and cool.

'He's starting a fever. We'll need to get that thing out of his arm.'

'I'll fetch something to grab it with. Is it metal?'

'It looks like wood.'

'Some kind of splinter.'

'No, there's metal in there, too. Who knows what he's been collecting? He probably fell on a shovel.'

'Oh, come on, Sigrid, he's been fighting!' Helga sounded concerned, at least.

'We'll need to turn him on to his front.'

A sudden chill as the blankets were pulled back, then hands again, not ungentle, against his skin, manipulating him into position. How many hands? It felt like dozens. Dozens of hands all fluttering around, holding him up, no need for a bed, a nest of hands. He landed with his nose in a blanket, and had enough sense to turn to one side so that he could breathe. The blanket scraped across cuts on his forehead, stinging sharply.

'Oh, nasty!' Helga again, more emotional than the other two. He felt a pang as fingers brushed something in the back of his right arm. Sword arm: not good. Where was his sword? Had he cleaned it? Where was his knife? Missing ... lost in Eirik's longhouse. A missing knife. Why did that seem significant? Must be like that woman ... Astrid. Had she lost a knife?

'Ready?'

'Ready. You holding him, Helga?'

'Oh, yes!'

'No need to sound as if you're enjoying it. Right, I'll do it, then.'

Confusion vanished into white hot pain as whatever it was was tugged from his arm. A cloth, wet with who knew what, was slapped over the wound as he jerked and gasped, and the bandage was tied firmly. Then those hands moved over his skin again, turning him once more on to his back, settling him before his arm had stopped screaming.

'Oh, should have restitched his leg before we turned him again,' said Rannveig.

'Look, we can reach like this.'

'Helga, leave his legs alone!'

The pain subsided into an insistent throb as he felt his leg being rearranged. Quick stabs reset the stitches. They felt like midge bites compared with his arm.

'I'll stitch his arm later, when we're sure there's no badness in the wound.'

'We need more wet cloths. He's starting to burn.'

'Water.' The word came mysteriously from his own lips. He felt almost at once a dab of moisture, an instant of bliss. Then his mind whirled into a roaring world of fire.

Gradually, he was aware of voices again, tiptoeing in his dreams.

'It's broken, he can sleep now.' Cool hands on his forehead again.

'Could we get a couple of dry blankets? He's sweated the Boardhouse Loch into these ones.'

'I'll see what we have.'

'Where did that thing go?'

'Oh,' a vague voice, 'I don't know. I put it down over there, I think.'

'Well, it's not there now. I just wanted to see what it was.'

'I didn't really look. Not a swordpoint, anyway.'

'Odd. He must have fallen on something, as you said.'

He smiled to himself. He had followed that all the way through, quite a complex little conversation. He wondered what it was they were talking about.

'Serve you right, you know,' came a whisper. 'You shouldn't go poking your nose in.'

What?

He tried to open his eyes, but there was a hand on his forehead again, just lightly touching them shut. Then it vanished, and he knew he was alone. Frowning, he fell asleep.

Things were clearer again when he woke. Sigrid was sitting by his bed, a pot of something green before her and a clean bandage in her hand.

'What's that?' he asked suspiciously.

'One of Rannveig's salves.' Sigrid spooned some of it on to the bandage, and leaned over to apply it to Ketil's arm. He dashed it away.

'No more bloody salves!'

She sat back, startled.

'You're still confused.'

'No more salves. I'm sick of salves.'

Sigrid turned suddenly to look at the longhouse door, slapped a clean bandage on to Ketil's arm and scooped up the salve-smeared one from the floor, jamming it into the folds of Ketil's pack just as Rannveig entered the house.

'He's conscious,' said Sigrid, unnecessarily.

'Wonderful! We have a tough one here!'

'Thrawn, anyway,' Sigrid muttered. Ketil struggled to sit up, trying to see the wound in his arm. 'What did you fall on?'

'I was in a fight – two fights – but I'm not sure how this one happened.' The memory was coming back swiftly, but he wanted to make sure he knew who was around before he began to discuss it with Sigrid.

'Two fights in one night? My, Kirkuvagr has changed since I was a girl!' Rannveig laughed. 'Did you meet Brodir?'

'Yes, I had a meal in the hall,' said Ketil. 'He sends his greetings to all here and on the Brough.'

'Oh, I suppose he's doing his best,' said Rannveig, 'though it can't be easy there at the moment. I don't know what's going on, but it feels … well, I shouldn't be surprised if Thorfinn has a bit of trouble around there, soon. And I'm not sure Brodir's the man to keep it under control. What did you think?'

'You may be right.' Rannveig was clever. Einar was a lucky man, he thought. She must have eyes everywhere, though if she came from Kirkuvagr indeed, she would no doubt still have connexions there. 'Thorfinn might want to send him a few men to help.'

'Well, we'll see, no doubt: it's not up to either of us! I mean, he won't be sending you for a bit, anyway.'

'No.' His sword arm. Damn it. His sword? 'Did I bring my sword back?'

'Oh, yes,' said Sigrid.

'Well, may I see it?'

'It's on your pack.' She glanced at his arm, and leaned over him to pull the sword in its scabbard within his reach. He held the scabbard with his right hand, and gently extricated the sword with his left. It was clean.

'Can't leave a warrior with a filthy sword,' said Sigrid, turning away. 'I assume it wasn't all your own blood all over you. You must have done some damage to someone.'

'Oh, yes,' said Ketil, though he was growing sleepy again. 'I think there was a man stumbled on to my sword while I was standing admiring it.'

'Aye, seems likely. There he goes, back to sleep,' she added, her voice fading gently away as he sank back down on the bed.

'It can't have been Hrolf,' came a thin voice into his waking ears. 'Those ribs are definitely broken. He could never have lifted Snorri over the wall.'

'Yet he's the obvious suspect.' It was Rannveig, helping Einar with his problems as usual. 'Hrolf or Hlifolf: they were the ones Snorri insulted.'

Einar sighed.

'They were the ones we know Snorri insulted. Let's face it, my dear, Snorri was not the kindest of skalds.'

Rannveig gave a soft laugh. Ketil woke enough to wonder what time it was – surely if Rannveig and Einar had retired for the night, so had Hlifolf. Was he not sleeping somewhere in the longhouse, too?

'Then it must have been someone who came back with us that night. That's Hlifolf, Hrolf, Bjarni, Afi, and Ketil, not counting the women. I don't think I could lift Snorri anywhere, either.'

'No, my dear, I don't think a woman did this, either. And Hlifolf … Bjarni and Afi seem the most likely.'

'The thing is, they both went back to their houses,' said Rannveig, her voice growing softer, 'but Ketil found the body, and Ketil admits he was the one who had arranged to meet him.'

Ketil's heart gave a little leap. That was interesting.

'But why would Ketil kill him?' asked Einar. 'He's a stranger here.'

'Maybe Snorri killed Ketil's friend Herleif.'

'But if he killed Snorri in revenge, he had only to say.'

'Then maybe there was more to it. Maybe Snorri knew something about Ketil. Snorri had travelled – maybe he had come across Ketil somewhere else.'

'But Ketil is Thorfinn's man!'

'He says he is,' said Rannveig reasonably, 'but what if he isn't? Thorfinn himself hadn't seen him for a couple of years. Anything could have happened in that time.'

There was silence as Einar considered this. Ketil held his breath, trying to let it out soundlessly when Einar finally spoke.

'We'll bury Snorri in the morning, anyway. I'll think about what you said. Where's Hlifolf tonight?'

'Visiting Hrolf.'

Einar sighed.

'Good. He thinks I'm a fool, you know.'

'Perhaps.'

That was interesting, Ketil thought. Many women would have denied it, soothed their husbands, but Rannveig was realistic.

'He thinks he'd be much better at running a hird, being chief.'

'You let him do so much, though.'

'Oh, I can't be bothered with these things any more. Training and ball games and arguments and deaths. I'd be quite happy if Hlifolf did take over, you know.'

'No, you wouldn't. You think he's a fool, too!'

They laughed together softly, and that appeared to be the end of the night's conversation. Whatever time it might be, they fell silent, and Ketil sagged back into sleep.

His next awakening was rather more strident.

'Where is he? Where is the poor injured warrior?'

Daylight blazed through the rooflights above him.

'He's asleep! You can't disturb him!' Rannveig's swift

defence made him wonder if he had dreamed her accusation of him last night, but Rannveig was no match for Ingibjorg in full flight – not Ingibjorg backed by her daughter Asgerdr and by Thorfinn himself. Dazed, Ketil struggled to sit up in his bed, pulling the covers tidy with his left hand and blinking as Ingibjorg thrust back the woollen curtains around him.

'Ketil! What have you been doing?' Her sheep-face loomed perilously close, fingers brushing at the scrapes on his forehead.

'Leave the poor fellow alone!' Thorfinn laughed. Asgerdr stayed modestly in the background, Ketil noticed. He was glad: coping with both of Thorfinn's womenfolk at once would be a strain.

'I will not!' snapped Ingibjorg. 'I know what Rannveig's nursing is like. I must look at your injuries and make sure that they are clean and properly treated.'

'They really are, my lady,' said Ketil at once, though he regretted the note of desperation in his voice. He saw the expression on Rannveig's face turn from outrage to smug satisfaction, and proceeded more carefully. 'But it's urgent that I speak to Earl Thorfinn just now, if I may, my lord?'

'Of course,' said Thorfinn easily, and shooed all three women from the longhouse. Ketil breathed a sigh of relief. 'Right, tell me what happened.'

Thorfinn squatted on the edge of the bed platform so that Ketil would not need to raise his voice. Ketil described, succinctly, his visit to Kirkuvagr.

'Your men there are loyal, but anxious and probably too few to cope with the growing support for Rognvald. Rognvald's supporters meet openly.'

'They're not too bright, though. Why attack with swords in the confines of a longhouse?'

'I've been thinking about that,' said Ketil, though he was not sure, between fever and pain, if his thoughts made sense yet. 'I think they were trying to drive me outside so that the one who attacked me in the street could do so without my seeing him. I think he started off in the longhouse but got out before I went in – perhaps someone had sent them a warning.'

'That would mean someone in Brodir's hall ...' Thorfinn frowned heavily.

'I suppose so, yet I should have said … Wait, though.' He rubbed his head, sorting his memories out again. 'Someone was following me in the street before I reached Eirik's longhouse. It was the old woman we saw at the Loons. I'm sure of it. I couldn't see her, but I could smell and hear her.'

Thorfinn looked puzzled.

'What were you doing there? At the Loons, I mean?'

'Trying to work out why Herleif was buried in the old way, with an eagle. With no luck, though.'

'So you think the old woman down there went to Kirkuvagr before you to warn Rognvald's supporters that you were coming?'

'Or to help set a trap, yes, possibly. I'm afraid she was dismissive of you and Einar and the Christian religion. She may well be a Rognvald sympathiser.'

'But Rognvald was a Christian, too …' The sorrow in Thorfinn's eyes was painful.

'She talked of bringing him back to life, though. Of how the old ways could do that.'

Thorfinn was silent for a long moment, elbows on his knees. Ketil did not move. It seemed callous to disturb him. How much must he long for Rognvald to be alive? His golden nephew, with whom he had once been so close, till Kalf's vicious rumours cut through the bonds that held them, more cruel than any sword.

'And the man who attacked you?' Thorfinn asked at last, clearing his throat noisily.

'I think he had no wish to be seen. Either he thought I would know him again, or he thought I would know him already. He must not have been confident of killing me, or for some reason not have intended to.'

'Did you injure him?'

'I think so. But there was already blood on my sword from the longhouse. I might just have caught clothing.'

'And your own wounds?'

'Just scratches. Apart from my arm, which ended up with something stuck in it. I wonder, though …' A thought had just struck him. 'The man aimed for my leg, where I was already injured.'

'You think maybe he was told about that, too?'

'Or he knew about it already. The more I think about it, the

218

more I wonder if it was someone I know. Someone from Einar's court.' He dropped his voice. 'It certainly seems to have been someone from here who killed Snorri. Einar and Rannveig know that, too.'

Thorfinn blew out wearily.

'Einar's not up to it any more. If it wasn't for Rannveig, there'd be a new chief here tomorrow.' Ketil said nothing. 'Who was around when you got the leg wound?'

'Hrolf, Hlifolf, Afi, Bjarni,' Ketil listed. 'And the rest of the hird watching, of course.'

'Of course. And who do they think killed Snorri? I'd willingly have throttled him myself from time to time, but to leave him for the pigs is too much.'

'They were saying Bjarni, Hlifolf, Afi – not Hrolf because Snorri broke his ribs. But their favourite murderer was me.'

Thorfinn fixed him with a look.

'And did you kill him?' he asked.

'No, my lord, I did not.'

'Good enough for me,' said Thorfinn, and stood. 'You look as if you need a rest. Take it while you can, but be careful. I've a feeling this is growing more dangerous, and not just in Kirkuvagr. But I'll send a few more men down there, anyway. Men with minds, as well as good sword arms. Whether Rognvald has risen from the grave or not, this needs to be stopped.'

When Ketil woke again, the light was brighter still. Rannveig was crouched by the fire, her back to him. He watched her in silence for a moment or two. Did she really think he had killed Snorri? He supposed it would be easier for her to accept than that Snorri had been killed by someone they had all known for years.

Rannveig looked up just as a figure appeared at the open door. It was Sigrid.

'Good morning!' said Rannveig.

'Just calling to see how the patient is,' said Sigrid.

'The patient is fine, and longing for some fresh air.' Ketil pushed his blankets aside.

'The patient needs to put some clothes on,' said Rannveig, with a critical glance behind her. Ketil pulled on his breeches, awkward with one hand, pushed his feet into his boots, and wrapped himself in his cloak. Sigrid regarded him quizzically, propped against the doorpost.

'I can't manage a shirt,' he said, and pushed himself out of the bed. He felt his head swim, and tried not to let his urgent grip on the bedpost be seen, but Rannveig was still busy with the fire and Sigrid had already turned to walk outside. He followed, keeping his steps slow and steady.

'Are you really feeling better?' Sigrid asked, as they made their way over to the paddock wall. 'You look trowie.'

'Thanks.' His right arm twitched and he winced, stopping it, then used his left hand to run over his scalp and chin. Two days without a shave: he would have to go to the baths. But the fresh air felt cleansing, too.

'Tell me what really happened, then.'

He described his visit to Brodir's hall, his fight with Rognvald's supporters, inside and outside Eirik's longhouse, and finally said,

'I think someone told them I was coming.'

Sigrid frowned.

'Someone from Brodir's hall?'

'Well, it could have been. They seemed more worried that I was a traitor, though, not keen to hide that they were.' He remembered the oily-haired man at the hall's door, pinning him against the stone wall.

'Who do you think it was, then?'

'I think it was the old woman from the Loons.'

'What?'

'It was her. She smelled the same, and she sounded the same. She said that Rognvald had come back from the dead – that they had raised him from the dead.'

'Really?' There was an odd expression on Sigrid's face.

'What's wrong?'

'I went back to see the old woman yesterday. Ketil, she was dead – she had been dead I reckon since just after we left her.'

Ketil felt his eyes gape.

'The old woman was dead?' He felt a shiver down his spine. Was the hag right? Were they resurrecting people – herself included?

'Well, yes and no,' said Sigrid.

'That's not helping.'

'It was an old woman, lying behind that horrible hut, with long, dirty grey hair. But I'm fairly sure it wasn't the same old woman.'

Ketil stared at her.

'There were two? No one said there were two.'

'But it does mean that one could have been dead behind the hut and the other could have been annoying you in Kirkuvagr.' She grimaced. 'Oh, she was stinking, the poor old thing.'

Ketil frowned.

'Do you know, that's odd?'

'What do you mean?'

'I mean there they were, living in that hut, in the marsh, and the hut was filthy and so were their clothes and hair. And you say the one you found stank. Well, the one that caught me in Kirkuvagr didn't.'

'Not at all?'

'I had her close to me, my knife at her throat – I cut her a little – and she smelled of that fire she had going. But she didn't smell as if she hadn't washed.'

Sigrid blinked.

'You don't suppose … could one woman have killed the other, then taken her place? Do you know, it looked as if the dead woman had been wearing a cap, like that pigskin one the woman we saw had. Her hair was all flattened and greasy – ugh, imagine taking that thing off a dead woman and wearing it!'

'I think you're jumping ahead too far,' said Ketil. 'We don't know there weren't two of them. They could have been sisters.'

'Well, maybe.' Sigrid sounded dubious, but Ketil had more important things in mind.

'Did you happen to see what it was they took out of my arm?'

'I did,' said Sigrid. 'Not closely, though.'

'Well?'

'Well what? Haven't you looked at it?'

'No.' Ketil was impatient. 'Someone took it away.'

'They took it out of your pack? Then it must have been important.'

'Out of my pack?'

She sighed, just as impatient as he was.

'Yes, didn't you see? I hid it in your pack, so that you could look at it later. It could just be a big splinter, for all I really know, but I knew you'd want to see whatever it was you fell on.' She looked him up and down. 'I'll fetch it, shall I? No point in you tiring yourself out.' She skipped off before he could think of a fitting retort. In a moment she was back, clutching a white cloth bundle and something solid. She waited until she was right beside Ketil again before she displayed her finds.

'What's that?'

'Oh! that's the salve you refused to have put on your arm. Remember? Rannveig came in and I hid it.'

'Is there nothing you haven't stuffed in amongst my belongings?' he asked.

'Well, it was handy. I'll take it home and get rid of it somewhere she won't see. Now, here's the prize you brought home so carefully.' She held out her hand.

'Not a splinter, then,' said Ketil in astonishment. His arm ached just at the thought of this embedded in it.

'No. That's the chape off a scabbard, isn't it? With a little bit of the scabbard, too, for good measure. You did know it's the sharp thing inside you're supposed to fight with, didn't you? Not the wooden thing you carry it in.'

He ignored her, fingering the bloodied fold of metal. Some of the dried blood wiped off under his thumb, and he scratched at more with his nail.

'What does that look like?' he asked, tilting it towards her.

'Some kind of bird. A raven? No, an eagle!'

'An eagle. This is someone's insignia.'

'Do you know whose?'

'As a matter of fact,' said Ketil, 'I do. Remember Ingibjorg's kinsman, who caused the rift between Thorfinn and Rognvald?'

'Kalf Arnason?' She nodded, but her face was pale.

'Kalf Arnason,' he said. 'Yes. This is Kalf's insignia.'

TUTTUGU

XX

A light rain began to fall as they stared at the chape in Ketil's hand. A shred of leather and even a tuft of wool from the scabbard's cover and lining were still attached. Ketil's upper arm ached.

'So Kalf is using rumours of Rognvald to rouse his followers,' Sigrid tried, 'so that he can try to seize the islands?'

'I'd say that seems likely.'

'We'll have to tell Thorfinn.'

'Yes,' said Ketil, 'but I want to think about that. After all, Ingibjorg is Kalf's kin. And Thorfinn often does what Ingibjorg tells him to do.'

'Not in this case, though, I hope?' Sigrid was shocked at the thought. Thorfinn could not be so stupid, surely? But Thorfinn had become so peaceable in the last few months: perhaps he would simply hand his earldom over to Kalf, and retire. Was that credible? Sigrid, her mind leaping, thought not, but then she would never have thought of Thorfinn cosying himself away on the Brough, either, and spending quite so much time in prayer. 'I wouldn't want Kalf as earl here,' she said at last. 'I don't trust him at all.'

'No, he's never been very reliable.'

It was all very well for Ketil to sound flippant, but she had to live here.

'Then we need to work out who's on his side, who's been helping him. What about these men in Kirkuvagr?'

'The ones I saw, the ones who attacked me in the longhouse, I wouldn't have called them leaders. I had the feeling they were all waiting for something all the time I was there, listening for orders from somewhere.'

'And you think you knew the man who attacked you?'

'I think that's why he waited to attack me in the dark, yes. But it could just have been that he didn't want me to know him again.'

For a moment Sigrid allowed herself to imagine trying to fight an armed attacker in the dark, in a strange place. She knew it was not something she could have done.

'I still want to find out more about the old woman,' she said, turning to the more familiar. 'Or old women. One or both of them seem to be on Rognvald's side. On Kalf's side.'

'Who told you about her in the first place?'

'Helga.'

'Helga?'

'Yes. I should go and see her, if she's in, about-going body that she is. I've nearly finished a braid for her, anyway.'

'No need to go and see her,' said Ketil with a smile. 'Here she comes – and by the look on her face, she's coming to see me.'

'Don't flatter yourself,' said Sigrid quickly. 'You know she just likes to sample every new piece of merchandise that comes into the harbour.'

She regretted the words the instant they left her mouth, but Ketil only grinned, and turned to greet Helga.

'This rain, eh?' said Helga. It was growing heavier. 'What are you doing standing out in this? Ketil, you should be in your bed!'

'I needed some fresh air,' said Ketil easily. 'But it's true, it might be time to go back in. Sigrid's glad to see you: she wants to ask you something.'

He turned and began his slow walk back towards the longhouse, then seemed to think better of it and headed instead towards the hall doorway. Sigrid pulled her cloak close and followed, with Helga beside her.

'I think he must be going to see Snorri's body. The funeral is today.'

'Yes: I came down to help Rannveig. Too many funerals just now,' Helga added carelessly, 'it's like a warm winter.'

'I know.'

Helga turned sharply with an indrawn breath, clearly remembering Sigrid's recent losses, but said nothing. Sigrid was glad.

'I nearly have that blue and green braid finished,' she said, helping Helga change the subject.

'Oh, lovely! I'm looking forward to that. It'll be beautiful - it's for a shirt for Hrolf. I bought some blue-dyed linen last summer.'

'Expensive!'

'Well, it was. But Hrolf has always allowed me my peedie purchases, you know that! Oh, and I left some bread at your place on the way past, by the way. Gnup said he knew where to put it.'

'Gnup is invaluable. Thanks.'

'He's a good lad, certainly. And if you married Bjarni he wouldn't have to leave, either.'

Sigrid had not considered the effect on Gnup of her marrying Bjarni. She realised at once that Gnup would not be as happy about it as Helga seemed to think. Gnup's worst nightmare would be to be absorbed back into his grandmother's household. She tucked the thought away for later consideration, and paused outside the door of the hall. Ketil had vanished inside.

'Helga, remember you told me about that old woman by the Loons?'

'The one who's died? Was it me who told you? I don't remember ever having reason to mention her to anyone.'

'Yes, it was. The day you went south to meet the silver trader.'

'What silver trader?' Helga's face went a little stiff, then she added hurriedly, 'Oh, yes, the silver trader. I never did manage to meet him.'

'Oh, that's a shame,' said Sigrid. The silver trader, she remembered, had been supposed to be coming north from Hamnavoe – on the road that she and Ketil had taken to go to the Loons. Interesting: what had happened to the silver trader? Had he existed at all? She shot a sideways glance at Helga, but her pretty face had returned to normal. 'Anyway, I was going to ask you about her. Did she live on her own?'

'On her own? Of course she did! Who else in their right minds would live down there with her in that stinking hut?'

Sigrid noted that Helga seemed quite familiar with the stinking hut.

'She didn't have, say, a sister? Or a daughter or mother?'

'She might have. No doubt she had a mother, once – though I'd be prepared to believe she just grew out of the marsh! But I've never heard of a daughter or a sister. She's always been there on her own, as far as I know. Which isn't very far, by the way: I've never even seen her, not close up. Not very close, anyway.'

The lie was not convincing, and Helga must have known it. She tried a different tack.

'Why did you want to know about her, anyway? You're very brave, going down there on your own! Different when Ketil was with you. You'd feel safe anywhere with him protecting you.' She gave a little wistful sigh, which Sigrid managed to ignore.

'We were trying to find out who might have buried Herleif – you know, Ketil's friend in the gully – with an eagle like that, as if they followed the old beliefs.'

'And did she tell you anything?' Helga's voice was untrustworthy again, even a little wobbly. But after all, she had told Sigrid about the old woman in the first place. She could hardly deny all knowledge of the old beliefs.

'Oh, this and that,' said Sigrid, remembering. The old woman had seemed to know a good deal of what was going on around the Brough and Einar's place. 'What's happening with her, do you know?' she went on. 'With all the fuss over Ketil, all I had the chance to do was to tell Einar she was dead, and leave it to him.'

'She's to be buried down by her hut. And I think Einar said something about burning the stuff that's in it.'

'She was killed, though: what about compensation?'

'Well, as I said, I don't think she had any family. And as far as Einar's concerned, whoever did it has probably done the community a service. He mentioned something about priests of the old religion being burned in Norway, in the time of King Olaf.'

Sigrid thought of the tiny body, gnarled and broken, thrown behind her home, and felt suddenly deeply sorry for the old woman. After all, it had not been that woman who had tried to drug them, who had worked against Ketil in Kirkuvagr. It looked as if she had been right, and someone had killed to take the old woman's place – and the foul pigskin cap.

She was distracted from her thoughts by a voice from the doorway.

'Ah! There you are,' said Hlifolf. 'Come to pay your respects to poor Snorri?'

'Of course,' said Helga briskly, and in they went.

Ketil was already kneeling, very straight, next to Father Tosti. His short-cropped hair made him look almost monk-like himself in the candlelight. His bandaged right arm was visible under his cloak, and Sigrid wondered if he would need help getting up again.

Lying on the table, on a clean cloth, Snorri had been stitched into his shroud but his face was still clear, his hair and whiskers glistening clean. He did not look right with his eyes closed. Those eyes had always been open, watchful, clever, mischievous at the very least, occasionally malevolent. Sigrid half-expected him to sit up and laugh at them all for falling for his trick. She knelt to pray, and felt Helga join her on one side, and Hlifolf, a little too close, on the other. She could smell his rosemary scent heavy in the air.

Gradually, the other members of the community joined them, including Einar and Thorfinn, and eventually Tosti rose to his feet and signalled for the bearers to bring the old bier. Ketil would probably be relieved not to have to help carry Snorri, who despite his legs had not been a small man. Sigrid saw Ketil rise and slip out, and return a little later shaved and somehow wearing his new shirt over his bandages. Rannveig must have helped him.

Tosti oversaw the arrangement of the awkward corpse on the creaking bier and made sure the stronger bearers, including Bjarni and Afi, were at the front, then made the sign of the cross over them for the commencement of their journey.

'In nomine Patris, et Filii –'

'Fili*ae*,' muttered Hlifolf beside her, just clearly enough for Tosti to hear.

'Et Spiritu Sancti, Amen.'

'Amen,' said everyone, except Hlifolf, who murmured, 'Spiritu Sanct*ae*, Amen,' after everyone else had spoken. He lifted his head to smile benevolently at Tosti. Tosti as usual looked discomfited at Hlifolf's corrections. Sigrid wondered why he still needed reminding. Hlifolf was always correcting him.

Led by Father Tosti, the procession set off towards the Brough just as Herleif's had done, not so many days ago. In a few minutes, only the women were left behind in Einar's hall. Rannveig nodded to her women, and they snuffed out the valuable candles, taking them away, and moved the table back into its usual place. The cloth was whipped up and folded, and taken for washing. The hall was a hall once again.

'I wonder how long they'll be?' Helga mused, watching as Hrolf left with the rest, stepping carefully with his arms wrapped around his broken ribs. Hlifolf paced with him. Ahead there was a pause as Bjarni changed places with one of the other mourners: Snorri must be a heavy burden indeed for them to change so soon.

'We can put the cold food out, anyway,' said Rannveig. 'Probably nothing more than that. There'll be plenty of folk on the Brough who'll want to toast Snorri at his grave: they could be there for a while. The stew is cooked, it just has to be heated, but we'll bring it in ready to put it over the fire. And we'll light the fire – no sense in being cold and miserable, even if it's a funeral. That rain is getting heavier. We'll set out the bread and the cheese – thank Heavens Lent is nearly over! I'm longing for a nice piece of sausage – and then I think we'll take a seat ourselves and drink a cup of wine to poor Snorri's memory.' She set her hands on her hips and surveyed the hall, her briskness suddenly sagging, a weary look on her face. 'Poor Snorri. We seem to be having a bad time of it, just now.'

'We will, until we find out who's doing all this,' said Sigrid absently. Rannveig flashed her a curious look, then recovered.

'Right! Who's brought bread? Sigrid, you know where the big serving plates are. Helga, I'm sure your bag is bulging with bread. You … Ragna's daughter. The cheese is over in the dairy. Bring it in and cut it up a bit, you know the way. Asgerdr,' Thorfinn's daughter jumped, clearly not expecting to be involved, but Rannveig's face was bland. 'You're young and fit, you can help me carry in the stew pots. Ingibjorg, maybe you'd be so good as to light the fire? There's a lamp over there if you need a start. Let's get organised, and then we can relax.'

Sigrid did as she was bid, as she always did when Rannveig took charge. The great soapstone dishes were heavy, so she trotted back and forth carrying them two at a time, arranging them on the tables, so that Helga could fill them with sweet fresh bread and Ragna's silent, nameless daughter could add lumps of sharp-scented, yellow cheese. Asgerdr, looking as if she would rather be anywhere else, strained to bring in her side of one of the large stew pots, but her face split into a wicked grin when she caught sight of her mother kneeling on the flag floor trying to blow life into the fire. Clearly Ingibjorg did not normally stoop to such things. Sigrid smirked to herself, and tried to look as competent as Helga and Rannveig.

In truth they were generally quick and competent, under

Rannveig's direction, and it was not long until they could share some wine and perch around the fire, taking a breath after their hurry.

'I'll drink this before we put the stew over the fire,' said Rannveig, comfortable against a table end with her knees up to her chest. 'Dear,' she added, fluffing over the fact she still could not remember the girl's name, 'how's your mother? How's Ragna?'

The nameless daughter cleared her throat, unused to speaking.

'She's still not well.'

'And it's her stomach still?' The girl nodded. Woman, Sigrid corrected herself – she was a widow, but Sigrid found it hard to think of another person claiming the status of womanhood in Ragna's longhouse. 'I'm sorry I haven't been to visit for a while. What with funerals and injured men ...'

'It's all right,' the girl whispered, 'she's not really ready for visitors.'

'But we could help,' said Helga, 'we could take some of the work from you and your sister.'

'Oh, we don't mind. Olvor's there now, and it's hardly any work.'

'But the extra cleaning and washing, I'm sure ...'

'No, no, nothing like that! It's no trouble at all.' The girl – woman – whatever her name was, but not Olvor – seemed determined. And she must have known how reluctant anyone else would be to step into that family and help. She would be used to managing, just she and Olvor, and feeding Bjarni and the rest just as usual.

'What on earth is wrong with her?' Ingibjorg asked, behind with the Buckquoy clash. 'She's my kinswoman: if she needs nursing, she should have sent for help from me.'

'No doubt she thought you would be busy, what with the building work, Ingibjorg,' said Rannveig diplomatically.

'It's not as if I can't leave them unsupervised for a little while,' Ingibjorg objected. Sigrid was visited by a vision of Ingibjorg up to her knees in mud, directing the placing of building flags. She smiled to herself, then saw that Asgerdr had noticed. But Asgerdr really was only a girl. Asgerdr, however, had already been distracted by her mother's next words.

'We'll go and see her straight after the meal is over,' she

announced. Asgerdr looked aghast. So, she noticed suddenly, did Ragna's daughter.

'She – she – really isn't very good with visitors at the moment,' she stumbled. Sigrid could imagine. The daughter would be terrified that Ragna would shout something unforgiveable at their Earl's wife. 'In fact she really prefers not to be disturbed: any upset, any change in routine, can ... can turn her stomach.'

'Turn her stomach?' Ingibjorg queried. It made sense to Sigrid, though. Ingibjorg turned her stomach regularly.

'Make her bock ...' The nameless daughter's voice faded as she probably thought of a dozen more appropriate ways to put it. But her meaning was clear, anyway. Or it was to Sigrid, with her vivid memory of Ragna vomiting over the remains of her dinner. Ingibjorg's face was a delight, but Sigrid thought the daughter was feeling the weight of the room's attention.

'So, Helga,' she said, trying to think of something to start at least a parallel conversation, 'as I say, that braid should be finished in the next couple of days, if I'm allowed to get on with it.'

'It couldn't be sooner, could it?' Helga asked sweetly. 'Only, you know, if I could finish the shirt in time for Easter, that would be lovely!'

'The vigil starts in two days, Helga. Have you actually made the shirt? You could have most of it done before you add the braid, and save yourself time.'

'Well ...' Helga hesitated.

'You have started it, haven't you?'

'I was hoping ...'

'Helga, I'm not making a shirt for Hrolf. That's a wife's job, or a betrothed. I'm not making a shirt for any man, just at the moment.'

'Oh, well, I suppose... Not even for Bjarni?'

'Not even for Bjarni. Not yet, anyway.'

'Not until Ragna dies, maybe?' Helga whispered it, but her eyes glinted with mischief.

'Helga! That's awful!'

Helga subsided a little, but she still looked pleased with herself. Sigrid was not at all pleased with her. That kind of rumour could lead to all sorts of trouble. She had better not go near Ragna until the woman was well again.

They heard voices outside, and Sigrid, who was closest, stood to see if it was indeed the funeral party back. It was: some of them were red in the face and others a little hilarious, but they had made it home, along with Thorfinn and some of his men from the Brough who had joined in at the churchyard. All of them were soaking, and Ketil looked pale – paler even than usual. Sigrid hurried them inside to the fire and to the food that would help them to some sobriety.

'You all right?' she muttered as Ketil passed her.

'Yes,' he said shortly, but she watched him sink gratefully on to a bench near the back of the hall, pushing his wet cloak back from his shoulders. When she turned back to the door, Tosti was slipping in, an anxious look on his face.

'What's wrong?' she asked.

'The new church,' he said, widening his eyes at her. 'I slipped in to see how things were going for Saturday, and the roof's leaking all over the floor. Well, not quite all over, but it's not good.'

'Oh, no! After all your work!'

'Well, all our rushed work,' said Tosti, with a quick look round for Thorfinn. 'A little more time and care might have been well applied.' He smiled. 'I've sent one or two men back up to fix it, but, well, it's wet, and they'd been toasting Snorri. It would probably have been better to wait, on the whole.'

'And pray for better weather for Saturday and Sunday,' Sigrid added.

'The perfect solution, yes! But if God wills that the roof should be tested, then the roof should not be found wanting!'

He grinned, and made his way modestly to the back of the hall, mopping water from his fringe with the edge of his cloak. She turned back to the door to see if anyone else was coming in: the hall was already crowded. Einar and Thorfinn were wrangling politely over who was to take the high chair at the head of the hall, while Ingibjorg stood by to make sure she had her place of honour, and was not reduced to serving ale. Sigrid grinned, and looked away, accidentally catching Hlifolf in the end of her smile. He nodded happily, and smiled back as she quickly straightened her face.

'Einar tells me,' he said, as he came over – it was his usual

way of making it sound as if he were Einar's particular confidant –
'that you were the one to find that dead creature at the Loons
yesterday?'

'That's right, yes.'

'That must have been so upsetting for you. And in all that
mist, too, really quite uncanny. You must have been terrified!'

'I didn't enjoy it, certainly,' said Sigrid, unwilling to accept
his comfort. 'But I'm sure the old woman had the worse part of it.'

'Oh, of course, Einar mentioned that, too – that you'd been
there before?'

'Only the day before, that was all.'

'And she was in good health then?'

'Yes …' She might have said that she was also a different
woman, but she was reluctant to give Hlifolf any more information
to add to his stores.

'That's so useful – to know at least a time after which she
must have died.'

'Yes, I suppose so.'

'Oh, naturally Einar is once more entrusting me with the
investigation – unless Thorfinn decides once again that your friend
Ketil should look into it. But of course Ketil is not at his best at
present, is he?'

'Not really, no,' she agreed reluctantly.

'Now, you'd been to see the woman the previous day? With
Ketil?' His voice was probably what he thought of as soothing, but
it came over as oily. Sigrid felt faintly sick.

'That's right.'

'And you were accustomed to visiting her?'

'Not at all. That was the first time I had been there or seen her.
I'd only found out she existed a few days ago.'

'But when you knew she was there, you rushed to see her?'

'We wanted to ask her something.'

'And did she answer you?'

'Up to a point.' Again, she had no wish to go further, but she
also wanted to make sure Hlifolf did not form the suspicion that
either she or Ketil was an adherent of the old beliefs. 'She talked
some nonsense to us about a local goddess. Ollinn, or something.'
Ullinn, she remembered quite well. She suppressed a shudder.

'But nothing that was helpful? Nothing … of the real world?'

'No, not really. Just silly things, vague, you know, like a fortune teller.'

'Of course.' He drew breath importantly. 'In my opinion – as I said to Einar – we are as well without people like that in the place. She'll be buried later today next to her hut, and the bruck within will be burned. I shall be supervising it myself.'

'In that case,' said Sigrid, 'what could possibly go wrong?'

Hlifolf, deaf to irony, smiled in satisfaction.

TUTTUGU OK EIN

XXI

Ketil watched as the funeral meal gathered pace around him. Watching was about all he felt he could do at the moment – he was drained. It had probably been foolish to walk to the Brough with the funeral procession, but he had hoped the drink at the interment might begin to open mouths and loosen tongues. Bjarni, Afi, Hlifolf and Hrolf had all stayed quiet, though, along with most of the others, only taking a few respectful mouthfuls of spirit. For all he had gained, he might as well have stayed in bed. And he had definitely lost recovery time.

Someone tapped his shoulder from behind, and he jerked round.

'Sorry!'

It was Hrolf's son, the King's Table player.

'Asgrimr! Sorry, you took me by surprise.'

Asgrimr took that as encouragement, and squeezed on to the bench beside Ketil.

'Father would be pleased.' He saw Ketil's puzzled expression. 'Me, creeping up and surprising a warrior. Hlifolf's been training me. Not that I was creeping, though, not deliberately. I was only coming to ask you if you wanted a game.'

Ketil hesitated. He was not sure he was alert enough to know which way up the pieces went.

'Oh, all right, then. But I doubt I'll make a very good opponent.'

'Father said you'd been wounded in a fight in Kirkuvagr,' said Asgrimr, already unfolding his table.

'Yes.'

'Badly?'

'It'll heal.'

'That's good. Father's ribs are healing well, too.' He laid the pieces on the cloth with deft respect, giving each one a little encouraging tap. 'I quite like it when Father's injured. He stays at home more, and Mother looks after him. It's peaceful.'

'It does sound good. He spends a lot of time here, I suppose, usually.'

'Yes, and then Mother shouts at him when he comes home. But it's worse when she doesn't.' He laid the last piece on the cloth, and looked up, but did not quite meet Ketil's eye.

'Doesn't shout at him? Is that what you mean? How is that worse?' Though Ketil, sometimes staying with his brother and sister-in-law, knew well that sometimes a wife's silence could be much worse than a blazing row.

Asgrimr shrugged.

'Sometimes it just means she's not there.'

There was something conclusive about the way he said it, and Ketil decided not to pursue it further. Perhaps Helga had relatives she retreated to, when Hrolf had left her at home alone for too long.

Ketil shifted a piece, then Asgrimr began with a flurry of moves as they took and countertook each other's soldiers. The board was quickly pared down, and Asgrimr paused to consider his next move with more care. Ketil took the chance to glance around for Hrolf in the crowd. The mourners, faced with the serious fast of Good Friday in the morning, were taking their chance to eat and drink to slightly beyond capacity. The gathering was turning raucous. Einar looked saddened: Thorfinn appeared cross, but Ingibjorg, her eyes all over a sturdy young warrior she was chatting with, had a white hand on his arm, firm as a grip on a tiller. Her daughter, bored, slouched to one side, an elbow on the table. She caught Ketil's eye and raised her eyebrows at him, a challenge he chose to ignore. He inclined his head slightly, and let his gaze wander on.

'There,' said Asgrimr, interrupting his survey. He turned his attention back to the board. Asgrimr's king was perilously close to reaching one of the corners. Ketil was not particularly interested in winning, but he had to make the effort. He studied the board again and finally shifted one of his soldiers to a space beside the king, gently threatening. Asgrimr grinned, and reconsidered.

Ketil located Hrolf behind Einar's chair, talking intently in the shadows with Hlifolf. Was it Ketil's imagination, or was he standing less carefully than he had been earlier in the day? Ketil glanced quickly around: no one was watching him, not even Asgrimr. He scooped a piece of cheese into his left hand, and flicked it hard across the hall. It landed at Hrolf's feet, or as near as he could make it. Hrolf looked down in surprise, then quickly and easily stooped to pick up the mysterious object. There was very little wrong with his ribs.

Ketil looked away, before Hrolf could realise the cheese had come from him, and concentrated on Asgrimr's next move. Asgrimr slipped his king across the board to a point where Ketil could do nothing to stop him, and in two moves had reached a different corner, and won.

'You're good at this,' Ketil remarked. The boy nodded, knowing it for a fact.

'To be honest, though,' he said, 'I'm not good at much else. If battles were played on King's Table boards, I would be Earl – if I wanted to be. But people don't always behave like the pieces on the board, do they?'

'Very rarely,' Ketil agreed gravely.

'And balls and swords and things, they're nearly as bad. They don't do what I want them to do. It's not like that for you, though, is it?'

Ketil shrugged.

'It takes a lot of practice.'

'Years, I should think. But there's more to it than that. When you threw that piece of cheese at my father – well, if it had been me, I'd probably have hit Einar instead. Or thrown it over my own shoulder.'

'Mm,' said Ketil. He had not thought that Asgrimr had noticed.

'Why did you throw it at him?'

'It was a kind of joke,' said Ketil after a moment. Asgrimr looked resigned.

'I don't really understand jokes,' he said. 'I don't see the point. But be careful,' he added seriously. 'People who make jokes against my father sometimes – aren't very lucky.'

'What do you mean?' Ketil asked, trying to sound less tense than he suddenly felt. Asgrimr shrugged.

'I just mean that often bad things happen to them. Maybe it's because he's Einar's counsellor: it's always useful to know powerful men, isn't it?' He was vague, and Ketil knew he had said all he could say. But his gaze wandered away to Einar, delicately perched on his chair beside Thorfinn, thin, ghostly, no doubt itching to be back with his books. A powerful man? He used to be, but was he still?

Asgrimr was optimistically laying out the pieces for another game, when Afi crossed the hall and propped himself on the table opposite Ketil. He grinned, contorting his scarred face into something that resembled a friendly troll, rock-born but benevolent.

'How are you doing, then, Ketil?' he asked, gesturing broadly to Ketil's injured arm.

'Improving,' said Ketil.

'I was thinking,' said Afi, improbably, 'when I was carrying the bier today: you were interested in the boat wreck we found last autumn near the gully. Low tide's early tomorrow morning. Are you up to coming along and seeing where the wreckage was? I can show you, and a few of the lads are happy to come along and see what else they remember. There might even be something the sea and us missed.'

Ketil ignored the warning ache in his arm.

'Yes, I'll come, if you're going. It would be good to see how far it was from the gully, anyway, though I doubt we'll find anything now.'

'You never know!' Afi gave a monumental wink. 'Right, we'll come and pick you up about dawn. See you then!'

It was only as he surged away that it occurred to Ketil to ask who 'we' actually were. Was he falling into a trap? After the attack in Kirkuvagr, he should probably be more careful. He let his mind wander while Asgrimr began the next game on the offensive, then decided. He would go – armed – and he would make sure to tell Sigrid tonight exactly what Afi had told him. Then at least she could report to Thorfinn, if something bad happened to him.

The way bad things happened to anyone who played a joke against Hrolf.

He hoped the cheese trap had not been taken the wrong way.

He beat Asgrimr a couple of times, surprised to find his

thoughts growing clearer just as he had decided it was time to retire for the night. Asgrimr did not grudge the victories, clearly turning over both of them in his mind to see what he could learn from them. Ketil did not ask Asgrimr not to mention the cheese-throwing to his father. He had a feeling that it would not even occur to Asgrimr to talk any further about the incomprehensible joke.

Sigrid was near the door, looking as if she had been planning to leave, too, but Bjarni had an arm casually propped against the wall, blocking her path. Ketil could not decide whether or not Sigrid found this annoying. In any case, he had to interrupt their conversation.

'I'm off with Afi in the morning to see where that boat's wreckage was found in the autumn,' he said without apology. 'We're going at dawn.'

She met his eyes and he was sure she realised why he was telling her.

'Do you think that's wise?' she asked, nevertheless. He should have known she would not let him away without some hindrance.

'We're not going far,' he said. 'And there are others coming.'

'Me, for one,' said Bjarni cheerfully. 'I helped salvage the boat, so I know where it was. Don't worry, Sigrid, I'll make sure he doesn't do anything stupid!' He grinned at Ketil, while managing somehow to move closer to Sigrid, ownership declared. Ketil smiled back.

'There, you see? It will be fine,' he said, and left.

But something about the encounter had unsettled him. He was not at all sure, he found now, that it would be fine. Not fine at all.

Dawn on Good Friday did not break so much as seep into the darkness, like traces of milk in muddy water. Yet he woke, as he usually did, easily enough, testing his arm and leg to make sure they were just a little better than yesterday. His leg was definitely on the mend, if he did not try it again. His arm still felt as if the chape were inside it. He seized his clothes and boots, made sure he had more than one knife, and slipped out of the longhouse.

The haar outside was a thick one: he could feel the drops against his skin. He washed quickly, combed his hair and pulled on his clothes, admitting to himself that he made much easier work of his tight-sleeved shirt than he had the previous day – his arm was still very painful, but at least it was more flexible. Breeches were still hard to manage with one hand, though, and he wished he had a nice pair of York boots with a toggle instead of long laces to manage. His ankles felt loose. But he was ready before Hrolf and Bjarni, arriving from their different directions, appeared to collect him, Afi loomed out of the mist from wherever he lived behind the hall, and all four walked along the landspit to where the steps led down to the harbour. Hrolf still held his ribs as he went.

'We'll take my boat,' he said importantly. 'Bjarni's is up for repair, and Afi's ...'

'Mine just about takes me, and no more!' Afi laughed.

'Where is your boat, Bjarni?' Hrolf glanced around the busy harbour.

'About as far over there as you can go, and not be out of the other side of the bay,' said Bjarni ruefully. 'There's a man there promises he can do something about that mast step. If he can't, I'll need a new boat.'

'Should have brought it to me,' said Afi comfortably.

'I suppose. I thought you were busy.'

'You're a boat-builder?' Ketil asked, interested in anyone who worked with wood.

'Oh, aye. Too busy to build myself a new one, mind!'

'There you are, then,' said Bjarni. 'But if the man can't fix it, I'll come to you for a new one anyway. You know the kind I like.'

'Aye,' said Afi, winking, 'small and fast, with no room for cargo!'

For a few minutes the men discussed boats, with Hrolf pointing out distinguishing features on some of the beached boats they passed. Ketil noticed the kvarr on which he had arrived was away, no doubt continuing down the coast to Hamnavoe or Hoy. He wished it well.

Hrolf's boat was neat and serviceable, and fairly new. It could have taken probably half a dozen men, or three men and Afi. Hrolf was clearly proud of it, touching the smooth gunwale before Afi and Bjarni took a side each to run it into the water, Hrolf keeping a proprietorial hand on the prow. The keel swished across the sand, eager to be back in the waves. Ketil followed, feeling a little superfluous, but hoping he would not have to row, not today. He need not have worried: once they had all scrambled on board, Hrolf would not even let Ketil take the tiller.

'For one thing, you'd need your right arm, and for another, the rocks around to the north are tricky. It needs someone who knows where we're going. Don't worry about my ribs,' he added heroically, 'I'll manage.'

'Well, if you're sure, then I shan't argue,' said Ketil, deliberately expressionless. He settled himself in the prow, though, out of the way. Afi and Bjarni took an oar each, and Hrolf himself saw to the steering. It would indeed have been awkward to use his left arm.

Ketil sat sideways, his hand on the prow, watching where they were going. He remembered from his arrival the sheared sides of the Brough's rounded head, the kitticks calling from the cliffs, the flashing aaks, the lyres with their bright bills, but there was much less to be seen today even than on the day of his misty journey. The haar was low and wet, the birds' cries bodiless, detached from the world, things you could weave into a harness for Fenrir.

'When do you think this will lift?' he called back down the boat. Hrolf shrugged, casting an assessing look at where the sky was supposed to be.

'Midday, I'd say. We'll be sticking to the coast, so it shouldn't bother us. Afi, remember to ease off a bit? Bjarni's strong, but we don't want to be going round in circles.'

'Sorry!' Afi tried to shorten his stroke a little, but it was clear he was uncomfortable.

'Tell you what,' said Bjarni, more than a little breathless, 'why don't I row there, and you row back?'

There was a moment of unsteady reorganisation amidships, and Bjarni took both oars. Hrolf nodded his satisfaction, and they set off again. Grinning to himself, Ketil turned back to see where they were going. It was good to be back on the water again.

They rounded the headland, and saw the bear claws of the dark brown rocks stretching out from the north side, layer after layer fading as they retreated into the haar. At low tide they were longer than ever, a comb fit for the most legendary of giants. Near the Brough itself the sharp cliffs above them were high enough to defend the settlements above from a northerly attack, some of the edges sharp all the way to the top. Ketil tried to work out where he had seen Sigrid the day he had arrived, moving stones somewhere near a stream ... there? Was that it? The stream was a thread of black and white down the cleft it had carved, and at its foot, where it splayed out over tilted flat rocks to be lost in the waves, he could see a couple of the slabs she had arranged. Hadn't Tosti, the little priest, said something about Sigrid building a bridge? To atone for her husband Thorstein's sins? This was what Ketil had pictured when Tosti had told him. What else, Ketil wondered, had Thorstein done?

Afi, squatting behind Ketil with his back to Bjarni's straining shoulders, peered through the mist to see precisely where they were.

'We must be close,' said Bjarni, gritting his teeth. Ketil wondered what he was trying to prove – no one would expect him to be as strong as Afi. 'Surely we're nearly there?'

'Och, nowhere near yet!' said Afi, winking at Ketil. 'It'll be a while yet. Is that not right, Hrolf?' He glanced back over Bjarni's shoulder, and Hrolf, suppressing a grin, agreed.

'Just keep going. I'll tell you when to stop,' he assured Bjarni.

Bjarni paused in disbelief, then redoubled his efforts. Then something on the land caught his eye, and he leaned back suddenly, shipping his oars.

'That's the Geo! We're well past the place!' He waved a fist at Hrolf, then turned and scowled at Afi and, by extension, Ketil. All three men laughed, Afi as if his immense sides would split. Bjarni swore imaginatively, and began to use the oars to poke the nearest rock, trying to turn the boat. The waves, lapping gently through the mist, made it difficult.

'You'll have to row on,' Hrolf suggested, just about recovered, 'and we'll turn in a loop.'

'We'd better!' Bjarni warned. 'Any messing about with that rudder and I'll be over there, and I'll not be paying any heed to ribs you've already broken!' Still, he rowed on willingly enough as Hrolf helped him steer, the boat relaxing into the camaraderie of a shared joke. Ketil found himself wondering if any bad luck befell those who played jokes on Bjarni, too.

When they had turned, and rowed back just a little, Afi pointed a broad finger.

'That's where it was, there. See that scrape down the cliff

face? I put that there to mark it, just in case the owner reappeared. But he most likely drowned: the boat was in pieces.'

Bjarni and Afi caught the end of a rocky outcrop, angling the boat between two teeth to avoid any damage.

'You want a closer look?' Bjarni asked Ketil.

'Since you've brought me all this way,' said Ketil, though he was not looking forward to scrambling out of the boat on to those rocks with only two useful limbs. 'Where's Sigrid's gully from here?'

'Just up there,' said Hrolf, turning and giving a convincing wince at his apparently broken ribs. The gully really was not far at all, though, as Sigrid herself had said, you would not want to try it carrying a sheep – or a dead body. And anyone crouching low, never mind a dead body lying under a scraping of earth, would not be visible from down here. Had Herleif landed here, for some reason, climbed to the gully and been attacked?

Ketil gritted his teeth, and swung himself over the low side of the boat, using his left arm to push hard against the gunwale to steady his balance. The rocks were as dry as they were ever likely to be, the dark brown of old, wet, wood, frilled with foam as the waves were shredded on them. Ketil had no wish to be shredded, too. He stood, and moved delicately forward towards the gully, trying to watch his step as well as look about him for any trace of the boatwreck that had been found there.

'Well, he has bones in his nose, anyway,' he heard Hrolf remark. He smiled to himself. Determined he might be, but probably foolish, too.

He saw no point in climbing up to the gully, fortunately: he had seen it before, and it would be easier to see it again coming from the land side. From here, it was clear how part of it had already crumbled away: the cliff was friable, mud and small stones, held together, it seemed, by nothing more than the grass at the top and the claw-grip of the rocks below. It would be more of a scramble than a climb to reach the top. Instead, he turned his attention to the serried rocks at his own level, sharp eyes trying to pick out anything the least unusual, or out of place. He had no idea what he was looking for. Something that proved that Herleif had been here? That the wrecked boat had been his? If so, the local scavengers had cleared the wreck, unaware that he was lying dead so near above them. He took a cautious step over another sharp ridge, scanning the next dip. Nothing. No – wait. Something. Something glinting, near the point where the ridges vanished into the friable cliff. What was it? Not the sunlight on water, anyway: it was as misty as it had been all morning. He edged along the hollow, licked by incoming waves, his boots soaking. When he reached it, he saw it had been worth coming. It was a knife.

It was not just any knife: it was Herleif's knife. He remembered the pattern, quite clearly, from when he had seen it last in Trondheim. The trouble was, it was not the knife he had seen in Einar's hall, along with Herleif's body. It did nothing to prove that the boatwreck had been Herleif's, but it certainly raised some questions. How had it come to be here, and not with Herleif's last remaining possessions in Ketil's pack?

He picked it up, conscious of the watching men behind him, and at the same time lifted a nicely rounded flat stone. Slipping the knife into his own belt, he turned carefully, gazed out to sea for a moment, then skimmed the stone neatly across the waves. It bounced eight times – fair for a left-handed shot – and vanished. He shrugged, and stepped back towards the boat.

'You find anything?' asked Afi, hopeful.

'No, nothing. As we expected. But at least I can see now how close the wreck would have been to the gully.'

'Aye, close enough,' said Hrolf. 'He could easily have climbed up there, if it was him.'

'If he survived the wreck,' said Afi sadly.

'Well, if it was him, Afi,' said Bjarni, 'he did survive the wreck, because he went up there and had his throat cut.'

'Oh, aye, of course.'

Afi and Bjarni changed places while Ketil made the best of climbing back into the prow. When he was ready, Hrolf and Bjarni helped push the boat back from its noust in the rocks, and quietened by their lack of success they set off back the way they had come.

Afi's strokes were so powerful that the boat seemed to skim over the waves, not bothered with the niceties of pushing through them. It was a shock, therefore, when he gave a yelp, and caught a crab, thumping backwards in the boat and pushing Bjarni forward with a cry of protest on to Ketil's hip.

'You'd better not have clipped a rock with that oar!' Hrolf complained, readjusting himself on his own perch. 'What do you think you're doing?'

'Look! What's that?'

Afi pointed. They were next to the sharp gouge carved into the fragile cliff by Sigrid's stream. Because of the angle of the cleft, only Afi, facing backwards, could see easily into it, but when the others turned to look too, they all gasped.

TUTTUGU OK TVEIR

XXII

After another restless night, Sigrid reluctantly conceded, at dawn, that she was not going to sleep any more. She pushed herself out of bed, and wrapped a shawl round her shoulders before venturing into the haar.

Back in the longhouse, her tousled hair jewelled with tiny drops of water, she moved slowly, rousing the fire, feeding the cat, letting the hens out. There was no rush: Gnup would be a while yet. She decided not to bother with breakfast until he arrived. There was small chance of being disturbed at this time of the day, and she could just about finish the braid for Helga. Letting her fingers find their own way, her mind and eyes still fogged with sleep, she settled by the fire and looped the work around her bare toe, released the tablets from their leather strap, and set to work.

When Gnup arrived, she was tying off the ends, taking care to plait them evenly, taking pleasure in the different combinations of colours in the finishing strands. Gnup helped himself with equanimity to baked eggs and yesterday's flatbread, and a kind of sauce Helga had made from dandelion and ramsons and hard cheese. Sigrid ate some, too, then pulled her foot hose and boot back on. She trailed the braid over both her hands, making sure her fingers were free of sauce.

'Done!' she said, with some pride. 'I'm going to take this up to Helga, if you're all right on your own.'

'Of course,' said Gnup happily. 'I can manage. It's nice.'

'Thank you. I'll maybe be a while,' she said, as an afterthought. 'I might go down and look at the sea.'

'Of course,' said Gnup, peeling another egg and not looking at her. Sigrid watched him. He probably knew about the bridge she was building for Thorstein, to atone for what he had done, but he knew better than to say. He was a good lad.

She bound her hair in her headcloth, slipped her back cloak

into the loops of her shoulder brooches, and rolled the braid into a piece of cloth to protect it from the damp haar. Already she was thinking of the lovely wool Helga had for her next work. She could feel in her fingers the yarn it would make, see the colours she would mix it with. She gave a little sigh of happy anticipation as she set off.

'Sigrid! Come in!' Helga wore the cheerful expression she usually had when Hrolf had gone out for the day. She hugged Sigrid, wafting the scent of rosemary around her. 'Hrolf's away in the boat – oh, he and Bjarni are showing Ketil where that wreckage was found last autumn, remember?'

'I remember,' said Sigrid. 'Children out, too?'

'Looking for eggs. The hens are wandering far and wide!' Helga returned happily to her fire, where she was baking. The longhouse was sweet with the smell. Sigrid crouched opposite her.

'I've brought your braid, the blue and green one.'

'Oh! Wonderful!' Flatbreads forgotten, Helga reached out a hand for the cloth bundle. She unwrapped it, and exclaimed with delight, the blue-green wave flowing through her fingers. And suddenly Sigrid knew.

'It was you I sold it to. The braid that was on the man in the gully.'

'What was that?' said Helga, her eyes only on the braid.

'Herleif's cloak had a braid on it that I made.'

'Lots of people make braid.' Helga's voice was soft, distant.

'And they all know their own. I do.' Sigrid sighed. 'Helga, how did you know Herleif?'

Helga gave the braid a final admiring stroke, then laid it down beside her, careful to see it was all on the cloth in which it had been wrapped.

'It'll make a lovely shirt for Hrolf.' Sigrid did not reply, and eventually Helga sighed in her turn. 'He arrived out of the blue one stormy evening. I'd never seen him before. Hrolf had taken the children down to Einar's hall – he spends more time there than he does here, as you well know, and I get bored. You can only make so many flatbreads.'

She flipped the ones she was baking. Sigrid made a face, not unsympathetic, but said nothing.

'He said he had walked from Kirkuvagr, and he was soaked through. His boots weren't muddy, though, and later I discovered he had wrecked his boat on the rocks under the gully. I found him some dry clothes, brought him in to the fire. Big, strong man, he was – not thin and muscular like that Ketil, but broad, well-built, capable looking, you know? He could build you a house, father your children, slaughter your enemies, and row you away, and not pause to draw breath.'

'And one thing led to another, no doubt?' Sigrid tried to keep the gall out of her tone. 'How did he come by the braid, then?'

'He was around for a while.'

Sigrid's heart leapt.

'All winter?'

'No, I mean a month or so – good heavens, he was in hiding! I don't think he could have managed it all winter. He was bored enough as it was, all that waiting. I kept him amused as much as I could.' She had the grace to blush just a little. 'I stitched the braid on to his cloak as a gift for him. His clothes were very plain.'

'Didn't Hrolf notice?'

Helga gave her a look.

'No, of course not. He knew nothing about Herleif.'

'Helga, why didn't you tell me you knew who Herleif was?'

Helga's next look was even more devastating.

'There's a reason Hrolf didn't know about Herleif. We were very secretive. And I haven't mentioned him to anyone. Why on earth would I? You're my best friend, and I didn't tell you.'

Sigrid sat back against the bed platform. Her head was spinning with questions.

'Did he tell you why he was here?'

Helga shrugged.

'He said he was waiting to speak to Thorfinn.'

'So Thorfinn was still away when he was here?'

'Thorfinn didn't get back from Rome till nearly All Saints' Day – remember? He wanted to celebrate it when he came back.'

'Yes ... but had Herleif gone by then?'

'He had. I mean, not long before Thorfinn arrived. He'd told me he might have to leave in a hurry, so I assumed he'd heard about Thorfinn coming and had gone to meet him.'

'But he never did, did he?'

'Well … I don't know,' said Helga. 'I didn't know anything about it until you found his body.' Her voice broke very slightly on the last word, but she held back the tears Sigrid could see in her bright blue eyes. 'I always hoped he might come back again.'

Sigrid frowned. She felt sorry for her friend, but irritated with her, too, and she could not show that.

'Do you know anything about the eagle?'

'Eagle?'

'The bird that was buried with him. An eagle.'

'No, I don't know anything about that.' She looked puzzled. 'But he liked birds, you know. He'd watch them for hours, he said, eagles, too. He could tell you all about them: he was as good as a sailor.'

Was there something in that? Sigrid was not sure. She rubbed her eyes with the heels of her hands.

'Ketil will want to talk to you, no doubt,' she said at last, ignoring the glint of pleasure in Helga's eyes. Helga would soon recover from Herleif's loss.

Sigrid stumbled down the path from Helga's longhouse, feeling lower than she had since the day she had found Herleif's body. She had known well enough that there was still a good chance Herleif had been killed in the autumn, but to have the proof there like that, proof that Thorstein could well have killed Ketil's man, had shaken her. She knew she had not asked Helga everything she should have, but no doubt Ketil would tell her what she had missed. She would look like a fool, as usual. And she had done no work on Thorstein's bridge for days, just when it seemed he had even more to atone for. She had let him down, too.

She strode blindly along the landspit, only half aware of the haar still thick around her. She was not quite near enough to the edge, at least at first, to be in any danger. When she reached the point where she could scramble down to her bridge, she did ease her stride, pacing carefully towards the cliff edge. The stream here was shallow, almost more bog than flowing water, draining the wettest parts of the Brough beyond. But it nibbled away at the cliff edge, a few feet from her path downwards, and she wondered how much longer it would be before this innocuous trickle of water would carve its way back into the landspit, maybe destroying her bridge as the rubble fell muddy down to the sea. She picked her way across the wet grass and stood on the other side of the stream, pausing before going down to work. The mist was thinning, but there was a glare in it, a fizzing against her eyes. She stood staring out at it, letting her sleepy mind rest. She would not jump today. She was too tired to bother. And anyway, she had to tell Ketil about Helga and Herleif. It was a small thing, but it was a purpose. The sea, steel grey, lapped below, braided with black and white. Maybe that was where Ragna had had the idea for Bjarni's cloak braid. She would have to find the white wool. Or maybe it was their hair she had thought of, her own so white, and Bjarni's so black. Ragna's white hair ... what was that little memory at the back of her mind?

The shove to her back came as such a shock she was outraged before she was frightened. Her feet slipped and her arms flailed as she scrabbled to find sound ground under her boots. She thought she cried out, but she was not sure: she half-turned, vaguely aware of a figure in the mist, already walking away.

'Help me!' she shouted, appalled. But she was already slipping fast, the treacherous cliff crumbling under her knees, her chest, her fingers ... She wound her fingers tight into the sharp grass at the cliff's edge, feeling some of it tear, wincing as it cut into her flesh. Her breath was coming in gasps, causing her to sway against the muddy cliff face. She tried to calm down, to give herself some chance.

Could she let herself slide down? Not from here: it was too far. She would be shredded, and there was no hope she would not break her legs, at best, on the jagged rocks below. A few paces to her left, and she would have fallen on to the path she had intended to take anyway. Whoever had pushed her knew where to push. And who had it been? The anonymous cloaked back, head lowered, disappearing into the mist, told her nothing. But there was something: she had caught that slight fragrance as the figure had swirled away. Rosemary. Helga had not wanted her to tell Ketil about Herleif. Now she felt more than angry, frightened, shocked. She felt betrayed.

And she would not be able to warn Ketil about that, either.

Her hands were slipping. Well, she would have to apologise to Thorstein soon enough for her failings. And Saebjorn – would he be there? Little Saebjorn, so innocent. Could he be in the same place as Thorstein? Would she really be able to hold him again? A flicker of something passed through her mind. Saebjorn was dead. Thorstein was dead. She was not, and however much she missed her little boy, she was not ready to join them yet. She took a deep breath, let go with one slipping hand, and flung it up to take a better grip.

There was a shout from below – from the sea? She could not afford to look down, but a spark of hope ignited in her heart. At the very least, she would not die alone.

No. She was not going to die.

Her arms were aching, but she was inching herself up to the cliff's edge. Her toes tried to find firm holds in the sharp pebbles of the cliff face. Beyond the sound of her own breathing she heard someone telling her to hold on. She managed to save her strength by not responding. Footsteps below. Something scrambling past on the path. Something touching her foot, supporting it in one hand, reassuring fingers holding tight. The relief was slight, but wonderful. Then a familiar face appeared above her head, strong arms reached down, and she parted company from the hands below as the hands above lifted her up, clear and safe.

There were moments of confusion. Bjarni hugged her hard to his chest, his damp cloak lapping about her. Behind her she was aware of Ketil, standing near the cliff edge, calling down to someone below. She turned to look at him, but he had his eyes averted, gaze fixed somewhere down near Bjarni's feet. He gave them a wide berth, edging around them. At last, Bjarni let her go, chilling her with the sudden withdrawal of his warmth but holding her to look into her face.

'You need a hot drink. Come on,' he said, 'the Brough is closer than Einar's place. Ingibjorg will look after you.'

Sigrid opened her mouth to protest, but Ketil seemed to nod. She had no energy to argue. Leaning on Bjarni's arm, with Ketil close on her other side, she went, shivering.

It was a mark of how dazed she felt that when she saw Ragna sitting with Ingibjorg and her women, she did not at first take her in. The men handed her over like a delicate parcel, and she was aware of them hovering. Ingibjorg waved her hands to cause a cup of hot wine to appear before Sigrid, and a warm blanket wrapped her from behind. Her teeth chattered against the cup, but she managed a swallow or two, and immediately felt better. She was, she told herself, more chilled than anything. She was certainly not injured, though a quick look at her hands showed blood amongst the grass stains.

'What on earth happened?' Ingibjorg demanded, gazing past Sigrid at Ketil and Bjarni. They were not standing close to one another.

'She must have slipped off the edge of the cliff, near the stream,' said Bjarni. 'We didn't see – we were rowing past, and saw her dangling there.'

'And rescued her! Wonderful!' Ingibjorg clapped her hands. Sigrid, coming around with a degree of resentment, was amused to see Ingibjorg's daughter stare at her mother in disgust. 'How lucky you were there!'

'You both came up from below, did you?' Sigrid managed to ask.

'We did. Hrolf and Afi are bringing the boat on round the headland.'

Sigrid looked at Ketil. He nodded.

'Then it wasn't either of you that pushed me over the edge,' said Sigrid. She shut her mouth tight as her voice trembled a little. She hoped no one had noticed, but Ketil had already met her eye. 'Nor Hrolf nor Afi.'

'Pushed?' said Ragna, with a glance at Ingibjorg. She adjusted a shawl at her throat, like a chief's cloak. 'That will be the shock, Sigrid. You will have been standing far too near the edge. I've seen you there before.'

'Not so near the edge that I don't know whether or not I've been pushed,' Sigrid responded sharply. Some memory was poking at the back of her mind again. 'I'm glad to see you up and about again, Ragna.'

'Oh, yes, Mother's been improving tremendously!' said Bjarni enthusiastically.

'She's looking very healthy,' said Sigrid.

'Isn't she?' said Ingibjorg. Neither she nor her daughter looked that delighted at Ragna's company, but she was about the only woman in the Brough or Buckquoy that Ingibjorg did not think utterly beneath her.

'Is Thorfinn about?' Ketil asked.

'Oh, I'm sure Thorfinn doesn't need to be told!' said Ingibjorg. The look she was directing at Ketil could have been put to verse and recited by Snorri after several strong ales. 'Sigrid will have imagined it.'

Sigrid could still feel the bruise on her back, and was quite sure she had imagined nothing of the sort. She looked at Ketil, but he was heading for the door.

'It's not about that, although I think he should know about that, too,' he called over his shoulder, and then grunted. Sigrid turned. Ketil had almost walked into Thorfinn. 'My lord.'

'Ketil? What should I know about?' Thorfinn might have found his religion, but no one could say he had lost his wits. He advanced up the hall to where the women were sitting, his broad shoulders blocking the light from the door. Ketil looked like a slip of a boy behind him. Sigrid turned away, already feeling safer. And the wine was helpful, too.

'My lord, the man who attacked me in Kirkuvagr.'

Sigrid saw Ingibjorg's eyes flicker from one man to another.

'Yes? You've found him?'

'I have, my lord.'

Thorfinn turned and stood in front of his high chair, and gave a brief puzzled glance at the women and Sigrid wrapped in the midst of them. Then Ketil had all his attention.

'Well?'

'This man. Bjarni Hrafn.'

Sigrid felt her jaw drop. But at the same instant, she noticed Bjarni's scabbard, poking treacherously from beneath his damp cloak. The chape had been ripped off.

Ketil was speaking, Thorfinn standing with one hand out to still Bjarni as Bjarni spun to confront them. Sigrid's memories were clicking into place like weaving tablets, and the pattern they were producing was true. She looked hard at Ragna, whose eyes were only on Bjarni. That face ... the great nose, and, slipping from her headcloth, the white hair, white as the haar over the sea ...

'My lord!' Bjarni was allowed to speak. 'I cannot imagine where Ketil has this idea from! I haven't been to Kirkuvagr for weeks, and as for attacking him – well, I was coming to think of him as my friend!' He turned a plaintive look on Ketil. 'You haven't been here long, Ketil, but we've had some laughs, haven't we?'

'Whatever I think of you, Bjarni, my loyalties are to Thorfinn. And yours are not. You have been working for Kalf Arnasson, to bring down Thorfinn's rule of Orkney.'

'How could you suggest such a thing?' Bjarni's tone was full of hurt, but Ragna suddenly laughed.

'Oh, let's admit it, Bjarni! You'll say anything for an easy life! Yes, we favour Kalf – Ingibjorg's kinsman, as are we!'

'What?' Ingibjorg looked like a sheep that had walked into a wall. 'What are you talking about?'

'Your uncle Kalf, my dear,' said Thorfinn, his voice grim. 'I knew he was trouble. He could never be trusted, not even to fight when he bothered to turn up for a battle. Bjarni –'

But Bjarni did not stay to listen to whatever Thorfinn had to say. He was already through the door. Ketil spun to follow him. He reached the door, but fell back. Hrolf and Afi, looking damp and bewildered, staggered into the hall, blinking.

'Well, get after him!' Thorfinn yelled.

'After who?' said Hrolf, looking about. 'Oh, Ragna! Good to see you've improved, madam. But Bjarni just ran off down towards Buckquoy – said he'd had a message you'd taken a turn for the worse?'

'Did he go to the harbour?' Thorfinn asked urgently, not bothering with explanations.

'No, why would he do that? His boat's up for repair. Has been for days, down the bay.'

'No, it isn't,' said Thorfinn. 'I saw it myself at Skipi Geo yesterday. He's escaping!' He pushed Hrolf aside, dodged around Afi, and strode to the door, collecting Ketil on his way. But again they met an obstruction, and Thorfinn cursed at the thin young man who appeared, panting, his hands still on the reins of his horse even in the doorway.

'My lord Thorfinn!' he gasped, his voice squeaking with effort. 'My lord Thorfinn! There's a fleet off Kirkuvagr, and it's hostile!'

'Whose fleet? How many ships?' Thorfinn snapped, spinning to face him.

'Nine large ships. We think it's Kalf Arnasson, my lord!' The man was hesitant, as if he expected not to be believed. But Thorfinn stopped a moment, and turned to stare at his wife. Ingibjorg flushed, then paled, her sagging skin unhealthy. She shrugged. Thorfinn, his face agonised, turned away.

'Right, you lot, let's get the men together,' he snapped. 'Hrolf, you gather the Brough hird. Ketil, go and tell Einar we need everyone he has. Afi, make sure everyone has weapons and shields. We meet at the harbour to sail for Kirkuvagr.'

Hrolf, Ketil and Afi left, wordless. Thorfinn paused again, eyes on the flag floor. Then he said, without looking up,

'Well, wife. My armour. My shield.'

'Yes, my lord.' Ingibjorg nudged her daughter hard and the two of them disappeared into the dark recesses at the back of the hall.

Thorfinn approached the few women left.

'Well, Ragna, what did you know of all this?'

Ragna grinned and shook her head, but Sigrid was ready.

'Ragna killed the old woman down at the Loons,' she said, 'and pretended to be her when Ketil and I went to question her about the old beliefs. Then she went to Kirkuvagr, and either delayed Ketil until Kalf's followers were ready for him, or warned them he was coming. Or both.' She stopped, hoping she was right. A look at Ragna's face confirmed it. She had not expected to be so easily uncovered.

'I can see you are not arguing, Ragna,' said Thorfinn. 'Tell me, did you kill the Norwegian soldier, Herleif, too? Or did Bjarni rouse himself to do that on his own behalf?'

Ragna was unimpressed.

'We did not touch Herleif. We did not even know of his being in Orkney until you dug him up.' She tossed the last words at Sigrid, as if Sigrid were in the habit of scraping through the kinds of places you would find abandoned corpses.

'But you tried to push me off the cliff just now, didn't you?' Sigrid said suddenly.

'Push you off the cliff?' Ragna looked appalled. 'Why should I do that? You are no threat to me, or to Bjarni! And you needn't think he's going to marry you now, anyway – if he ever was.'

'He certainly isn't,' said Thorfinn. 'If he escapes my sword in the next few days, he'll be exiled. And you will go with him.'

'Not if Kalf wins,' said Ragna, too smug by half. Sigrid's hand itched to slap her. Ingibjorg appeared with Thorfinn's armour, clumsy hands removing his cloak to add the protective layer of his leather and steel byrnie. The cloak went back over it for now, and Asgerdr, trying not to show that she was struggling with its weight, handed him his shield. Thorfinn took it lightly, and looked down at Ragna.

'Lock this woman up till my return. My return, Ragna, not Kalf's. I shall not let him get away with it this time.'

TUTTUGU OK THRÍR

XXIII

Out in the broad bay before Kirkuvagr, blocking the entrance to the harbour, Kalf's great ships began to emerge, dull black hulks on the misty water. Ketil shook rain from his cloak, but kept low. The minute Thorfinn's ships appeared around the coast, keeping close to the rocky shore, he and the men from Buckquoy were to advance on Eirik's longhouse.

The mood on the ships, he knew, was tense. No one had really been expecting an out-and-out fight, and though weapons were always to hand, armour had had to be dusted off and shields dug out from kists, and down at the harbour it had been madness for a while, preparing, launching, manning the ships. Thorfinn had a dozen ready there, and had sent messages to Toun o' Firth and Hamnavoe for reinforcements, just in case. He had stood above the harbour near Einar's hall, conversing quietly with Einar, watching the men below, rounding up the last of the men above. Hrolf, Hlifolf and Ketil stood nearby, Ketil wondering, if it came to a fight, how well he would manage. Hlifolf's mind was on other things.

'My lord, this is Good Friday! Tosti, isn't it?'

'Yes, of course it is.' Tosti was small and miserable, propping himself on a light processional cross. He was more snappish than usual. Ketil recognised first-battle nerves, and edged to stand beside him.

'I trust you're not thinking of fighting on Good Friday, my lord!' Hlifolf persisted. 'It's very bad luck!'

'Hlifolf, you're a fool,' Thorfinn stated. 'If you can't find something useful to say, then save your breath for the fighting.'

Hlifolf went a little pink, and shuffled over to Ketil and Tosti. Ketil shrugged, and dropped his voice.

'You know Thorfinn's father died on Good Friday, at the battle of Clontarf.'

'Of course I know that,' said Hlifolf, even more pink. Ketil
sensed he was lying. 'That's precisely why I mentioned it. Father
Tosti, remember which way round that cross is to be carried!' He
tipped his head back, dignity restored, and marched off, back to
mutter with Hrolf. Hrolf, Ketil thought, did not seem as
sympathetic as usual.

'You're not coming with us, are you?' Ketil asked Tosti.

'Thorfinn wishes it.' If words could sound pale, Tosti's did.
'I've travelled a good bit, Ketil, and I've seen a few things, but up
to now I've – ah – I've never had the good fortune to participate in
a battle. I'm sure it will be tremendously exciting and indeed
informative.'

'Oh, always,' said Ketil solemnly. 'I've been both excited and
informed on a number of occasions. Sometimes quite violently.
Perhaps you might find it just as exciting and informative if you
take your cross off to one side and watch from a safe distance?'

'Do you know,' said Tosti with a nervous giggle, 'I believe I
should?'

Ketil glanced away, fastening off his sleeve bands, and caught
sight of Sigrid hurrying back towards Buckquoy. She seemed to
see him but did not pause, then, as if torn, she ran over quickly to
him.

'Don't want to distract you, but Ragna says they didn't kill
Herleif. Didn't know he was around.'

'Then who?'

She glared at him.

'I'll do my best. Just try to avoid any more wounds. It's better
to have more than one working limb, most of the time. Leave the
fighting to the people who can.'

She waved a hand, and disappeared towards Einar's
longhouse, leaving Ketil with his mouth open to reply.

'Still trying to defend her husband?' Tosti asked, happy to be
distracted.

'I suppose so.' Ketil was not sure. Had Ragna pushed Sigrid
over the cliff? If so, why had Bjarni rescued her?

Thorfinn grumbled about Kalf's timing as they boarded the
ships, muttering that he wanted to be back for the Easter vigil. His
face was contorted, a mixture of anger, urgency, and something

like hope. Ketil did not like to see it. He found a quiet spot and tightened the bandages over his wounds, praying they would not burst open again. In fact, he prayed for some time, first with Tosti, partly for Tosti's own comfort. Then for a while he prayed alone, deliberately, thoughtfully, then in a half-conscious stream of one or two words repeated and repeated at the back of his mind, that carried on through the rest of the journey and his preparations. He settled his scabbard against his right thigh, and rearranged his cloak over his right arm. It felt odd, draughty on his left side, but he had done it before. No shield, though: that was not a happy thought.

Darkness, the thin spring darkness, swept over the sea before they had reached Kirkuvagr, and Thorfinn kept his ships back, hidden in rain, hugging the coast, waiting for dawn. Kalf was blocking the harbour, almost within touching distance of his allies at Eirik's longhouse – and perhaps of Bjarni, too. Thorfinn had wanted them kept separate if possible: it looked as if they were too late for that, so he decided to squeeze them together instead.

While the men fox-slept in their cloaks, hands on knives, and the lookouts stared into the darkness until dripping monsters lurked in the corners of their eyes, Ketil and thirty other men, including Einar's Buckquoy forces, slipped off to the shore, landing to walk softly around the coast to huddle inland of Kirkuvagr. They were close enough that Ketil could smell the harbour, dead fish and freshly-worked wood. Were Kalf's allies all in the longhouse where he had been attacked? Or were they scattered about the town, waiting for some signal to come together? Where was Bjarni? The men from Brodir's hall, relieved and sheepish, had joined them as soon as they had appeared, glad of the reinforcements but anxiously counting heads in the dusk.

'Ships, too,' Ketil whispered, nodding out to sea. Brodir grinned, nodding. 'Any more sign of Rognvald?'

'Nothing since you were here last. Good to see you, by the way – my lad thought you didn't look well when you collected your horse, but you were dead keen to go, he says.'

'Needed to get back,' Ketil agreed. He had no wish to remember that journey back to Buckquoy.

'There must be a score or so in the longhouse, unless they're all gathered in there to wait for Kalf. Did Thorfinn know Kalf was back from the Western Isles?'

'I don't think so.'

'No, it came as a surprise here.' Brodir was in a chatty mood, maybe nervous. Raindrops lined his long hair. Ketil wondered how Tosti was feeling. 'Do you think the man we think is Rognvald is actually Kalf?'

'No. I don't think he would have risked that.' Kalf was never one to put himself in harm's way until he was sure which way the wind was blowing. 'Eirik is the right colouring, or as near as anyone is going to get, but he's far too short for Rognvald. But I think he may have contributed to the deception.'

'How do you mean? Oh, by getting people to say they'd seen him?'

'I think it was a little more material than that,' said Ketil, but his eyes were on the bay. The light was growing, and the nine great ships, a centipede of shields along each side, took on colour gradually, as if dye were leaking into cloth. A thread of peat smoke came from the longhouse by the harbour.

'Maybe they're going to have breakfast before they fight!' said Brodir, with a hint of laughter.

'Maybe they'll feed us, too!' Ketil suggested, hoping Brodir would not panic. Afi, looming out of the rain behind them like a hairy standing stone, grinned sedately. Hrolf was pale, and Ketil could see his lips moving – perhaps he, too, was praying. He had been completely withdrawn on the journey, and it was clear that Hlifolf found it odd. There had been no mention of his mysteriously unbroken ribs. Einar was still, no more substantial than a thread of the mist, watching the sea.

As the light grew, Ketil was filling in his brief memories of the settlement, the harbour's edge, the alleyways between longhouses, the middens and the animal enclosures. Open battlefields were much easier to plan for, but there was shelter here – that would work for and against them. He sensed a movement out on the water, and squinted against the mist. Thorfinn's hastily prepared fleet was appearing, slipping along the coast, edging towards Kalf's motionless ships. An instant later and a torch appeared at the prow of the nearest ship, waved back and forth three times, and vanished. And the attack began.

They had been outmanoeuvred. Eirik's men sprang from

behind them, driving them down towards the water. It took a few minutes of confusion, of running and fighting and dodging, for Ketil to realise that Kalf's supporters had needed the advantage of surprise. They were thin on the ground.

Thinner once Afi had knocked two of them together and dropped them into a midden, faces first. But Brodir was spitting blood, the back of his neck slashed by a knife. Ketil stabbed back with his own knife at the assailant and twisted when he met flesh, pulling away sharply as a screaming body fell behind him. Brodir slumped to the ground, choking, rain and blood mingling on his face. Angling himself along the wall of a darkened smithy, Ketil moved towards the harbour where Eirik's longhouse still sat shadowed and silent. His left hand familiarised itself with his sword hilt, finding the dents and ridges his right hand knew so well. The blade was already bloodied.

There was a cry, half-strangled, and Hrolf hurtled past him, wild-eyed. Ketil turned to see what he was fleeing but there was nothing: Hrolf launched himself at a black-bearded man peering round the longhouse corner, as if he had given him personal insult, hacking and stabbing furiously. Ketil met Afi's eye – the big man was equally baffled, but shrugged and moved on. Ketil was still trying to assess who was where: he had seen Eirik himself, fighting somewhere to the left. He recognised a couple of the others he had seen in the longhouse that night, before he was attacked. But others were missing. Where were they? Behind them, stalking them? Off on the ships with Kalf? Or still in the longhouse?

The threads of smoke had faded and the longhouse was lifeless. The open space before it seemed miles across. Ketil lingered, assessing the distance, the proximity of other fights and who in them had the upper hand. Hrolf had destroyed his opponent and flung himself into a fight between Einar and a couple of Eirik's men, nearly as much danger to Einar as to the others. Was anyone available to back Ketil up? Not really, but the house had to be investigated. He took a deep breath, and stepped out from his shelter.

As if drawn back by some giant hand, the mist lifted. The sun burst through the shreds and glistened, just over the roof of the longhouse, blinding him. And a figure appeared, light dancing on golden hair and steady blade, and stood, easy and glorious, in the centre of the open ground.

Ketil blinked rapidly, and found he was holding his breath. Surely it could not be?

His face was in shadow. Ketil stared so hard he only barely registered the figures running behind him from the longhouse – the rest of Kalf's, or Eirik's, or Rognvald's hird. There were plenty of them: now Thorfinn's men were outnumbered. He heard cries and renewed beating of swords and shields. How well prepared were the men from the Brough and Buckquoy? Perhaps more than he was, Sigrid would tell him.

But the figure in the open space was not content with standing looking splendid. He beat his sword upon his shield, one sharp thud, calling for attention. A voice rang out.

'Oh, this is not good enough! Where is Sigurd's son? Where is my uncle Thorfinn?' He spun on his heel, surveying the place. 'Find Uncle Thorfinn!' he called with authority. 'Tell him it's past time for revenge!'

Ketil stepped forward, his sword at the ready, his feet light on the sandy ground. He knew that voice.

'Earl Thorfinn Sigurdarson is not here. He is where he should be, on his ship. Whatever help you expected from Kalf Arnarson, expect it no longer.'

The golden-haired man laughed. Ketil blinked again. It was strange to hear that recently familiar voice coming from a figure he had not seen since he had buried Rognvald Brusason. He knew he had buried Rognvald. This was not Rognvald.

'Thorfinn will come! He will not be able to keep away! He hates himself for killing me: he will not be able to resist the hope that I am still alive!'

'That hair,' said Ketil, turning his sword in his left hand, trying not to draw attention to it, 'I suppose it was Eirik's, originally? I noticed he'd had a close shave.'

'I don't want to fight you, Ketil,' said the figure dismissively. 'I want to fight Thorfinn. I want to beat him in a fair fight.'

'So that you can become Earl, Bjarni?'

Bjarni snatched the mat of golden hair off his head, revealing the black raven wing of his own hair. The golden crown went spinning high, catching the light, only to land ignominiously over the smoke hole of the longhouse roof. Loose threads glittered as they waved in the warm air.

'There's no reason why not. Not with Kalf's help.'

'And why would Kalf help you?'

'He's my kinsman. Our kinsman. Ingibjorg and Kalf and Ragna my mother – all kin.'

'Ingibjorg, though. Ingibjorg is married to Thorfinn – surely Kalf won't act against Thorfinn?' It was a stupid question – Kalf only acted for Kalf, and he had hurt Thorfinn before. But Ketil was playing for time. He knew his strength was limited, and Bjarni was an excellent swordsman. And he treated the question with the contempt it deserved.

'Kalf has never been interested in following Thorfinn. Thorfinn should go back to Caithness, and his precious Scottish grandfather, and leave Orkney alone.'

'An interesting idea. Yet Thorfinn's father was Earl – ' He broke off as Bjarni lunged at last. It was almost a relief.

As far as he could tell, no one else was paying them any attention. It was a shame, in a way: Bjarni had a glittering look in his eye, just on the edge of madness, that said he would probably enjoy an audience. And that an audience would distract him.

Ketil was still hopeful, though. After a few thrusts and parries, Bjarni muttered,

'Oh, but you're not left-handed, are you?' Ketil would have expected him to remember, particularly as they had fought twice before. Any good warrior would, and in normal circumstances, Bjarni was indeed a good warrior.

As he now showed, by using Ketil's injuries against him, as much as he could.

He drove Ketil backwards with a few neat, sharp jabs, and Ketil's feet found uneven ground, a bank of weeds and grass at the foot of a wall. He winced, doing his best to hide it, as his injured leg took the strain, but the bandages held. He pushed himself back off the wall at a good angle to slip out under Bjarni's sword, turning the fight so that Bjarni faced into the wet sunlight.

It was Bjarni's turn to wince. Ketil had caught his thigh on the way past, slicing through his breeches and a good nail-depth of flesh. Blood oozed. Ketil snatched his chance and, spinning, cracked his sword hilt down between Bjarni and his shield, jarring the fingers open. The shield fell with a thud and rolled under their feet, causing them both to stumble. Bjarni drove his elbow into Ketil's right side, aiming for his injured arm, and stepped back to draw his knife with his shield hand.

Ketil swore inwardly, wishing he could trust his right arm. Two blades against his one was a challenge he could do without. But Bjarni seemed wary, nevertheless. A patch on his right leg was sodden dark with blood, and Ketil wondered if he was letting the pain affect him. Or he was letting Ketil believe he was, luring Ketil into an attack for which Bjarni was more than ready. Bjarni's eyes were still bright and alert: he was fresh, not tiring at all. Ketil could feel both his arm and his leg like logs, not quick to his command, potentially fatal flaws. But, facing Bjarni, he could not afford to think that way.

Bjarni was pushing forward again, gently, almost imperceptibly. What was behind Ketil? Oh, yes: Eirik's longhouse, with the cooking fire lit. Ketil had no happy memories of fighting in there. And if Bjarni was keen to try it, more than likely he had some reason, or at least an ally or two lying in wait. A trap for Thorfinn, no doubt, but just as easily allowed to close around Ketil. After all, a trap could catch more than one victim.

Ketil let himself be pushed, but very slightly changed his position so that he was backing to a point somewhere away from the longhouse door. He had no wish to be pinned against the wall, either, but it would give him more room for dodging than a hostile doorway. But if he dodged again now, he would look weak, as if he were allowing Bjarni to chase him around. He needed to leave this position on his own terms.

He allowed himself a moment to take stock. Ahead, he could see Afi doing something nasty to Eirik, while the big man with the oiled hair who had threatened him that night was heading purposefully towards the harbour. Hrolf ran past like a berserker, crimson sword flying. By contrast, two of Thorfinn's men lay with their guts spilling out over a low wall, one of them moving spasmodically. Ketil thought they were on the whole winning, but that did not mean he was not on his own here. Bjarni, fortunately, seemed to think he could handle Ketil without help, too.

Ketil glanced again to one side, looking as if he might be considering which way to dodge. Then without noticeably drawing breath, he hurled himself forwards, straight between Bjarni's two blades.

Bjarni was quick, but having a left-handed opponent was clearly throwing him. His hands seemed to disagree over which one should parry Ketil's blow, and he ended up taking it on his left forearm. Ketil's sword slit through the sleeve bindings but somehow failed to go further. He managed to tangle his right hand in the loose bindings, tugging and swinging back, and jerked the knife from Bjarni's grip. Bjarni's fingers must still have been bruised from losing his shield earlier: he shook them hard, blinking, but his sword was ready.

Bjarni slashed and struck, and Ketil parried, unable for the moment to push on. They were close, very close – too close to fight sensibly. Then Bjarni surged forward, spinning his blade across to swipe Ketil's sword from his hand and drive him back, too fast. Ketil's foot slipped, and he fell.

The ground slapped his back and took his breath away. Bjarni surged above him, taking a second to breathe, knowing Ketil was going nowhere. Where was Ketil's sword? His head scraped on the ground as he tried to see it. Oh, of course: off to his right. His right arm lay just clear of it, but he could not get it to move.

Bjarni gave a breathless laugh, pleased with himself. He lifted his own sword, prepared to enjoy the moment.

Ketil closed his eyes. Then he writhed sideways like an eel, all the movement in his shoulders. His reluctant fingers closed on the sword hilt. He grabbed it, and swung.

Pain exploded behind his eyes, in the depths of his arm. Pain in his ribcage, too, as Bjarni's weight fell hard on top of him. The rasp of blade on bone echoed for a moment, and was gone, replaced by a deep, desperate gurgle.

TUTTUGU OK FJÓRIR

XXIV

Sigrid and Rannveig watched, blank-faced, as the men from Buckquoy and the Brough disappeared down towards the harbour. Hrolf and Hlifolf, solemnly nodding encouragement to the younger warriors; Tosti bearing a thin cross, almost visibly shaking; Afi cheerful, chatting to his neighbour; Ketil quite calm, though still favouring one leg. Sigrid was praying, silently but fervently, while her mind was whirling. Should she pray for Bjarni, too? She was hardly ready to think about him at all yet. When he had rescued her, she would have married him on the spot – well, maybe – but if he was a traitor, and a trickster … and a murderer, too? Ragna said they had not killed Herleif. Thorfinn had not yet asked her about Snorri. But who else would be murdering these people? If Ragna had spoken the truth, then was there someone else in alliance with them who had known what Herleif knew, who had wanted to prevent Thorfinn knowing?

But wait, she thought, as the last man followed his companions down the harbour path. Wait. Why would Ragna and Bjarni, or anyone involved in spreading that rumour of Rognvald's return, why would they want to prevent Thorfinn knowing about it? The whole point of the rumour was to have it spread to as many people as possible, and to Thorfinn in particular, to cause uncertainty, dismay, hope … No one who knew Herleif was there to tell Thorfinn about the rumour should have wanted to kill him. It defeated the object entirely.

Rannveig moved and broke the spell, blew her nose and nudged Sigrid.

'What about a cup of wine?'

Sigrid nodded. Another cup would not go amiss. She shifted her shoulders as she walked after Rannveig. Now that the shock had worn off, her neck and arms ached. And as for her hands …

she held them out in front of her. The thin grass cuts stung viciously. Working with wool would not be comfortable for a few days – yet another interruption to her business. She put the thought aside.

So Herleif had been killed for some other reason. Well, she thought, making herself face facts once more, Thorstein could have done it. He could have met Herleif by chance, quarrelled with him – she should know, more than anyone, how Thorstein could find a quarrel under a pebble – and killed him, and scared to tell Sigrid or anyone else Thorstein buried the stranger in the gully. But what about the eagle? And why bury him at all? Why not just leave him, or roll him over the edge into the sea?

And now she knew that Helga and Herleif had been lovers, the idea of Thorstein picking a random fight, the mystery of the eagle, could be tucked once again into the back of her mind. Surely this was a much more interesting proposition, much more likely. Helga had said so confidently that Hrolf had not known about Herleif, but perhaps she was wrong? After all, Hrolf had quite a temper, too: she remembered with a shudder how he had attacked Snorri at Thorfinn's supper. It was well for Hrolf that his ribs had been broken, or he would certainly have been the first in line to be blamed for Snorri's death. But if she could find out that he definitely knew about Herleif … well then, that would be something worth telling Thorfinn. And Ketil.

She shook herself. She was thinking about condemning her best friend's husband. A man she didn't like much, true, but still Helga's husband. And if he were to be exiled, Helga would probably have to go too, losing her not only a friend but also a valued customer – and she supposed that Ragna would not be commissioning much tablet weaving from her now, either. Could she ever really have married Bjarni and been taken into Ragna's household? She felt as if she had been sleepwalking into it. In that case, she had had a very lucky escape.

But what if – what might happen at Kirkuvagr? Would Kalf attack Thorfinn? Would he dare? Sigrid had never thought much of Kalf, always slipping on to the winning side as soon as he had worked out which it was. If he did attack, surely Thorfinn would win. But Thorfinn had been taken by surprise, and they had no way of knowing how many men might be ready in Kirkuvagr, waiting for Bjarni to help in the fight. Kirkuvagr had always been Rognvald's stronghold. If there was still sympathy for him in the islands, it would be there. But of course Rognvald was dead. Would they really fight for Kalf?

She found herself sitting opposite Rannveig at the longhouse fire, not really aware of walking there. Rannveig's face reflected the kind of thoughts, the confusion, that Sigrid was suffering. Maybe they should talk about it. Rannveig was always sensible. As if she heard her thoughts, Rannveig looked over.

'It's always the worst time, isn't it? When they leave? It's fine for them, I mean: they're as cheery as boys with their first cup of strong wine. But we're the ones left with the hangovers.'

'I thought Einar wasn't going to fight any more?' Sigrid asked tentatively, hoping she was not stepping on sensitive ground.

'Well, when Thorfinn asks … you know? It's not so easy to say no. And it's one thing to go raiding, I suppose, and another to help defend Thorfinn's lands.'

'I suppose so, yes.' She hesitated. Rannveig was clearly worried about something. 'Do you think he's going to be all right?'

Rannveig looked up from her wine cup in surprise.

'Einar? Oh, yes, I should think so. After all, no warrior reaches Einar's age without some idea of the best way to get through a skirmish.' But there was something there, all the same, Sigrid was sure. She knew that Rannveig had been particularly careful of Einar recently. Did she think, perhaps, that Einar was growing confused? That he might not indeed remember the best way to get through a skirmish?

Well, whatever it was, she was sure Rannveig would deal with it without her help. Rannveig always managed everything well. And it was comfortable, sitting here in her warm longhouse, sipping wine, but Sigrid reminded herself that she had work to do – and she could make a small start right away.

'I didn't see Helga come to wave Hrolf off,' she said. 'Is she all right, do you think? Did Hrolf mention anything?' She tried to keep friendly concern uppermost in her tone. Rannveig raised her graceful eyebrows and shrugged.

'No, I don't think so. Perhaps there was something with one of the bairns?' She reflected for a moment. 'It's a funny thing, though: Hrolf did look nervous. Well, you know what he and

Hlifolf are like: before heading off to anything at all dangerous they like to put on a swagger – I doubt it lasts into the battle. But Hrolf was quiet today, wasn't he?'

Sigrid nodded, thoughtful. Her back and shoulders ached still, in spite of the wine. Had Helga really pushed her? That smell of rosemary … Perhaps Hrolf used it too. But Hrolf had been down in the boat below the cliffs. He could not have pushed Sigrid off, whereas Helga could easily have followed her in the haar along the cliff path and taken her chance. She would have to go and speak with her, however comfortable she might feel here by the fire.

The sea to the north was only hinted at ahead of her as she walked back towards her own longhouse from Einar's hall. She wondered if Gnup had found food and drink to sustain himself through the day, and thought he would probably be all right. Gnup usually was. She was lucky to have him: the farm would have gone to wrack this last while if he had not been there to work it. But what would happen to Gnup if Bjarni and Ragna were exiled? Would he have to go too? The thought appalled her: she was used to Gnup. She knew it would appal Gnup even more.

She glanced at her longhouse, then up in surprise at the roof. Smoke was seeping from the smoke hole under the ridge. If Gnup was cooking, she had better make sure all was well: she had never seen him cook, but her absence must have driven him to it. She hurried up to the door, sniffing the air for a burning smell.

She stopped. There was a figure crouched at the fire, but it was not Gnup.

She took two paces into her own house, and the figure heard her, and turned. It was Helga.

The bruise on Sigrid's back throbbed once, hard, as if in warning. Helga's eyes were dark and huge and she kept them focussed on Sigrid. Sigrid found she could not move.

'I started your fire again,' said Helga at last, her light voice sounding unreal. 'I hope you don't mind. I was cold.'

She had no cloak on, nor even a shawl, and her arms were folded tight around her as she crouched. Sigrid was suddenly reminded of Herleif's body, curled on its side in the tawny earth. She knew Thorstein would never have gone to all that trouble. Thorstein had not killed Herleif. But Helga could have. Everyone carried a knife. Herleif would presumably have trusted her. A lovers' quarrel? Had he threatened to leave? Or rejected her? Helga liked to have what Helga wanted. But to kill for it?

Well, if she had, she had tried to kill again. That swirl of rosemary scent ... and here she was in Sigrid's longhouse. Was Sigrid going to end up in the gully, too? Funny, she thought, the idea of that gully being her last resting place was somehow worse than the thought of death itself. She wished she had taken the time to say more to Ketil before he left, to tell him what Helga had told her. Stupid of her: she had been thinking about Ragna and Bjarni, about what had just happened on the Brough. She should have said. Now, if she disappeared or was found dead, no one would be any the wiser. Stupid, stupid.

Sigrid swallowed, more noisily than she liked, and tried to remember what Helga had just said. Something about the fire ...

'Oh, yes,' she said, her words creaking. 'Of course.' She stepped up on to the bed platform so that she could pass Helga's huddled form without going too close. She could not see Helga's hands. But this was her friend, something was telling her. Her friend. She could not be a killer, and if she were, then surely there was a good reason? Herleif could have attacked her? But then she could just have gone to Einar and reported it. Unless ...

'Did Herleif attack you, Helga?'

'What?'

'I was just wondering ... did Herleif arrange to meet you, and then attack you, and you didn't want to tell Einar Herleif was dead because then you'd have to tell Hrolf you'd gone to meet him? Herleif, I mean?' The words tumbled out over the fire, so that she had the odd impression the flames should have wavered with their clumsy weight. Helga's eyes gaped.

'What are you talking about, Sigrid?' She looked baffled.

'About Herleif's death. Are you sure you don't know who killed him?' She made herself squat down at the side of the fire, not far away. Helga was holding her hands out to the heat, and Sigrid could see that her knife was, as usual, attached to the brooch on her shoulder. No immediate threat. Sigrid wondered if her heart would realise that before it burst out of her chest.

Helga had not replied. She stared into the fire, and the flames flickered in reflection in her extraordinary eyes. Her face was white, that dead white that sometimes goes with red hair, but not usually on Helga's healthy skin. She looked ill. Sigrid resisted the temptation to reach over and touch her arm.

'Helga?'

'I was sure,' she said, wretchedly. 'I was sure. If you'd asked me earlier, I'd have been sure. But now ...'

'What's happened?'

There was another silence. Sigrid held her breath.

'You know the men have gone to Kirkuvagr? Did you hear? Something about Bjarni ... I didn't understand. Hrolf came back home for his sword and shield and said ... But why would they be fighting Bjarni?'

Sigrid felt they were wandering off course, but she kept her peace with difficulty, not responding. There would be time later to explain what Bjarni had done, when Thorfinn held him to account. If Thorfinn catches him and defeats Kalf, came a little voice – but the other outcome did not bear thinking about. Sigrid put it to the back of her mind, and focussed on Helga.

'Hrolf came back for his sword ...' she prompted, taking Helga back to the last apparently relevant point.

Helga drew a deep breath.

'Hrolf came back for his sword and shield,' she repeated. 'And I'd been thinking about what we'd been talking about when you came with the braid. About Herleif, you know.'

'Yes ...'

'And ... well, I accidentally told him.'

'You accidentally told him?' Sigrid struggled to imagine it. 'Do you mean you told him about you and Herleif? Or you told him that you had told me?'

'Well ... both,' said Helga miserably. 'The thing is, I think telling him I'd told you was worse. He was – well, he went very strange. He actually pushed me out of his way. And – and he swore at me.'

Sigrid suddenly thought she knew why Helga still cared for Hrolf. Pushing out of the way and swearing would have been a mild day, with Thorstein. Maybe Helga was luckier than Sigrid had ever realised.

'I was wondering,' Helga went on, unaware of Sigrid's thoughts, 'if maybe he really had known already? About me and Herleif?'

Which was the point at which Sigrid decided Helga didn't need sympathy – she needed shaking.

There had been no point in even asking Helga if she had tried to push Sigrid off the cliff. It was clear that her mind had been on other things ever since Sigrid had left her. Sigrid shook her head as Helga, wrapped in a borrowed shawl, disappeared back into the haar to her own longhouse, furnished as Sigrid herself had been earlier with a cup of hot wine. Now what? If Hrolf had known about Herleif, then he was the most likely killer. Again, she thought of telling Ketil – but Ketil and Hrolf were in Kirkuvagr. Then a thought struck her. Hrolf had been the one to stab Ketil in the calf. Had that really been an accident? Had he been trying for something more serious? Or had he, perhaps, just been warning Ketil off growing close to Helga, too? She shook her head, and returned to the fire. The cat, abandoning the corpse of a mouse outside, came and joined her, licking its whiskers. It never felt the need to go reporting its killings, or to bury its dead in odd fashions. If the cat had come across a dead eagle it would simply have picked out the best bits and eaten them.

'But Herleif liked birds … Well, cat,' she said aloud, 'I need to talk to Ketil. Or rather, I think, I need to talk to someone. Helga is obviously not that person. I need someone intelligent – not you, though, I think, as you can't answer back. Though maybe that's a good thing. Hm.' She considered. 'No, I need someone else's opinion, that's what I need.'

But at that point, the door slammed shut. She jumped up, suddenly aware of the sharp rise in the wind. That must be why the cat had come in so readily before dusk. She hurried to fasten the door before it caught the wind again, but it was snatched from her hands. Gnup belted in, accompanied by what felt like a bucketful of rain. The weather had turned.

'Freezing!' cried Gnup, holding out blue hands. Sigrid resigned herself to cooking, and took him over to warm by the fire.

She had tossed about in her bed all night. The heather had never seemed so prickly, nor the furs so determined to bundle themselves in corners, and her head and shoulders were solid with pain. Gnup had stayed, the weather his excuse, though what he might have been going home to with neither Bjarni nor Ragna there was a good question. She had not plucked up the courage to discuss it with him, but he seemed to know what had happened. She was not sure, but she doubted that Bjarni and Ragna had his sympathies.

The wind had blown itself out by morning, but the rain had greater stamina. Sigrid looked at the wool she had spun to nailbind a hat for Gnup, but for once it had no appeal for her. She had gone over, once again, from the perspective of knowing their guilt, all she had seen and heard of Bjarni and Ragna over the last weeks. Bjarni's seeming attachment to her, probably false; Ragna's illness, just when she and Ketil wanted to talk to her – but how could she have known they were heading her way? All the old woman had said, down at the Loons, now to be re-examined in the light of it being Ragna talking. No wonder she had known so much about Buckquoy gossip. Had she known what to do with the old woman's herbs to make the fire produce that strange smoke? That did surprise Sigrid. Ragna had never been much of a woman to make salves and medicines. In fact, having the skills to make herself deliberately, carefully sick - Sigrid would have thought that beyond her. Sigrid herself had some knowledge of plants – not as good as Helga or Rannveig, but enough certainly to know how to dye wool or linen – and she would not have been confident with an emetic, not to time it perfectly, anyway. And, she suddenly remembered, there had been that instant of fear in Ragna's eye when she stood, just the moment before she vomited. Did she think she might perhaps have got it wrong?

Yes, she needed to talk all this over with someone intelligent. And when it came to intelligence in Buckquoy, Rannveig was the obvious choice. Sigrid tucked her headcloth and cloak around her, bade goodbye to Gnup, and headed down to Einar's place.

Einar's place was quiet. Of course, the men were not back: no one would have expected it yet. If, as seemed likely, they had planned a dawn raid, they would probably still be fighting. Yet there seemed to be very few women about, either. Rannveig usually had her team of brewers and dairy workers busy about the place. Perhaps there had been some work planned on the fields or with the sheep that the women were now doing in place of the absent men. Sigrid hoped Rannveig herself had not gone, too.

But Rannveig was in the longhouse, clearing up alone after breakfast. She did not seem to have fed many people, either.

'Sigrid.' Rannveig did not rush to offer hospitality. Indeed, if anything she looked disappointed when she saw who had just come in. But Sigrid needed help.

'Have you time to talk, Rannveig? I'm trying to sort out everything that's happened recently. I didn't sleep, thinking about it all.'

'I thought you and Ketil were dealing with that,' said Rannveig, a slight twist of a smile on her lips.

'Well, he's not here, obviously.'

'No, of course.' Rannveig sat back, wiping her wet hands and leaving the soapstone dishes to drip. She nodded to a place on the bed platform, and Sigrid took a seat. 'What's bothering you?'

'The main thing,' said Sigrid, trying to sort out her thoughts, 'is that Ragna said they hadn't killed Herleif – Ketil's man in the gully.'

'Perhaps they didn't,' said Rannveig reasonably.

'I don't think they did. It doesn't make sense for them to kill him, even if they knew he was around. They wanted the rumours of Rognvald's return to spread, to reach Thorfinn. Killing Herleif only slowed that down.'

'Then she was telling the truth.'

'Then who did kill him?'

'Ah.' Rannveig met her eye. 'I see your point.' She glanced towards the door.

'And the other thing is,' said Sigrid, 'I don't think Ragna and Bjarni were working on their own.'

'Well, no. Obviously there are people in Kirkuvagr.'

'I know, but I think there was someone else helping them here. Otherwise – well ...' Would it take too long to explain about Ragna's well-timed vomiting?

'One of those daughters? What are their names again?'

'I have no idea,' said Sigrid, and they both laughed. Rannveig glanced at the door.

'Can I get you a cup of wine?' she asked. 'I think this talk might take a while.'

'That's what I was thinking,' Sigrid agreed. 'Yes, please!'

Rannveig went to a hanging shelf and poured wine into a cup, fumbling at it. Sigrid wondered if Rannveig had slept badly, too. The wine might send them both to sleep, she thought, taking a deep draught.

Someone thumped the door, and Rannveig jumped up as if someone had poked her with a knife. Heavy footsteps sounded on the flags outside. Something made Sigrid stand to see what was happening.

An old man, familiar from the Brough, entered, his sword sheathed. She relaxed a little. With his one arm, he drew Ragna into the house. Close behind her was a boy with his knife drawn, an anxious look on his spotty face.

'Here we are, Rannveig,' said the man, nodding to her. 'Ingibjorg sends her thanks. As you know, the usual cell is being rebuilt, so she says it's been – awful awkward.' Clearly those had not been Ingibjorg's exact words, but the man was being diplomatic. A small smug smile squirmed across Ragna's face.

'We'll keep her secure here until Thorfinn comes back,' Rannveig reassured the man. 'Thank you for bringing her. Will you take some ale? There's plenty in the hall across the way - help yourselves.'

The man had obviously heard about Rannveig's ale. He grabbed the boy by the shoulder and vanished from the house, relief in his broad grin. In the longhouse, suddenly, there was silence.

'Take a seat, Ragna,' said Rannveig at last.

'What's she doing here?' Ragna asked, nodding at Sigrid. Sigrid's heart began to beat sharply.

'She came to talk,' said Rannveig.

'She can talk all she likes,' said Ragna, establishing herself by the fire. 'I assume the wine is drugged.'

'Of course. I'm not sure what you would do without my drugs,' said Rannveig. Sigrid looked at her blearily. She felt a sudden urge to sit down again.

'Yes, dear, you're very useful,' said Ragna, as if Rannveig was a mere girl. 'You're not going to kill her, are you?'

'No, no,' said Rannveig. Her voice seemed to come from a very long way away. Sigrid felt dizzy. 'She'll sleep till we get clear, down to Kirkuvagr.'

'I don't think Bjarni would like her killed. Even if he's made his choice elsewhere.'

Rannveig's face came abruptly into her vision, a pleased expression on it. She seemed to be staring into Sigrid's eyes, but for some reason Sigrid found it hard to stare back. Her eyes were closing. She should really have had more sleep before coming here. She felt very confused.

'And of course, when you marry Bjarni, you will do what he and I want you to,' Ragna was continuing somewhere, with her usual helping of self-satisfaction. Sigrid almost laughed. The new look that passed over Rannveig's face said something very different. Maybe they were less friendly than they had suddenly appeared? What was going on? Rannveig had drugged her. The thought gave her a moment's clarity. Rannveig said she wasn't going to die, but Rannveig was clever – and careful. Oh, God. Was she dying? She thought she struggled, but maybe she had not moved at all. Her limbs felt as if they belonged to someone else.

'Right,' said Rannveig, and her voice echoed in Sigrid's head, 'she won't be going anywhere for a while, and those two guards will soon be out of it. We'd better get moving. The horses are ready behind the hall.'

She seemed to grow smaller. Ragna moved somewhere. The fire diminished somehow, and the longhouse fell silent. And a great darkness billowed into Sigrid's tired head, and she knew no more.

TUTTUGU OK FIMM

XXV

Ketil lay still, panting, pushing the agony back into its place. He closed his eyes against the brightness of the sky above him, then began the awkward task of pulling himself out from under Bjarni's corpse.

Eirik was dead, his skull split by an axe blow wielded by the man with the oiled hair – his hair was now spiking out in an interesting shape and covered in clinging dust. He gave Ketil a nod that seemed to say 'Aye, well, but I still have my eye on you, right?' Ketil nodded back, finding his neck was stiff. He refused to look at his arm.

Eirik's corpse was laid out beside Bjarni's near the longhouse. Ketil thought Thorfinn would probably want to take Bjarni back to Buckquoy, but Eirik would be buried here, where there was a little chapel. It had been built by Rognvald: it seemed appropriate. Three or four more of Eirik's men were being held in the longhouse itself, guarded by some of Thorfinn's men. Ketil glanced up: Bjarni's golden wig, tossed so casually up on to the roof, seemed to have lost its lustre.

Einar, a dutiful ghost, was kneeling in prayer over the corpses of Thorfinn's men, laid out a little away from Kalf's supporters. Hlifolf stood by him, head bowed in self-conscious piety, gleaming sword propped before him. Ketil wondered if he had used it at all. Hrolf was sitting against the midden wall where Thorfinn's men had died, wiping his own sword with a handful of grass, a curious look of despair across his face. His strange rage during the battle had vanished: he was a diminished figure.

'Does he do that a lot?' Ketil asked, nodding at him. Afi glanced back.

'Berserker? He has a temper, but I've never seen him do that before. He's a careful man in battle.' He winked at Ketil: for 'careful' Ketil should take 'cowardly'. It was what Ketil would have expected. Hrolf had been acting very oddly.

Ketil and Afi were now standing by the harbour, trying to work out what was happening out to sea. Thorfinn's ships were hanging back, perhaps saving themselves until Kalf's ships might surge into the harbour so his men could land to fight Thorfinn's men in Kirkuvagr. But Kalf's ships were not moving, either, prows dipping and lifting gently like cattle grazing without urgency.

'Why does Thorfinn not go on and sink the bastard?' Afi asked, without rancour.

'It's his wife's uncle. It puts him in an awkward position.'

Afi nodded thoughtfully.

'Aye, you don't want to go against the wife. Otherwise where would your farm be when you're off on a raid? Aye, aye, he's right to hang back,' he added generously. Ketil wondered what Afi's wife was like, to be able to manage him like that. 'Aye, but look, Kalf's off!'

They blinked out at the sea. Afi was right: Kalf's ships, oars out, were turning. But they were not turning towards Thorfinn's ships. Instead, almost politely, they slipped one by one past Thorfinn's fleet, keeping to the east, so close to the coast they must have scraped the rocks by the Bay of Weyland. As they grew more distant, Afi mumbled, but Thorfinn seemed to have no inclination to pursue them. Instead, his ships turned too, gliding quickly towards Kirkuvagr's harbour. It was only minutes before Thorfinn himself was jumping ashore.

'Well?' he said at once.

Ketil, with a glance at Einar's continued prayers, reported quickly, helped by Afi's affable input. Thorfinn was already striding towards the longhouse to assure himself, presumably, that his enemies were truly dead this time. Conscious of that, Ketil tentatively pointed out the golden hair on the roof. Thorfinn called for a long stick, and soon the hair was flicked down on to the sandy ground. Thorfinn poked it with his foot, scowling.

'Kalf fled, of course, as soon as he saw things were not going his way.' He spat. The spittle caught on the golden hair, and he kicked it over to lie beside Eirik and Bjarni, the hair that had been cut from one and worn by the other. Tosti, who was dutifully seeing to Kalf's dead, made a face. 'Better send the prisoners off to join him, I suppose.'

'Where's he going, my lord?' asked Afi.

'Back to the Western Isles, I suppose. Or to Norway, to see if the King's forgiven him this time. Let him run, for now. I want to get back to my new church. The Easter vigil is tonight. Tosti, you'd better start hearing confessions as we sail back.'

Tosti, tucked up in the prow of Thorfinn's greatest ship, was busy as the men made their way to him one by one, taking turns at the oars. Even though they tried not to listen, the litany of killing and maiming, and occasional other muttered sins, flowed back over the ships, whispering into all their ears, echoing their own words. When Ketil himself confessed to killing first an unknown man, then Bjarni, Tosti's fingers tightened in prayer, his face flushed with emotion.

Everyone was quiet. Hrolf stared out to sea. Hlifolf was cleaning his knife, a neatly shaped one with a leaf-pattern handle. Bjarni's confession and escape, and their rush after him and the skirmish at Kirkuvagr, had kept all their minds busy. Now, cooling from the heat of battle in the fresh breeze of Eynhallow Sound, they had time to reflect on the man who had been their friend and sword-brother. Shock set in, and in one or two faces there was a hint of hostility towards Ketil. Had he been sure, before killing Bjarni? Had he been sure? But others, by contrast, slapped Ketil on the shoulder (remembering, mostly, to keep to his left), acknowledging his difficulties, pleased, to an extent, that he who had not known Bjarni so well had relieved them, his erstwhile companions, of the task. Ketil said nothing. He was not sure what he could reasonably say. The soothing sigh of the wind, the rhythm of the oars and the faint whispering of atonement conspired, and soon the ships were soft with the snoring of those lucky enough not to be rowing. The oarsmen were for the most part kind, and let them sleep.

Thorfinn did not sleep. Ketil watched him, dark and stern, his brow drawn in thought. He would be considering what to do about Kalf, what to do with Ragna and her daughters. Ragna, though, had told Sigrid she had not killed Herleif, and Sigrid seemed convinced. So the mystery remained, even if the main challenge had been met. Ketil wondered if he would ever get back to Norway. Should he offer to follow Kalf, to speak up against him in

Thorfinn's defence? Would Thorfinn even consider it necessary, though? The King of Norway would not have difficulty in remembering what a slippery customer Kalf had always been in the past. He would hesitate to trust him now, whatever he might think about Thorfinn himself.

The wind had dropped by the time the land passing them began to look familiar. Ketil looked up to the cliffs and saw a figure in a headcloth, huddled against the rain, watching them go by. Sigrid? His heart skipped, remembering Sigrid's fall yesterday. But no, when he looked more closely he was sure it was not. In fact, it seemed to be Helga: there was a child by her side, and she was waving to the ships. Ketil glanced around for Hrolf. Hrolf was slumped in the next ship, just visible, staring ahead, not rowing. Ketil roused himself and waved back, hoping to reassure Helga before she drifted backwards and out of sight.

The ships rounded the head of the landspit with practised ease, skimming across the dimpled water. Gannets on the cliffs spread their wings in welcome, fierce-eyed sulas glared, and kitticks rattled. The Brough swelled above them. As they came about the final point, Ketil held his breath and Thorfinn tensed: would Kalf have taken his ships around the east of the mainland, through Scapa Flow and up to the Brough's neat harbour? No: he could not possibly have reached it before them, and look, the harbour was empty of warships. Thorfinn's little fleet came ashore, and the men, weary, slid out on to the sand, helping to haul the boats high up the beach. Einar wavered, and his face was exhausted. Thorfinn nodded to him, and caught Ketil's eye: the war party split, with the Brough men heading back with Thorfinn and Einar's men following him back up to Buckquoy. Ketil kept a close eye on Einar, stumbling up the path before him, but the old man – he suddenly seemed old – made it to the top without falling.

At the top of the path, Helga was waiting, along with some of the other women. Ketil glanced around. No sign of Sigrid, but perhaps she was off trying to find out more about Ragna and Herleif.

'Where's Rannveig?' asked Einar suddenly.

'Is everything all right?' Helga demanded. 'What happened? Where's Hrolf?'

'Hrolf's here,' said Ketil. 'He's fine: he fought bravely, and I don't think he's wounded.' He did not add 'but he's not himself, either'. Helga would notice that soon enough. Ketil saw Hrolf arrive with Hlifolf at the top of the path, and raise a hand to salute his wife, but his eyes looked glazed. Was he ill? Ketil was not sure.

'Where's Rannveig?' Einar asked again. Helga, drawing back from Hrolf with a puzzled face, turned to him.

'I knocked on the longhouse door when I came down here, to tell her I'd seen the ships pass. There's no one there, though. She must be out in the fields somewhere.'

'No one at all?'

'Well, I didn't look in every neuk!' Helga laughed, a little nervously. Einar looked stern. 'But the fire was tamped down, and no one came when I called. One of the beds had the curtains drawn: I looked, in case she was lying down sick, but it was empty.'

Einar, finding some reserve of energy, pulled himself upright and strode over to his longhouse. Hrolf and Hlifolf, Ketil and Afi followed, with Helga trotting to keep up. Einar flung open the door and paused before stepping inside. He called Rannveig's name, but there was no reply.

'Dairy?' offered Hlifolf. Hrolf said nothing, and he and Helga did not quite touch as they stood in the doorway. 'Brewery?'

Einar turned and left the longhouse, his long paces taking him quickly to each outbuilding in turn. As they passed the pig sty, Ketil felt a shiver pass over his shoulders as the memory of Snorri's chewed corpse came to his mind. Reluctantly, telling himself there would be nothing there, he stepped closer to the wall and looked over.

Sigrid was lying on the muddy ground, her headcloth askew, hair escaping, gown rucked up, bare legs filthy. Ketil did not remember crying out, but the others were with him in a moment.

'She's breathing,' snapped Ketil. He said it, but he did not quite believe it.

'We'll get her out,' said Einar, with uncharacteristic efficiency. He nodded to Hlifolf and Hrolf. 'The pig must be in the shelter.'

'No, look,' said Helga. 'The gate's broken.'

It was true. The wooden frame that leaned against the gap in the wall was smashed. The pig, thought Ketil, must have decided there would be more interesting things than Sigrid outside her sty.

They crouched by Sigrid, Helga feeling her throat gently for a pulse. She looked up, nodding and smiling.

'Let's take her inside, then,' said Einar, and frowned. 'The horses have gone.'

'Could someone have attacked the place?' Hrolf's voice sounded unused and creaky. Hlifolf proprietorially pulled Sigrid's skirts down around her legs, and smiled with the kind of satisfaction Ketil found he wanted badly to punch. Between Hrolf and Hlifolf, Sigrid was lifted and brought fairly carefully into the longhouse, where Helga revived the fire and fetched water. She looked up at the waiting men.

'It's all right, I can manage now!'

'But what's wrong with her? What's happened?' Einar demanded. Helga turned Sigrid's head gently.

'There's no sign of any injury, except for a few scrapes probably from being thrown down on the ground. No blood ...' she checked Sigrid's clothing. 'Or none that I can see yet.' Helga considered. 'She's sort of ... sleeping, really.'

'Drugged?' asked Ketil. A waft of the heavy scent from the old woman's fire, down by the Loons, seemed to flicker past his nose. Memory? Or was there something of it here?

Helga moved to look at him, and her foot rattled against something. She bent, and picked up a wine cup.

'What's that doing on the floor?' asked Einar. 'Rannveig would not leave something like that lying around.'

'Horses,' said Hlifolf suddenly.

'What?' Einar asked, but already they could all hear it – hooves outside. Einar's sword flashed, and Hlifolf, looking worried, drew his own. Ketil moved his right hand then remembered, drawing his with his left hand again. Hlifolf nudged Hrolf: belatedly he did the same.

There was the sound of feet hitting the flag threshold, and a knock at the door. Einar looked about at the others, and relaxed a little, only to tense immediately as Thorfinn strode in. He blinked when he saw the weapons raised against him.

'My lord,' said Einar, and they all resheathed their swords, a little sheepish.

'An unusual welcome,' said Thorfinn, then through them saw

Sigrid lying on a blanket, being tended by Helga. 'Something happened?'

'Rannveig is missing, my lord. The place is abandoned, two horses have gone, and Sigrid was cast aside in the pig sty. Helga thinks she may have been drugged.'

Thorfinn frowned, taking in the information. Then he said,

'Right. Now my news. Ragna was brought down here this morning, at Rannveig's suggestion. Ingibjorg thought it sensible, and sent two men – well, an old man and a boy – down here as Ragna's escort. They have not returned.'

'Then where are they now?' said Hlifolf waspishly. 'And why would Rannveig send for Ragna?'

'The cells on the Brough are being rebuilt. Ragna was apparently causing trouble. Rannveig's suggestion was not only sensible: I believe it was very welcome.' Thorfinn's expression was bland. Ketil could well imagine Ingibjorg's impatience at having to guard even her own kinswoman.

'Is there any chance,' he asked quietly, 'that the man and the boy were sympathetic to Bjarni?'

Thorfinn looked at him assessingly, blowing up from his bottom lip as he often did.

'You mean you think Ragna and they are off to join Bjarni? And they've taken Rannveig … as a hostage?'

'We can hope so, my lord. That way at least she is safe.' Not cast aside like Sigrid, he added to himself, though Sigrid was still alive.

'I didn't look in the hall,' Einar said suddenly.

The men turned and went as a body to the doorway of the hall, and Hlifolf, first in the line, hurried inside.

'Here are your men, anyway, my lord – sleeping it off, by the looks of it!'

An old man, his right arm long gone, and a lad of no more than ten, were splayed about an ale barrel. Beside them on the floor, laid out like bacon in the making, the missing pig snored.

'Drugged, too,' said Einar. 'Then they were not Bjarni's men.'

'Ragna tried to drug Sigrid and me, down at the Loons,' Ketil said. 'And Sigrid believed she had made herself sick when we wanted to ask her some questions.'

'She's more skilled in medicines, then, than I had thought,'

287

said Thorfinn, nodding. 'She may indeed have drugged your Rannveig too, then, to make her more compliant for the journey. Two horses gone? It looks as if Ragna has taken Rannveig and gone to join her son.' He sighed. 'If it were only Ragna, I'd say let her go. But we cannot leave Rannveig to her mercy, can we?'

Einar looked torn. He clearly wanted to find Rannveig, but he was physically exhausted from the day's work already.

'I'll go, my lord,' said Ketil. 'If you want to go on to the vigil?'

'I do ... I wonder how far they've gone? You might even make it back in time, if you hurry. And you'd better take two or three men with you, just in case you run into trouble. Some of the Kirkuvagr men may have escaped before we rounded them up.'

'More than likely, my lord,' Hlifolf agreed with a weighty sigh. Thorfinn rounded and glared at him.

'You probably want to fancy yourself up for the vigil, so you can't go. And you look as if you're asleep on your feet,' he added, turning to Hrolf. Hrolf seemed to look through him. 'Ketil, you'd better find that giant Afi and a couple of others. Einar probably has a few more horses to lend you, if you're lucky.'

So Ketil, who had thought he might have time to rebandage his arm and leg and see how they had survived the fight with Bjarni, instead found himself back on the road to Kirkuvagr in the afternoon rain, with Afi jogging along on one side – no horse in Buckquoy could take him - and a couple of Einar's men from the ball game riding at the other.

The men had taken Ragna to Buckquoy in the early morning, Thorfinn had explained. Even walking, the women could easily have reached Kirkuvagr by now. And what would they do then? Ragna would find that her side had lost, that Bjarni had died, and his body had been brought back to the Brough. Would she think it worth keeping her hostage then, or would Rannveig become an unnecessary burden?

With that in mind, they made a good pace, stopping only to ask people they met if they had seen two women with decent horses heading for Kirkuvagr. Several of the people said they had, enough to confirm that they were on the right track. And just beyond the toun o' Firth, they saw in the distance on the curling shoreline the two figures they had hoped to find. Their horses fresher and stronger, it was a matter of minutes to catch up with the women, who pulled up and faced them.

'It's too late, Ragna,' said Ketil. 'You've lost. Bjarni's dead.'

Ragna's face was stony.

'We heard. You killed him.'

'I did.'

'Then let us go. What harm can two women do?'

'In your case, my lady, I'm sure you could do a great deal.' Ketil had no illusions that Ragna was a weak female.

'But Thorfinn will only exile us anyway. Why not let us go?'

'"Us"?' Rannveig broke in. 'Why "us"? Drugged me and snatched me from my own hearth! I suppose she wanted a hostage!'

'Well, you're safe now,' said Afi cheerfully. 'Come on away from her, lass, and we'll make sure Ragna does no more harm.'

'Just let us get to the toun o' Firth,' Ragna said, ignoring him. 'We'll do no harm – we can get a boat there and leave.'

'"Us" again!' Rannveig spat in disgust. She edged her horse closer to Ketil's. 'Please, just take me home, Ketil. Home to Einar.' The neck of her horse was across his own mare's nose, her hand reaching out for his bridle as if to urge him on. There was something odd about her face – was it whatever drug Ragna had given her?

Ragna. With a burst of action, Ragna's horse shot off past the men, hurtling towards the boats in the toun o' Firth's little harbour. Ragna cried out in delight. Rannveig looked confused, still clutching Ketil's reins, and Afi was on the wrong side, but the other two dug their heels into their horses' flanks and charged after Ragna.

The chase was not a long one. Ragna's horse, so close to bolting, stumbled. Ragna fell, white hands splayed, white head cloth ripped back, white hair a dandelion clock in the air as she spun, landed, and crumpled. The Buckquoy men reached her and one jumped down to examine her more closely. He shook his head, and looked back to Ketil for instruction.

Ketil bowed his head for a moment, eyes closed. Too much death.

'Put her over the back of the horse, if the horse will take her,' he called. 'Bjarni's at the Brough: she should be there too.' He looked at Rannveig. She met his gaze in relief.

'It's very sad,' she said quietly. 'The son and the mother both, and so unnecessary. Those poor daughters.'

'Come on,' he said, thinking that Rannveig was being particularly charitable. The daughters, at least, might be quite pleased their mother was dead. 'I'll take you home.'

Einar's place was almost as quiet, when they reached it, as it had been when they returned from Kirkuvagr. This time, though, in the longhouse Einar himself leapt up when his wife appeared at the door, taking her into his thin arms. Helga, too, was there, still keeping watch over Sigrid.

'She's still sleeping,' Helga said quickly when she saw Ketil arrive. 'But otherwise she seems all right.'

'Ragna drugged her, too, but I don't think it was the same thing,' said Rannveig, breaking away gently from Einar to look to the latest casualty. 'Sigrid was trying to stop her getting away – and of course, she was not so valuable as a hostage, so she wanted to leave her here. I'll take care of her now, Helga. You'd better get on to the vigil.'

Helga's remarkable eyes closed.

'I'm not sure. I'm not sure Hrolf is going.'

'Not going?' Einar was shocked, and a little annoyed. 'He has to go, unless he's ill.'

'I think he might be,' said Helga in a small voice.

'Then off you go home and look after him. I'll take care of Sigrid,' said Rannveig again. She was fetching a cup from a hanging shelf. 'Ketil, you're chilled, after that ride. Some wine?'

'Thank you, Rannveig.' He took it gratefully.

'I'd prefer you to come with me, Rannveig,' said Einar mildly. 'If Helga is happy to stay here, and if Hrolf really isn't going – which does not please me – then you can come with me, can't you? You'll be all right here on your own, Helga, won't you? You know where everything is, and now that Kirkuvagr is back under Thorfinn's control, there should be no danger.'

'I'm sure I'll be fine,' said Helga, with a glance at Ketil. On the blanket beside her, Sigrid stirred slightly, then settled again. Rannveig knelt at her side, concern on her face. But Einar reached out a long arm.

'Come, my dear, we'd better go or we'll miss the beginning. Ketil, if you're ready?'

Ketil glanced back as he left the longhouse behind the others. Helga was lighting a lamp. The flame flickered and steadied, casting long shadows on Sigrid's pale face.

TUTTUGU OK SEX

XXVI

'Urgh ...'

Sigrid's dreams surged and ebbed, and became woven around with a strange, insistent moaning. She swallowed, and the moaning stopped. It seemed to be her own. She opened her eyes.

The room lurched sideways and spun. Frantic, she turned her head to one side and was sick, coughing and choking. Her eyes were sticky, and there was a stench in her nostrils – vomit, yes, but wine too, and, strangely, pig dung. Where was she? She had no pigs. She was sure of that, though for a moment she was not quite sure who she herself was.

There were lamps lit, little bubbles of light hovering somewhere above her. A shadow passed between them and her stinging eyes, paused, loomed large, and became familiar.

'Helga?' Her voice was sticky, too.

'Here, drink this.'

A cup appeared, wobbled, and steadied.

'No wine ...'

'No, it's not wine. I thought you'd like some cool water. Would you like wine instead?'

'No, no.' She pulled her head up, and carefully sipped, while Helga hands busied themselves with rags to clear up the mess she had just produced. Was she ill? Well, clearly. And Helga was looking after her, as no doubt she would have done if it had happened to Helga ... whatever it was. Had she eaten something bad?

She shut her eyes, letting the swirling in her head settle for a moment, then opened them again more carefully. It was very slightly better.

This was not her own home, no. But nor was it Helga's. Yet it looked vaguely familiar.

'You had a good sleep, anyway,' Helga was saying, and she

suddenly realised that it was addressed to her. Should she have been listening? She remembered that she was supposed to be being cautious, wary of certain people – or everybody? What was it? Had Thorstein killed someone again?

Her mind pursued that thought for a while, then she remembered Thorstein's dead body, his funeral at the Brough church. No, Thorstein was dead. Saebjorn was dead. Her eyes filled with tears. How long ago? She had no idea.

The water tasted good, took away some of the nasty taste, but there was still that strange, piggy smell. She licked her lips and swallowed.

'Pigs?' she tried. Helga blinked.

'What was that, dear?'

Sigrid summoned all her strength.

'Pigs!'

Helga looked blank, then surprised.

'Oh! Yes, we found you in the pig sty. Isn't that awful? Just where poor Snorri was found ... well, anyway, the pig wasn't there, and you weren't dead, so that's all right, isn't it?'

Sigrid felt nauseous again, but this time she had no wish to be sick. She struggled to raise herself a little from what seemed to be a blanket on the bed platform, but there was nothing behind her to rest her head on. Seeing what she was doing, Helga pulled over some more blankets and made a kind of cushion for her head. She sagged against it in relief.

Rannveig's house, that was where she was. Well, if she had been found in the pig sty (pig sty? What on earth had she been doing there?) then this was probably the nearest house. And Helga was her friend, looking after her. But where was Rannveig?

She looked about her, more in an effort to keep her eyes open than anything else. That was Hlifolf's bed, she knew. And that was Ketil's bed there, where they had treated him and looked after him after someone attacked him in Kirkuvagr ... the thing they had pulled from his arm, that had belonged on Bjarni's scabbard. So that ... that meant Bjarni had run away, and they had all gone after him ... that bit was very hazy. There was going to be a fight, though, that much seemed clear.

'Who won?' she asked, and her voice sounded as hazy as her mind felt.

'Who won what, dear?' asked Helga. 'Oh! Do you mean the fight in Kirkuvagr?'

'No, no,' said Sigrid, thinking she meant the one she had just been thinking about, the one where Ketil had been injured. 'Bjarni ... oh, yes, Kalf, too. That one.'

'That's what I meant!' Helga tutted. 'They found them in Kirkuvagr. Half of them went round in the ships to stop Kalf getting away, and the other half – our men, the Buckquoy men – went round by land to stop Eirik getting away. Like grabbing something hot from the fire.'

'Yes, yes,' said Sigrid. She was not that stupid: she had understood the basics of the fight. 'But what happened?'

'Hm, well. Thorfinn's men and Einar's men won, thank goodness. Both of them are home and uninjured. Hrolf's fine, though he's very tired. Hlifolf is all right, though knowing him he maybe just sat back and advised, you know?' She laughed. 'Father Tosti managed to keep clear of trouble, too. Afi's fine. A couple of Brough men died, oh, and you know Bjorn down the Hamnavoe road? He's lost his other ear.'

'Careless,' Sigrid murmured.

'The bad news is, though,' said Helga more gently, sitting by Sigrid's blanket and taking her hand, 'there is bad news, I'm afraid, Sigrid.'

Sigrid, still confused, found her heart beating like a hammer on an anvil.

'Who's dead?' she asked. She struggled to think who Helga had not mentioned. Awful thoughts surged in her mind. She clutched Helga's hand. 'Who is it?'

'It's Bjarni,' said Helga, her eyes full of sympathy. 'Bjarni's dead. Ketil killed him.'

'Ketil did?' Sigrid could not help sounding surprised. 'But Bjarni was the best swordsman!'

'Well, I haven't heard the whole story, but Ketil killed Bjarni. Thorfinn brought his body back here for burial. You'll be able to say goodbye, at least.'

'I don't want to say goodbye to Bjarni Hravn,' Sigrid snapped, some part of her mind coming back to life. 'He was a traitor.'

Helga sat back, shocked.

'But he saved your life! He was going to marry you!'

'He never asked me,' said Sigrid, pushing herself up a little further on her pillow, 'and I have reason to believe he was in love with someone else all along.'

'Bjarni was?' cried Helga, even more surprised, but for the life of her Sigrid could not remember why she thought this. Who else could Bjarni have been showing an interest in? Who on earth was it? And who had told her?'

'He would never have married me – and I have to say, if I had taken his mother into consideration, I would never have married him,' Sigrid declared, but the effort tired her out again. Helga looked at her dubiously, then tucked her hand back under the blanket again.

'Well, if that's how you feel about it … He was so handsome, though!'

'Well, yes,' Sigrid admitted sleepily. 'Very handsome. Better for decoration than anything else though, really, don't you think?'

Helga giggled. Sigrid opened one eye, but Helga was up and wandering around the longhouse, poking into the contents of hanging shelves and baskets, pulling out curtains to admire them.

'Rannveig has some nice things,' she remarked. 'This blanket's lovely. I wonder where she got it?' Folding the blanket neatly, she moved on to another hanging shelf. 'Lots of little bottles and jars. She's so clever, isn't she, Rannveig? Her ointments and medicines always seem to be the best.'

'And her ale. Don't let Ingibjorg hear you say that!'

'No, indeed!' Helga giggled again, but something stirred anxiously at the back of Sigrid's dozy mind. 'I wonder if she has any love potion? Or maybe you can tell me – what kind of thing does Ketil like, then?'

'Ketil? I thought you'd given up on him.'

Helga shrugged.

'Well … he's quite hard work. And I thought Hrolf was watching for a bit, there.'

Sigrid looked at her, with her wonderful dark eyes. Why was Ketil hard work? Surely men flung themselves at Helga's feet? Was it that she was married, or was there something wrong with him?

'Tell me about Herleif,' she said, closing her own eyes again. 'What was he like?'

'Oh,' said Helga, making herself comfortable by Sigrid's side, 'Herleif was nice!'

'Handsome? As handsome as Bjarni?'

Helga considered.

'Different.' She smiled, evidently remembering. She did not, Sigrid noticed, seem to be grieving much. It was unfair: she was still grieving for Thorstein, who had been bad-tempered, violent, difficult, and, frankly, expensive. Helga had happy memories, and was unaffected. How did that work?

'He was just here for a little while,' Helga said, almost as if she had heard Sigrid's question. 'Neither of us took the other too seriously, I think! I just wanted a little excitement – the men can go raiding and fighting and have all the fun in life. I mean, I don't want to fight, but I just want to feel my heart beat that little bit faster, you know? And he was big and strong and good-looking, and he wanted me just about the same as I wanted him. That makes it easier, doesn't it?' She did not seem to need an answer, which was good. Sigrid had never been unfaithful to Thorstein – would never have dared, even if the opportunity had presented itself. The thought of what he might have done if he had found out was disturbing even now, when it could no longer happen.

'He was gentle, too, which was a bit strange. I mean, he was ordinary, really,' she added hurriedly, as if Herleif's gentleness might indicate unmanliness. 'But, well, it was birds, really, that intrigued him. He loved all kinds of birds. I even saw him tend to injured ones – not just hens or ducks, but wild ones that he just found. He just seemed to know how they worked, how to handle them. He used to tell me all about them. He was … Well, I liked just spending time with him.'

'He sounds nice,' said Sigrid, half asleep. 'But what would have happened if Hrolf had found out?'

'I know! It doesn't bear thinking about, does it? Hrolf's temper!' She shook her head in disbelief. 'But I don't think he knew about any of them.'

'Any of them?' Sigrid echoed irresistibly, then pulled back. 'No, don't tell me: I don't want to know. Not just now, anyway. You said earlier,' she hauled herself up again, another wave of clarity sweeping her head, 'you said earlier that you thought maybe Hrolf had known all along?'

'Did I?' Helga looked away. 'I'm not sure.'

'I was sure you did. And I meant to tell Ketil … Where is Ketil?'

'Oh, don't worry,' said Helga, grinning again. 'Ketil came back safely from Kirkuvagr. A bit tired, maybe, but he was able to go running off after Ragna and Rannveig.'

'He's safe, good.' Sigrid let the end of the sentence slip for now. It made some strange sense, somewhere. 'And where is Hrolf, did you say?'

'Oh, I sent him home. He looked very strange – sickly, I thought. He had no business going off to Kirkuvagr with broken ribs, that's what I told him.'

'But wasn't he rowing around the Brough yesterday morning?'

'Oh, no,' said Helga at once. 'He was just steering.'

'Well … Are you sure he's gone home?'

Helga sighed.

'You're always asking me if I'm sure about Hrolf doing this, or Hrolf knowing that. How can I tell? I only see him here and there! If he did know about Herleif, he certainly didn't do anything about it. Did he?'

'Like murder him, perhaps?' Sigrid managed to meet Helga's eye. Helga went white. The possibility had obviously never occurred to her. She really was quite stupid.

'Oh, Hrolf would never have done that!' she breathed at last. 'Never!'

'Not even in a temper?'

Helga shook her head emphatically.

'Never.' Wide-eyed, she seemed still to be trying to picture the scene. 'Anyway, Herleif would have beaten him. You know what Hrolf's like in a fight. He would probably never have taken Herleif on.'

'But what if he had taken Herleif by surprise? Attacked him from behind?' Sigrid made herself sit up, giving the room a second or two to stop going round. 'Listen, Helga, are you sure Hrolf's at home?'

'He certainly should be,' said Helga, just a little uncertain now. 'But Sigrid, apart from us, everyone is at the vigil. What harm could he do? And who would he harm? I don't know what you're worried about.'

'The trouble is, nor do I ... Helga, you haven't even told me what happened to me. Why do I feel so weak?'

'Oh!' Helga gave her face a moment's attention. 'You look strong enough now, I suppose. I didn't want to alarm you when you had just woken up.'

'Well?'

'Well, when the men came back from Kirkuvagr there was no one here, we thought. We looked around, and there was no sign of Rannveig or her women, which was odd.'

'Yes, it would have been.' Sigrid was losing patience.

'Then we found you in the pig sty, and you'd obviously been drugged. Then what came next? It was busy enough! Oh, yes, then Thorfinn came back down from the Brough and said Ragna had been brought down here by two of his men because the cells were being rebuilt up on the Brough. He said it was Rannveig's idea, but that Ingibjorg thought it was a good one so down Ragna had come, apparently. Well, I didn't see her, but then I was at home, of course. Anyway, Einar realised two of his horses were gone, and there was no sign of Ragna, and then they found the two men who'd brought her down here drugged in the hall – with the pig, which was your good luck. So Thorfinn sent Ketil off after the horses and they came back with the horses and with Rannveig. They'd rescued her from Ragna along the road, and Ragna had bolted on her horse – I don't think I ever saw Ragna on a horse in my life, so she can't have been that good a horsewoman – and fell off and broke her neck. So they brought her back too, and Father Tosti's going to bury both of them up at the church on Monday.'

Sigrid frowned. There was something wrong in what Helga had told her, but the fog in her mind was like the fluff that accumulated around her weaving tablets when the holes were too rough. It blocked her thoughts, stopped them from running smoothly. She had to stop to disentangle things.

'So Thorfinn thought Ragna and Rannveig ...'

'Ragna took Rannveig hostage, and tried to go and join Bjarni at Kirkuvagr,' Helga explained, speaking slowly.

'And Thorfinn sent Ketil after them. I hope Ketil was all right. His leg wasn't much use for riding the other day.'

'He seemed fine,' said Helga happily. 'And before they went

off to the vigil, Rannveig gave him a cup of her hot wine. She wanted to stay here and look after you, but, well, I suppose Einar wanted her close after all that. And I was happy to stay with you. I'm not that fond of vigils, you know?'

'Yes ...' A thread came loose in Sigrid's head. 'Rannveig gave Ketil hot wine?'

'You know what she's like: it's her favourite remedy, isn't it?'

'She gave me hot wine ... oh, no. No.' Sigrid kicked away the blanket, finding herself in only her shift. 'Where's my dress?'

'It's filthy. Here, take it easy, Sigrid! You've been drugged, remember?'

'I need to get to the Brough.' She clutched her forehead. 'Where does Rannveig keep her dresses?'

'What are you doing?'

'I need to warn Ketil. He's been drugged, like me. The dresses?'

Helga was already there. Rannveig was taller than Sigrid, and a little slimmer, but Helga found a pleated dress that was open at the sides. Quickly, as Sigrid propped herself against a wooden pillar for balance, they slipped the brooches with their accoutrements off Sigrid's own dress and on to Rannveig's. Sigrid picked up the skirts, tucked with a belt, and shoved her feet into her boots.

'Listen, Helga. If Rannveig comes back, tell her I've gone home. All right? Keep her away from Ketil, and from me. It's Rannveig, Helga. Rannveig drugged me. She was running away with Ragna and Bjarni – well, with Bjarni, anyway. I don't think Ragna would have survived for long. And now, if I'm right, Rannveig has drugged Ketil. And they're both on the Brough.'

The buildings at the entrance to the Brough were dark and quiet: Saturday baths had been taken, the smithy was cold, the building work which seemed never to stop these days was silent, even around the back of the church where the monks were supposed to be housed, if Thorfinn ever persuaded them to come. Sigrid paused. Her head was still swimming a little, and the rush through the cold wet air had not helped as much as she might have hoped. Now the clouds had parted, and the moon was out, the washed-out white light bathing the Brough in confusion. She wanted to be sick again, but swallowed hard: she needed to find Ketil. But she turned her head to the wall next to her and retched helplessly. She felt dreadful.

An owl, pale wings spread, loomed from the darkness and swerved with shock at the sight of her. Up ahead was the church, the doorway out of sight at the other end, miles away, it seemed. Touching the wall for support still, she made her way more slowly than she would have liked up between the buildings, keeping her gaze steady on the far corner of the church, her goal, as if she were seasick and fixed on the horizon. It was not altogether helpful.

Then she saw a figure emerge from behind the church, no better than she was. Tall, limping a little, he slumped against the church wall. It was Ketil.

She was about to cry out, even from this distance, when she saw someone else appear from the shadows and approach him. A man, she thought, squinting hard: a man who seemed to have been waiting specifically for Ketil. That did not necessarily bode well. She stopped moving and tried to see more clearly. Stockier than Ketil, shorter, too – not Bjarni back for revenge, anyway. She would not like dead men walking to become the fashion on the islands.

Ketil seemed to be struggling to push himself away from the wall. His shoulder must be in agony, she thought: it could not possibly have healed enough in those few days for Ketil to be doing everything he was doing – never mind his leg. The foolish man seemed to consider pain to be a trifling inconvenience, not a message to stop and get better. Ketil staggered off, disappearing around the corner of the church, perhaps trying to go back inside and escape the stocky shadow following him. Sigrid told her feet to be steady, picked up her overlong skirts, and stumbled after them both.

She rounded the church faster than she had expected, but the two men had not gone back inside. Instead, for some reason she could not fathom, they seemed to be scrambling up the spoil heap left by the building work for the monastic quarters. For a moment they paused on the top, the stocky man a step or two behind Ketil. He muttered something, and moved his arm. Ketil slipped.

There was only a faint cry as he fell. Sigrid gasped. But he could not have fallen far: the digging had not gone deep, relying on rock beneath for the foundations. He would hardly be injured. But what happened next left her breathless.

The stocky man picked up a shovel, and began flinging earth down over where Ketil must have fallen. Furious in the moonlight he laboured, scoop after scoop of wet, rocky soil – she could hear it scraping the metal – spattered down on the far side of the spoil heap. And she could not seem to find her voice to cry out.

Instead she ran, ran round the spoil heap. Something sensible told her to avoid that flying shovel, but she could protect silly, inept Ketil. She found toeholds in the flag wall, clung to its coping, and threw herself into the building site. Yes, there he was: flailing on the ground, half-covered already in earth. There was a cry from the spoil heap as she rushed over to him, crouched with her back to the slope, pawing mud from his face, his eyes, his open mouth. He was not breathing.

She pushed him on to his side, slapped his back, hauled him back, scraped out his mouth again, tried to clear his nose. More earth fell around them, pattering damp and cloying, covering his legs, her cloak, her head. Her hands were frantic as if she were quickly moulding his skull from soapstone, turning him again, slapping him again, ordering him to breathe, to try, at least. The rain of earth came faster, relentless, it seemed, and she could do no more than hold Ketil's head to her chest, sheltering it from the onslaught. Then something heavy hit the back of her head, and she slumped forward into blackness.

TUTTUGU OK SJAU

XXVII

There was shouting.

He could not quite make out the words – his ears seemed muffled. Wary as ever, he kept his eyes shut and waited to see if he recognised a voice. There was a weight over him, heavier than blankets. Something made him wonder if it was Bjarni's body, but when he thought about it, this seemed lighter than that.

'What in God's name is he doing? Put that down!'

Well, they couldn't be talking to him, he thought. For some reason, he seemed to be weaponless. He moved very slightly, and some of what was covering him fell away. Earth? Was he buried? He gasped, choked, and flung himself on his side to cough. More earth fell from him, and the weight that had lain on his chest shifted and moaned. He was too busy trying to clear his nose and mouth to pay much attention.

'What's that?' Thorfinn's heavy voice. Ketil struggled then to wake up. Thorfinn as usual sounded as if he were in control of things. Though that did make Ketil wonder why he had then been buried. 'There's someone under there!'

'I'll see what it is.' Hlifolf, confident, keen to be in the midst of things. Ketil felt large hands on his face, wiping away the dirt. 'It's that Ketil again! I thought he was in the church!'

'Was,' said Ketil, in his own defence. He knew he had started in the church, and then what? He struggled to his knees, and spat out even more mud. Thorfinn's dog – Rognvald's dog – came and sniffed at him, clearly surprised at bones that dug themselves up.

'Get him some ale.' Thorfinn was annoyed. 'This vigil is ill-starred.'

'Hold on,' said Hlifolf, who had stood back from Ketil, presumably trying to keep his good clothes clean, 'there's someone else here!'

'Ow! Get off my foot!'

The muddy lump that had tumbled away from Ketil took on some kind of life. Ketil blinked in surprise. Sigrid's face was relatively clean, but her headcloth and shawl were filthy. She scrabbled for a footing in the rough ground and stood up, brushing off her hands and skirts to very little good effect. Her headcloth slipped back completely and she shook it off, her hair tumbling out the way he remembered it. He knelt for a moment longer in the mud, head swimming with memories and with – what?

Oh, yes. He had left the vigil because he had been feeling ill.

'Drugged, too, eh?' Sigrid, elbows on her hips, looked down at him.

'Drugged too?' Thorfinn echoed. 'Ketil, were you?'

'It makes sense,' Ketil agreed. He pushed himself up on to his feet, sleeve to his mouth to quell the nausea. The world looked no steadier from there, but he tried to see who else was around.

There was quite a crowd. It seemed that the vigil was temporarily suspended. Even Father Tosti hovered, anxious, by the church door.

Einar and Rannveig, Hlifolf, Afi, Thorfinn and Ingibjorg and their family, the delicate Asgerdr looking appalled at Ketil's appearance. No doubt he had slid down in her favour. He felt a slight smile on his lips, and was fairly sure he was going to be all right. Then he looked up at the spoil heap to his right. On the top was Hrolf, white-faced, wild-eyed, held by two sturdy men from the Brough. One clutched a shovel in his free hand.

'So it *was* Hrolf …' he heard Sigrid murmur in slightly irritating satisfaction. How had she known? And if she had known, why had she not told him?

'Hrolf, what are you doing?' Hlifolf's voice was baffled, hurt even. He stepped out of the crowd. Sigrid seemed to be looking past him, back where Einar was standing, her expression now uncertain. What was wrong?

'I needed … he was going to …' Hrolf's teeth were chattering ferociously. He was so far from the furious warrior of the morning that Ketil could hardly believe they were the same man. But at last Hrolf drew strength from somewhere, and pulled himself straight. 'Ketil was going to accuse me of killing his man Herleif.'

Thorfinn gave Hrolf an assessing look, then turned to meet Ketil's eye. Ketil raised his eyebrows – dislodging more dirt – and glanced at Sigrid. She shook her head very slightly.

'I was not, my lord. I don't believe he killed Herleif.'

'But …' Hrolf's knees went weak. 'But you kept asking … and Helga said …'

'Man, you're making no sense,' said Hlifolf, taking another step towards his friend. 'I think you're not well. You were acting very strange this morning.'

'Maybe *he's* drugged.'

Sigrid's words were loud and clear, and everyone turned to her, Ingibjorg with an indulgent look on her sheep-face. Ketil saw Sigrid straighten her shoulders, ready for something.

'Why do you say that?' asked Thorfinn, as a prompt more than as a real enquiry.

'Ketil was drugged and I was drugged – by the same person. I don't know why, but maybe she had a reason for drugging Hrolf, too?'

'She?' Einar asked. 'You mean Ragna? But she left hours ago. How could she have drugged Hrolf?'

'No, not Ragna,' said Sigrid, not looking at Einar. She drew breath, but before she could speak Rannveig cried,

'Oh, Helga! Oh, no, and I left her to look after you! I'm so sorry, Sigrid!'

Sigrid glared at Rannveig, exasperated.

'Not Helga, Rannveig. You!'

'Me?' Rannveig was shocked. So was Ketil – but it had been Rannveig who had given him that delicious hot wine, just what he had needed when he came back from rescuing her from Ragna … or had he not rescued her at all?

'Ragna said she and Rannveig were escaping together, going to meet Bjarni,' he said, his head beginning to clear. Sigrid flashed him a grateful look. 'Ragna kept saying "us", and Rannveig kept trying to distance herself from Ragna.'

'Well, wouldn't you?' Rannveig snapped. 'Honestly, Ketil –'

'And didn't you say, my lord, that it was Rannveig's idea to have Ragna held at Einar's place, rather than here on the Brough?'

'But that made perfect sense, Ketil,' Ingibjorg put in. 'Our cells … well, even when they're in one piece they're hardly a fit place for someone like Ragna. She's my own kinswoman!'

Thorfinn gave her a look of deep disgust.

'Yes, it was Rannveig's suggestion – though it was welcomed here, too.' He considered. 'I never knew Ragna had a reputation for her medicines,' he said after a moment. 'You, Rannveig, however … your skills are well known.'

'But I only use them for good, my lord! The very idea that I might run off to Bjarni – to Kalf's camp – why would I do that? My place is with my husband!'

'Overhearing his deliberations and passing on secrets, yes,' said Ketil, the picture growing clearer. 'You always were clever, Rannveig.'

'Rannveig?' Einar's voice was low, his thin face pale as he bent towards her. 'Rannveig?'

'Take your wife home, Einar,' said Thorfinn.

The crowd watched in silence, moonlit faces all turned the same way, as Einar and Rannveig walked slowly round the church, and out of sight. Ketil wondered what Einar would do. He was not a man who suffered betrayal well, however gentle he might have become. Ketil shivered.

'But she didn't kill Herleif either, I think,' said Sigrid. Thorfinn turned to her again.

'How do you make that out?'

'If she's on the side of Kalf and Bjarni, it was in their interests to spread the rumour of – of Rognvald's reappearance, not to stop you hearing it. And anyway, she would probably have poisoned him, not cut his throat.'

Thorfinn nodded thoughtfully. Ketil, too, approved the reasoning. Sigrid had always been quite bright.

'That makes sense,' said Thorfinn. 'But if you know so much, Sigrid Harald's daughter, then tell me who did kill Herleif? And who killed my skald Snorri?'

'Well,' said Ketil, praying he was right, 'that would be Hlifolf.'

There was a collective gasp from the crowd. This was better than a vigil, even with candles. Hlifolf allowed a shocked look to pass across his face, then shook his head.

'It's the after-effect of the drugs, I suppose. Look, even by the moon you can see. Both their eyes are black as pitch!'

'I know by your knife, Hlifolf.'

Hlifolf opened his mouth to respond.

'Rosemary!' Sigrid cried suddenly. 'You wear rosemary too! You pushed me over the cliff!'

'He killed them for me ...' Hrolf said unexpectedly. Hlifolf looked across at him, seemed to consider for a moment, then turned and ran.

It was a mistake. Everyone there was tired, but everyone there was tense. He was caught in seconds, and brought back.

'Right,' said Thorfinn, with a stern look at the empty church. 'Everyone – hall.'

The assembly did not take long. Thorfinn was not in the mood for delays, and sat alert, the dog on his lap close as a counsellor. Ketil took Hlifolf's knife from one of his guards, and showed it to Thorfinn.

'This knife was in Herleif's grave. It wasn't Herleif's – I found his on the rocks below the gully yesterday. This one was brought back to Einar's hall with Herleif's body, but it was in Hlifolf's custody, and it quickly disappeared. And here it is.'

'You don't know that,' Hlifolf said haughtily.

'I might not have known it. But the fact that you took it is a clue.' Ketil tapped the knife on his hand. His arm was feeling better. So was his head, sorting out some information Sigrid had slipped him as they walked to the hall. He just wished these things did not have to be aired in front of so many people. He was not happy performing to an audience.

'You killed Herleif because –'

'Don't say!' pleaded Hrolf suddenly.

'... Because he had insulted Hrolf.' Ketil had no wish to bring Helga's name into disrepute, grateful though he was that Sigrid had told him. There were a few puzzled noises from the crowd. No doubt rumour would fill in the story anyway. 'Snorri died for the same reason, didn't he?'

'Snorri was an offence to good Christian men,' said Hlifolf. 'It's followers of the old faith who think Christians are – aren't real men.'

'Followers of the old faith, like you?'

'What?'

'The way you buried Herleif,' said Ketil. Hlifolf laughed uneasily, glancing sideways at Thorfinn. 'The eagle.'

'Oh, that?' Hlifolf tried to sound relaxed. 'That was just a trick. Herleif – well, was he a real man? He liked birds. I'd found a dead eagle, told him about it, said I'd heard he liked birds. He went down to the gully to look at it – he may have thought it was only injured,' he added innocently. 'He bent over it. It made him easier to reach.' Hlifolf seemed rather pleased with his trick, pleased enough to let the charge of murder lie over him.

'How did you know he liked birds?' Sigrid asked, alarmed that she had missed something.

'I had my sources,' Hlifolf smiled. 'Sources close to Hrolf.'

Sigrid gasped.

'Asgrimr? You had Helga's son follow her?'

'I knew you were quick,' Hlifolf sighed. 'I wish I had managed to push you harder. You clearly knew too much.'

'And the old faith?' Thorfinn spoke from his high chair. He was not going to let that drop. The dog growled.

'My lord, obviously not! Where was I this evening? At the vigil! I attend services as often as Tosti here holds them! I confess my sins,' he paused, as if trying to remember when he might last have committed one. 'I obey the commandments! No one can fault me!'

'Father Tosti?' Thorfinn gestured the little priest forward. Tosti gripped his rosary nervously.

'Hm, well, my lord, yes, I suppose so.'

'What do you mean, you suppose so, you ignorant priest?' Hlifolf snapped.

'He's certainly attentive. And his corrections are always very ... well meant,' said Tosti, flushing scarlet.'

'You mean they're wrong?' Thorfinn demanded.

'Well, yes, my lord, that would be a good way of putting it. But a man should not be condemned on the quality of his Latin.'

Hlifolf looked as if he felt he had been. Thorfinn, Latinless himself, was more prepared to be merciful on this charge. He nodded.

'Put him in the most complete cell and guard him well,' he ordered. 'And take him to confession and mass in the morning, and on Monday I'll decide what to do with him. You killed Snorri because he offended you and Hrolf?' He gave Hlifolf a very sharp look. Hlifolf's gaze dropped. Thorfinn snorted. 'You're a pathetic excuse for a man. Take him away. Hrolf, you're nearly as bad. Go home to your lovely wife.' He watched the men leave, an expression of disgust on his face. Then he turned to Ketil.

'Satisfied?'

Ketil nodded.

'Yes, my lord.'

'Anything else?'

Ketil looked to Sigrid, eyebrows raised.

'No, my lord.'

'Then let's get to this vigil, before dawn beats us to it.'

In borrowed clothes, faces freshly scrubbed, Ketil and Sigrid left the church after the Easter morning mass, breathing in the fresh air after the night of close-packed bodies and burning wax. Ketil rubbed his eyes, and looked out to sea.

'Well, there you are,' said Sigrid. 'You can go back to Norway at last.'

'Away from these damned islands, yes.' He thought of his men in Trondheim, wondering what had happened to him. He'd have to tell them about Herleif, at least. The sea was grey and empty of ships on this holy day. He longed to be on it, off north, to trees and mountains, the smell of pine on the air. He smiled, and turned back to her. 'Will you be all right?'

'Oh, probably. We'll see what Einar does with Rannveig. If he believes her and not us, I'll no doubt be poisoned within the week.' She made a face that was only half-joking.

'And Bjarni?'

'You were the one who killed him, I heard.'

'I was.'

'I suppose he was tired after all his exertions.' She smiled too. Perhaps she was beginning to suspect he was not such a bad swordsman, after all. Maybe one day he would have the chance to show her. 'Listen, Ketil, I was never going to make a shirt for Bjarni.'

'Really? Because it looked very like courtship to me, here and there.'

Sigrid blushed, and looked sternly out to sea.

'I'd have come to my senses. If I was ever out of them. Imagine being in the same house as Ragna!'

'Gnup will be pleased.'

'He will.' She sighed, and pushed a stray curl off her cheek. Her eyes met his, something there he could not quite read. 'Well, don't go without saying goodbye.'

Dismissed, after all they had been through. He pressed his lips tight together. But then, he wanted to go.

Some people go, and come back. He remembered what he had told her.

And some just go.

Outlandish words in Tomb for an Eagle:

Aak - guillemot
Arbie – sea pink
Bairn – child
Barkit - dirty
Bonxie – great skua
Briz – squeeze
Bygg – bere, a form of barley grown in Orkney
Dunter – eider duck
Dwam – daze or dream
Gippesvig - Ipswich
Gutter – mud, muck
Hacksilver – assorted bits of silver used as rough payment before the use of official coinage
Hamnavoe – Stromness
Hassfang - dogfight
Heithabyr – Hedeby
Hod – a telling-off
Ill-luckid - unlucky
Keek - look
Kirkuvagr – Kirkwall
Kittick – kittiwake
Kvarr   - merchant ship
Lyre - puffin
Peedie – small
Skeldro – oystercatcher
Skon – cake of cow dung
Sula – gannet
Teeick – lapwing
Toun o' Firth - Finstown
Trowie – ill looking (or troll-like!)
Tuim - hungry
Yow - ewe

About the Author

Lexie Conyngham is a historian living in the shadow of the Highlands. Her historical crime novels are born of a life amidst Scotland's old cities, ancient universities and hidden-away aristocratic estates, but she has written since the day she found out that people were allowed to do such a thing. Beyond teaching and research, her days are spent with wool, wild allotments and a wee bit of whisky.

The sequel to *Tomb for an Eagle* will be *A Wolf at the Gate*, in 2019. You can if you wish follow her professional procrastination on Facebook and Pinterest, or at www.murrayofletho.blogspot.com, or you can even sign up for newsletters by emailing contact@kellascatpress.co.uk.

The Orkneyinga Murder series:
Tomb for an Eagle
A Wolf at the Gate

The Murray of Letho series (set in early 19th. century Scotland):

Death in a Scarlet Gown
Knowledge of Sins Past
Service of the Heir
An Abandoned Woman
Fellowship with Demons
The Tender Herb: A Murder in Mughal India
Death of an Officer's Lady
Out of a Dark Reflection
A Dark Night at Midsummer (a novella)
Slow Death by Quicksilver
Thicker than Water

The Hippolyta Napier series (set in mid 19th century Deeside):

A Knife in Darkness
Death of a False Physician
A Murderous Game

Also by Lexie Conyngham:
Jail Fever
Thrawn Thoughts and Blithe Bits (short stories)
Windhorse Burning
The War, the Bones, and Dr. Cowie

Made in the USA
Middletown, DE
09 September 2023

38247195R00187